CITY
OF
NUMBERED
MEN

THE BEST OF PRISON STORIES

Off-Trail Publications
Elkhorn, California

With thanks to fellow gangsters-in-arms
Mike Ashley, Doug Ellis, John Gunnison,
Will Murray, and Steven Rowe
for valuable contributions

Front cover artwork by
Walter M. Baumhofer
from *Prison Stories*, March 1931

CITY OF NUMBERED MEN
THE BEST OF PRISON STORIES
Copyright © 2010, Off-Trail Publications
ISBN-10: 1-935031-11-2
ISBN-13: 978-1-935031-11-6

OFF-TRAIL PUBLICATIONS
Elkhorn, California
offtrail@redshift.com

Printed in the United States of America
First printing: February 2010

CONTENTS

— — § — —

— — § — —

STORIES FROM INSIDE THE BARS

ILLUSTRATED

PRISON STORIES

Published by HAROLD HERSEY

| VOL. I | NOVEMBER, 1930 | No. 1 |

Imprisoned Pulp
John Locke

THE PULP MAGAZINES WERE ALWAYS CONSIDERED DISREPUTABLE, an affront to literature, an insult to civilization. To many of the readers, they were a guilty pleasure to be hidden from the reproachful eyes of parents, school teachers, ministers, mayors, and other right-thinking citizens. Pulp stories served the dessert of thrills without requiring the meat and potatoes of moral understanding. By the time he started his own company in the late-'20s, publisher Harold Hersey understood the nature of the pulp magazine all too well. He had long since surrendered to the desires of his readers. They wanted excitement, not enlightenment, and if he cared to remain in business, that's what he would give them.

Among the early offerings of his Good Story Magazine Company were a pair of magazines featuring violent tales of the new breed of outlaw created by Prohibition: *Gangster Stories*, which debuted with the issue of November 1929, and *Racketeer Stories*, February 1930. They raised more than a few eyebrows when they emerged, and raised them even higher when they proved successful. Could the already-disfavored pulps sink any lower? Hersey's brazen new titles answered loudly in the affirmative.

Critics and censors answered back. Criminals were being glorified. Crime was shown to pay. Our youth were being taught to disrespect the law. Hersey modified the product to make sure that criminals never triumphed over the law. (The complete story of the gang pulps, and the attendant conflicts, is told in *Gang Pulp*, OFF-TRAIL PUBLICATIONS, 2008.) Still, it must have grated on him to be forced into compromise after finally fulfilling a dream of publishing his own magazines, a dream of independence.

Thus, when he introduced an offshoot of the gang pulp, *Prison Stories*, with the issue of November 1930, it may have seemed that Hersey was having the last laugh. All the bad characters, all the vice and violence, was moved behind the bars of government institutions, and no one could argue that crime had profited the criminal. One simple move—and a dubious moral dimension had been restored. All the potential for excitement remained. Cons could fight cons—with shivs replacing Tommy-guns. Gangs could battle gangs. Guards could be as corrupt as cops on the take. And wardens could be as sadistic as any police interrogator. You will note from this collection, however, that cons couldn't murder guards. The censors were still lurking.

These factors may have entered into Hersey's thinking when he created *Prison Stories*, but if so, it's far from the whole story. As we usually find, when digging into Hersey's affairs, there is method underlying his madness.

In the years leading up to *Prison Stories*, Prohibition had put issues of crime and punishment front and center as never before. In an address given to the Welfare Council of New York in February 1929, Lewis E. Lawes, Warden of New York's Sing Sing prison, and a well-known reformer, said: "We begin this year of enlightenment with more laws to prevent crime than ever before in history, and more people breaking them. . . . Every week the tragic evidence that social morality cannot be legislated into existence passes before you with the week's consignment of criminals."

What had Prohibition wrought? A simplified narrative goes like this: Prohibition criminalized ordinary behavior. Prison populations swelled. Outraged at the lawlessness, defiant legislatures lengthened sentences, swelling populations even further. Prisons became dangerously overcrowded. A bad meal was enough of a spark to ignite the powder keg. Realistically, there were more variables: the rising national population alone would increase prison populations; issues of education, unemployment, etc., affected conditions contributing to criminality; and many crimes were not directly related to Prohibition and its consequences. But the simplified narrative is close enough, and reflects widespread public perception at the time.

Nineteen-twenty-nine started with a big prison story. On January 13, at the Philadelphia County Prison, 600 inmates rioted for twenty-four hours, holding the guards at bay with table legs and other makeshift weapons. Squads of police eventually subdued them with tear-gas bombs after a three-and-a-half-hour battle. How had it all begun? The food was unfit to eat.

New York state had its own conditions. In 1926, the "Baumes law," named for State Senator Caleb H. Baumes, increased prison sentences. It mandated sentence length, removing the decision from judges and parole boards. It required that a fourth felony conviction would automatically result in a life-sentence, even if all four felonies were property crimes. Murderers and shoplifters were treated alike. The population at Sing Sing steadily grew; by the middle of 1930, it had reached record levels, no trivial statistic for a prison built in 1825. By 1930, similar laws had been enacted in twenty-three states.

Sing Sing, twenty-five miles "up the river" from Manhattan, was New

November 1930   Cover art by C. Wren

A pretty girl is gently escorted to her death. The electric chair was the modern method of execution in New York. Other states still used hanging.

York's most famous prison, but not its toughest. Incorrigible prisoners were transferred from Sing Sing and other state institutions to Clinton Prison at Dannemora. They called it "America's Siberia." On July 22, 1929, 1,300 inmates rioted in a massive escape attempt, Dannemora's "wildest disorder" since opening in 1845. The battle raged for five hours; buildings were set on fire; a few inmates escaped; guards eventually drove the prisoners back into their stone cell blocks with grenades, tear-gas bombs, machine guns and rifles. Experts debated the cause, but enlightened consensus settled on the dangerous overcrowding.

John S. Kennedy, of the State Commission of Correction, attempted to tie the underlying causes together: "Within the last year or two the State prisons have received a large number of professional gangsters. Some of them never were detained before for long periods of time. Now they find themselves confronting ten, twenty, and thirty year periods of confinement. These men have been used to no little luxury, a free and restless existence. They are appalled by the prospect of what seems endless punishment. And it is this type of men who organize and try to carry out desperate efforts to escape."

Prison unrest could be a contagion. News spread. Warden Lawes reported that one out of six Sing Sing inmates subscribed to daily newspapers; the other five out of six—if they knew how to read—got their newsprint secondhand. Some prisoners had state-of-the-art communication devices— radios. An additional source of information was the "grapevine telegraph," a "mysterious means of communication known only to the underworld."

Thus it can be understood why New York's prison system soon received another shock. After several days of tension following the Dannemora unrest, a riot erupted at the state prison at Auburn. Inmates took over the prison arsenal, capturing riot guns and ammunition. Seventeen-hundred inmates battled guards in another five-hour affair. Buildings were turned into smoking ruins; prisoners went over the wall. It took a force of 800 to quell the outbreak. News trickled to the nearby State Prison for Women, turning it into a "howling bedlam."

Auburn melted down on a Sunday. Come Thursday at noon, an insurrection erupted at the Leavenworth Penitentiary, Kansas. The rioters, armed with improvised weapons, numbered 3,758, as it was reported. They were driven back to their cells with riot and machine guns. The pandemonium of shrieking, cursing, and breaking glass continued after nightfall. Three causes were theorized: bad food, the news from New York, and the daily temperature of 100°. Not in dispute was the prison population: double capacity.

Over the following months, more riots occurred. October 3-4, the Colorado State Penitentiary in Canon City; two days, thirteen dead. December 11, Auburn again; desperate prisoners held the facility for six hours. The warden was captured and beaten by rioting prisoners. He

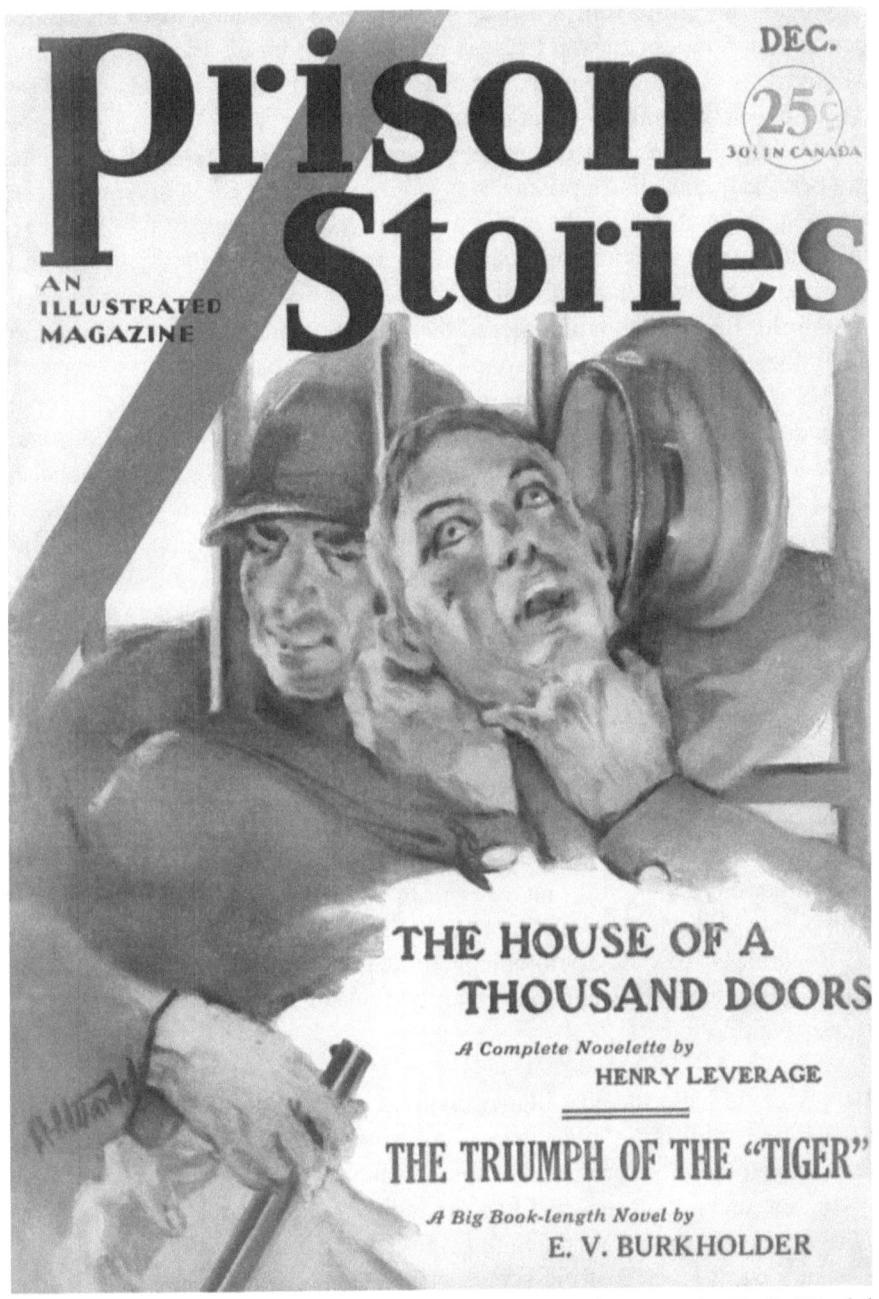

December 1930   Cover art by R.C. Wardel

*Henry Leverage was the heart and soul of the magazine. An ex-con himself
(Sing Sing 1915-18), he contributed numerous stories.*

resigned his position in January, citing his injuries. February 1, 1930, Canon City again, where prisoners had been threatening to "burn down the whole penitentiary" unless the warden was removed. March 26-27, Jefferson City, Missouri; two days, two riots; the cause on day 1, bad food; the cause on day 2, day 1; the warden installed new "hard boiled" rules. April 19, Rhode Island State Prison; two gangsters posing as visitors smuggled guns into the prison; the ensuing uprising was subdued by tear gas. On April 21, at Ohio State Penitentiary, the wave of riots reached an appalling climax in the aftermath of an abortive escape attempt; 318 men burned to death, and hundreds more were hospitalized as brick-and-wood cell-blocks condemned as unfit for human habitation blazed through the night; many men burned to death locked in their cells. The population: triple capacity.

These crises elevated prison reform into a major national issue. People argued about causes and solutions. Reformers wanted a return to rational sentencing; conservatives called for more prisons, not shorter sentences. Warden Lawes measured the temperature of the times: "Never before, in America, has there been such wide discussion of crime and prison problems."

But riots weren't the only prison stories in the news. There were the trials and sentencing of notorious criminals, routine escape attempts, racial conflicts, chain gangs, rock piles, and the macabre drama that hung like a dank, dark cloud around the frequent executions. Not every story was gloomy; some came with a touch of humor. On March 1, 1929, a fresh tunnel was discovered beneath the Sing Sing yard. It came within five feet of the outer wall. They dubbed it the "Sing Sing Subway." In September, the pole vault was dropped from the annual field-day exercises at Sing Sing in September—the Sing Sing Games—for fear that the wall would be breached from above. Now if that wasn't a pulp story waiting to happen . . .

Regardless of the sociological dimensions, by now the dramatic possibilities should be apparent. The prisons of the era were hotbeds of stories waiting to be told.

Hersey could have staked a bigger claim to originality if he'd made *Prison Stories* one of his initial titles in late-'29 instead of late-'30 but, as was often the case, Hollywood took a larger role in shaping the pop culture landscape. Note that several successful films, including *Underworld* (1927) and *The Dragnet* (1928), had done much to inspire Hersey's gang pulps.

The first in a wave of big-screen prison stories was *Condemned*, which premiered November 4, 1929. It, perhaps, should be given honorable mention in the current discussion. The film starred Ronald Colman as a Parisian thief condemned to Devil's Island, appropriate to the prison genre, but not topical to the problems in the United States. *Prison Stories* would include a

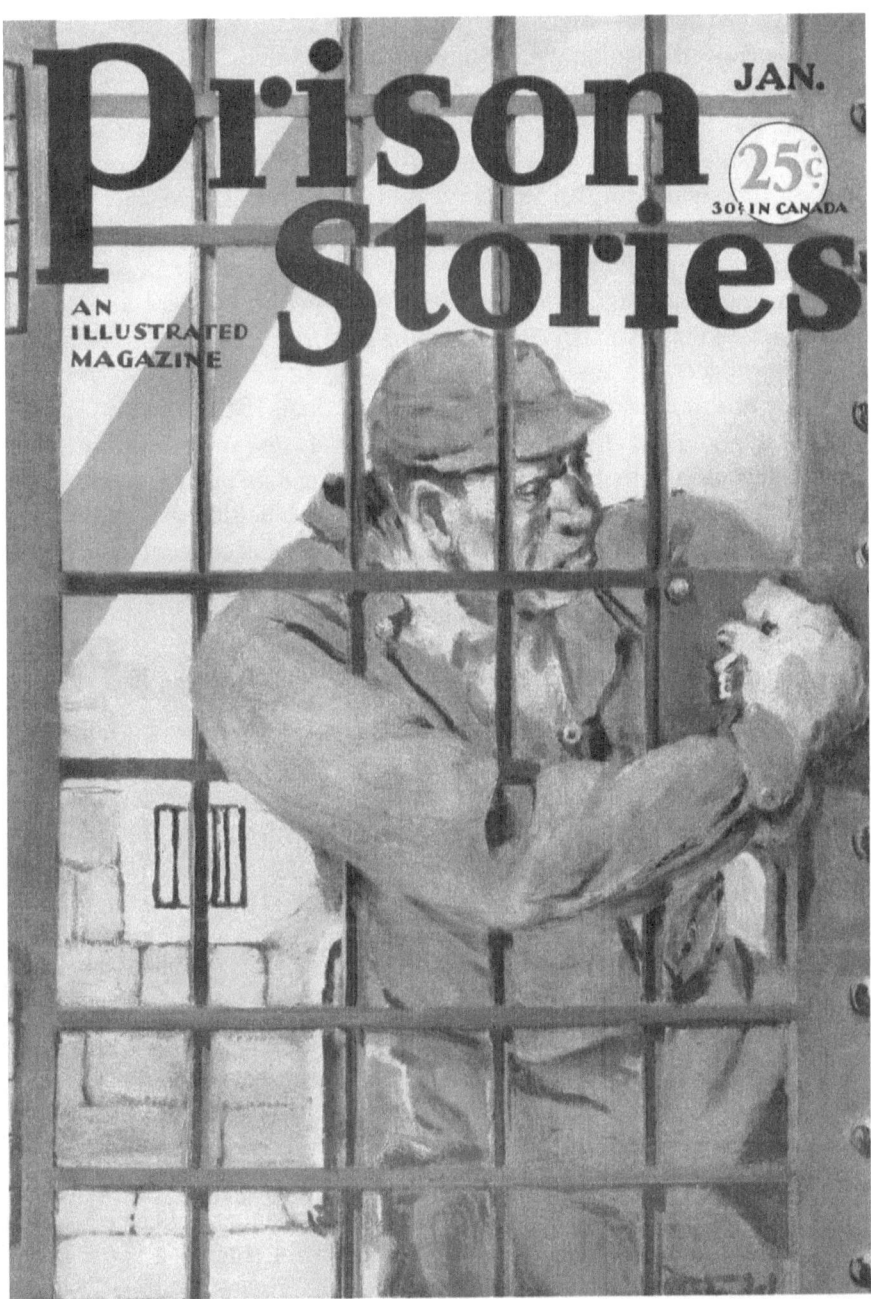

January 1931   Cover art by R.C. Wardel

A gorilla-like convict frees himself from captivity.

Devil's Island story, Walt S. Dinghall's novelette "Island of Forgotten Men" (January 1931).

At the cost of opening with two honorable mentions, the next entry was not a Hollywood movie, but a Broadway play, *The Last Mile*, which opened on February 13, 1930, a death-house tragedy based on the true story of Robert Blake, executed in Huntsville, Texas on April 19, 1929. The playwright, John Wexley, did significant research on prison conditions. He was particularly influenced by October's Canon City riot, and by a tour of Sing Sing hosted by Warden Lawes, who shared Wexley's anti-capital punishment stance. The play was quite successful and it's fair to presume that New Yorker Hersey knew of it; he may even have seen it. *The Last Mile* reached the screen from a minor producer, but not until 1932.

Three prison films hit New York screens in June 1930. Shot on location in San Quentin, *Numbered Men*, based on the play *Jail Break*, was the story of an innocent man framed for counterfeiting. Sending away a framed man was a convenient way of creating a convict-hero. The title was an obvious influence on "City of Numbered Men," included in this collection.

In *Shadow of the Law*, William Powell played a man sent up for manslaughter. He escaped, and got the girl and a happy ending out of the deal.

The third June prison picture, *The Big House*, was one of the year's box-office and critical hits. It's a direct product of the real-life turmoil in the prison system, and probably the single biggest link connecting the actual riots to *Prison Stories*. The producers went to great lengths to achieve a realistic portrayal of prison, and were praised for their efforts. The character of the warden makes speeches complaining about prison overcrowding. And the film culminates with an all-out riotous jailbreak. The success of *The Big House* guaranteed that the prison-riots story, which was fading in the news, would be kept alive in the public consciousness.

Another prison film, *Up the River* was released October 12, 1930, too late to have influenced *Prison Stories*. It was destined to be the only film featuring both Humphrey Bogart and Spencer Tracy. Tracy's film career had been launched by his stage role in *The Last Mile*. *Up the River* also featured a true insider, Joan Marie Lawes, the warden's eight-year-old daughter.

Two of the best-known prison films of the era were *20,000 Years in Sing Sing* (Tracy again), based on the book of the same name by Warden Lawes, and *I Am a Fugitive From a Chain Gang*, derived from a series in *True Detective Mysteries*. Both were released in 1932, long after the demise of *Prison Stories*.

Prison Stories, then, began with a strong public awareness and interest in prison issues. The June release of *The Big House* provides a plausible point

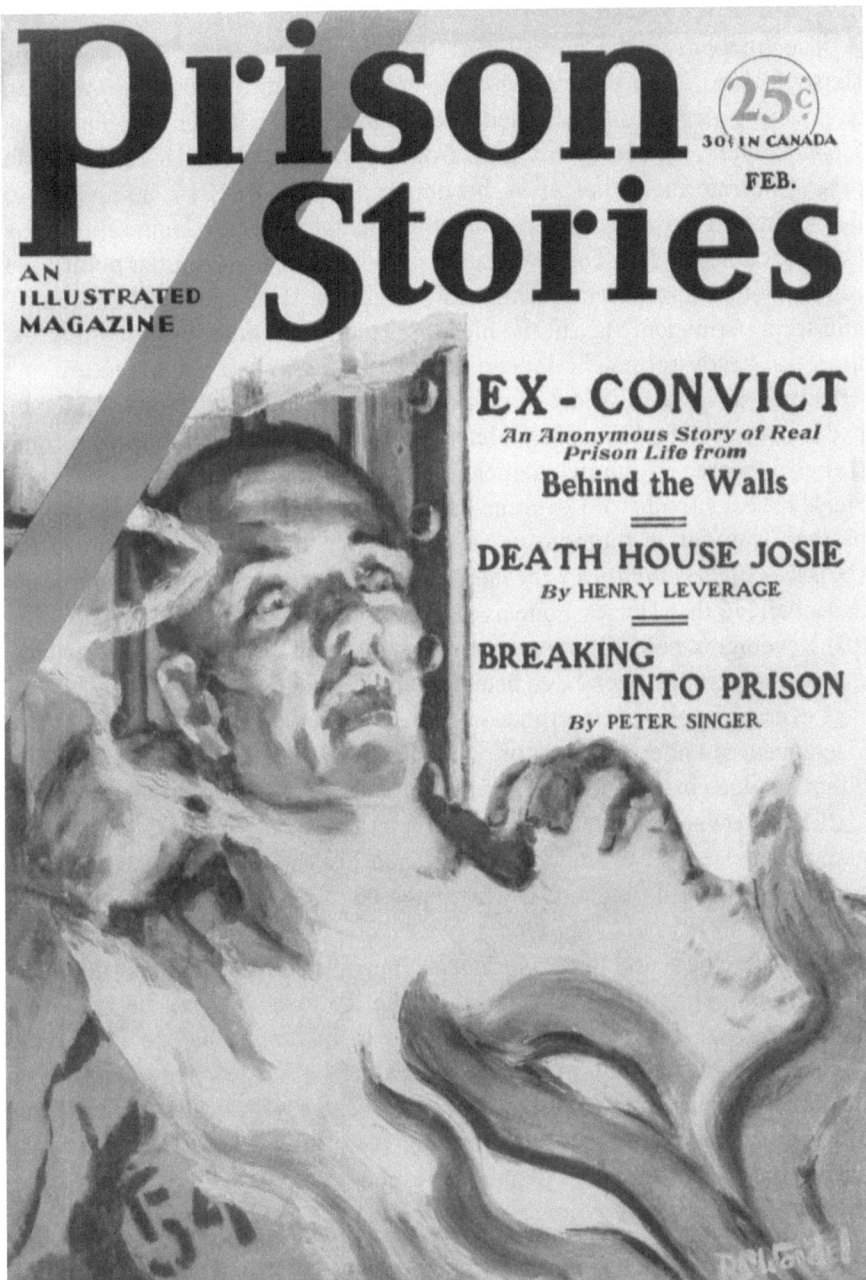

February 1931   Cover art by R.C. Wardel

Fires were a frequent result of the calamitous prison riots that dominated headlines in 1929 and '30.

at which Hersey would have begun planning and gathering material for the new pulp.

The linchpin to the project may have been pulp writer and long-time Hersey friend, Henry Leverage. Leverage was an Englishman with an engineering degree and a varied background who was sent to Sing Sing for auto theft. He served his time from approximately 1915-18. While in prison, he reformed himself by becoming a writer. In 1916, he applied to the Authors' League of America for membership. Hersey, representing the League, came to visit. The two stayed in touch. Leverage started publishing stories with some success while still in prison. His talent didn't qualify him for a permanent stay in the big-time, and he eventually settled into the life of a steady-selling fictioneer. During the '20s, he sold adventure and detective stories to a variety of pulps, including Clayton titles where Hersey had become chief editor. When Hersey started his own companies, Leverage stories appeared in the magazines. In his 1937 memoir, *Pulpwood Editor*, Hersey speaks fondly of Leverage but fails to mention *Prison Stories*, which by then was only a footnote to his career. But a close examination of the six issues of *Prison Stories* reveals Leverage's heavy presence, which leads us to believe that Hersey conceived *Prison Stories* with the understanding that Leverage would supply ample material based on his own experiences. *Prison Stories* may even have been Leverage's idea.

Leverage appeared five times in *Prison Stories* under his own name. He also appeared under a variety of pennames, which can be connected to him either by clues in the pennames or the stories. Some were easily determined. Carl Henry, who appeared four times, is an abbreviation of Leverage's full name, Carl Henry Leverage. Leverage had been using the name since the early '20s. Edward Letchmere, who appeared twice, is the main character in Leverage's 1919 novel *The White Cipher*. Peter Singer appeared three times, and is only to be found in *Prison Stories*. Specific story elements in common between Singer and Leverage stories make the match. There may be other names in *Prison Stories* that also belong to Leverage, but no immediate connections are obvious. As Hersey wrote of Leverage: "His manuscripts made up in brilliance what they lacked in neatness. A deal of editing was always required to put them in shape for the printer." Thus, with the prose altered to some extent, confident matches may not be possible in every case. (Additional detail on Leverage and his pennames can be found in the *About the Authors* section.)

Prison Stories ran for six issues: November, December, 1930; January, February, March, May-June, 1931. They had 160 pages each, in line with Hersey's other pulps at the time, making a total of 960 pages. Creative content—fiction, pseudo true stories, and illustrations—account for 794 pages. The remainder is made up of nonfiction features, the letters column

Prison Stories

25¢
30¢ IN CANADA
MARCH

AN
ILLUSTRATED
MAGAZINE

LIFE!
By
D. B. McCANDLESS

BULL'S EYE
By Henry Leverage

**BIG HOUSE
BOOMERANG**
By Margie Harris

March 1931   Cover art by Walter M. Baumhofer

*According to Leverage's story, the worst convicts—the demons—had bull's
eyes on their backs, to make them easier targets during escape attempts.*

Kites from Stir, ads, and miscellaneous material. Leverage's known contributions, minus illustrations, come to about 214 pages, or 28% of the creative content of the magazine. The next closest contributor was gang-pulp regular E. Parke Levy, with just over 90 pages, or about 12%. Most of the remaining space was filled with other Hersey regulars like Margie Harris, John Gerard, and Walt S. Dinghall.

Another Leverage pseudonym, Winfield Byrd, is a special case. He had two stories in *Prison Stories*, "City of Numbered Men" and a serial, *Public Enemies*, which centered around Chicago racketeers imprisoned in England. The serial ran for four parts from the third (January) through the final issue (May-June). In the midst of this, Leverage died on February 14, 1931. At the end of the fourth installment of *Public Enemies*, Hersey ran a boxed announcement: "We regret to announce that due to the death of the author, Mr. Winfield Byrd, we will be unable to continue this story." Several conclusions flow from these circumstances. The saddest is that Leverage's death, at a relatively young 46 years, was quite unexpected. (His death didn't receive much attention and the cause is unknown.) We know it must have shocked Hersey, not only because Leverage was his friend, but also because he was running an unfinished serial—a gamble, a publishing disaster, and a certain embarrassment, which may explain why the details receive no airing in *Pulpwood Editor*. It's a shame Hersey didn't publish an obituary for Leverage, but perhaps the use of multiple pennames, which would have been revealed by such a notice, was too big a secret to let out. Hersey did remark in *Pulpwood Editor*: "[Leverage] continued to contribute stories to magazines almost up to the day of his death. He was a most charming, entertaining fellow. I miss him often when I go to make up an issue. He never failed to come in with just the right yarn for the right place." One last conclusion is that Leverage's death was the main or leading cause for the demise of *Prison Stories*. Once the Leverage backlog had been published the magazine folded. There is no doubt Hersey could have filled *Prison Stories* from the contributions of other regulars, but Leverage's loss combined with unrewarding sales probably killed Hersey's enthusiasm.

(Note that *Prison Stories* skipped April. In the absence of other evidence, we would have guessed that Hersey delayed the issue while weighing the implications of Leverage's death. But, in fact, the switch of *Prison Stories* to every-other-month publication, along with three other Hersey titles, had been announced prior to Leverage's passing. The March issue should have been dated March-April, an anomaly common to the pulps. The May-June issue announced that there "should be" another issue in two months," but no details were provided.)

The prison crises would fuel many of the tales in *Prison Stories*, but Hersey,

May-June 1931   Cover art by Walter M. Baumhofer

A one-eyed brute with a shiv, the weapon of choice in stir. The possession of a firearm by a convict was considered extremely serious.

regardless of his view of America's problems, never forgot that he was an entertainer, not a politician, and that many of his readers were adolescents. The stories would offer virtually no attempt to explore the reasons for crime and punishment, other than acknowledging that certain rough people made themselves unfit for society and that prisons existed to sequester them. Riots are mentioned, sometimes in passing, sometimes as a central plot element, but only distilled to pure adrenalin; the overcrowding that turned the prisons into tinderboxes gets discarded as a byproduct.

In the first year of the gang pulps, Hersey attempted to mollify the censors with vague but earnest editorials to the effect that only by understanding criminals could the crime problem be solved. The actual stories had more to say about the sounds of Tommy guns than the souls of sinners, but that is in the eye of the beholder. *Prison Stories* published a cursory Hersey piece in the second issue (reprinted in this volume). Getting to the heart of the matter, Hersey laid out the mission of the magazine, an emphasis on characters: "PRISON STORIES tells how it feels to be a four-time loser, a die-hard, a demon, a lifer or a desperado." The magazine was following well-established norms: "Half of literature contains something about a crime." Society would benefit: "This magazine is a lamp on a dark subject that concerns everybody." Whether the readers were likely to be illuminated by the contents of *Prison Stories*, that again is in the eye of the beholder.

"Wait Outside," by Don Murray, is an excellent example of how the excitement of the prison insurrections could be separated from the context of the events. ". . . with a shout which carried clear to the outside walls, the seventeen hundred freedom-mad prisoners surged to their feet, throwing chairs aside or seizing them to beat down the guards who opposed them." The figure of 1,700 was not chosen haphazardly; it figured prominently in the headlines following the first Auburn riot. Later in "Wait Outside," the burning of wooden buildings on the prison grounds evokes the Ohio State Penitentiary disaster. However, the story never explains the riot other than as a spontaneous uprising inspired by some of the worst inmates; nor does it question the inherent danger of the ancient, wooden buildings.

"City of Numbered Men" stresses the danger faced by a new warden: "Two-fisted, square-jawed, shrewd-witted, he realized he was up against the biggest fight in his life. The warden before him had perished in a riot. The one before that was knifed by an insane inmate." The narrative hints that his mission is reform: "When the governor of the state sent Big Tom down to Penthouse he instructed him to break the mutinous spirit there, build the new cell houses, and keep that prison out of the newspapers." To a politician, newspapers—publicity—present the biggest threat. The only underlying problem at issue was the character of the convicts and the prison employees:

[The governor] forgot to add that Penthouse contained the choicest collection of die-hards, lifers, con-men, demons and schemers in captivity. He neglected to state the facts concerning graft so strong that the Principal Keeper went home every night with a three-pound porterhouse steak under his uniform and the guards came to work in expensive sedans.

Henry Leverage's "Bull's Eye" builds the entire story around a riot:

The riot at Black Ridge Prison had all the elements of a battle in France. Seventeen hundred convicts held the prison and the walls. They were armed with machine guns, rifles and revolvers taken from the arsenal. Smoke from burning shops floated above their impregnable position.

Surrounding Black Ridge was a ring of steel. Soldiers, gun guards and a detachment of the state militia occupied dugouts and trenches, under a withering fire from the rioters.

They sat down to starve the inmates out, at governor's orders. He was a reform executive who didn't want "his boys" slaughtered.

Most of the convicts were not "boys." They were "die-hards," demons and lifers.

That figure of 1,700 again, the weapons captured from the arsenal, and the burning buildings, all evoke the Auburn riot. Leverage, for an ex-con, is strangely unsympathetic to the prisoners. He tells the story from the state militia's point-of-view. They stand in armed opposition to the rebels, who are abetted by the reformist governor's misguided minimal-violence strategy. Perhaps, as someone who patiently did his time and returned to society's good graces, he had no tolerance for insurrection, regardless of the fuel feeding the fire. So he ignores large-scale issues and focuses on personal conflicts between troopers. Or, perhaps it's as simple as, cops are good guys, convicts are bad guys. Because this is the pulps.

Prohibition remains one of the best illustrations of "the law of unintended consequences." Intended, among other things, to reduce crime and corruption, it had the opposite effect, of which the prison crises were an ugly reminder. The crime and punishment equation had become very obviously unbalanced, which added to the momentum for Prohibition's repeal. That was accomplished in 1933, pushing Hersey's gangsters and convicts into the archives of memory.

Harold Hersey
Tales of an Ink-Stained Wretch
John Locke

HAROLD HERSEY, THE PUBLISHER of *Prison Stories*, worked as an editor from the age of 16 until his death at 62, a near-half-century of service during which he supervised or edited an astounding number of magazines (our current tally hovers around 140). He's best-remembered as a pulp-magazine editor and publisher, which dominated his career in the '20s and '30s. In the late-'20s and early-'30s, a period of fecund growth in the industry, he launched his own pulp chains. While his formula didn't ultimately make him a major player in the field, his bold experimentation with new genres and titles, like *Prison Stories*, made him a legend in the colorful history of the pulp magazines.

In 1937, he published *Pulpwood Editor*, one of the few contemporaneous memoirs of the pulp era, though it's more industry analysis than autobiography. We would have hoped for this book to explain many of the behind-the-scenes events that compelled his many career shifts, but most of the interesting questions go begging for answers. The same holds true for the numerous articles he supplied to the writers' magazines. He's most forthcoming in "Looking Backward Into the Future," a long article published in the fanzine *Golden Atom* in 1954. The article focused on his involvement in the 1919 Street & Smith pulp *The Thrill Book*, but also included many biographical details. A follow-up article on his involvement in other science-fiction pulps was completed but never published and the manuscript is considered lost.

In a detailed examination of his career, the suggestion of conflict with his various business partners arises at different points; of particular note is 1927-39, a period of frequent change in which his ultimate goal of establishing himself as a publisher fell short. He maintained professional decorum throughout, however, and kept his private business affairs out of the public arena. In the end, magazine publishing relies on circulation, and we can assume that numbers—of copies sold, copies returned, dollars earned, creditors calmed—governed Hersey's destiny much more than his professional relationships, but many of the details are doomed to remain secret.

In the mid-'30s, a reputation for failure attached itself to Hersey, owing in part to his many short-run pulps, and endorsed by his self-deprecating humor in owning up to his shortcomings. Over time, however, this view of him has expanded to interpret any claims he made to *success* as exaggeration or self-aggrandizement, as if he had, by definition, failed in everything. In truth, he had a wide mixture of wins—of varying duration—and losses. Furthermore, we can find no basis in his many scattered writings that he overstated his role in any venture. *Pulpwood Editor*, for instance, the central document in the Hersey story, is not contradicted by the record—which makes it all the more valuable as an expert view of magazine publishing as it stood at the time. In the book Hersey cheerfully admits to several of his failures, e.g. "a title that nauseates me every time I recall it: *Loving Hearts*. It deserved to fail; it did"; or "I failed miserably with *Detective Trails*." But not every short-run title was a failure in the least-charitable meaning of the word. Many titles were started to test the public appetite for new concepts; a one-out-of-four survival rate was actually considered a success. Other short-runs were essentially publishing-on-demand services that Hersey provided to second parties.

If, at times, Hersey comes across as a braggart for mentioning all the noteworthy things he was involved in, or all the famous people he counted as friends, the record bears him out. He led a remarkable and unusual life that had many dimensions outside of the pulps and was well-known in publishing at large. The pulps were simply "one of the magazine worlds that I've lived in and out of." What is undeniable is that he lasted for some forty years in the mercurial business of magazine publishing, and if survival is any measure, he was indeed a success.

Hersey's father, Augustine Haynes "Doc" Hersey was born about 1850. He migrated from Maine to Montana in the 1870s. Harold's mother, Adelaide Carpenter Johnson, born approximately 1868, also came west in the '70s. The couple married in Montana in 1887. Harold wrote a lot about his father, but seldom mentioned his mother. He notes that his father had been a "sheriff, miner, druggist, prospector, etc." In 1887 he ran a store in Butte, A.H. Hersey & Co. He appears to have been active in Montana affairs. He became a journalist; his first known article was published in 1888. He reported for Montana's legendary *Anaconda Standard*, a newspaper closely associated with the mining industry. There are two deceased children in the family history, which may explain the six-year gap between marriage and Harold's birth. Harold Brainerd Hersey was born on March 29, 1893 in Bozeman, not far down the road from Anaconda, Butte, and the state capitol of Helena. *Pulpwood Editor* notes that he "was born on a billiard table—an auspicious start for a man who has regarded life as a game of mingled luck and skill." From November 1895 to about March 1896, Doc Hersey put out a weekly newspaper, *The Montana Transcript*, suggesting that the publishing bug would be passed from father to son. Harold's sister, Lois R., was born about 1897. In 1898, Doc had relocated to Washington, D.C., while Adelaide attended business college in Helena. In 1899, Doc was a roving newspaper correspondent, traveling around the U.S. and abroad, with Harold in tow. In due course, Adelaide and Lois relocated to Washington, D.C. A second girl, Charlotte Frances, was born about 1900.

Our earliest record of Doc's reporting is an April 1899 dispatch from Puerto Rico. The article reveals knowledge of broad sections of the continental U.S., from southern California to Florida to the northeast, suggesting that Doc had been traveling and reporting for some time. In 1903, Doc reported on the aftermath of the Mount Pelée volcano eruption in Martinique. Harold suggests that much of their travel in this period covered Mexico and the West Indies. Father and son spent the majority of 1903 in New Orleans:

> In New Orleans, I had heard the first of the great jazzmen, without any idea, of course, that they were making musical history. Years later, when I was co-editor with Art Hodes of *The Jazz Record*, it was my good privilege to get to know "Pops" Foster and other old-timers I had listened to as a foot-loose boy of ten, when I hung around places where we youngsters weren't supposed to go and accompanied my father on many a riverboat excursion.

They left New Orleans in 1904 "to go to the Orient, via Atlanta and the St. Louis World's Fair." Doc had been assigned to cover the Russo-Japanese War (1904-05). "I wandered as a boy," wrote Harold, "through the Philippines, China, Japan, and as far south as Anam, Siam, and Australia." Harold's first published story appeared in *The Manila Gossip*. He was eleven. Doc Hersey nourished his son's imagination:

> I deem myself most fortunate in having had a father who encouraged a natural interest in literature by telling me the stories written by the immortals some time before the average lad between eight and thirteen years of age reads them on his own initiative. He also made up stories from the whole cloth of his rich imagination that was always equally graced by a keen sense of humor. Some of them were told in serial form as I trudged along, clinging to his hand, while we took long walks through the streets of New Orleans, Mexico City, San Francisco, Honolulu, Manila, Shanghai and New York. These are but a few of the places we visited. I was often left to my own resources, while he covered an assignment. . . . Once, to my acute embarrassment, he left me in Canton, where, not being able to speak the language, I was unable to ask the way to the bathroom.

The eighteen-year age difference between Doc and Adelaide, and Doc's constant travels, may have put a strain on the marriage. At any rate, the couple divorced in 1906, with the judgment filed in Montana. In 1907, Doc's travels were over. He and Harold settled down in D.C. Doc worked in the Press Gallery of the House of Representatives; then died in the Fall. In Washington, Adelaide was employed by the Agriculture Division of the Census Bureau. In late 1907, Harold was a Corporal at the Winchester (Virginia) Military Institute. This may not have lasted long, for Harold went to work in the Library of Congress as a messenger boy. In 1908, he published his first magazine. At the LoC, he was promoted to clerk, then at age 16 became editor of *Part Four, Copyright Catalogue*. He continued to hold this job while completing night studies at George Washington University. He noted that through working on the *Copyright Catalogue*, he "learned to edit copy and read proof with a vengeance during seven long, doleful, monotonous years." In addition to work and university, he contributed to magazines:

> When I worked with the Copyright Office . . ., I used to prepare [filler material] and sell it regularly to the magazines. I had a tiresome job in those days. . . . Over me was a tight-minded, officious chief clerk, whose delight seemed to be to walk back and forth in the aisles, watching the slaves at their oars. Permit me shamefacedly to confess that I developed a system of cards by which I could slip my copy for magazines under the cards I was writing by way of routine work. When this "gent" sniffed around I was always ready for him. I worked fast and my office work did not suffer. . . . For five years I wrote brief articles for particular magazines and I made as high as a hundred dollars a month so doing. My practice was to get to know the editor as well as the magazine, *by mail,* and then after trying him out at broad intervals with set pieces I gradually worked up to steady production until I was looked upon as an asset and was often called in by special request to help with issues containing much filler space. I never wrote short stories. I merely did this sort of work to supplement the low government wage I received and also to gain experience in magazine making.

He also briefly published a magazine called *The Open Road*. As in the previous quote, he reveals a developing independent streak:

> [*The Open Road*] was the most successful magazine I've ever issued; it had a verse in it that hymned the tragic lives of the prostitutes when the red light district was closed in Washington. It was promptly suppressed. I nearly lost my precious job at a time when I had not got over the fears of a white collar slave.

One senses conflict with the aforementioned "officious chief clerk."

Hersey would have an active love life. The first indication comes in 1911, when Hersey was 18, and probably living with his mother. He and his longtime friend, the 17-year-old Dorothy Koerth, fled Washington at noon for Baltimore to get a quickie marriage. When Dorothy's mother came home that afternoon and found the girl gone, she suspected as much and phoned a number of local police departments, including Baltimore's. Forewarned, the marriage license clerk in Baltimore relayed news of the couple's arrival back to Washington. Mrs. Koerth appeared on the scene before the license was issued; wedding thwarted. She had no issue with Hersey, just considered her daughter too young. Any further progress in Hersey's relationship with Miss Koerth remains unknown.

On July 19, 1913, Harold married Merle Williams. Both of their mothers worked in the Census Bureau. Merle, born in 1889, was four years Harold's senior, and had been married before. She was the daughter of a Methodist minister and had attended the Methodist-founded Willamette College in Salem, Oregon. Their only child, Dorothy Merle Hersey, was born on December 7, 1914. Another Dorothy in Harold's life.

Harold had written poetry since "early youth." In his latter years in Washington, he published several volumes of poetry, all privately printed. He also found opportunity to travel: "Visited Europe first in 1914 via cattle boat from Philly." Whether Merle came with him isn't known.

Degree in hand, Harold came to New York in 1915 as assistant to Eric Schuler, secretary of the new Authors' League of America; he helped edit the *Authors' League Bulletin*. We have no evidence that Merle came with Harold. On the contrary, he gives every indication of living as an unattached single man. Like his father, he appears to have given his literary ambitions priority over family obligations. Meanwhile, Merle held a number of secretarial positions in Washington, e.g. secretary in the Horticultural Board of the Department of Agriculture, secretary to Illinois Congressman George E. Foss. Her last known position was stenographer in the Bureau of Education, 1922-23.

In New York, Hersey became active on many fronts. He appears to have had no single longstanding employment, instead engaging "in many another ambitious enterprise." He worked in a restaurant, "typing menus to pay for meals," where he met many authors and artists. His friends were "mostly poets or painters." He freelanced. His byline turns up on poems and brief sketches in *The Smart Set*, *Breezy Stories*, *The Parisienne*, *Saucy Stories*, and numerous other magazines. He maintained a Washington connection through his association with a magazine, *The Minaret*, in 1916; he was advisory editor, and contributed a series, "Silhouettes of the City," and other material. He edited a New York fashion magazine, *Le Dernier Cri* (*The*

Latest); this may have lasted several years, but his only known bylines are in 1917 issues. He determined that writing fiction was not his likely destiny: "Courtland Young paid me fifteen dollars for the one and only story I ever wrote for a pulp" ("The Locked Door," *Young's Magazine*, February 1917). He also had a story, "The Dead Book," in *Le Dernier Cri*, which he later reprinted in *The Thrill Book*.

Hersey referred to his early years in New York as his Greenwich Village period and, indeed, he became a well-known figure in Bohemian and literary circles. In 1917, he helped launch a literary magazine, *The Quill*, the "house organ of Greenwich Village," an "idealistic venture" on which he served as editor for the first issue. He was advisory editor on another Village publication, *The Spectator*. The May 1917 issue included his article, "Patchin Place, a Little By-Way of New York." Patchin Place is a historic cul-de-sac in the Village that has been home to many famous writers, particularly in the early 20th Century. Hersey lived there, among "Patchinese" neighbors like John Reed (*Ten Days That Shook the World*). Hersey recalled how they "and many others lived in that narrow street off Jefferson Market Prison and struggled with our destinies, each in his individual way."

Hersey's broad experiences in this period introduced him to a great many people, including some prominent figures. One was Theodore Dreiser. Hersey had been a fan of the novelist, and written about him, thus when in 1916 the New York Society for the Suppression of Vice, and new chieftain John S. Sumner, sought to ban Dreiser's *The Genius* on grounds of obscenity, Hersey, on behalf of the Authors' League, immediately joined the defense. Hersey and H.L. Mencken sent out hundreds of letters to prominent writers, publishers, editors, academics, etc., seeking signatures for a leaflet protesting the ban. Hersey did most of the clerical work while Mencken applied the personal touch to famous authors. But Hersey's efforts threatened his position with the League when "respectable" members opposed the defense. According to Hersey, he was "forced out," after which he began a closer association with Dreiser. That ended sourly, however, when Hersey announced he wanted to publish an account of the defense effort; Dreiser thought he was abusing their friendship to advance his literary career. They remained friends, however. Years later, when Dreiser was complaining that he had to defend *The Genius* single-handedly, Mencken reminded him, "Young Hersey sweated for you like a bull."

Another prominent associate was Margaret Sanger, the pioneering birth control advocate. Hersey became friends with her in the prewar years, and was a great admirer. His laudatory poem, "Margaret Sanger," is included in his 1917 collection *The Singing Flame* (from the publisher of *The Spectator*): "Her presence lingers like a work of art/Which has expressed the untold mystery of life." In 1919, Hersey "serve[d] her and the cause on a volunteer basis." The two had a brief love affair in the early '20s. In 1921-22, Hersey helped edit her magazine, the *Birth Control Review*. He also contributed poems, book reviews, even a satiric one-act play.

After leaving Dreiser, Hersey went to work for the Britton Publishing Company, New York. He ghost-wrote the bestselling *Laugh and Live* (1917) for actor Douglas Fairbanks.

A number of people Hersey met in this period would cross paths with him during his years as a commercial magazine editor, to mutual benefit. In 1916, he went to Sing Sing to visit Henry Leverage, who had requested membership in the Authors' League. Leverage was doing time for auto theft, and remaking himself as a writer. They hit it off and the prolific author would eventually publish many stories in Hersey-edited pulps until his death in 1931. A minor example was Clement Wood, an assistant editor on *The Quill*. Wood became best known as a poet, and for his many books on the craft of poetry. He also wrote detective stories for the pulps. His short in the debut issue of Hersey's *Racketeer Stories* (February 1930), an anomalous item on Wood's résumé, is explainable primarily by his acquaintance with Hersey.

In March of 1917, Hersey turned 24 while America manned up for the Great War. Wyndham Martyn, the editor of *The Parisienne* who had published Hersey poems, introduced him to the Colonel of the Army's 9th New York Regiment. Hersey enlisted as a buck private, cutting short his editorship of *The Quill*. He was motivated to oppose "the repeated inhumanities of armed automatons in the service of a Government without honor." Notwithstanding its Bohemian tradition, Greenwich Village exhibited its own patriotic fervor; there was even a war benefit in Patchin Place. A week after Hersey's birthday, the U.S. declared war on Germany, but, though expecting to be called to the front, he would never see action: "Got lieutenancy three months later, assigned to general staff work; as lecturer (damn 'em) and had the dubious pleasure of lecturing instead of seeing the fun abroad." From 1917-19, he wrote a number of books for Britton. Unlike the Fairbanks ghostwork, most of the books had military themes, e.g.: *An Introduction to Military Science* (1917), *Do's and Don'ts In the Army* (1918). He contributed articles on military matters to *Scribner's* in late-'18 and early-'19. Two of these were expanded into *When the Boys Come Home* (Britton, 1919). In the book, he predicted that returning soldiers, transformed for the better by their experiences, would have a positive impact on domestic institutions. Hersey, in like fashion, had used his army service to advance his domestic literary career.

Hersey spent his last three months of army service in New Orleans, a welcome transfer. Discharge in hand, he returned to New York on Christmas night, 1918. "By and large, I hadn't enjoyed military life either as a volunteer in the ranks or as an officer. The train bringing me back to Patchin Place in Greenwich Village seemed to move at a snail's pace." He spent the evening "meeting old friends and acquaintances, visiting favorite eating places and wandering the streets of Greenwich Village."

> One disappointment marred this long-looked-for occasion. The lady who had written me so often and at such fulsome length, telling me how she lived only for the day of my return, answered my knock at her door by opening it just wide enough to see who it was, and screaming as she hastily closed it again. That I felt extremely sorry for myself, knowing she was not alone, goes without saying.

Hersey reconnected with Theodore Dreiser. Dreiser had visited him at Fort Hancock, New Jersey, and "talked over plans to organize a militant league of writers, painters, composers and others in the world of the Seven Arts"; now with Hersey back in New York and "all for starting a crusade against the moralists," they held meetings in Dreiser's apartment with author and editor Frank Harris, and many other personages from the arts, in attendance. But their ambitions fizzled, though Hersey "had a lot of fun accomplishing precisely nothing."

Instead, Hersey faced "the age-old problem of how to earn a living. . . . Bohemia had lost much of its charm. . . . I wanted just a plain job with a regular weekly salary, on a magazine, preferably, but if such was not to be, any job would do." In February 1919, at Margaret Sanger's home, he met W. Adolphe Roberts, editor of *Ainslee's* magazine:

> I hadn't an idea . . . of the sort of magazine for which I'd like to work. Certainly, I didn't envision myself as the editor in charge of a national publication of any sort. The job of assistant, or reader, was about all I could expect, and even this possibility seemed more like a dream than a reality. I would be 26 years old in a few weeks. Everyone, that Saturday afternoon, appeared so confident, so sure of themselves. Fresh out of the Army, with no feeling of security in this after-the-war period, and so many men much better equipped than I was, getting out of uniform day by day, I remember smiling somewhat foolishly when Margaret introduced me to Roberts, saying that she felt sure I would make a good editor if I had an opportunity to prove it. . . . Roberts surprised me by saying that over at his shop, Street & Smith, [they] were seriously considering the launching of something really new in the way of magazines. The title hadn't been decided upon, nor had they hired an editor as yet. He suggested that before I got embroiled with another "little" magazine I drop by the following Monday for a further chat. He might be able to introduce me to the General Manager, William Ralston, provided, of course, that we both agreed beforehand that I could handle the job.

Ralston and Hersey "hit it off" immediately. Ralston was satisfied with Hersey's experience despite its lack of commerciality. "He took me on, I think, more because of my energy and enthusiasm and my love for the printed page in any form, than for what I'd learned as editor of a Government publication and of such 'little' magazines as *The Quill*." Ralston's other concern was Hersey's affinity for fantastic literature, but this was a field Hersey was well-acquainted with, thanks to his father's influence. Hersey had read Verne, Wells, Poe, all the big names in the field. He'd even seen Méliès' *A Trip to the Moon* on a movie screen in Manila in 1905. Hersey was in the Street & Smith offices the following day. Only after he'd been "assigned a desk and instructed in the routine daily work at Street & Smith" was Hersey told his assignment. The new magazine was to be *The Thrill Book*, and it would focus on science fiction and the fantastic. Such material had appeared with increasing frequency in the Munsey pulps, but this magazine would be the first to center on the concept. Hersey burrowed into the job.

Hersey's future role with Bernarr Macfadden's magazine chain has its origin in a meeting from this period. Newsman Fulton Oursler was a newcomer to New York in 1918. In his autobiography, he tells of meeting Hersey, the most colorful description of Hersey from this—or any other—period:

> Back in my Baltimore days, Frank Blackwell had bought some of my yarns for *Detective Story* magazine. Now I was asking if I could write for him again. With great kindness he encouraged me to try; also, he told me, they were about to launch a new type of story magazine, the name of which must remain a secret. He introduced me to the editor of this budding storybook, Harold Hersey, a young man with bushy hair, gleaming eyes and a sardonic laugh. He told me he was a poet.
>
> "I live in a little cul-de-sac called Patchin Place," he told me, "behind the clock tower and the misery of Jefferson Market Court. I live in an attic there with an electrifyingly lovely mistress. Come and join the party this very night." It sounded like a speech from Murger. I could hardly wait for nightfall and set out from my rooming house as early as I dared.
>
> That night I had the feeling that I was visiting in the Elysian Fields of the land where I would make my home. Harold Hersey's garret was the vestibule of heaven, and he Saint Peter who let me through the pearly gates. Here Hersey lived for years with a succession of lovely ladies, quite in the pattern of Rudolph and Marcel and their fellows of *la vie de Bohème*. Of course, the bohemians never really existed, and neither did Hersey and his friends—not in the way they thought they existed. They made imaginary characters of themselves

and convinced me of their reality.

That smoky room is a haunting picture now. Men and women, some few on chairs, but most of them squatters on the floor, with little cakes to chew on and with thick china cups filled with red wine. Some called it Chianti; others called it Bordeaux; some insisted that it was Burgundy; you could call it anything you wished. And while we chewed and drank, Harold Hersey read his poems aloud in tones of such soft cadence that they should have been reserved only for the lines of William Shakespeare, but which he could impart to no other lines but his own. They sounded swell.

Other poets read their verses, too, and there was high talk—not about sociology or the rights of labor, but gossip about the soul of things. Today you can see their faces in the pages of the book reviews—and almost anywhere—for some of those men and women are famous now. Others, no one can ever see again, except in memory. Still others you can come upon, hidden away in little offices of magazines, preparing the copy of more fortunate writers to be printed and spread abroad.

Oursler gives the mortal's view of a god; the god, who had so many mortals at his feet, provides a more prosaic memory:

When I was mis-editing *The Thrill Book*, and making all the mistakes on the calendar, a slender, energetic fellow who made an immediate appeal to my heart called on me with a poem. As much as I hate to admit it, I did not buy that particular poem, but I did take such a fancy to its author that he came down to my tiny apartment at Patchin Place many times, and a friendship that has never lost its favor was born in those days. This was Fulton Oursler.

Oursler did have a short item in *Thrill Book's* fourth issue, however. Oursler went on to become Macfadden's Supervising Editor in 1921, a job he held continuously for twenty years, except for a brief period during which he relinquished the position to Hersey. The two men had strong elements in common. Both had literary inclinations, but would ultimately surrender much of their time and energy to the world of commercial magazine production. In time, Oursler's editing and writing career would be much more significant than Hersey's, but in 1919 Hersey was the one living the dream. The cheap digs of Patchin Place were soon to be a memory, though, as Hersey, perhaps because he had a real income from Street & Smith, soon found a better place on West 11th Street in the Village.

Other Macfadden figures surfaced in this period, such as John R. Coryell, the originator of Nick Carter, and a long-time editor and writer for Macfadden's *Physical Culture*. Hersey ran his novel, *Strasbourg Rose*, as a

4-part serial in *The Thrill Book*.

W. Adolphe Roberts was another figure who would land with Macfadden. He was on the editorial staff when Hersey became Supervising Editor, and would later appear in Hersey pulps. Milo Hastings, another compatriot, wrote for Macfadden magazines: articles on food for *Physical Culture*, a science-fiction serial for *True Story*. At about the time of Hersey's employment with Street & Smith, Hersey and Hastings wrote a short fantastic novel, *The Book of Gud*, presumably intended for *The Thrill Book*. They previewed the work for a mutual friend, songwriter and showman, Billy Rose, who dismissed it as "too big for your talents." Hersey eventually published *The Book of Gud* in his magazine *Main Street* in 1929, with Hastings' name changed to "Dan Spain."

Hersey lists multiple reasons for what proved to be a rapid failure for *The Thrill Book*:

> The sub-title of *The Thrill Book* was a compromise. We conferred about it again and again. Our final choice shows, indeed, how timidly we approached the great subject of science fiction. "A Delightful Number of a New Type of Magazine" was the way it read on Vol. 1, No. 1, dated March 1, 1919. This compromise was what destroyed the project in a short time. I blame no one but myself. I feel sure that had I been more daring, more certain of myself as an editor, and had I been better equipped with a wide knowledge of science fiction, I could have convinced Bill Ralston and the others in the "front office" of the need for a magazine almost 100 per cent devoted to this subject from the very start. I was not forced to bring out the first issue so quickly. I know I would have been allowed plenty of time in which to get in contact with the writers I needed, as well as develop others along the lines I had in mind. As has been so often the case with me, I rushed into print without stopping to consider every angle.

The boldness of the intention had not been matched by boldness of execution. This is in contrast to Gernsback's *Amazing Stories*, launched in 1926, which put science fiction on every cover and didn't dilute the contents with other kinds of material. Hersey concluded: "We did dream of publishing what is now known as science fiction. But about all we did was dream."

Ralston dismissed Hersey after half of *The Thrill Book's* sixteen issues had been published—incidentally, with *Strasbourg Rose* at its midpoint. Hersey never shrank from citing *The Thrill Book* as one of his failures: "It flopped. I was fired." The magazine, test marketed in selected states, simply failed to sell. Sam Moskowitz, in *Under the Moons of Mars: A History and Anthology of "The Scientific Romance" in the Munsey Magazines, 1912-1920*, points to another reason for Hersey's departure:

Murray Leinster, a close friend of Hersey's, asserts that the main reason he was dismissed was that an inordinate quantity of stories and poems published in *The Thrill Book* was discovered by Ralston to have been written by Hersey, and some even by his *mother*, under a wide variety of pen names.

Indeed, there is much material in *The Thrill Book* bylined under house names, during Hersey's reign and afterwards. In *Golden Atom*, Hersey lists some three-dozen poems he published in *The Thrill Book*, all but two under pseudonyms. Several were reprinted in Hersey's collection *Gestures in Ivory* (Britton, 1919). As Hersey admits, only one of them belonged in a magazine devoted to the fantastic. Four other *Thrill Book* poems were by Harry Kemp, a staff-writer for *The Quill*. It may have looked to Ralston that Hersey had fallen back on his Greenwich Village sensibilities, instead of fulfilling the primary goal of the pulps: entertainment, first and last. "Frank Blackwell . . . had tried to din this into my thick skull during my short stay with his house." The experience taught Hersey a much-needed lesson about the commercial world:

> When I began editing fiction sheets I had the notion that the readers were ignorant citizens who didn't know any better. My first experience as the editor of a national pulp taught me that the majority of them might be ignorant in a cultural sense, but not as to what they wanted to read. I started by attempting to teach them the finer things; I ended by being educated instead of educating, and, to add to my misery, I flunked the entire course.

Despite Hersey's occasional, brief, but cheerful, references to *The Thrill Book*, he may have harbored some resentment toward the experience. His April 1927 *Author & Journalist* bio mentioned he "worked as full editor in 'sweatshops,' where magazines are turned out as if they were shirts," a clue made more derogatory by its failure to name the house. He couldn't have been talking about Clayton, as he was currently employed as chief editor there. He must have meant Street & Smith, with their high output of weekly and semimonthly pulps; indeed, their reputation as the "fiction factory" mirrors Hersey's slur. In *Pulpwood Editor*, he backhandedly compliments Street & Smith as "good shoemakers."

Hersey quickly rebounded from the disaster by hiring on with William Clayton in June 1919. Clayton had broken into the pulps with *Snappy Stories* (1912-21, then sold) and *Romance* (1914-16), and was starting a new chain. The first title, with Hersey as the initial editor, was *Telling Tales*, a pulp aimed at women; a moderate success, it ran for six years and 91 issues. The magazine featured a large number of shorter items: stories, poems, and features. Numerous well-known names of the time could be found therein, e.g. H. Bedford-Jones, George Allan England, J.U. Giesy, Robert W. Sneddon, Octavus Roy Cohen, Murray Leinster. Some of Hersey's pals showed up, as well: Clement Wood, Harry Kemp, Henry Leverage. Hersey, himself, appeared with poems and features.

Hersey described his apprenticeship:

> When I joined this organization I was like a college graduate. I had the theory but not the practice. Mr. Clayton was a kind but stern teacher. He forgets more in one night about the practical making of magazines than the average publisher learns in a lifetime. The privilege of being Mr. Clayton's general advisory editor is due to those close years when he and I did all the work ourselves with only the help of one stenographer, a circulation man, and an office boy. I cut my eyeteeth then. [*The Author & Journalist*, May 1927]

With Clayton, Hersey would enjoy his longest period of steady employment since the Library of Congress.

In 1921, Hersey took a long trip to Europe, returning June 10. In London, he contributed material to *The English Review*. He lectured on American poets and history. Upon his return, he and Clayton were ready for a male-oriented pulp. They introduced *Ace-High Magazine*, the first of several successful magazines that would outlive the company. The first issue, dated September 1921, featured W. Adolphe Roberts, Henry Leverage, and Hersey on the contents page. Roberts had published Hersey's poetry in *Ainslee's* (and opened the door at Street & Smith); now Hersey returned the favor. Initially, *Ace-High* was positioned against *Adventure* and *Short Stories* in content: "All stories must be of the virile, out-of-doors, adventure type of appeal to red-blooded men. Western, adventure, detective, sea and sport stories are particularly desired." A banner above the title read "Western, Adventure and Sport Stories." Later, the comma was dropped to indicate a narrowed focus, in respect to the booming popularity of western fiction.

In 1922, Hersey had his own radio show for six months, on WOR, Newark, New Jersey. He spoke for an hour on topics in American history such as "The Growth of Arkansas." After the show ran its contracted course, Hersey turned his material into an *Ace-High* feature, "The Making of America: State by State." As he lamented in *Pulpwood Editor*, "I was still afflicted with the idea that the public would accept education along with entertainment. I was soon to be disillusioned. . . . Clayton used to say that *Ace-High* succeeded in spite of my articles, not because of them." The transition from Bohemian to editor was complete. From then on, entertainment would be Hersey's foremost goal.

Clayton hired Bina Flynn to help with the editing; western authors Ray Nafziger, W. Bert Foster, and J. Edward Leithead were kept on staff to generate fiction to mix in with material from freelancers. The next, and greatest, success, *Ranch Romances*, was inaugurated with a first issue of September 1924. Conceived by Clayton and Hersey, it established a romantic subgenre to the western. So successful was it, *Ranch Romances* outlived several owners, running into the early-'70s, the last of the pulps. It was soon followed by *Cowboy Stories* in May 1925, which "cost me many a headache before it succeeded." *Cowboy Stories* tilted the western in the direction of more action, the opposite track taken by *Ranch Romances*. The worldly Hersey may have seemed an unlikely figure to be presiding over an expanding empire of western yarns, but as he reminded people: "I was born in Bozeman, Montana, and raised on stories told by a father who went to Montana in the sixties and a mother born in Minnesota and who went West in the seventies." Perhaps to emphasize the point, he published the occasional humor item under the byline "Montana Bozeman."

Following the prevailing winds, Hersey started writing western poetry; a collection, *Singing Rawhide: A Book of Western Ballads*, illustrated by Clayton cover artist Jerry Delano, appeared in 1926. The book left an unusual legacy. One of the poems, "Lavender Cowboy," poked fun at an underdeveloped cowpoke: "He was only a lavender cowboy/The hairs on his chest were two." It was turned into a song for the 1930 Bob Steele movie *Oklahoma Cyclone*. From then on, it evolved into a minor country & western standard, sometimes with modified lyrics, sometimes with authorship listed as "traditional," as if it came from beyond memory. It was recorded by country artists as early as 1938. In 1940, it was banned from radio with many other "blue" songs. It was subsequently recorded many times, mostly in the '50s and '60s, most notably by Burl Ives.

The Danger Trail, an adventure pulp, was issued by Clayton in February 1926; in October, the detective pulp *Clues* joined the line-up, the last new magazine under Hersey's charge. With *Telling Tales* defunct, a victim of the success of the western magazines, Clayton had five major pulps, which may seem a modest number for a "chain," but most of the magazines were bumped up to twice-a-month publication after showing viability as a monthly. The combined circulation was in the range of two-million a month.

Curiously, Merle came to New York and began working in the cheap magazine field. In 1925-26, she edited the titillating *Artists and Models Magazine*. In 1929, she joined Harry and Irving Donenfeld at the Irwin Publishing Company, and became the well-known, and long-suffering, editor of a string of girly pulps: *La Paree Stories*, *Gay Broadway*, *Snappy Magazine*, etc. In 1931, Irwin turned into the Merwil Publishing Company, the name derived from "Merle Williams"; the shift was undoubtedly a dodge to shed Irwin's creditors, including unpaid authors, but Merle had also become a principal in the company. In 1933, the group revived the old pink-sheet *Police Gazette*, the "Barber's Bible," which had gone bankrupt in 1932. With Merle, a minister's daughter, editing, the revival garnered national attention. In 1934, she began developing a series of pulps for the company, which presumably became the *Spicys: Spicy Detective, Spicy Adventure*, etc.

Harold and Merle were probably still married as late as 1921, but were definitely divorced by early 1926, when Harold married Elinor Post, daughter of author W.H. "Billy" Post.

In the December 1926 *Author & Journalist*, western author Albert William Stone wrote of meeting the editor in the Clayton offices:

> Hersey is an impressively masculine man, with his heavy shock of gray-streaked hair, his close-clipped mustache, his athletic build, and his vigorous bass voice. The latter fairly booms. . . . Mr. Hersey likes authors. His enthusiasm is contagious—and lasting. He knows their problems, and he rejoices in their triumphs

When Hersey left Clayton, he cited *Ace-High, Ranch Romances, Cowboy Stories, The Danger Trail,* and *Clues* as the company's successes. He was generous in sharing credit for their creation, especially with Mr. Clayton. Early on, Hersey had been a hands-on editor; over time, as staff filled in below him, he became editor-in-chief, managing the chain. Essentially, he had risen to perform the same role that Fulton Oursler played for Macfadden Publications.

Thus, it was natural and reasonable, when Oursler resigned his position in March 1927, that he recommend his old friend Hersey to replace him. Oursler's surprise resignation quickly followed the surprise success of his Broadway play *The Spider*, which lured him into pursuing his dream of full-time freelancing.

Hersey's view of his own abilities had actually been moving in the opposite direction from Oursler's. As Oursler was embracing his dream of being a Real Writer, Hersey was surrendering to his role as mere editor:

> I didn't fail at writing and take up editorial work by way of revenge. Such an editor is almost as offensive as the college boy who drifts in regularly looking for an editor's job to fill in for the holidays, who offers as proof of his ability the fact that he edited the *Rah Rah Tic Tac* of good old Haryale. I have been associated with magazines since my thirteenth year, with certain interruptions—these interruptions being sorehead periods in the early days when I suddenly decided to write advertising copy, walk through Europe, or lecture to groups of

misunderstood ladies. Each interruption was a rank failure except in experience. Thus, I have been driven to realize that I am incapable of being anything else. Put this down on your mental ledger in either the debit or the credit column—it doesn't matter which; for, like the Old Man of the Sea, I am going to stay "until the last galoot's ashore." When my whiskers trail on the floor I will doubtless be clicking my heels together in a publisher's office the while I get a lacing for some story I purchased that displeased the Boss. [*A&J*, May 1927]

His attitude probably helped land him the job, as Bernarr Macfadden would have been overly sensitive to the possibility of hiring another man with bigger dreams than the job offered. To the July *A&J*, Hersey contributed an exuberant 900-word homage to his predecessor titled "My Friend Fulton Oursler." It was loaded with praise for Oursler's talents as editor and writer, and full of great expectations for his own future with Macfadden:

> When I learned that Mr. Oursler . . . had recommended me to Mr. Macfadden to succeed him as supervising editor of one of the largest publishing houses in the world, I was filled with hesitancy. My admiration for the man and my love for the man were equaled only by my admiration for his work. The mere fact that he felt that there was a possibility of my filling his shoes in this great organization was both flattering and disturbing. We discussed the matter many times in detail. It was only after I had the pleasure of meeting Mr. Macfadden and knowing that here was a man I could admire personally as well as officially that I had the courage to accept his offer.
>
> Among the many things that have happened to me during my life in New York, one of the things that has not occurred has been a sophistication of soul. I am still meek enough to admit that I have much to learn and much to gain by learning. In taking over this work I feel that I have an opportunity both to profit by my experience in editorial work and to perform a real service to humanity at large. I have long been an admirer of *True Story* as an element. I feel that it serves a great purpose in life and I feel that there is justification for the public taking it so to heart and buying the Macfadden magazines in overwhelming quantities.

Ominously, Oursler's break with Macfadden wasn't absolute. As Hersey continued:

> Both Mr. Macfadden and I are going to miss [Oursler] during his coming vacation in Europe and when he returns we are going to hold him here as an adviser so that we can benefit by the processes of his mind and the value of his experience, as well as burning enthusiasm for all that is decent and fine in life.

Nevertheless, Hersey suddenly found himself at the helm of the freewheeling Macfadden Publications, a far cry from Clayton's budget-conscious pulps. *True Story* alone had a circulation equal to the entire Clayton chain. Not to mention *Physical Culture*, *True Detective Mysteries*, *True Romances*, *Dream World*, *The Dance Magazine*, and *Ghost Stories*. There were nine magazines in all, and several newspapers. Hersey was in charge of hundreds of people, including old friend W. Adolphe Roberts, a staff editor.

When Oursler returned from Europe, Hersey was at the dock to greet him, one editorial titan to another. Oursler had no intention of returning to Macfadden, but his expenses were mounting. He was already paying significant alimony to his first wife; on top of that, *The Spider* attracted a raft of plagiarism suits. They were eventually proven groundless, but the legal bills were burdensome. So, approximately eight months after assuming control of Macfadden Publications, on December 23, 1927, Hersey was out and Oursler back in. Was Macfadden unhappy with Hersey's performance? Macfadden stayed discreetly silent on the subject. We can fairly say that Oursler's departure, which severed an excellent working relationship, had been a huge disappointment to Macfadden, and Oursler's return would have been welcome and comforting. Oursler remained quiet, as well. It must have been an uncomfortable moment in his relationship with Hersey, especially after having lured him away from a solid position with Clayton. As for Hersey, he played the good soldier and never divulged the terms of his departure, only describing it as a resignation; a fig leaf, perhaps, to mask a humiliating turn of events. In *Pulpwood Editor*, he strings together a long list of memories of the Macfadden experience, many of them negative, e.g.:

> The desk pool "with hundreds of eyes boring into my back"; "always seeing new faces and the feeling that I was once more an adjutant in the army and that outside my office were hundreds of sergeant-majors and clerks detailed to the task of handling myriad shifting, changing men who were nothing more than numbers to me and never could be anything more"; "the sudden realization that power, now that I had come into it, was a bore"; "conferences, eternal conferences"; "scratching my name or initials a thousand times a day on a thousand different documents"; "the visitors, oh! those dull, interminable conversations"; "deadlines, deadlines, deadlines— forever the slave of schedule"; "red tape and tiresome expenditure of precious energy handling routine instead of making magazines as I had been trained to do"; etc., etc.

It sounds even worse than Street & Smith's "shoemaking." These comments bolster Hersey's position that he had resigned, by laying out the reasons while still not divulging the particulars. He did retain his respect and affection for Bernarr Macfadden, and refers to the experience as a "postgraduate course" that prepared him to eventually strike out on his own. Still, the comments are surprisingly candid given Hersey's typical circumspection. It could be he was merely echoing what he had already confessed to Macfadden.

When Hersey left Macfadden, he was "the proud possessor of around $500 and a lot of dreams—with perhaps more hope than faith." He went to his mother's country home in Highland, New York, eighty miles up the Hudson River, determined to get out of the "editorial game." But the bug was too big to squash. After ten days, he established a new publication, *Swap—The Swapper's Magazine*. He described it as the logical extension of the readers' departments found in magazines like *Ace-High*. It would be "a medium of exchange for articles and ideas." It would also include fiction. The *Author & Journalist* solicitation blurb called for "short-stories with swapping or trading plots." A western serial would begin in the first issue. To contributors, *Swap* would pay a paltry half-cent a word. In *Pulpwood Editor*, Hersey described *Swap's* fate, lesson learned, and benefit gained:

> *Swap* lasted for three issues, but I have never looked upon it as a personal failure. It was my first venture as an independent publisher on a national scale and it was the means of introducing me to an enterprising group who, although they did not encourage me to go on with *Swap,* did listen to the more ambitious scheme I had long entertained of establishing a string of pulps over my own name.
>
> Incidentally, it taught me a lesson in the financial psychology of the Boom Days. I learned not to approach Money with a small though practical magazine proposition based on the American propensity to trade—even to swapping horses while crossing a stream—and which required but little financial support. Unless one promoted something *big* there wasn't a Chinaman's chance of securing cash or credit.

He must have been sensitive to criticism at this time. In *A&J*, he answered back:

> All that I can say about [*Swap*] is that it was the third failure out of twenty-one years of successes. [*The Thrill Book* and, presumably, *Telling Tales*, were the other two.] Of course, my enemy friends and my friendly enemies can look at the failure and forget *Ace-High, The Quill, Cowboy Stories, Clues, The Ledernier Cri* [sic], and others, since I started editing and mis-editing. Here in New York there is always much more excitement about a failure than there is about a success.

During the Highland period, Hersey also took over an established magazine, *Elite Styles*, his first venture into fashion since *Le Dernier Cri*. Another step toward independence, Hersey would share in the profits . . . were there to be any. One Hersey-edited issue of *Elite Styles* made it out before financial troubles sunk the enterprise.

It had been a rough patch, the sudden departure from Macfadden, followed by two quick-failing magazine ventures; but it was the bridge Hersey needed to set him on the path from employed editor to independent publisher. After rejecting offers from publishers, he joined the Eastern Distributing Corporation as general editorial adviser. This seems to have been a temporary arrangement. Hersey busied himself buying material for *Brief Stories* while he plotted the birth of his own chain of pulp magazines. The timing was excellent for such an enterprise. The conservative old-line distributor, the American News Company, offered reliable service, wide reach, prompt payments, and took a modest return. But independent distributors, like Eastern, were rising to challenge the ANC. They arranged credit with manufacturers, advanced credit to the publisher, paid shipping, handled returns, and took a bigger commission. What they needed was product; all the publisher needed was a little cash, $5000 in the case of Hersey and his backers, a shoestring. As he noted in *Pulpwood Editor*, "the scramble to get out magazines, good and bad, became so intense, so hysterical, that it seemed for a while that all one had to have was an idea for a new magazine in order to embark upon a publishing career." So, barely half a year after leaving Macfadden, Hersey was an editor-in-chief again, this time for his own brainchild, officially called Magazine Publishers, and unofficially the Hersey Magazines. Once again, he was living his dreams.

The chain was launched with four titles which began appearing on newsstands in late-August, 1928: *Flying Aces*, *Western Trails*, *The Dragnet*, and *Under Fire*, a war pulp. ("The average pulp is launched in the late summer so as to benefit by a running start when cold weather comes.") Macfadden entered the all-fiction field at the same time with *Red Blooded Stories* and *Flying Stories*, prompting *A&J* to observe, in regard to both companies, "there seems no limit to the number of fiction magazines that can be swallowed up by the American public." The total print run for Hersey's first four issues was 400,000. New pulps sold in unpredictable quantities, thus justifying the multi-title approach. Hersey noted: "Fortunately, my creation of *Flying Aces* was an instantaneous and lasting success. It carried the weaker titles."

Hersey tried to attract authors with a novel approach to payment: the word-rate was tied to an issue's sales. A 50,000-issue seller would net the author a cent-a-word; at the top end, a 125,000-seller would pay three cents. Unmentioned in that plan was the term "payment on publication," often the hallmark of the fly-by-night operation; established authors expected to be

paid on acceptance. What "payment on publication" said about Hersey's
financial position was that, as a startup on a shoestring, he couldn't afford to
invest in the future, not even in the next month's issue.

New titles were added in quick succession. Hersey bought the reprint
pulps, *The Golden West* and *The Underworld*, from Carwood Publishing
and converted them to original-fiction magazines. Over a five-month period,
another six pulps were added: *Sky Birds*, *Spy Stories*, *Fire Fighters*, *Aviation
Stories*, *Murder Mysteries*, and *Loving Hearts*. *Spy Stories* and *Fire Fighters*,
in particular, demonstrate the trend toward extreme specialization then
underway in the pulps. Hersey issued such magazines as experiments, bait
for untested public fancies. The concept alone wouldn't sustain the magazine,
however; execution mattered. He blamed the failure of *Fire Fighters* on
impatient handling in "a money-mad decade." Hersey also tried his luck
with two mainstream magazines: *Famous Lives*, a magazine of biographical
material, and *Main Street*. The latter, a quarterly devoted to American arts
and letters, Hersey co-edited with his wife Elinor. A film magazine was
announced but never issued. The circulation for the entire group quickly
approached a million-and-a-half copies a month. Later, singling out some of
the successes of Magazine Publishers, Hersey said:

> *Underworld* magazine doubled in sales during the time that I
> edited it. *Flying Aces* sold over 90,000 copies with the third issue.
> *Western Trails* reached an average of about 50,000, making a profit,
> but a small one.

Despite these small triumphs, Hersey resigned from the company in the
summer of '29. *Writer's Digest* called it "agreeing to disagree." Hersey was
as inscrutable as always. Perhaps his backers—who he never named—felt
that too many of the titles were experimental, and too few successful. Perhaps
they wanted more control over his decisions. Perhaps Hersey bargained hard
for everything he wanted because he knew, that if negotiations failed, he
had a better deal waiting in the wings. Our best idea of what the backers
wanted is what happened to the company after Hersey left. New editorial
management was hired, half the titles were shed from the roster, and the
company rebranded itself as the Ace magazines. It remained viable for two
decades. "It is functioning today under extremely able management," Hersey
conceded in *Pulpwood Editor*.

As soon as Hersey left Magazine Publishers, his next venture sprang
up, the Good Story Magazine Company. There would be no soul-searching
about his future in the "editorial game" to delay matters. It's the dramatic
suddenness of this event which suggests Hersey might have known he had
another deal waiting. All he would admit publicly is that he was "amply

financed," a divulgence to reassure freelancers that they ran no risk in submitting stories. The '20s had been littered with low-paying, slow-paying, or non-paying magazine publishers.

In the summer of '29, Hersey started soliciting fiction for the new venture:

> What I am most interested in now is in securing Western, detective, crook and underworld, as well as flying material—short-stories, novelettes and serials. I will not use detective short-stories, but will only want detective novelettes and serials. Aviation stories will go easy on the woman interest, but strong on action and the technical sides of flying. Western stories should either be of the two-gun type or humorous in characterization and plot. Crook stories—and I will use many of them—must have a strong feminine interest, playing up the gun-girl as well as the crook.

Industry interest must have been high—and wide—forcing Hersey to make these remarks in the October 1929 *Author & Journalist*:

> Many of my good friends have been writing to me to say that they have received word that my new string of Red Band Magazines are either selling well or not selling at all or just getting along. This information about the selling of my new string has held me spellbound—these rumors are beautiful because of the fact that the first of the new string of magazines is not even on the newsstands at the time of this writing. Thus is Dame Rumor, the past mistress of rum, Romanism, and rebellion—or what have you? During the past two years, as Mark Twain might say, rumors of my death have been grossly exaggerated. Rumors have flown hither and yon, like swallows, and if I had tried to keep track of them and followed them to their various sources, I would probably have joined some pleasant mad-house near by.

He laid out his ambitious plans for the forthcoming year, with failure factored into the calculation:

> Our hope is to get at least one success out of every four titles issued and in the fall of 1930 to experiment with further titles with the same percentage of success in mind. . . . It would be a wise man indeed who could predict the future of any title. The making of a magazine has been my business for over twenty years. I have had a large proportion of success, about 80 per cent. But the 20 per cent of failures have been my greatest teachers.

Over a five-month period spanning 1929 and '30, Good Story issued a dizzying eleven titles, easily the most audacious debut of any new company in the history of the pulps. The red-hot genre of aviation was represented by three magazines (*Flight, Eagles of the Air, Complete Flying Novel*). Of course, there had to be a detective title (*Detective Trails*) and a mainstream western (*Quick-Trigger Western Magazine*). There were experimental one-shots: *Lucky Stories*; *Love and War Stories*, a cross-genre pollination; and *Thrills of the Jungle*, for which Hersey claimed inventor's credit for "the joining of the adventure and sex themes." Since some titles were planned for ten-issues-per-year publication, the company never had eleven pulps come out in a single month. The top months (judging by the slightly misleading cover dates) had nine.

(In the thick of this activity from Good Story, Hersey issued a one-shot named *Popular Engineering Stories*, April 1930. The publisher was listed as the Magazine and Book Corporation, but Hersey's name is not to be found within. The layout of the magazine and the use of regular Good Story writers, and artist W.C. Brigham, brands it a Hersey product, and Hersey alludes to it in *Pulpwood Editor*. But the motivation for segregating it from Good Story isn't clear.)

Most noteworthy in Good Story's launch was Hersey's introduction of a new genre, the gang pulp, which had gestated in *The Underworld* and *The Dragnet* with "crook stories"—tales told from the point-of-view of Prohibition's illicit profiteers. The magazines created to present this new world of Tommy-gun action, unscrupulous gun molls, gang murders, and all-around violence were *Gangster Stories* and *Racketeer Stories*. Hersey even pushed the concept of lawless entertainment to the other side of the Mississippi with *Western Outlaws*, as if to show that crime in America was a well-established tradition. The gang pulps, which portrayed criminality as if the law barely existed, were an "instantaneous and spectacular national success" and quickly received a censorship backlash from Sumner and the New York Society for the Suppression of Vice, the very same group that had stymied Dreiser in days of yore. Hersey was forced to make editorial concessions. Also, the indicia of the pulps switched the publication office from New York City to Springfield, Massachusetts, probably on advice of attorney, since the NYSSV's jurisdiction was New York state. (The controversy is dealt with in detail in *Gang Pulp*, OFF-TRAIL PUBLICATIONS, 2008.)

At this point, we can examine the issue of Hersey's financing for this significant undertaking. It seems to have been an open secret in the business that Bernarr Macfadden was backing Hersey, but the two principals kept the arrangement very hush-hush, never discussing it publicly. A main point of evidence is the quiet migration of magazines from Macfadden's company to Hersey's, which took place for more than a year. It started with two transfers:

1) *Love and War Stories*, edited by war correspondent Burnet Hershey, was a genre-blending minor entry. It had been announced as a new Macfadden magazine in early '29; but came out as a Good Story pulp with a cover date of January 1930. It survived for one issue, suggesting poor sales and the possibility that it had been issued simply to get a return on already purchased material. 2) A floundering Macfadden pulp, *Tales of Danger and Daring*, had been announced as the renamed *Jungle Stories*, but then ended up as Good Story's *Thrills of the Jungle* (December 1929). After the first flush of new Good Story magazines, Macfadden's pet project *Flying Stories* (he was an aviation enthusiast) came under Hersey's control. This was soon followed by *Ghost Stories*. The last Macfadden issue was March 1930; the first Good Story issue was dated April, continuing it the same format without interruption. Two Macfadden nonfiction magazines came over later. *The Dance Magazine* joined Hersey's group in the late summer, and *Model Airplane News* joined in 1931. The implication of all this is that Hersey's company was a Macfadden subsidiary which would create its own titles and attempt to give second-life to magazines failing at the parent company.

Further evidence of the Macfadden-Hersey connection comes from the correspondence of author August Derleth. Derleth tried unsuccessfully to sell to *Ghost Stories*. In 1929, he received letters from *Ghost Stories* editor Daniel E. Wheeler on Macfadden letterhead. In 1931, he received several letters from Wheeler on Good Story letterhead. Later in '31, Derleth received correspondence from the new *Ghost Stories* editor, Stuart Palmer, on Macfadden letterhead; subsequent Palmer letters used Good Story paper. All of this suggests a mingling of resources—from editorial staff to stationary—between the two companies.

An outright confirmation—of what should otherwise be obvious—came from pulp-writer Arthur J. Burks. In 1929, he sold stories to both Macfadden's *Flying Stories* and Hersey's *Spy Stories*. In 1930, he supplied a steady stream of fight-racket novelettes to *Gangster Stories*. A New Yorker at the time, he'd visited the Good Story offices to talk shop, as made clear in the following dispatch in the October 1930 *Writers' Markets and Methods*. He also gives some insight into the chaos inherent in launching a pulp chain from scratch:

> I have heard considerable complaints among writers lately about the *Good Story Magazine Company*, Harold Hersey, editor and publisher. This is a Macfadden subsidiary, its debts underwritten by that organization. I've always got my money from this group, though I have waited, and even got more money by waiting and refusing to quarrel with a harassed editor who has a huge job on his hands. While it is confidential, as to the inner details, I happen to know something

of the inner workings of this office, and about the various inside things that have cropped up to cause some discontent among writers about the way they have been used. My word for it, the inner discord of this group has been straightened out, and you will get a square deal there if you'll practice a little forbearance. After all, the beginner gets a chance to get into print with this group far sooner in his development than anywhere else in the game. Also my word for that.

Macfadden's backing is clear and it's not hard to fathom his motives. One is that Hersey was qualified for such a job; Macfadden must have concluded that in 1927 or this later arrangement wouldn't have come about. Another is that Macfadden had huge financial resources, had failed to make successes of his own all-fiction magazines, felt it was an important market, and saw Hersey as his rainmaker. The last is that Hersey's unfortunate experience as Macfadden's Supervising Editor—ditching his position at Clayton only to be haunted by Oursler's unexpected return—left Macfadden feeling indebted. The Good Story venture also makes it clear that Hersey burned no bridges upon leaving Macfadden's employ.

The more problematic question is why Macfadden and Hersey kept the partnership such a secret. One naturally suspects financial motives in business dealings, but none are obvious in this case. Reformulating the question as, What were they trying to hide? raises another possibility. Bernarr Macfadden is famous as "the Father of Physical Culture"; it's the bedrock of his enduring fame. A much less-appreciated aspect of his life, because it never got very far off the ground, was his lofty political aspirations, up to and including the Presidency. He first dipped his toes in the waters in 1928, hoping to run for Governor of New York. Other attempts at high office were yet to come. It's fair to say, though, that in 1929, as Hersey's financier, he would have been briefed of Hersey's plans in detail, and would have greatly preferred not to have his name associated with Hersey's dubiously moral gang pulps lest it be raised against him in a political campaign. If protecting Macfadden's name was a priority, it would also explain why Hersey reacted swiftly to the vice bureau's assault on the magazines. It further explains why Hersey continued to remain vague about Good Story's backing in *Pulpwood Editor*. When the book was published in 1937, Macfadden's political aspirations were still very much in effect, and Hersey may have considered vows of privacy to be equally in effect.

Throughout 1930, Hersey tinkered with the lineup. *Western Outlaws* was renamed *Outlaws of the West*; *Quick-Trigger Western* changed to *Quick-Trigger Stories of the West*, though its last issue was January 1931. Several titles, in addition to the experimentals, were dropped: all the aviation magazines, *Detective Trails*. The gang pulps were working, though, and, per the original plan, more titles were added later in the year. *Mobs* and *Gangland Stories*, two similar themes, were added simultaneously in the summer; *Mobs*, presumably the weaker seller, was dropped after two issues. *Prison Stories* was added later in the year, with much of the content supplied by ex-con and Hersey favorite, Henry Leverage. However, Leverage died in February 1931, taking the magazine down with him. In all, Good Story published 76 issues in 1930 (judging by cover date, not street date). A rolling twelve-month average shows the company putting out a consistent 6-7 issues a month.

Hersey was the face of the company, which leaves the impression that he edited all the magazines himself. He may have personally edited many issues but he did, in fact, have a staff, which he refers to numerous times in *Pulpwood Editor*, e.g. "my editor" for *Gangster Stories*. He recounts several anecdotes about firing editors, including one incident that implicitly came to blows:

> And there was the editor who changed the magazine's policy during my absence on a swing around the country. He had not consulted anyone except himself. He dropped his regular writers without giving them a warning, substituting an untried group. He was fired by long distance telephone. He waited at the front door for my return. Our argument was settled in that comforting fashion so popular among schoolboys. He stayed fired, nonetheless.

Unfortunately for history, only a few of the names of his staffers leaked out. *Ghost Stories* had Dan Wheeler and Stuart Palmer, as noted. *Flying Stories* had Eugene Clancy, whom Hersey had met at Street & Smith while he edited *Thrill Book* and Clancy handled *People's*. Additionally, a Hersey ad in the June 1930 *Author & Journalist* mentioned: "Mrs. Hersey and I personally read every story that comes in." A September item in *Writer's Digest* added:

> Mr. Hersey's . . . rather peculiar when he sends you back a yarn—he doesn't use rejection slips of any kind! But don't imagine your story hasn't been read thoroughly nevertheless, even if you do get it back in your return envelope with nothing but the script. Mr. and Mrs. Hersey both read every yarn carefully, and you'll get fast decisions. A wonderful market for the clever unknown writer—Mr. Hersey doesn't give a darn about big names—it's the *story* that counts with him, first, last and always.

Combined with her role on *Main Street*, the references to Elinor Hersey imply that she had been intimately involved in the Hersey operation all along.

In early '31, *Complete Gang Novel Magazine* was introduced. It looked and felt like a Hersey gang pulp, and featured the same talent, but the publisher was listed as the Complete Gang Novel Co. Hersey's involvement was hidden at first, then later admitted, and the imprint changed to Good Story. *Complete Gang Novel* listed Kenneth Owens as editor, but that may be a Hersey pseudonym. The motives for the secrecy aren't clear. The pulp ran for ten issues into 1932.

The gang pulps, *Ghost Stories*, and *Outlaws of the West* continued to run through '31, but there were to be no more successful new magazines. There was, instead, a proliferation of new Good Story titles that quickly died: *Miracle, Science and Fantasy Stories* (originally announced as *Astonishing Stories*) (2 issues), *Speakeasy Stories* (4), *Riders of the Range* (western-love) (4), *Zoom* (4), *Murder Stories* (3), and *Courtroom Stories* (6). Added to *Complete Gang*, they represented a second wave of seven new titles over six months, almost matching the company launch. Good Story continued to put out 6-7 issues a month, but since the second wave didn't produce a few winners like the first wave had, we can assume that overall sales were falling. The second wave may even represent a note of desperation, an attempt to generate new revenue to offset falling sales of the first wave.

Why was Good Story failing? Hersey struck gold with the gang pulps but, over time, it proved to be a claustrophobic genre; the stories were confined to a narrow fictional universe. In that respect, it resembled the Western Front fiction that had been the rage in the late '20s and had already run its course with the public. There were only so many fresh stories that could be told about men in a trench—or a speakeasy. Hersey and Macfadden had been right about the timing for an explosion in the pulp field; but they were wrong about the formulation of the product. Good Story pulps smacked of '20s style with their white-backgrounded cover designs. Hersey argued for his approach in *Pulpwood Editor*: "I have found that the vignette is superior in sales value to the overall, or bleed painting that takes up every fraction of an inch on the cover." The development of the pulps in the '30s argues otherwise. Full-color took over the newsstands; vignettes became the exception. New companies like Popular Publications carefully crafted their covers for eye-appeal, including *Gang World*, which came on the market in late-'30 and was a nickel cheaper than *Gangster Stories*, to boot; it only lasted several months longer than *Gangster*, but it must have cannibalized some of Hersey's gang sales. And there was plenty of other competition on the newsstand: reliable Street & Smith, Fiction House, Dell, Clayton, with the Thrilling chain just coming onto the market in late-'31. The often crude artwork on the Good Story pulps put them among the worst-looking of the lot. Hersey couldn't afford the name writers, either. His stars, like Anatole Feldman, had to be homegrown. Even Hersey's own Magazine Publishers, now doing business as Ace, were winning the beauty contest at the cheap end of the spectrum.

All things considered, this announcement from the November '31 *Author & Journalist* probably came as no surprise to the industry: "Harold Hersey has retired from the Good Story Magazine Company, and its affairs are being closed up." Macfadden must have withdrawn his support and the reasons are easy to fathom. Good Story had proven to be a poor investment, and any sense of indebtedness to Hersey had been paid off. Macfadden had other poor investments to consider, especially his tabloid the *New York Evening Graphic* which continued to bleed millions from company coffers. Plus he had just purchased the major national weekly, *Liberty*. Good Story may have been one annoyance too many. But it wasn't quite the final word. The shutdown announcement had been premature. Hersey purchased the titles and forged ahead as a true independent, as of November 1; as of January 2 he took over distribution in partnership with a J.V. Rafferty. Hersey: "I had the cows, so I bought the delivery wagons." He continued the second wave of futile title creation with *Headquarters Stories* (2 issues), *Front Page Stories* (4), *Blue Band Magazine* (1), *New York Stories* (3), and *Speed Stories* (2). They, and the preexisting titles, were published under imprints like Headquarters Publishing and Blue Band Publishing.

Hersey's relationship with Macfadden wasn't severed, however, as he performed a publishing favor for his benefactor which, though the timing is hazy, appears to have occurred *after* Hersey's purchase of Good Story. Macfadden had feuded in 1930-31 with George T. Delacorte, founder of Dell Publishing. Dell had been issuing confessional magazines along the Macfadden lines (as had other publishers). Macfadden's irritation apparently reached a boiling point in '31 when Dell brought out a new title, *My Story*. Macfadden threatened to create a competitor, *Your Story*, and *My Story* was dropped. In the summer of '31, Dell came out with a humor magazine, *Ballyhoo*, which was a surprise success, quickly reaching two-million copies in sales. Hersey: "Boy, weren't we disgusted when [Dell] scored so emphatically with *Ballyhoo*." Macfadden struck out for revenge using Hersey as his proxy. Hersey issued an imitation called *Tickle-Me-Too*, which didn't last long. In December, Hersey had his own humor magazine on the newsstands, *Slapstick*, edited by Hugh Layne, one of Hersey's associates on *The Dance Magazine*. Another humor title, *Haywire*, was added a few months later.

Being in charge of the show allowed Hersey to indulge his long-smoldering desire for Real Writerhood. He returned to his literary roots with a magazine of letters, *The American Autopsy*. Intended as a quarterly, it lasted one issue, January '32, and featured a novel and nearly 100 pages of verse, all unsigned; all by Hersey, as he admitted in *Pulpwood Editor*.

He referred to magazines like *Main Street* and *The American Autopsy* as "magazines born of pride rather than of common sense."

By the summer of '32, the Hersey gang pulps had wound to a halt. *Gangster* and *Complete Gang* ceased publication; *Racketeer and Gangland Stories* was a consolidation that lasted three issues before expiring. *Outlaws of the West*, the western gang pulp, was one of the last to fold, with a final date of August '32. Meanwhile, Hersey maintained a shred of publishing respectability with the Macfadden holdovers *The Dance Magazine* and *Model Airplane News*. He was going through tough times. In *Golden Atom*, he mentions "having to walk back and forth to the printer after selling my Pierce Arrow car and giving up my New York penthouse apartment."

An odd item in the Hersey oeuvre is the final issue of *Gangster Stories*. The last issue in the continuum was dated July 1932. Four months passed and this issue reappeared on newsstands with a November date on the cover and contents page. The stories were all the same. Another significant alteration was the box on the contents page advertising the next issue. The July issue announced an "All-Star August Issue"; the November issue announced an "All-Star November [sic] Issue of Greater Gangster Stories." The promised stories, including Anatole Feldman's "Tanbark Racketeers," were the same in both. In the interim, Hersey had sold the *Gangster Stories* title (and *Model Airplane News*, and presumably the rights to all his titles); the November reissue of *Gangster* appears to have been the first number from the new management. *Greater Gangster Stories*, which ambiguously promised either greater gangsters or greater stories, finally appeared on the newsstands with a February 1933 date, and highlighted "Tanbark Racketeers" on the cover. The publisher was listed as the See Publishing Corporation, which is probably the corporate mask for George C. Johnson, listed in the magazine's indicia as President. Material for the pulp was solicited in the writers' mags by the Jay Publishing Co., which no doubt represents Jay P. Cleveland, listed as Secretary. The editor was Hugh Layne. Hersey's name is not to be found in any of the issues, nor in the legally precise Statement of Ownership in the November 1933 issue. In all respects, however, the pulp was similar to *Gangster Stories*, in cover style, title logo, featured authors, etc. Thirteen issues of *Greater Gangster* came out, the last dated May '34, by which time Prohibition, which created the climate for bootleggers and gangsters, had been repealed.

As Hersey's publishing enterprises had struggled along, he supplemented his income with a variety of enterprises, as described in *Pulpwood Editor*:

> I was not only the head of a publishing business, but a central distributing agency, as well, which serviced the wholesalers over the country with magazines owned by other publishers and those of my

own such as the *Dance Magazine, Model Airplane News, Slapstick* and the pulpwood sheets. I was also distributing razor blades, playing cards and similar products that sell both in drugstores and on the newsstands.

He issued an exposé magazine for a friend, *Medical Horrors*, with articles like "The Drug Racket." He took care to conceal his role as publisher, but when word of his involvement got out, he cancelled the magazine after one issue (January '32) rather than risk offending his drugstore clients. He increasingly turned to work-for-hire publishing jobs, including a short-lived title which he edited in '32, *Screen Humor*. With his magazine chain swallowed by history, he appears to have lacked a dominant source of income, cobbling together a living. He worked on an oddball magazine, *Strange Suicides*, for another publisher. Two issues, dated January and February 1933, came out. "If I grow to be a hundred I will never live down *Strange Suicides*—my friends and enemies, God bless them both!—have no intention of ever letting me forget it." He served as business manager for a weekly tabloid of New York news, *Knickerbocker Jr.*; it was edited by others and probably didn't last long.

Also, in the second half of 1933, he became marginally involved in the publication of girly pulps, or "sex magazines," the risqué fiction magazines that often featured nude photography and sold under the counter, the kind of magazines that ex-wife Merle had made her name in. In *Pulpwood Editor*, Hersey describes the business aspect of this "pseudo-pornographic nonsense" in great detail, but is near-silent about his own involvement. He only goes as far as listing the titles, and his role. For four titles, such as *French Night Life Stories* and *Jo Burton's Follies*, he notes that he served as advisory editor; on a fifth, *Harlem Nights*, he was publisher. Despite the similarity in material, there's no known connection with these magazines and Merwil Publishing.

Later in the year, Hersey edited a new pulp, *The Twice-a-Month Love Book Magazine*, which featured art that wrapped around the front and back covers. The contents were cheap, though, and only one issue is known to have been published. In this venture, Hersey shared an office on 42nd Street with the publisher of another ephemeral experiment, *Detective*. Within several months both concerns were out of business.

Hersey's activities from 1934 to mid-'36 are largely unknown. He had to have written *Pulpwood Editor* in this period, although at 74,000 words it's unlikely to have occupied the entire period. It was published June 3, 1937, which probably means Hersey turned the manuscript over to his publisher a year before that, give or take a few months. How he supported himself while writing the book is a mystery.

In the middle of '36, Hersey returned to the magazine game with a trio of titles based on popular comic-strip characters. It appeared to be a low budget operation. Hersey's address was "Room 1104, 49 West 45th Street." *Writer's Digest* noted that "he is to be found there only at a few stated hours." At least one assistant editor was involved. The name of the company was C.J.H. Publications. Hersey's mother's name was Adelaide Carpenter Johnson Hersey, Johnson being her maiden name, and that's our best theory to explain the initials. Two of the magazines were standard pulp-size, *Dan Dunn Detective Magazine* and *Tailspin Tommy Air Adventures Magazine*. Their cover art looked like color comic-strip panels, as opposed to the typical painted pulp cover; color interior illustrations also distinguished them from standard pulps. The first issue of *Dan Dunn* was dated September 1936, and it alternated months with *Tailspin Tommy* for two issues apiece with one skipped month. In that slot (December), Hersey issued a larger saddle-stitched magazine, *Flash Gordon Strange Adventure Magazine*. It ran only one issue. A Joe Palooka magazine was announced but never came forth. Before the bottom fell out, Hersey absorbed *Mystery Adventure* from its distressed publisher, changing the title to *Mystery Adventures*. It lasted for five issues under Hersey's guidance, a number equal to all the comic-based pulps.

The sale of *Pulpwood Editor* may have whetted Hersey's appetite to return to writing, since by the fall of 1936, he was absorbed in work on a project he had "long dreamed of," a biography of old friend Margaret Sanger. Sanger wrote him on October 20, after learning of his efforts. (Information on this period comes from Sanger's correspondence.) The timing would have come at about the time the last of the comic-based pulps had been put to bed; *Mystery Adventures* continued to appear, dividing Hersey's attention. Sanger didn't take Hersey seriously at first, but when she learned in January and February, 1937, that he was conducting interviews she became alarmed. She had been working on her own story and feared the potential contradictions and complications that might arise from having a competing book out at the same time, a version by a former lover, no less. As she wrote a friend:

> Well Hersey did go out to Corning [New York] & my brother said he was cheap & awful— He ran about wild talking to everyone over 80 that he could find. He has a complex which makes him avoid talking to intelligent people. He caters to the poorest, most ignorant & likes what they say . . . He is no biographer but a pulp journalist & I'm finished. I've written his publisher & to him. He gives me a pain so there—

To defuse the animosity, Hersey agreed to submit the manuscript for her approval. Later, Sanger met Hersey and his publisher, Robert Speller, for drinks at the Ambassador Hotel in Manhattan. But Hersey reneged on the offer to share the manuscript, later blaming his "stern pride." Sanger was angered and remained so for many months. As she wrote one of her two ghost-writers on October 19: "I hoped against hope that Hersey would drop dead or have some other calamity befall him before he finished what he calls a Biography." She got her wish, more or less. Fate—disguised as economics—intervened, as it did so often in Hersey's affairs. Speller ran into financial difficulty and dropped the book. Hersey, doubly disillusioned by Sanger's disapproval, abandoned the project. In 1939, he donated the unpublished manuscript to the New York Public Library, where it was discovered in 1969 by Margaret Sanger's grandson, three years after her death, and finally published. As the only Sanger biography written by a contemporary from her formative years, it has a special significance. Sanger needn't have fretted about the content, however; the book is not a "tell all," rather an adulatory work focusing on her life as a crusader.

For the period of 1937-38, all we know of Hersey's activities are the wrapping up of C.J.H. Publications and *Mystery Adventures*, and the Sanger biography. Since neither was likely to have provided much income, it's again a mystery as to how Hersey got by. *Pulpwood Editor* had been widely, and positively, reviewed, so that may have helped.

In 1939, he made one last stab at the pulps with *Fact Detective Stories* and *Fact Spy Stories*, novel only in the respect that they packaged nonfiction in a pulp-size magazine, an experiment that had been unsuccessfully tried by others. Hersey didn't fare any better. *Fact Detective* had only two issues, March and May; *Fact Spy* had three, April, June, and September. The company, Fact Magazines, shared offices with Frank Armer's Trojan Publications, publisher of the *Spicys* and other pulps, which led to some initial confusion.

At this point, we should note that Merle W. Hersey severed her relationship with Merwil Publishing in mid-'34, and became the independent publisher of the *Police Gazette*. She also purchased the titles *Bedtime Stories* and *Tattle Tales* from Nuregal Publishing. But by early-'35, *Police Gazette* had failed and Merle had filed for bankruptcy. However, *Bedtime Stories* and *Tattle Tales* continued with the editor listed as Gloria Grey, which is almost certainly a mask that Merle employed to avoid the past. Merle Hersey's name thereafter disappears from magazine publishing, but the listed editor of Harold Hersey's *Fact* magazines was none other than Gloria Grey. Assuming this was Merle Hersey, it's the only known time they worked together in their strangely parallel publishing careers. "Gloria Grey" turns up one last time in our records, in 1942, as editor of *Stocking Parade*.

Hersey traveled a bit on the public speaking circuit in 1939-40, regaling women's groups with insights on the publishing business, for example his

Wednesday afternoon address on December 6 to the Woman's Club of New Rochelle, on the subject of magazines. We know of four such engagements, including one as far away as New Castle, Pennsylvania, over 300 miles from New York City, making it likely he was paid for his appearances.

Hersey had long since given up writing poetry. His last published collection had been *Bubble and Squeak: A Book of Light Verse*, published in 1927 by *The Author & Journalist* while he was supplying them numerous articles. But in 1939, he published *Verse*, a collection of his best works. The book included an introduction by Fulton Oursler, which is our first evidence of contact since Oursler's return to Macfadden, and Hersey's ouster, in late-'27. Oursler began:

> In the gallery of my recollections, the portrait of Harold Hersey hangs in a position of special honor. He was the first poet that I met in the flesh. . . . Early memories of him are among the fondest that I have.

The remainder of the introduction was an early version of the magical meeting of Hersey that Oursler used in his autobiography (quoted previously). The occasion of Oursler's introduction to *Verse* may have rekindled a long-dormant acquaintance, for in early 1940 Hersey was back at Macfadden, presumably working for Oursler, who was still Supervising Editor and by then famous as *Liberty's* editor. Hersey's assignment was a new magazine, *True Pictorial Stories*. The concept was original—sort of. It was yet another first-person confessional aimed at women. The subject was dramatic stories of glamorous and newsworthy women. The originality was all in the form: the stories would be told with captioned photographs. It's hard to imagine that Hersey had much enthusiasm for the assignment; it sounds like something Oursler gave him as a favor for old-time's sake. Two issues hit the newsstands, and perhaps no more; Hersey's second spell with the company was even shorter than the first.

Hersey began his final act in mid-'41 when he became general editor for a new company, H-K Publications, also known as the Hardy-Kelly Group, for publishers Joseph J. Hardie and Raymond J. Kelly. Hersey presided over H-K's chain of magazines until his death in 1956. As Centaur Publications, Hardie published the pulp *Conflict*, which lasted for four issues in 1933-34. In 1938, an apparently revived Centaur bought out a comic book company. In the comics boom of 1939, they re-emerged as the Comic Corporation of America with *Amazing-Man Comics* and, in 1940, *Stars and Stripes Comics*. As H-K, in 1940, the company issued a science fiction pulp, *Comet*, choosing that name, perhaps, because of its resemblance to "comic." The fifth and final issue of *Comet* roughly coincided with Hersey's arrival. Hersey presided over the demise of the existing comics while also introducing *Man of War*, and a fact-based comic, *World Famous Heroes Magazine*. The entire comics line was defunct by early '42.

Hersey's key creations for the company were magazines aimed at the armed services. *Too-Hoo*, *Khaki Wacky*, *Jeeps*, and others, were digests featuring service-related jokes and cartoons. *Army Life* and *Khaki Humor* were humor magazines which culled material from the many Army camp magazines then springing up. Hersey built up a collection of these magazines, some of which were only mimeographs. One service-humor magazine served as an example of how quickly H-K could implement a new idea. *Black-out* had been dreamed up on December 10, 1941—no doubt a reaction to Pearl Harbor—and was on New York newsstands by the end of the month. As with Hersey's pulp chains, titles would come and go as the market dictated.

Under the name Harle Publications, the company published crossword puzzle magazines like *Dime Crosswords* and *Championship Crosswords*. A regular-sized magazine, *All-American Band Leaders*, featured photos and biographies of popular music figures. There were also the famous Hersey one-shots. A magazine aimed at teenage girls, *Miss America*, made only a single issue after a year of development.

In 1944, Hersey published *G.I. Laughs: Real U.S. Army Humor*, a book collection of the best Army camp material. It was quite a success and only wartime paper restrictions kept it from selling better. *More G.I. Laughs* came later in the year. It would be the last book Hersey published under his own name.

There were more H-K titles in 1944, humor magazines like *Mirth*, *Zest*, and *Keep 'Em Laughing*. From 1945 into late-'50, we have no record of his employment with H-K. He was, however, involved in several other enterprises. In 1945, he edited paperback murder mysteries published under the Diamond Library label. Only two titles are known. Also in 1945, he edited *Pictorial Detective*, a true-crime magazine from Rural Home Publishing of Louisville. One issue is known. From 1946-50, Hersey edited magazines for Charlton Publishing of Connecticut (the parent company of Charlton Comics). The known titles are *Hit Parader* (1946-48) and *Country Song Roundup* (1949-50). He edited a 1949 televison programming weekly, *Tele-Week*; it lasted two issues and may have been a Charlton magazine. As an apparent side project in 1947, Hersey stepped in to help jazz pianist Art Hodes edit the faltering magazine *The Jazz Record*.

In late-'50, Hersey returned to H-K, where he would spend the rest of his working life. He had another popular music magazine in 1951: *Melodyland*. The last known publication for which he was hands-on editor was *Boat Sport* (first issue, May 1952).

"I would not choose to relive one single day out of the past," he wrote in 1954. "I have lived a full life. The world owes me nothing."

He died on a Saturday night, March 17, 1956, in a Manhattan Veterans Administration Hospital, after an illness of several months. He was survived by his widow, Alexandrina, his two sisters, and his married daughter, Mrs. Dorothy Wiley of Wichita, Kansas. When Elinor left the picture, and Alexandrina entered, remain mysteries. Hersey married at least one other time, in the '40s, to a Marian Kieley; another mystery.

Merle W. Hersey died in 1956, as well. She was buried by Dorothy in a cemetery near Wichita. Dorothy was buried near her mother in 1997.

Hardie and Kelly ran Harold Hersey's obituary in the June 1956 *Boat Sport*, concluding, "His place in our affection and in the publishing world will be mighty hard to fill." The bulk of the column, however, cribbed copy from Hersey's *New York Times* obituary, suggesting that his employers didn't have any special understanding of his past.

Hersey's autobiography would have been most welcome, and undoubtedly fascinating. When he put together the *Thrill Book* piece for *Golden Atom*, he became aware, to his surprise, that people were interested in his past publishing ventures. It started him thinking about writing his autobiography, but he hadn't kept notes, and his memory for the myriad details was hazy, and his collection of first issues had been sacrificed through many changes of address. *Golden Atom* publisher Larry Farsace had provided Hersey with notes and outlines that made the article considerably easier to write, and far more accurate. A comprehensive autobiography would have taken a major effort by Hersey. "God willing, I'll get around to writing these and many another chapter in what has truly been an exciting and vari-colored life of one ink-stained wretch who never knew any better and never wanted it in any other way."

About the Authors

PRISON STORIES PUBLISHED A NUMBER OF LONG NOVELETTES in the 40-50 page range. Because of length restrictions, only one is reprinted in this collection: "Big House Boomerang" by Margie Harris. Many of the shorter pieces were written by Henry Leverage, under his own name and various pennames. Thus, this collection, aiming for a cross-section from all six issues, ended up with a higher percentage of Leverage material than the actual pulp. It seems an appropriate outcome, however, since, he was a well-known ex-con author, and his death and the demise of *Prison Stories* go hand in hand. He was the heart and soul of the magazine.

Below are all the authors (and pennames) who appear in this collection, with their backgrounds and identities unraveled to the extent possible.

Bell, Thomas (Spence) [unknown birth and death dates] ("The Black Warden"): Bell appears to have been an associate of Henry Leverage, due to both of them using the penname Winfield Byrd (see Byrd entry). Nothing is known of Bell's identity, but his work continued to appear long after Leverage's death in 1931, so he is a separate person. He had short stories in *Story* in the mid-'30s. He copyrighted a three-act farce in 1935. His three copyright entries (including the two in 1930 under the Byrd name) list Los Angeles area addresses. In the '40s, Thomas Bell stories appear in *Collier's* and the women's magazines, *Ladies Home Journal* and *McCall's*. The last known Thomas Bell story appeared in the Spring 1954 *Thrilling Wonder Stories*. It's enough of an anomaly to leave open the question of whether these several Thomas Bells were all the same person.

Byrd, Winfield ("City of Numbered Men"): A penname for Henry Leverage. The only two known published stories under this name are in *Prison Stories*, "City of Numbered Men" and the unfinished serial *Public Enemies*. The prison newspaper angle in "City of Numbered Men" firmly points to Leverage, who edited the Sing Sing newspaper, *The Star of Hope*. At the end of the fourth installment of *Public Enemies* (May-June 1931), the magazine printed this boxed item: "We regret to announce that due to the death of the author, Mr. Winfield Byrd, we will be unable to continue this story." Since Leverage died in February, this leaves little doubt as to the identity of "Byrd."

There is another wrinkle to the Byrd name. Leverage's story *The Green Spectre* was adapted as a three-act mystery comedy by Thomas Spence Bell, writing as Winfield Byrd, and copyrighted in 1930. Another three-act comedy, *Little Scarface*, by Bell writing as Byrd, was also copyrighted in 1930. Three Thomas Bell stories appear in *Prison Stories*. Presumably, Leverage recruited Bell to the magazine. Leverage may have borrowed the Byrd name for unknown reasons, or perhaps the Byrd stories are Bell-Leverage collaborations.

Grove, John Harold [unknown] ("The Warden's Dollar"): No biographical information. Grove had three known stories published, two in *Prison Stories*, and a third in the June 1932 issue of *Racketeer and Gangland Stories*. Possibly a penname.

Harris, Margie [unknown] ("Big House Boomerang"): Margie Harris was the unlikeliest of gang pulp authors, a woman whose prose was as tough as it comes. Her first known fiction appearance was the novelette "Death's Trapeze" in the May 1930 *Gangster Stories*. For several years, she appeared exclusively in Hersey gang pulps, *Mobs*, *Racketeer Stories*, *Gangland Stories*, *Complete Gang Novel Magazine*. "Big House Boomerang" was her only appearance in *Prison Stories*. She eventually provided Hersey with forty stories, most of them long novelettes. Her stories occasionally featured female protagonists, e.g. "Cougar Kitty" (*Mobs*, June-July 1930), "The Angel from Hell" (*Gangster Stories*, April 1931).

When Hersey sold *Gangster Stories*, Harris continued to appear in its successor, *Greater Gangster Stories*, providing another nine sagas. Through the remainder of the decade, she branched out to other publishers. There were more gang stories—to Spencer's *Gang World*, Carwood's *The Underworld Detective*—but that genre was all but dead. She began appearing in detective pulps like *New Detective*, *Ten Detective Aces*, *Super-Detective*, *Clues*, *The Feds*, etc. When Winford attempted to revive gang pulps in the latter part of the decade, Harris had a brief return to glory in *Double-Action Gang Magazine* and *Ten Story Gang*. Her last known published stories appear in 1939.

Judging strictly from her publishing record, several things stand out. She seems to have been attracted to the pulps by Hersey's gang magazines, as no prior published fiction is known. Their emergence may have given her the "I could do just as well" inspiration to try her hand. She also seems to have come to the field fully formed. She entered writing longer, well-plotted stories; and her prose is more polished than much of the hackwork in the gang pulps.

Personal information on Margie Harris has proven extremely difficult to come by. The only good source thus discovered is this remarkable letter she provided for the June 1931 issue of *Gangster Stories*, at Harold Hersey's request:

Dear Ed:

A biographical sketch of Margie Harris?

Scram, Baby; whaddyuh think I am, a canary—yelpin' on myself?

I got your slant, though, somebody's maybe asked "Who's this frail who cracks wise from the inside?"

Just another twist, sisters and brothers—maybe, but look out for my lipstick. You know some of the sugar Molls carry one for their own use, one for "the other jane"—and that one has cyanide in it. So look out for my lipstick, too.

How did I get that way? Maybe newspaper work; maybe just associates. I never got a dirty deal from a "digger" or a gambler in my life. I've had plenty from the other kind.

I've known some great guys. I interviewed Tiger Jake Seidenwand after he'd done four years "solitary" in San Quentin. I wrote a Sunday Mag. series on Sontag and Evans, the California bandits; Morel, their waiter-partner used to be my pal. I met Charlie Becker at the Sausalito ferry the day he got out of San Quentin after the Crocker National Bank forgery. The Bankers' Association hired him at $500 a month as a bad-check expert—and to make him be good.

In Chicago, I "palled" with Jim Colosimo and his wife, Dale Winter, before somebody shot Jim out from inside his shirt. Mossy Enright, Ike Bloom—Wise Guy of the South Side—Dion O'Bannion; I knew 'em all. And on the other side, Maclay Hoyne, the Chi. district attorney. Ike Bloom taught me how to "stack" Canfield solitaire and how to run up the big mitt in poker.

I've flitted from Coast to Coast—border to border, and across. I know Tia Juana, Mexicali, Juarez, Laredo, Reynosa and Matamoras like a country boy knows the way to town. Maybe I know more mokkers and lollygows than senators, more frails than Vanderbilts—but I like 'em.

And it's nice to write yarns for you inquiring ones—and the rest, too. I'm not going to tell you whether what I write saves my life by providing food, or what I don't write saves my life because I'm trusted. Two guesses. You can have 'em both.

Somebody asked if I ever wore a badge. Witness declines to state at advice of attorneys. Anyway, I haven't one now, and nobody has my fingerprints.

I know a slue of coppers too. Some of 'em I've liked; others, not so good. Among these is the New Orleans dick who said: "Quit writing them crook yarns, girlie; whyn't you try goin' straight?"

Maybe your mother and sister wouldn't like me—but I could show sister how to build a Mickey Finn.

Anyway, I try to be regular. I never turned up a pal in my life. A crippled grifter can take me for my back hair, but when they get a hypocritical reformer on the rack, I'll trample a lot of folks to get in and give the wheel one good twist on my own account.

I'm not "nice," nor am I "awful." But I'll bet four seeds I know a better story than YOU for I've made Broadway George laugh and he's the undertaker's assistant who told the first Pat-and-Mike story.

Anyway, thanks for being interested.

MARGIE HARRIS.

The letter dovetails neatly with our deductions. Her journalism background and acquaintance with criminals and underworld figures made her a natural candidate for the gang pulps. Some possible experience in law enforcement may have given her additional perspective. It's hard to tell from the letter, though, whether she's being cagey from sincere motives, or simply to create a mystique for her readers.

Apart from the scattered travels she alludes to, her discoverable background breaks into two periods, California and Chicago. The names which she assumes are familiar to readers of the '30s, are not so well-known today. But pinning down their records gives a rough idea of when she may have lived in their respective areas.

From the California period, San Quentin prisoner Tiger Jake Seidenwand appears to be the notorious murderer, Jacob Oppenheimer, also known as the "man-tiger," "the human tiger," or "the prison tiger." Serving a fifty-year sentence, he was moved from Folsom to San Quentin in 1898. After attacking prison guards, his sentence was upgraded to solitary confinement for life. He was confined to a cell above San Quentin's jute mill, which figures so prominently in "Big House Boomerang." By 1911, Oppenheimer was back at Folsom, where he was executed in 1913. Harris' interview would have to have been sometime between 1903 and 1911. Seidenwand and Oppenheimer aren't remotely similar names, but that doesn't preclude a memory error on Harris' part.

John Sontag and Christopher Evans were two railway robbers of the San Joaquin Valley who faced off against law enforcement in a bloody battle on June 11, 1893. Sontag died as a result of the wounds received. Evans recovered from his own wounds and received a life sentence. "Morel" was Edward Morrell who busted Evans out of the Visalia jail after the trial. Evans was recaptured and eventually released in 1911. He died in 1917. Morrell served sixteen years of a life sentence in Folsom and San Quentin, resided in solitary confinement near Jake Oppenheimer, published a book about Oppenheimer in 1912, and went on the lecture circuit to talk of his experiences from the point of view of a prison reformer. Harris' Sunday articles sound more like a retrospective than firsthand reporting.

Charles Becker, the "King of Forgers," was released from San Quentin on September 28, 1903 after serving four-and-one-half years.

From the Chicago period, Vittorio "Big Jim" Colosimo was the boss of Chicago's Levee district. Dale Winter started out in Chicago as a singer in Colosimo's Café. Big Jim divorced his wife and married the beautiful Dale. A week after returning from the honeymoon, on May 11, 1920, Big Jim was murdered in his restaurant, a crime that was never solved. Dale became a stage actress.

Maurice E. "Mossy" Enright, the labor czar of Chicago, was murdered on February 3, 1920. Isaac "Ike" Gitelson Bloom was a power in Chicago Democratic politics; he died December 15, 1930. Dion O'Bannion, known as the "King of the Beer Runners," was shot to death in his Chicago florist's shop on November 10, 1924. Maclay Hoyne served as Cook County State's Attorney for two terms, 1912-20; he died October 1, 1939.

"Broadway George" couldn't be identified.

If Harris was a journalist in California right after the turn of the century, and we also assume she was young at that time, a birth date around 1880 seems plausible as a working estimate. That would have made her about fifty when she started appearing in the gang pulps. Her publishing record is fairly consistent throughout the '30s, but slows down slightly in 1938-39.

Her last known whereabouts was Houston, Texas, 1935. Also, she bylined a Texas-based true-crime article for the October 1937 *American Detective*, published by the same people who issued *Greater Gangster Stories*. It's her only known nonfiction piece.

She'd made a handful of appearances in Standard's *Thrilling Detective* and *Popular Detective*. Her last known published story was "Problem for a Ranger," an 18-pager in the December 1939 *Popular Detective*. She then either quit publishing or died.

Henry, Carl ("Hanged by the Neck"): Penname for (Carl) Henry Leverage. Leverage used the penname as early as 1922 for the Hersey-edited *Ace-High Magazine*. Four stories written under the Henry name appeared in *Prison Stories*. Note the twist in "Hanged by the Neck" which reflects Leverage's background as an electrical engineer.

Letchmere, Edward ("Cell Number Seventeen"): A penname for Henry Leverage, used three known times, once in the Hersey-edited *The Dragnet Magazine* (November 1928), and twice in *Prison Stories*. "Edward Letchmere" was a character in Leverage's 1919 novel *The White Cipher*.

In "Cell Number Seventeen," inmate Mike Harrison is described: "He's the stir's detective—an inside sleuth. Chess player, chemist, mathematician, psychologist, electrician. He graduated from three colleges before he reached this one." That may have been Leverage describing himself, more or less.

Leverage, (Carl) Henry [1885 - February 14, 1931] ("Brothers in Stripes," etc.): Leverage was a graduate engineer, a member of the Royal Society of Engineers of London and the American Institute of Electric Engineers. In 1914, he was convicted of car theft and sentenced to three years, nine months. The harsh sentence was based on three previous convictions which led to him serving sentences in Washington, Baltimore, and Philadelphia. Leverage told the court: "I admit that I have been an ocean card sharp and a general crook, and that I did not have to steal. When I wanted to I could always earn a good living in my profession. After I got started on the wrong road it was hard to get back again. I have tried several times, but all in vain."

Other descriptions of his background provide a jumble of information. His *NYT* obit noted that he married May Collins in 1911. Harold Hersey wrote that Leverage "let fall hints about experiences in China and Europe, anecdotes of sailing before the mast and adventures in the far West." A 1926 syndicated column noted that: "Leverage . . . is a London-born American, who ran away from his Denver home and spent a winter on the San Francisco waterfront. He tried the sea for a while, hunted for gold in Alaska, worked in a railroad office in Denver and then went to New York to write."

In Sing Sing, Leverage edited the prison magazine, *The Star of Hope*. He also sold stories to pulps and slicks from prison. He applied to the new Authors' League of America for membership in 1916, and received a visit from Hersey, then assistant to the League's secretary. Hersey notes that Leverage "had pictures of Joseph Conrad, Kipling, and other well-known authors on the walls. There was a small library on a shelf over the tiny table where he kept his typewriter. He had special permission to write by candlelight after hours." The two began a life-long friendship.

Leverage wrote the story and screenplay for a 1916 film, *The Twinkler*, a drama of underworld and prison life. Leverage's jailbird status was emphasized in advertising for the movie. For instance, a newspaper ad described *The Twinkler* as "A big drama in five acts, written by Henry Leverage, a prisoner in Sing Sing."

In 1917 and 1918, his stories began appearing in *Short Stories* and the Munsey pulps. He also began selling to *The Saturday Evening Post* in 1918. His murder mystery in the May 25, 1918 *Post*, "Whispering Wires," proved to have long legs. Upon its newspaper serialization, the *Kansas City Star* wrote: "In this newest type of [scientific] detective story Mr. Leverage writes of new inventions, such as the war has brought out. Being an electrical engineer with an imagination, Mr. Leverage combines his abilities in both lines successfully as he builds one of the really gripping mysteries of the season." In February 1919, Leverage, by then out of prison, received an offer of $2500 for the film rights. Just as he was about the sign the contract, his agent came up with an offer of a $500 option for dramatic rights. Leverage took the smaller offer, which presumably offered better long-term benefits. However, the option expired after six months and was not renewed. Leverage tried fruitlessly to sell the story to Broadway, Fort Lee, New Jersey movie producers, and Hollywood. He went broke—so the tale goes; his stories continued to appear in the pulps. To his rescue came playwright Kate L. McLaurin, who offered to adapt "Whispering Wires" into a play in return for a split of the proceeds. The finished play was sold on the spot and became a hit on Broadway in 1922-23. It eventually was performed regionally and in 1926 found new life as a film from Fox. Leverage and McLaurin tried to follow up their stage success with a play based on Leverage's 1919 novel, *The White Cipher*; it never got off the ground.

Leverage's pulp work was a mix of detective and adventure stories. He sold to most of the publishers, including Harold Hersey at Clayton. When Hersey started Magazine Publishers in 1928, Leverage became a presence in *The Dragnet, The Underworld, Under Fire, Western Trails*, and others. When Hersey started the Good Story Magazine Company in 1929, Leverage began appearing in its notorious gang pulps, *Gangster Stories* and *Racketeer Stories*. The Hersey-Leverage relationship reached its culmination with *Prison Stories*, which debuted in late-'30. The pulp had almost certainly been created with the expectation that Leverage would supply a quantity of authentic stories under a variety of names. When he died unexpectedly in February 1931, Hersey folded the magazine soon thereafter.

Leverage's death drew little attention. He was survived by his wife, May, his mother and a sister.

Murray, Don [unknown] ("Wait Outside"): Only known story. No other information. The writing style is distinct enough that the name doesn't suggest itself as a Leverage penname.

Pierce, Elwood F. [~1887 - June 1, 1940] ("A Square Deal"): Elwood Pierce was a descendent of a pioneer family of Chester County, Pennsylvania. As a youth, he wrote short stories, and entertained his friends with his work. He began a life-long career as a newspaperman in 1905 when he joined the Chester *Morning Republican* as a cub reporter. The town of Chester is on the outskirts of Philadelphia. In 1909, he joined the *Chester Times* to head the sports department. In about 1910, he became the state editor for the *Philadelphia Inquirer*. He resigned and enlisted in the Army during the World War, and was stationed in St. Nazaire, France through 1919. Upon his return, he became managing editor for the *Chester Times*. In approximately 1920, he moved west and became telegraph editor for the *Los Angeles Chronicle*. At some unknown date, he moved on to the Los Angeles office of the International News Service.

He has nine known published short stories. The first was in the Second August 1924 issue of *Breezy Stories*. He hit the July 1925 issue of *Weird Tales* with "The Dream of Death." He had several stories published in *Everybody's*, and two in *Battle Stories*. "A Square Deal" appears to be his only sale to the Hersey pulps. His last known story is "Torture Chamber" in the September 1932 *Underworld Magazine*.

In 1928, he published his only known book, *Give a Boy Luck*, a juvenile novel about newspaper reporting.

He died at his home in Hollywood of a heart ailment. He had been employed as night editor for the International News Service. He was survived by his widowed sister, Mary L. Wolf, who had been living with him for several years. She died of a heart attack several months later.

Singer, Peter ("The Electric Warden"): Presumably a penname for Henry Leverage, based on similarity of style and distinctive story elements. E.g. references to a Prisoners' League turn up in Leverage's stories, as well as in Singer's "Con Con Carney" (not included in this collection). Also, the only four known Peter Singer stories are in *Prison Stories*.

A Square Deal
Elwood Pierce

A square deal—that's all these two escaped criminals wanted—and traveled all over the country to get one—but they shouldn't have traveled in box cars.

JIM GALLANT WENT OVER THE WALL AT SAN QUENTIN. It was a fancy bit of work and the liberty he gained required two years of effort. Not far from the outer barrier he fought it out with two guards. He fired three times and one of the guards fell. He was confident that he wounded the other.

His escape from the California prison was, of course, an outside job. That, too, is how he came to have the revolver. When he stood up and exchanged shots with the guards he was desperate, for he was determined that he would not return to San Quentin alive.

In time he made his way out of California. He zigzagged through Nevada. He negotiated Utah in the same way and without incident. And he managed to hurdle Colorado and enter Kansas. It was the season of harvest and armies of migratory workers moved about. One scarcely could get a hand hold on a freight train for them. They spread over Kansas like a pestilence and so made the way easier for Jim Gallant. Mostly a hunted man is safe when he takes to the road. The cleverest bull in the world couldn't find him, and Jim Gallant knew it.

He was going home. Home to New York.

In time the path of this escaped criminal would cross the trail of Pete Dennison. Pete already was on the way. And he too was going home—to San Francisco. In San Francisco Pete would get protection from the old crowd in the Mission. He had left stone walls behind—as effective and as efficient stone walls as the state of Vermont boasted. In Vermont stones and stone walls are common enough.

They had tried to make him serve seventeen years for a holdup and he knew to the last drop of sweat and blood what it means to do a stretch in stir.

Pete's cross-continent passage had not been difficult. He had money and good clothes provided him by friends. He did not travel the usual lanes. His was the road of vagabondia. He joined the countless horde of men that eternally drifts over the face of America.

Pete shot by way of the underground into Canada. In a few days he had recrossed the border and was back in the States. In time he was in Illinois, studiously evading Chicago. He rattled through Missouri and found himself on the outskirts of Topeka. Soon he would meet Jim Gallant, although he had no idea that such a crossing of paths was in store for him. He was not strong for Kansas.

Pete was picked up by the swarm of harvest hands and whirled along. Like a June bug. Or a moth. He felt that his way to the coast was clear. He had visions of the night he would cross the bay from Oakland to San Francisco. Lights twinkling. Or appearing suddenly out of a mist.

In the harvest season the railroads encouraged the vagabond, for the hobo may be induced to lend a hand with the crops. No one bothered Pete, late of Vermont, where stones are plentiful and prison walls are thick.

"Going to make Topeka?" someone asked Pete.

"I ain't sure," the fugitive replied. He swung from the train at a water tower. He had been riding long enough and wanted a change. Sometimes a man needs variety after a stretch in prison. It was like that with Pete, late of Vermont, who was on his way for a crossing of paths.

II

PALS

IT WAS AFTERNOON AND PETE WALKED AIMLESSLY. He had money and money brings security. He washed and shaved, achieving respectability. He'd find a quiet spot and have a few hours of peace. He was fed up on dirty-necked hoboes and plain bindle stiffs. Solitude was what he wanted, so he could think and decide an issue or two.

Pete's body was perspiration-lathered. He cut across a road to where a tree cast delicious shade. He threw himself on the ground before he knew that someone was back of the tree. A man stepped out and said: "Hello."

"Hello!" responded Pete. He sprawled on the ground and eyed the stranger curiously, listing him for what he was.

"Hot," declared Jim Gallant, traveling from California. Jim switched at a horse fly that played about his nose.

"Hot as hell," Pete smiled. He liked this stranger—liked his looks and liked his voice.

Jim Gallant contemplated Pete, who still puffed after his disagreeable walk across the scorching field. He smiled at him with his eyes. Pete smiled again, and with his whole face. It was the first time he had smiled since the judge said: "Seventeen years."

Jim Gallant, formerly of San Quentin, threw himself on the ground by Pete's side. Thus was the crossing of paths made a reality.

Jim did not tell, and Pete did not tell, although there must have been much of each other's careers that they guessed. Men who have been ground between stones of their own making do not have to describe the stones. There was an instinctive bond between the two men. In an hour they were friends. The days were to find them together. It was like blood finding blood.

"Where to?" Jim asked as they rested under the tree.

"I'm going to get set for the winter. It may be early to think of that, but there's nothing like California sunshine when it's rip snorting cold in the east."

"Tough going, though, especially in Los Angeles," Jim warned. He added: "And they don't like a guy none too well in Frisco."

Pete did not say too much. It was not his purpose to talk. "I'll get another rig," he declared, "and hang myself up to dry in a small town. I'll buy a safety razor and get sanctimonious. I'll get next to a hymn book. Once in a while I'll sort of bust things open and go in for an odd job. I wouldn't be guilty of stealing a hymn book, and they cost money."

"Well, I'm winding up on this stuff," said Jim. That was his game—to pass as a hobo. He continued: "You never get enough in this business. But I'm quitting, even if in time I come back for more."

"You can't quit the road. You got to go on."

"That's the worst of it; you got to go on." Jim ventured the big question: "Where you been?"

"Around," said Pete. "New England. In Canada."

"How were the bulls?"

"Fair. Only had trouble twice. Once a bull pulled a gun. He was real hostile. The pickings are poor up Canada way."

"I ain't been east since last year," Jim lied.

"Lay off it," Pete warned. "Keep to the west."

"Last year I did two months in Hartford."

"That's a hick town," Pete sympathized. "I don't go in for that stuff. The big houses ain't in my line. No walls and iron bars, thanks. The bulls and I ain't sending each other visiting cards."

Jim, who was twenty-seven, with light brown hair suspiciously short, shook his head knowingly. He passed his hand over his nervous mouth and it was a hard hand. Then he drew his lips into a thin line.

"There ain't nothing to the big house," Jim admitted, playing a sly game. "It's this way with me: I don't get excited over what you might call reform, but I only play the safe cards. I'm mother's angel child, and a de luxe edition of 'Now I Lay Me Down to Sleep.'"

"That's me, too," asserted Pete in a burst of confidence. He was saying more than he intended, but he had to talk. He looked more than his twenty-five years, and the smile that sometimes came into his eyes was a furtive smile. He talked from the side of his mouth, as Jim Gallant noticed. Pete concluded, smacking at a fly: "None of the high walls for yours, respectfully."

It took them a week to get beyond that stage conversationally.

Pete Dennison and Jim Gallant loafed on the outskirts of Topeka for ten days. They slept and they talked. They talked and they slept. And they lay for hours exchanging scarcely a word. They did not act like criminals.

There was no question about their being pals. "I know how to stick by a guy," Pete said as an inducement. "Better come with me to the west coast. I know people who will see to it that everything is jake with us. There'll be a string of fatted calves a mile long. All I have to do is to say you are a friend of mine."

Jim smiled his queer smile. "Can't do it," he protested. "I'm traveling east. It's an important trip." He smiled queerly.

It was night. They rejected the cover of a barn for the open atmosphere of a pile of hay on the ground. They were talking quietly about nothing in particular.

From a house across the field came a girl's song and the languid barking of a dog. Soon a lantern flashed, only to disappear in a barn. Shortly a group of men passed along the road, some two hundred feet from where Pete and Jim were lying. Their voices were subdued but excited. They carried lanterns.

Pete asked: "What's that mean?"

"Looks strange," said Jim, drawing his head under the hay. The men turned into the field and walked close to where Pete and Jim were hidden. They were making for the farm house. The fugitives watched them as they were swallowed up by the darkness.

"Did you hear what that guy said?" Pete asked.

"Yes, I caught it. He said: '*They* can't be far away.' "

"That gang must be looking for somebody."

"Seems so."

"Well, we ain't done nothing."

"No, we ain't done nothing," Jim Gallant nodded. He had a vision of high walls in California. He added: "But sometimes that don't matter. All the guys that go to prison ain't guilty. I ain't in no mood to take chances. Somebody might get a broken head. I'm rough when I start. I forget myself."

"I ain't no sap, either," Pete declared. "I can handle any pink tea that anybody feels like organizing. I been up against it before."

Lights flickered about the barn and excited voices came across the stillness of the field.

"Yep, they're on the hunt," observed Pete decisively. The old hard lines returned to his face.

"We better break a few handsome necks and get out of the way."

"We're about as safe here as any place."

"I ain't sure of that," Jim Gallant contradicted. He said: "Maybe we better move. I ain't going to get caught in no jam." Suddenly he asked: "What are you carrying?"

"This!" Pete slapped his hip pocket.

"I'm fixed!" For a moment Jim exposed his weapon.

"We better get rid of them. Dangerous to get caught with gats in this state. They railroad you on the lightning express, and they don't make station stops. After that they throw the key away."

"They ain't never going to put me in prison again," Jim said bitterly. "They ain't never going to, and I mean it. They ain't never." He had not intended to say that.

They looked at each other knowingly, their histories exposed.

"They ain't me never, either," Pete echoed. He thought, in a confused sort of way, of the stone walls in Vermont. "Not by a hell of a sight."

They walked across the new hay stubble. "We might get to Topeka; or what do you think?" Jim asked.

"We'll beat it back the way we came," Pete ordered. "We'll keep off the road and not get caught sleeping."

They walked for an hour but finally lost their sense of direction in the darkness. At last they agreed they were far enough from the men with lanterns to be safe.

"What do you suppose them guys was up to?" Jim asked.

They crossed a road and entered another field. Unconsciously they circled and encountered a barn with a great haystack and a silo at the side. They heard voices and around the side of the barn came a man with a lantern. Then a dozen men, all carrying lanterns.

"Who's there?" called a voice. "Hey! Who's there?"

Jim and Pete turned to run.

"Don't move," another man yelled, "or we'll shoot. We got you."

The fugitives did not heed the order. There was the crack of a rifle and the explosion of a weapon of less modern make.

"Stop! Stop!" All of the men seemed to be yelling.

"Run! Run!" Pete Dennison's words were husky from hard breathing.

Jim Gallant tripped and fell. He was up in an instant. He thought he heard footsteps back of him. Men running. "My God," he panted, in panic. He had come so far—from the walls in California—only to meet a situation like this. He knew now that he should not have quit the railroad. Freight trains are safer with their armies of moving men.

"Don't shoot unless you have to," Pete directed. "We'll get away from them." His body was wet. "We're all right now."

Late the next morning they entered Topeka.

III

A CLOSE CALL

THE NEWSPAPERS TOLD WHAT THEY HAD ESCAPED. Two robbers had entered a farm house and when the farmer's wife tried to battle them, they had shot her to death. Posses were searching the countryside. Highways were watched. It would be impossible for the criminals to get away. Such was the newspaper story with a description of the slayers.

"They could have sent us up easy," observed Pete. "Couldn't they?"

"I've known it to be done," Jim answered.

"You're the best pal I ever had," said Pete, his voice falling. "You and I got to stick it out for good. We were meant to go it together. It don't often happen this way, but sometimes it does."

"It sure has happened," Jim agreed. "Shall we beat it east? To New York, say?"

"No can do," responded Pete. "It's me for Frisco. What's the matter with you and the west coast?"

"No can do," Jim answered. His white teeth were revealed in a smile. "I guess you might as well know why. I'm trusting you to be on the level."

"Ah," said Pete, as the story ended. "That makes a difference. Now let me tell *you* something; long as you see fit to trust me." So he spoke of the walls in Vermont.

Jim's reply was emphatic although his words were spoken low. He thought of the guard he had shot—probably killed. "No more of the big house for me," he said. "I'll die before I'll go back."

They did not converse for a time after that. They smoked innumerable cigarettes. Both were jumpy. Every sound made them listen.

Finally Jim said: "The dope is we better split up, much as I hate to. But I got to go east and you got to go west."

Pete chewed on imaginary gum. There were times when his face was not pleasant to look at. "Can't we forget that for a while?" he asked. "Two fellows like you and me don't often catch up with each other."

Jim Gallant turned his face to the wall to hide his emotion. He did not want to appear soft, but Pete Dennison's words had touched him. Touched him, the criminal.

"You see," said Pete, "the trouble is I didn't tell all. Out in Frisco I got a lot of stuff hid away. Nobody knows where it is but me. I had a partner, but the cops punctured him a few and he's dead. There's a lot of money among the truck. That's why in hell I'm bound for Frisco."

Jim's eyes were dulled by evil—by selfishness. "You don't mean you got all that hid?" He struggled; his heart seemed to wither and die. "Well," he decided, "I got to keep clear of the Pacific. San Quentin's hell. I ain't got nothing ahead much, except some business in New York that may pan out, provided I can find a certain person. But you—you're going to sit like a robin over a barrel of worms when you get back to Frisco? Ain't you?"

Pete meditated, dropping the subject. He said: "We'll lay low for a few days and loaf." He had observed the look of greed and envy that had had birth in Jim's eyes.

"This," said Jim, "ain't such a bad dump." He referred to the Topeka lodging house where they had a room. They were comfortable but not safe. They would never be at ease.

There was an hour of silence. "It gets down to this," Pete finally commented, "no prisons for me." He said that over and over. And he added: "I'm playing safe after this."

"They'll have a sweet time landing me again," Jim agreed. "My jobs are going to be air tight. I'll use my brains. They can't get you if you use your brains. Too many people get stuck on the methods they use and make fancy blunders."

The lodging house was suffocating and foggy with tobacco smoke.

"It feels good," said Pete, breaking the silence. "It feels good, flopped like this . . . with a bed."

"What was that?" Jim questioned, becoming alert. "What's all the noise?"

Someone in the corridor outside was protesting: "This is a decent house, I tell you! I don't take in people like that, and you ain't got no right to come here rousting my lodgers. It ain't right. . . ."

"A bunch of thieves and yeggs, that's what they are," came the loud reply to the unfinished protest. "Now get busy and exercise them passkeys of yours. Open every room in the joint. We know they're here, and you're hiding them or you'd—"

Pete was out of bed in an instant while Jim Gallant had his ear against the door.

"Cops!" breathed Jim. "In the hall—right outside!"

"And us with gats!" Pete Dennison was looking wildly about him.

A trap. They couldn't afford an encounter with the police.

"I—I ain't hiding nobody," whined the landlord outside. "I don't have to open until I—I see a search warrant."

"You'll see stars. You'll open up them doors right now—all of them—or we'll bust them in such a way that the Carpenter's Union will give us a rising vote of thanks. Say, what are we fooling with this monkey for?—"

There was a thump. Plainly the landlord was being thrown violently against the wall. "Don't hurt me. I'll open them!" Then the metallic click of keys.

"I want to see this'n first—not that. This one—open here!"

The door had an old-fashioned lock and Jim gave the key a quarter turn. Someone was unsuccessfully jabbing with a pass key on the outside. Pete had the window open. "Fire escape!" he called, fright gone now that action was necessary.

Pete was the first out. Jim followed. They were on the second floor and reaching the ground was a simple matter. Their room had been a back one. Pete swung ten feet from the fire escape. Jim dropped after him. They were in a yard littered with boxes, barrels, cast-off articles of furniture and refuse characteristic of the neighborhood. In the rear was a high wooden fence with a mean alley beyond. The only illumination was an incandescent light well up the alley.

Then, out of the darkness, two powerful hands grasped Pete Dennison. He twisted about with a gasp of astonishment. He was in the steel grip of a policeman. Pete tore himself loose and had his captor by the throat to stifle an outcry. They struggled, muscles strained, both bent on death.

Jim saw Pete's predicament. He whipped out his revolver and with a leap was on the struggling antagonists. His first blow missed, for he did not strike from a point of vantage. His second swipe was different. The butt of his revolver clicked sharply against the policeman's skull. The officer crumpled and fell.

Men shouted from the windows above and four shots were fired.

Pete and Jim trampled the policeman in panicky retreat. More shots and shouts. The yard was peopled by shadows and the two fugitives, their bearings lost, ran about confusedly. They plunged head-on, seeking each other's throats with excited hands, but realizing their mistake, made for the high board fence.

Another fusillade of shots, a scream and then all was quiet.

Jim, fleeing, was overwhelmed by a sense of tragedy—he was human enough for that. Pete Dennison had been shot. He was lying back there in the yard dead. That was his thought.

Jim muttered: "*They won't take me!*" He passed from the alley through an open gate and into a rear yard, stumbling over an ash can, then walked through a maze of alleys to a side street. By this time he had recovered his nerve. He was thankful that these were not well lighted thoroughfares.

Pete Dennison was dead. Jim's imagination ran riot. He had been a good pal. They had become friends so quickly and Pete was the real article. Jim felt very much alone. But he had to go on. He couldn't go back. Pete must necessarily be left to his fate.

Then out of the darkness came a form. Jim was ready to fire. He did not like the actions of this man in the darkness. But suddenly he recognized the form.

"I thought they'd got you," said Jim. "After those shots I was certain I heard you scream and fall."

"I never scream," said Pete. He added as they sped away: "I heard that; I thought it was you."

"Keep your hand on your gat," Jim instructed. "We're not going to get caught now."

"Not by a hell of a sight," Pete Dennison declared.

IV

SUSPICIOUS

"CLOSE CALL," SAID JIM, WHEN THEY WERE OUTSIDE OF THE CITY.

"We ought not to keep together," Pete warned. "Someone in this neck of the forest seems determined to pick up two men. Someone appears to want to arrest two men bad. Looks like it ain't good medicine for two men to be traveling together."

"Kansas ain't healthy," said Jim.

"I ain't kidding myself into believing that I got a charmed life. Not enough to make me take chances on going back behind the walls. The big houses are all alike, in Vermont or any other place. And they ain't going to take me. Not while I can shoot," Pete said.

"Maybe we better grab the front end of a passenger," Jim suggested.

"Too dangerous. Better stick to the regular way."

They boarded a freight train without inquiring its destination. They wanted to get out of Kansas. They had found the Kansas method of treating strangers a bit too thick.

The train had two empty cars, both crowded with blacks, whites and a sprinkling of Mexicans. All had heard the call of harvest cash.

Pete complained of feeling ill. He said: "It's my head. That cop must have biffed me a couple. I hope he feels twice as sick as I do."

They watched for a convenient spot and at noon, finding it, jumped off. At a farm house they asked for work. The farmer was agreeable.

"Only," the farmer said, "you got to sleep in the barn."

The fugitives were not choosy.

"I need hands and you two look pretty decent," the farmer observed. "You treat me right and I'll see that you get a square deal."

Pete echoed: "A square deal. That's what I been traveling all over the country to find. But they seem to keep it under lock and key with the family jewels."

"I hope you ain't a pair of them dynamiting Reds?" the farmer asked suspiciously.

Pete and Jim had supper with the harvest hands and sat back of the barn smoking until it was time to seek the comforts of the haymow.

"I'm going to get a drink," said Jim, remembering the location of the pump. "Come have one on me. Then we'll drop into the hay like feathers."

The well was just outside the kitchen door. Jim and Pete could hear a voice within—the farmer's voice. The windows were open. He was telephoning.

"They're two suspicious eggs and look bad," the farmer was saying. "I've given them jobs so as to hold them. They answer the description in this morning's paper. Better come over, sheriff, and see what you make of them."

The convicts looked at each other blankly.

"Come on," ordered Pete. "We got to beat it."

"Suspicious, eh?" Jim repeated. In the night an evil look came to his eyes—a look that the night hid. "Suspicious, eh? I'll make him think we're suspicious."

As they passed the barn Jim threw a lighted match into the hay. From a distance he and Pete watched a blaze light the sky. "Suspicious, eh?" Jim said.

He had been true to the seed of San Quentin.

V

A CLEAN RIDE

PETE DECLARED: "I MUST BE BRINGING YOU BAD LUCK." They were fortunate in being alone in a box car that was clean because it had been used to haul grain. They had waited for hours for the train after leaving the dangerous farm house. It was the evening of the next day and the rattler was a haven of refuge.

Jim responded: "It's me that's the hoodoo." He wanted to do the right thing by his partner. "You'd have been in Frisco long ago if you hadn't caught up with me."

Pete waved his hands in the darkness. "That's all right," he said, going through the emotional process of lighting a cigarette. "Just so you and I understand each other. I call it good luck from the start—running into you. Meeting you was the only thing I can think of that would keep me away from Frisco. You're the best pal I ever had. Why, in Frisco—"

"Right back at you," said Jim meaningly.

Pete yawned. He said: "I'm ready for sleep." He crawled up in a corner. "I don't think we'll stack up against any more jams. And I liked the way you paid that farmer back."

Jim practised silence. The rattle of the train would not disturb Pete but Jim Gallant's voice would. He too tried to sleep. He had not felt so free in a long time. He'd pass a few more weeks with Pete, then he'd follow the trail to New York. There were folks in New York he wanted to see. He thought of Pete's hidden loot.

At last he slept.

The two men did not stir for hours.

It was daylight when Pete awoke and aroused Jim. It was hot in the box car with the door closed. The train, Pete noticed, was no longer moving.

Pete ordered: "Better stir."

"Where do you suppose we are?" Jim asked, rubbing the sleep from his eyes.

"God only knows. I hope there's food not far away. I feel like sausage and fried potatoes. And some good coffee."

"What I want is about ten pounds of rare beefsteak, with quite a few other things. Including enough coffee to keep Lindbergh awake on a hop to Paris."

Pete struggled with the door and in a moment Jim was helping him. The door rolled open with a shriek.

Outside stood a man with a rifle over his shoulder, walking up and down. Pete gasped and Jim gasped. They made a dash for cover. The man with the rifle spied them.

"Hello!" was his surprised exclamation. He walked over to the car and looked in.

"What place is this?" Pete asked for want of a better question.

The man with the rifle was silent. He chewed gum copiously. Then he laughed.

"Oh, this is only the state prison," he chewed. "Your palace car must have been shunted through the side gate during the night.

City of Numbered Men
Winfield Byrd

When the governor of the state sent Big Tom Collins down to Penthouse, he instructed him to break the mutinous spirit there, and keep that prison out of the newspapers. He forgot to add that Penthouse contained the choicest collection of die-hards in captivity— That's why he couldn't pull a long face when he learned how Collins squelched them!

IN THE STRONGEST PRISON ON THE MAP, in a city of numbered men, where hate and passion and silence ruled behind concrete walls, the new warden sat clenching and unclenching his huge gnarled fingers.

Big Tom Collins was the proper figure of a man. Two-fisted, square-jawed, shrewd-witted, he realized he was up against the biggest fight in his life. The warden before him had perished in a riot. The one before that was knifed by an insane inmate. The history of the wardens of Penthouse resembled the record of a suicide squad in Flanders.

When the governor of the state sent Big Tom down to Penthouse he instructed him to break the mutinous spirit there, build the new cell houses, and keep that prison out of the newspapers.

He forgot to add that Penthouse contained the choicest collection of die-hards, lifers, con-men, demons and schemers in captivity. He neglected to state the facts concerning graft so strong that the Principal Keeper went home every night with a three-pound porterhouse steak under his uniform and the guards came to work in expensive sedans.

Along one wall of the office where Big Tom Collins sat twisting his fingers, ran a rogues' gallery of the inmates, with their photos, records, red marks and other information. It was like an animated hotel register.

Big Tom squinted under his shaggy brows toward the door leading to the guard room. It was locked. The night-captain was outside, probably smoking a cigar. The screws were off the walls and every inmate was locked up with double security.

Slowly Big Tom got out of his chair and listened. There was no sound in the city of numbered men. He moved around the table and approached the Bertillon racks. His eyes roamed over the photographs until his fingers touched one. Jerking it out he lunged toward the table and light.

Minutes passed while he scrutinized every detail of a prisoner's features and record.

"It's him," Big Tom gulped. "He's gotta do it—if he's got any guts left in his miserable body."

The night-captain was startled when the warden's steel door opened and Collins beckoned to him. "Come here!" ordered Collins. "I want you to go in the East Cell Block and bring this inmate to me."

Big Tom never called his charges "cons." He knew they detested the word.

Gulping in astonished silence at the warden's request the night-captain took the Bertillon record of inmate C.45, otherwise known as Ed Fletcher. He clicked his heels, turned and strode obediently toward the guard-room's inner gate. Collins went back to his quarters, sat down heavily, and eyed the half-open steel door with a do-or-die expression.

"I gotta do it," he muttered. "These birds in this stir, from the P.K. to the yellow livered stool-pigeons, are putting it over on me."

There were mutiny, riots, disgrace, danger of explosives, guns at large in Penthouse Prison. Tom Collins' pride, the new cell block, which he had designed and almost finished, was in danger of being blown up any minute. He felt like an engineer seeing a great bridge toppling.

After C.45 was thrust in the warden's suite and the door closed, the night-captain paced the guard-room for an hour before the door opened again. He wondered through the smoke of three cigars, what was up. The warden called him again.

"Take him back! Lock him up and don't say anything to anybody about bringing him to me."

A change had come into the warden's face. Another change stamped C.45's features. A conflict of tremendous intensity must have taken place in the privacy of the suite, concluded the night-captain. A mental one, more devastating than any physical one. Had C.45 something on Tom Collins?

Jabbing C.45 roughly, the night-captain forced him through the gate and up the iron flights to the topmost gallery of East Cell Block. The captain unlocked the gang-lever, threw it in an open position, and inserted a key in a cell door.

"Get in!" he snarled at him. "Th' doctor says there ain't a damn thing wrong with you, Fletcher." This last declaration was a ruse to any listening inmates to throw them off guard.

When the key twirled the bolt in the lock, a covered head darted from the cell's upper bunk. White, straight-browed faces were pressed to the bars of adjoining cells. The cell at the right of Fletcher's was inscribed "Tia Juana." It contained two humorous hijackers. The cell on the left had a more studious aspect. Over its door was chalked "St. Anne de Beaupre." A forger and a church thief dwelt in that cloister.

Fletcher sank his weight on the lower cot. He placed his head in his palms. The footsteps of the night-captain echoed through the old cell block. Again the inmate on the upper bunk darted outward. A tiny match struck. It ignited a shielded lamp on a book shelf.

"Hello, Fletcher?" the inmate whispered. "Where've you been? The boys are going to think you ratted on somebody."

Leaving a cell after midnight was a suspicious move in Penthouse Prison. C.45 stared around the stone cell. He blinked at the rays of the student's lamp. His eyes fastened on signs of education—a folding desk, a brief-bag, a dictionary above him.

His cell-mate was editor of *The Star*, an inside publication distributed to convicts and screws. Tod Gaynor was a graduate of a university and two reform schools. He was serving ten years at Penthouse for a crime he admitted being guilty of.

"Where have you been?" repeated Tod.

C.45 whispered: "To see the doctor."

The expression of incredulity on the editor's features was reflected in the voices of the other inmates. They had the sharp ears of mice. Said Spike, the lesser in bulk of the two hijackers.

"He ken go tell that to Sweeney, Roscoe. Wot a chance gettin' out of one of these cells after th' gang-lever is pulled. Wot a chance. That guy's turnin' stool—an' I wuz goin' to vote fer him as our next Johnny-Up."

Roscoe grunted.

"You can't always tell, Spike. He's got a lot of explainin' to square himself wid me."

The grip of a profound silence came reaching into the old cell-block. Screws went by like padded prowlers. C.45 waited, sitting hunched on his bunk. He heard Tod Gaynor puff out the lamp with a yawning gasp.

Over the prison the dawn gradually paled and softened its harsh outlines. Through the bars C.45 studied the outer windows and the almost completed cell-block that was to be Warden Collins' pride, a monument to advanced penology. It had risen like a phoenix out of the ruins of a former cell building.

Clang! went the morning gong. Fifteen hundred die-hards and desperate men groaned and yawned in unison. It was like a breath from the great deep. A protesting breath that foretold no good for those in authority at Penthouse.

C.45 stood at the grated door, two fingers extended when the screw went by for the count. Above him Tod's fingers wiggled in the guard's face.

Again a gong clanged. The count was correct. The doors swung open simultaneously.

Marching in a snaky formation across the prison yard, C.45's company went into the mess-hall, had coffee, bread and molasses, waited for the bell and filed into the print-shop where *The Star* was printed, as well as ballots and letter-heads. Adjoining the print-shop was a long building filled with stamping machines for making automobile license plates.

C.45 acted dazed that morning. He did not comprehend his duties until Spike, the hijacker, nudged him and thrust a broom in his hands. "Better get busy, Fletcher. Th' Johnny-Up'll be here in a minute—an' y've had two scraps wid him. Some day, when you take a few more boxin' lessons, yo'll be able to knock his block off. You got it in you—but you need guts."

Sweeping between the presses and type-racks, C.45 encountered his cell mate, Tod, who had donned a linen coat. His tow-head was capped with a studious-looking visor.

"This is an honor shop," Tod remarked. "Y'u know why we haven't got a screw over us, Fletcher? The warden trusts us. Come clean about last night. You weren't at the hospital. The print-shop gang want to know where you were. They say you ratted to the P.K."

"About what?" evaded C.45, with a shrug of his huge shoulders.

Tod glanced about the shop. His office was invitingly close. In the door of it stood a burly inmate waiting suggestively. He was Pete Mullen, the prison Johnny-Up, a thug with a record for keeping order.

"It's no con's damn business where I was!" said C.45.

"Well—it is," insisted Tod. "I like you Fletcher—always did—but there's Mullen an' he's hot inside. There's going to be a scrap here—if you don't come clean."

"I can lick Mullen," C.45 declared. "I think I'll do it now."

The members of the print-shop company saw a change come over C.45. He peeled off his shoddy-coat, after dropping the broom, and strode to the Johnny-Up.

"What are you sizing me up for?" he shot between gritted teeth. "You needn't think because you're head of the League you've got a right to my business."

Mullen, who caught the note of defiance in C.45, laughed unsteadily. He glanced about the shop. The company were edging from their work. Forgers, hijackers, dope-fiends and prowlers goaded him at C.45.

"I'll bust this rat fer th' third time!" he announced. "Then I'm goin' to drag him to th' P.K. an' have him thrown in th' cooler. Th' dirty stool-pigeon!"

C.45's features flamed. He went at Mullen with his left extended and his right held low. Mullen went backward, tried to seize the door's edge, and fell across Tod's editorial desk. His fingers clutched at papers and carbons. Slowly he straightened himself.

"Fer that Fletcher, I'm goin' to—"

C.45 waited. He met Mullen's bull-rush with uppercuts that gashed that gangman's face to ribbons. He knocked out three of Mullen's teeth. He socked him in the left kidney, a killing blow, and sent him reeling out among the type-racks.

"Have a heart!" cried Tod, dancing about. There'll be a screw here in a minute. You two birds are gumming up my next issue."

The finishing-up and polishing off of Mullen came when C.45 mopped the blood from his own features and started milling, like a cooper at a barrel. The blows became well-timed. They bit. Gradually Mullen felt his knees sinking. He grasped the corner of a bench. C.45 waited.

"Got enough?"

"Naw—I'm only gettin' me wind—you rat!"

C.45 sidestepped, poised his weight on the ball of one foot and sent crushing another kidney blow, the most dangerous in boxing.

The P.K. came elbowing his way into the print-shop in time to see Mullen receiving a bucket of cold water that partly revived him. Heller's brows lifted in interrogation. He wondered who could have taken the Johnny-Up's reputation as a thug-ugly.

Then he saw C.45 washing his face and hands in a basin.

A crook of his finger brought two screws to his side. He whispered instructions to them. They seized Mullen. "To th' cooler fer you," one announced.

They shoved Mullen out into the yard.

"That dirty stool-pigeon!" he shouted to the print-shop company. "Don't this prove it, fellows?"

"Having finished washing the blood from his face and hands, C.45 saw suspicious eyes encircling him. Spike and Roscoe, the hijackers, reluctantly pulled some token money from their pockets and passed it to Tod. "That guy's improved in form," Spike remarked. "I'm a form-better, I am. That's why I went broke followin' the ponies an' took th' chance that landed me in this dump."

"He chiseled me out of ten bucks," Roscoe gulped. "I'm as big a sucker as you were, Spike. I bet Mullen would win."

C.45 picked up his broom and started sweeping.

He wondered why Tod had backed him to whip the Johnny-Up. The editor of *The Star* had a shrewd pair of eyes behind his glasses. He called C.45 into the office just before the noon whistle. Two proof-readers sat at desks. Tod gave a knowing glance at them. They were the forger and the church thief who celled next to C.45.

"Fletcher," Tod said evasively, "I wouldn't exercise in the yard, if I were you, unless you get a couple of strong-arm inmates to protect you from Mullen's gang. You might be knifed or beat up."

C.45's jaw squared. "Let 'em come! I'll be ready for them."

"I'm spreading the word," went on Tod, "that you're not a rat. I vouch for that—I know you didn't go out to the front-office, last night, to stool on anybody. Some of Mullen's mob wanted more proof from me. They didn't get it. Your secret is your own. So, protect yourself!"

C.45 wondered how much Tod really knew about the nocturnal visit.

"We'll exercise together, after eating," he proposed to Tod. "I want to look that new cell-block over. I'm taking an interest in it. Maybe, when my bit is done, I'll start fresh as a builder."

"Umph!" Tod remarked. "Yesterday, you didn't give a damn about anything in this stir. You've changed in more ways than scrapping. Come on, there's the noon whistle."

Tod had an inspiration when emerging from the mess-hall. He motioned to Spike and Roscoe to fall in behind. "Those two hijackers," he told C.45, "have got guts. They're with me. Most of Mullen's mob are yellow. A hijacker is doubly-bad to them, because they have the reputation of sticking-up stick-ups."

Penthouse Penitentiary now lay before C.45's searching eyes. He was seeing it from a new viewpoint. Perhaps the fight with Mullen had made him see things. He walked with a bold stride and out-thrown chest. The prison-cap he wore was pulled down well over his brows. Marks from the Johnny-Up's fists still disfigured his features.

Curiously, now and then, the college-educated Tod studied C.45. Once he used the word "sir," when answering a question. "Say," came from Spike trailing close, "you two guys is gettin' polite. Callin' a con 'sir.' Wot's th' big idea, Tod."

"Any man who can come back after two beatings from Mullen's fists and make him whine the third time is 'sir' to me," laughed Tod.

C.45 put a hand out and stopped. He looked upward where the towering concrete of the almost-finished cell-block rose above the old stone wall. His eyes grew sanguine when he noted the large air cells, the many windows, the breathing space inside the structure.

"A sermon in stone," he remarked.

"Maybe," said Tod. "But I heard there's soup enough in this stir to blow it up."

Tod's declaration came as a shock to C.45. He ground his teeth and turned, facing the editor. His swollen fists clenched tightly.

"Soup?" he repeated. "You mean dynamite?"

"Yes. Some cons call it soup and some dinny and some nitro. It's nitroglycerine extracted from dynamite sticks, by soaking the sticks in alcohol and getting out the sawdust, or whatever they use as a binder. I'd say there's two hundred pounds 'loose' in this prison, right now."

"For the love of Mike!"

"Fact. So there's the cell-house you've taken an unusual interest in. Up in smoke if certain cons start blasting. And the stuff, I've heard, was brought in by a contractor's wagon."

"You mean the contractor wants to undo his work?"

"Not the one who's got the contract. He's a square-shooter. Fletcher, there's wheels within wheels in this stir. The contractors who failed to get the million dollar appropriation are scheming with Mullen's mob, I think. They want a riot, a good job of dynamiting, and new contracts drawn. They'll get it unless that soup is found."

The interest C.45 had taken in the construction work seemed to master him. "Dirty, yellow graft!" he muttered. "I know, Tod, we're on the lid of hell as far as fire and riots are concerned. I didn't think they'd plan to destroy my—"

"Future home, eh? They are. Instead of a nice steel cell, with running water, and a real cot, the rats who nobody can point out are going to keep us all in those old stone coffins, unless there's a squealer among them."

"It's a dirty bird that fouls its own nest," admitted C.45. "Why didn't you tell me about the soup before, Tod?"

The editor looked at C.45's grim features queerly.

"I didn't know you were interested before. Now you act just like I act with *The Star*. I want to make a big thing out of it. I want to get permission to circulate it outside these four walls. They won't let me. Once in a while I feel like a fool that's editing something nobody sees."

"Can you get the low-down," whispered C.45, "on where that soup is? It's worth a—a thousand bucks to know."

Tod shook his tow-head emphatically. He removed his glasses and rubbed them on the sleeve of his prison uniform. Putting them on he glanced around at Spike and Roscoe, matching token-coins. None of Mullen's gang were near enough to hear him declare: "A 'grand' won't uncover it. It's in liquid form. Mullen's old armorer, the lieutenant of his outside mob, is serving seven years in here. His name is Peterman. He's in the concrete-mixing squad. And, Fletcher, it's my prunes against your mocha tomorrow morning, he's delegated to wreck the cell-block when the word comes through."

Adding hotly: "It's a damn shame, isn't it? Blooey goes three years' work and we inmates will be blamed. I can tell by the way certain cons are acting that the time is short. One of Mullen's low-brows warned his broad in the visiting room to keep away. That wasn't a natural action."

"Afraid of quick action?"

"Sure. Say, two hundred pounds of soup is an unstable menace."

"How about the warden's daughter? She lives near enough—"

A flush came over Tod's features.

"What's one girl more or less to Mullen's mob? But if they blow her up, I swear to God I'll croak Mullen!"

The determination that came over C.45's features attracted Tod's attention. He watched his cell-mate turn away from the construction work and stare toward the front-office. A mob of milling inmates, taking exercise, blocked the view that might be had of the administration building. C.45 wheeled around. He got out a pencil and paper. Spike and Roscoe nudged each other. The hijackers quit matching token-coins. They stepped nearer C.45.

Thought you wuz drawin' a picture," grinned Spike. "Looks more like a kite to me."

C.45 hastily crammed the note he was writing in a pocket. His cheeks flushed.

"It was a drawing of the cell-house, with description," he evaded. "Come on, let's cross the yard."

There was a box, near the administration building wherein convicts dropped protests that were supposed to reach the warden directly. The P.K. usually read them first. C.45 neared this box. He was roughly elbowed by one of Mullen's mob. Others of the locked-in leader's gang came swiftly in C.45's direction.

"Lay off him!" rasped Roscoe. "Beat it, youse!"

Spike picked up a stone. Tod seized a piece of timber. The tension was at breaking point when the inner gate to the guard-room opened. The P.K. came out followed by the warden, wearing a blue uniform and gold braid.

A "cluck" of warning sounded in Mullen's gang. They dispersed. The warden stopped directly before C.45. He hesitated, then thrust out his right hand.

It was almost a con's life's worth to be seen shaking hands with a warden, at Penthouse Penitentiary. C.45 clasped hands. To Tod, watching, he sensed that the note was passing from palm to palm. Then the warden went on.

"That's a bad break" said Tod to C.45. "You'll never be Johnny-Up after that move. What did the warden say?"

"Congratulated me on the fight with Mullen," said C.45.

Tod shook his head. "To hell he did, Fletcher. But it's your business, not mine. I didn't like the way the warden looked. He's been drinking. I thought he was sincere about improving our conditions, especially the cell-blocks. If he keeps on boozing, this bunch in here are going to take advantage of it."

C.45 pulled his prison-cap further down over his brows, and walked with Tod toward the print-shop.

What was on his mind, the editor wondered? Had he ratted about the nitro? Was he concerned about the warden's daughter? Tod grew hot when he thought of the frail girl, almost at the mercy of the prison die-hards. Lucile Collins was more than a friend to the editor of *The Star*. She was an inspiration, one he cherished. Her attempts to get the magazine outside the walls had almost been successful.

The whistle blew. The inmates went to work, some sullenly.

This sullen attitude, the following morning, was turned to glee and jeering at the screws, when the escape siren sounded soon after the first count. The blare of the whistle on one of the factories caused Tod to say to C.45:

"We'll probably be locked in all day. Some inmate is hiding out."

"Maybe he got out," said C.45.

"Nobody could get over the wall at night. They keep the guards on it, and it's electrified."

C.45 pressed his unshaven features to the bars. A thorough search was being made of the institution. Screws flitted in the dawn, carrying lanterns. They entered the damp cell-building and began examining every cell. Some climbed on top of the cell-block.

"Who blew this can?" Spike whispered.

His answer came from the forger on the right hand side of C.45's cell:

"Tony Conderilla. Workin' in th' dynamo room. That's queer, ain't it, Tod?"

Tod pressed past C.45 and answered the prison's comedian who had once been a jockey at Agua Caliente and Tia Juana.

"Conderilla, Spike? Sure, that's queer! He's only got about a stretch to do—maybe a year and a half. He wouldn't hide out." Tod looked at the lanterns in the yard. They resembled fireflies. He turned and studied C.45. "They're starting a big frisk, all right. I saw a couple of guards on top of the print-shop. A convict couldn't hide there. Strange—"

It occurred to the editor of *The Star* that there might have been a connection between the note passed by C.45 to the warden and the hiding-out of Tony. What relation could there be? C.45 seemed greatly concerned—watching through the bars every few minutes.

The P.K. came by the cell at noon. His face was dour. To Tod, watching, there was some sort of signal between C.45 and the P.K. A negative one—a shaking of the P.K.'s head.

After the grub was pushed in under the locked door at noon, Tod heard the screws letting out certain prisoners. No one opened his door. "I guess they don't trust us," he remarked. "But they haven't found Tony—and they're enlisting those they do trust in one grand search."

"I hope they find Tony."

"Hell," said the editor. "You know, Fletcher, it's more than Tony that would keep us locked in all day. It's the nitroglycerine they're after."

C.45's face was in a shadow. Tod could not see his cellmate's expression.

"Perhaps it is, Tod."

"You know it is! And that note—"

A pair of gripping hands closed around the editor's arms. "*Sisst*," breathed C.45. "Don't want me to throttle you, do you, Tod? Keep mum about that kite! I'm not a rat. I'm working for the good of the institution."

The search extended throughout the afternoon and evening. Nothing was found except a few bottles of booze, a half-dozen knives, and one rod without cartridges. The doors opened and the stiff-jointed, indignant inmates snaked their way to the mess-hall. While exercising, before going to the shops, the word went sweeping among the cons that Tony had been discovered sleeping on top of a cold boiler.

Spike grinned at Roscoe. "Ain't that a joke, fer this stir? Why, I saw them screws wid me own eyes lookin' in water-pipes fer th' wop. Maybe they thought he'd turned to a liquid—an' wuz poured there."

"I wish to cripes I knew where that soup was, Spike," shuddered Roscoe. "Suppose it's in th' print-shop?"

Having apparently "discovered" Tony, the front-office bunch, consisting of the P.K., the day-captain and deputies, tried a new angle in the attempt to uncover the hiding place of the nitro. The gang working on the new cell-block were herded in the chapel. The almost completed block was gone over inch by inch with sharp eyes.

Tod, who had the run of the inner prison, told C.45 nothing had been found in the construction work. The editor saw that his cell-mate seemed more concerned than the screws over the search. He was always staring out of the many windows of the print-shop.

"Maybe, Fletcher, it's a stir-yarn about that soup," suggested the editor.

"Not on your life! We—I know it's no false alarm now."

Tod walked away from C.45. He saw the P.K. and deputies approaching the print-shop. They came in, closing the door. One deputy went the round of the windows, closing each tightly. Steam sizzled in the radiators, although it was not cold outside.

"Some crazy idea," Spike gasped, mopping his bald head. "Say, Tod, maybe that P.K.'s springing a new kind of third-degree on us. Tryin' to sweat out th' truth. It lets me out, 'cause I never told th' truth in me life."

The print-shop grew hotter by degrees. The inmates removed their coats. They watched the alert P.K.

The ink-rolls began to soften. Butter oozed from a package on Tod's desk. A deadening pall of mist filled the print-shop and gathered on the metal surfaces. Louder, the radiators sizzled and hammered. C.45 came through the fog. He perched himself on Tod's desk and started fanning himself with a copy of *The Star*.

"If the P.K. wants to start trouble he's going the right way about it!" declared the gasping editor. "They're doing it in the mat-shop and the brush-shop. It's about a hundred and twenty in here now."

"Watch every inmate," said C.45. "See if any of them show unusual fear. Brixton moved away from his press just now. Why did he do that?"

"Say," Tod blurted, "you're acting like a screw, Fletcher! What's the object of heating this shop up until it'll catch fire?"

"Don't you know?"

"Of course I don't know." Tod dashed the beads of perspiration from his high forehead, and glanced at the inside telephone. "I got a notion to 'phone the warden or his daughter. I don't believe they know—"

Stopping his improvised fan from moving a moment, C.45 laid a detaining hand on Tod's arm.

"Lay off that 'phone," he said deep to his throat. "The warden gave orders to have every shop's temperature raised to the exploding point."

"Does he want to start a riot?"

"As an editor," remarked C.45, "you show considerable ignorance in human psychology and fear. Don't you see their game? Nitroglycerine and fulminating caps have a detonating point. If there's any hidden in this shop the extreme heat will explode them. They are trying to get the inmate who knows where the soup is planted to cave and confess."

Tod gripped C.45's brawny arm.

"I've been watching that linotype man of mine, Goldman. He's acting goofy. Take a look at him. He knows something—"

An explosion shook the print-shop. A second one followed the first. A plank and splinters shot up from near the linotype machine. Goldman ducked and slid toward the back of the shop. He was stopped by the alert P.K. "I got you!" throated the prison officer.

"Thems caps went off!" cried Spike. "Let's get out of this bake-oven!"

An investigation made by a deputy while Goldman struggled with the P.K. revealed an answer to the explosions. The deputy held up a shattered beer-bottle. Goldman had made home-brew with raisins and sugar. The temperature caused the containers to burst.

"Aw hell!" panted the disgusted Spike. "Them screws are on a bum steer—tryin' to put th' fear of God in us."

The P.K. ordered the windows opened and the radiators shut off. He strode out of the print-shop showing his temper by kicking Goldman ahead of him.

"I'll chalk you in!" he shouted.

Tod leaned out the window in the office and breathed the cooler air. He called C.45. "Well, your prize cell-block's still standing," he said. "I may finish my 'bit' in it yet. I haven't much time to serve here—but—"

The editor of *The Star* bared his left arm. "See the sweat coming out of that tattoo mark, Fletcher. That mark's going to settle me for a stretch in Lansing, Michigan. I wonder how I can get it off? It fits the description that a bank-teller gave of an arm that reached through the cage and snatched up a bundle of century notes. I must have been crazy!"

"That and the job you're serving for now are your only ones?" C.45 asked sincerely. "You aren't a born crook."

"About all!" Tod admitted.

"I'll see the governor. I mean I'll help you—"

"Say, *who are you*, Fletcher? After that fight with Mullen you've changed. I'm beginning to believe you're not what you pretend to be. Handing notes to a warden. Concerned as hell about the new cell-block. Getting me sprung. What's the mystery?"

Tod drew his head in from the window when C.45 refused to answer.

"Wonder what they found in the other shops?" he asked Spike.

"Nothin' at all. They didn't break one con down."

After Tod was locked in that night with C.45 he thumbed over some galley-proofs of *The Star*. "I'll have to skip an issue," he started to say when he heard light steps on the gallery.

A shadow came to the bars. Tod's galley-proofs dropped to the floor of the cell. He stared with mouth agape.

C.45's broad back blocked the view through the cell-door. A girl's hat moved and Tod saw the warden's daughter. She was apparently distributing books to inmates. Her whispering to C.45 caused the editor's ears to tingle. Suddenly she looked in at him.

"Good evening, Tod. Here's a corking book for you to read. *Queer People*.

It's all about Hollywood." *

Tod reached out and took the book. The girl's features flushed when he touched her arm, through the bars.

No note dropped out of his book, but from between the pages of the volume she handed C.45, a white object fluttered to the lower bunk. C.45 snatched it up and concealed it.

After the girl had gone, Tod said jealously:

"She distributed those books to get that kite to you. I never knew she ever gave you a second look. Looks strange to me."

A chuckle came from C.45. "She's got a right to give me a kite. I'll tell you why she has, some day. Our little prison angel is twenty years younger than I am. That lets me out, Tod."

"She ought not to be allowed in here with these gorillas. It's bad judgment on the part of the warden."

"Y—es. The warden has used bad judgment, several times."

A tune struck up when Roscoe played a soft harmonica from the cell labeled Agua Caliente. A protest rose from the forger in the St. Anne de Beaupre cell. Tod listened at the anathema passing between the cells.

"We're between Paradise and Hell," he said. "Wish I had that Lansing rap beat. I'd rather enjoy that slang Spike is slinging."

C.45 crumpled up the note. He chewed it to a pulp with a strong grind of his perfect teeth.

"Forget that rap, son," he said half absentmindedly. "Puzzle your brains and see if you can locate that nitro. It's certainly well planted."

Tod began to see that his cell-mate had grown myopic concerning the explosive brought in to destroy the contractor's work. C-45 roamed the yard next day with his head down as if the 'soup' was in the ground. He braced and muscled through several of Mullen's gangsters.

Mullen's armorer, Peterman, came up to C.45 while he stood eyeing the new cell-block. "Goin' to rent a room there, eh? You've been pipin' th' block off as if you wuz buildin' it. Thinkin' of th' poor cons, eh, who have those swell cells instead of livin' in wet coffins? Keep on thinking Fletcher, it's a pipe dream!"

"What do you mean?"

"Wot d'I mean? I mean th' lousy block ain't safe. It'll fall down. Th' contractor that's buildin' it is graftin' plenty. He's a white-collar guy who took th' gravy away from some honest lads, I know?"

Peterman's features twisted evilly. "Better keep away from it, Fletcher. I tell you it's goin' to fall down, an' it's goin' to crush th' Administration Buildin' when it lets go."

* Bestselling 1930 novel that savaged Hollywood.

The armorer slouched away. C.45 watched him. He went in the direction of the isolation cells where Mullen was confined. A screw came out and talked in whispers with the most dangerous con in Penthouse Penitentiary. They seemed friends.

Suspicion that Peterman was the lead to the nitroglycerine, caused C.45 to approach the P.K., who was strolling, with a deputy, near the new cell-block. C.45 climbed over a girder. He raised his right hand, a signal required of inmates when approaching an official.

"Can I lay off this afternoon, P.K.? he asked. "I don't want to go to my cell or the hospital. I'd rather join the idle company."

The P.K. nodded. "You can have anything you want," he whispered too low for the deputy to hear him.

Joining the idle company was a ruse to spy on Peterman. That mobsman, with three others of Mullen's gang, had pull enough to keep them from working. The idle company usually hung out in the frame grandstand at the ball-grounds. C.45 stretched himself along a plank. From beneath his prison cap he watched Mullen's armorer playing cards with the trio.

A word, now and then, reached C.45's ears. He shifted his head. One gangster looked in his direction suspiciously. Did they know the exact locality of the liquid dynamite? wondered C.45. Peterman indicated he did when he laughed and said brutally:

"Wot th' hell do I care about th' moll. She gets th' works if nothin' slips. An' so do th' rest of that front-office bunch."

Pretending to snore, C.45 lay rigid. The card game went on. A cripple climbed down the grand-stand and went under it, with his crutch tapping the planks. A drop of rain spattered C.45's resolute jaw. Other drops came down. The card game came to a finish.

Suddenly Peterman exclaimed: "Pipe wot's comin' from th' stone shed! Th' truck wid a screw in a raincoat drivin' it. It's goin' through th' front gate. I never saw that screw before. He's a con, fixed up wid a screw's uniform. A bunch is makin' a getaway wid our truck."

Then a surprising thing happened too swiftly for C.45 to grasp. The heavy truck, which went in and out of the prison at times, mounted a grade to the gates. The pseudo-guard at the wheel waved a hand at a wall-tower wherein was the lever that unlocked the gate. A screw came out in the rain. He was an aged man with poor eyesight. Two blocks of apparent stone on the truck satisfied him that everything was all right. He went back to the lever, pressing his weight on it.

Peterman, leading two thugs, lunged at the truck. They cried to the wall-guard:

"It's a getaway! Don't open that gate, you sap!"

The truck driver attempted to ram the gate. He was thwarted by the slow speed required to climb the grade. The crash that followed brought guards running across the yard. The two blocks of "stone" slid backward and broke open. Out of each crawled an inmate. C.45 gasped when he recognized the forger and the religious student who celled next to him.

Roughly a deputy yanked the driver from the crumpled-up seat of the truck.

He was an inmate mason who worked in the stone-shed. His features twisted in rage toward Peterman.

"You dirty rat! Squealed on me. I thought you wuz one of Mullen's men. You yellow-livered—"

The four gangsters cleared the stone-like boxes away from the rear of the truck, ignoring the captured con's biting oaths. A screw looked at them and scratched his head. C.45 felt his heart thumping wildly when he reviewed the accident.

Why did a supposedly right-guy, like Peterman, a famous armorer with a score of bumpings-off to his credit, turn informer on the impulse?

The answer to that question might be the unlocking of the nitro puzzle. C.45 heard the signal for all inmates to form in files and hurry to their cells. He joined Tod as the editor climbed the gallery steps.

A guard was already in the cell marked "St. Anne de Beaupre," frisking it for evidence against the forger and his pious companion.

"Are they the two?" asked Tod.

"Yes. This stir is full of surprises," reflected C.45.

Jammed in their quarters by the excited turnkeys, C.45 and Tod sat down on the lower bunk. The inmates began cat-calling and jeering. Crossfire of conversation ran through the old cell-block. "Who'd of thunk Peterman an' C.98 an' them two rodmen who gave Richscob, th' gambler, 'th' works,' would of welshed on a swell getaway?" Spike shouted to a pal. "Who'd of thunk it?"

"Peterman ratted?" came from the pal. "You're stir-crazy. He's a right guy!"

C.45 gazed at Tod. "He *is* a right guy," he remarked reflectively. "He's got the same reputation among the police as Mullen has. I know that. They never took the trouble to third-degree either man. It would have been useless.

"Yet he squealed on our next-door neighbor, the paperhanger?"

"Yep," C.45 bowed his head in thought. He ran his fingers through his chin-bristles, that were as prickly as points on a metal music-roll.

"I'm trying to put two and two together," he mused. "Tod, a strange action, one out of tangent, like Peterman pulled, is a clue. Peterman won't dare go in the yard after this. The cons will mob him."

"Perhaps they won't," said Tod. "There's a code of ethics among gangsters that's hard to understand. The two who tried to make that getaway aren't in the gang. They're occasional offenders. High-brow! Peterman, Mullen and the others who control the inside politics are low-brows."

Relentlessly C.45 kept at his point.

"The unusual action calls for an unusual explanation, Tod. We're getting close to the whereabouts of the nitroglycerine. It might have been in that truck. Say, I believe it is!" C.45 sprang from the cot. He began pacing the floor of the cell. "Where could it have been planted in the truck?" he asked. "It wasn't in those imitation blocks of stone. It couldn't be around the engine or crank-case. Heat would have exploded it. The floor of the truck is steel. It isn't hidden there. Yet, Peterman didn't want the truck out of the yard. That's why he welshed. He didn't want—"

"You've struck something!" Tod exclaimed. "Where the mind is—the treasure is. Though, in this case, one couldn't call nitroglycerine treasure. Hardly!"

"Peterman intended turning it into big money—by blowing up the new cell-house. Big money from some crooked contractor. I wish I could get out and look that truck over again, Tod."

"Nobody'll get out of these cells tonight—after that attempt to escape. The P.K. and warden are wild men."

"I—could get out—"

"Eh?" queried Tod.

"Yes, easy enough. I won't try. It will attract suspicion. We'll have time enough in the morning to examine the truck. You're not going to print *The Star* for a month, are you?"

Tod ignored the question. He examined C.45's unshaven features. He got up and trimmed his tiny oil lamp, that could be used after the electric globe went dark at nine o'clock. Then he lay down on the upper bunk, with his hands clasped behind his head.

The gong rang through the cell-block. The count was correct. An hour passed with Tod in the same position and C.45 thinking deeply. Finally C.45 declared: "I know you're not sleeping, Tod. Thinking of the nitro, eh, an' that rap against you when you finish this bit. Well, pal, take it from an older man than you are, that I'll show you that glycerine in the morning! I'm going right after it! You forget *The Star* and come along. Finding it will help a heap springing you and I'll be able to get a moment's peace. The governor will take care of both of us. You see, I've a secret pride in that modern cell-block."

"You act as if you own it," yawned the sleepy editor.

In the morning, after the screws finished the count, C.45 discovered that a clever brain-worker had blocked his plan to be first at the truck. The key to the cell-door lock refused to work. The print-shop company filed to the mess-hall without Tod and C.45. "Checkmated," said the exasperated editor.

"Some inmate plugged the keyhole with an obstruction."

The locksmith was sent for. He dug out bright particles of metal. "Tin-foil," growled the screw. "Taken from a tobacco can."

Lunging out on the gallery platform, when the door finally opened, C.45 rushed down the flights of steps. He heard Tod after him. They emerged to the yard. Turning swiftly C.45 pointed at the stone-shed.

"I see the truck's still there. Hurry, Tod."

The inmates had already reached their respective shops. C.45 strode into the low shed. He examined the truck's engine, after lifting the hood. He got down and looked under the pan. The floor steel was too thin for any hiding place. Backing a tire he exclaimed:

"Where are the spares, Tod?"

"At the back. Look. They're big ones, on a sort of shelf. Two of them. Could the soup be in them?"

"It could," came from C.45 grimly. "It's the last place anybody would search for it. Don't they bring liquor back from Canada in spare tires? Don't yeggs carry nitro in hot-water bags, for safety? There can't be much chemical action between pure rubber and pure nitroglycerine."

Tod and C.45 examined the twin tires which were covered with mud.

"A crooked contractor," mused Tod, "could have switched these tires for the regular spares that were on the truck when it made one of its outside trips. Are they the same make as on the wheels? The treads look different."

"They are different!" C.45 doubled up his fists. "Open one of the valves, Tod. Let see what comes out."

The excited editor unscrewed a cap, pressed a match against the plunger, and fell over backward when a jet of an oily substance struck the truck-frame and spattered against his glasses. He got up, staggering blindly.

"Oil, eh?" gritted C.45. "Nitroglycerine resembles oil. Smell the stuff."

Tod sneezed. "I smell it," he gulped. "There's a test for nitro. It'll make your head ache if you rub some on your palm."

C.45 looked around for a flat rock. There was none under the shed suitable for striking a drop of the "oil" with a hammer—a surer test than Tod proposed. He glared at Tod's oily sleeves. "Come on, we'll go to the doctor, quick. He'll be able to tell us if this "oil" is nitroglycerine, or not. Hurry, Tod!"

Reaching at the shift-lever before he rushed from the shed, C.45 announced: "The truck's transmission is locked. A guard must have done that last night, after the truck was driven in here. Great! No one can move it without a key."

The prison doctor sniffed Tod's oily sleeves. He rubbed a particle of the liquid between his professional fingers. "Where did this come from?" he asked in astonishment. "It's what they've been searching for around here."

"Hold on," be added too late to prevent Tod and C.45 from running down the hospital steps. The dazed editor reeled across the yard. He grabbed C.45's arm. "The truck is backing out of the shed. Look! That isn't a chauffeur at the wheel. He had a key—but, it's—"

"Peterman!" C.45 throated. "The armorer disguised in a workman's overalls! He's turning. He's racing the engine. He's heading for the space between the new cell-block and the administration building. That alley! It's all up—unless we stop him."

"I'll get him," Tod panted. "I'll stop him before it is too late."

A mastering resolve electrified C.45's giant frame. He plunged away from Tod, taking the direction of the administrating building. One wing of it was occupied by the warden's daughter.

C.45 crashed a window glass with his fists.

"Elsie!" he bulled. "Run out the front gate! Run for your life! The nitro is going to explode. Do you hear me, Elsie?"

A uniformed man came to the broken window. "Get Elsie outside the walls, George!" C.45 shouted. "Carry her out! There's going to be an explosion."

The man hesitated, dumb with surprise. Then he acted wildly, as if struck by fear for himself. The girl's voice came to C.45. She was being urged from her quarters.

Ducking and lunging in the direction taken by the truck, C.45 brushed a guard aside and looked between the administration building and the cell-house. Tod had broken Peterman's hold from the steering wheel of the truck. The armorer lay across the driving compartment of the track. A series of flames poured upward from the rear of the vehicle, where the nitro-filled tires were. The muffler-pipe, in some clever manner, was directed against the rubber.

C.45 grasped that it was too late to prevent an explosion. He hurtled himself at Tod, who had the engine racing.

"Look out!" the editor warned him. "Get away, Fletcher! I'm going—"

Tod dropped into first speed, let go the clutch pedal, and fell forward when the truck jerked forward. Peterman rolled to the ground. A wheel passed over his neck. He squirmed in death's throes as C.45 backed away and avoided the flames from the blistered tires.

Down over the yard, bouncing and crashing, clearing a way through shoring-timber, the five-ton juggernaut roared with open muffler. It rounded the print-shop, showering planks in every direction. It missed a gang of staring cons and seemed to leap a stone pile at the head of a wharf that jutted out into a river. Bars were at the end of the wharf, and a guard tower.

Tod rattled over the wharf planks. He missed the tower's base by inches and bucked the bars until they buckled and almost gave way.

C.45 ran in the direction of the wharf. He cried a warning to the inmates near the riverbank. The warning cries died in his husky throat. He stood stock still when a sheet of flame, resembling a volcano's, rose and blotted out the light of day. A wind sucked him toward the inferno. It threw him back, flat. He got up amid falling fragments of the dock. He cleared his eyes.

The truck and Tod had vanished. Receding water from the river revealed a weak swimmer trying to keep afloat in the debris. C.45 went through the broken bars with a plunge. He swam to Tod and ran a hand under his singed mop of hair. One of the editor's arms, the left, had been blown away.

"Keep cool," coughed C.45. "Lay on your back. I'll get you ashore."

Dragging the half-conscious editor to where a guard stood with a rifle, C.45 lifted him on the bank. He bent over Tod—shook his head. At first there seemed no life left.

The guard stood puzzled. "Lift him up!" commanded C.45. "Carry him to the Administration Building. Hurry, drop that rifle!"

"Who the hell are you to be giving me orders?"

"Do as I tell you! Pick him up!"

"I'll take no instructions from a con. Wait till th' P.K.—"

"I'm no con," said C.45. "I'm the *warden* of this stir!"

"Th' wot?"

"The warden! I assumed my brother's place in order to find out what was really going on inside here. And *found out*," added Jim Collins grimly.

Tod was carried by the astonished screw into the administration building. Elsie cleared her bed and pointed to it. "Put him there until the doctor comes," she breathed excitedly.

Leaning over the wounded editor, C.45, better known as Warden Tom Collins, examined the lacerated left shoulder. "You've gotten rid of the evidence that might have settled you for that Lansing job, Tod. The tattoo mark on the left arm. That's good. And, cell-mate, I'm going to get you paroled from here—soon as I can."

Tom Collins looked around at his brother.

"This boy saved the new cell-block, George. An' he saved Elsie. He's a good example for you."

Weakly Tod hinged himself upright on the bed.

"I don't know what this is all about," he said with his eyes on the girl, who whispered:

"I'm going to tell you afterwards, Tod. After the doctor comes. You remember the king who went among his subjects to find out the real situation in his kingdom? Well, that's dad! He took his brother's place. And he found plenty, didn't he, Tod?"

"I'll say he did!" answered Tod.

The Prison Demon

LETHAL CHAMBER

Carl Henry

Ralph Hurley had always known that a rich murderer can get out of stir quicker than an innocent dupe. But a hell-roaring two hundred pound bob-cat didn't need any dough—he was every bit as dangerous as Death—and he knew he could beat her racket!

WHEN RALPH HURLEY ENTERED SAN JACINTO PENITENTIARY it was like an irresistible force meeting an immovable object.

He became the prison demon in one, red night after he had been unhandcuffed by the deputies who brought him from Silverside. His escape to the yard began with a riot and ended with a conflagration that almost destroyed the institution. He was brought down in the morning, bleeding, bruised, shot in a score of places, but still defiant enough to pound his hairy breast with his fists and curse his captors.

Throwing him in the snake-hole took the strength of five burly screws.

"An' there you rot!" spat the Principal Keeper. "Rot, damn you, until you enter the lethal chamber! Cyanide's too good for you!"

The lethal chamber was peculiar to San Jacinto. It consisted of a limestone mosque, domed on top, with a sealed door. It stood in the white glare of a sun-baked yard.

Inside was a chair, stapled to the wall, a half dozen rawhide straps, a shallow pan filled with cyanide crystals and a bottle of acid. The pouring of the acid on the crystals produced a vapor—the most deadly known.

Condemned men had the choice of a firing squad or gas, at San Jacinto. The warden decided to give Hurley no voice in the matter. He notified the doctor to get the lethal chamber ready.

Taking savage strides about the snake-hole Hurley wiped the blood from his bruised features. He sniffed the smoke from burning buildings. Thirty other cons, who joined him in the rioting, were crowded in cells adjoining the snake-hole. Guards stood with rifles on their hips, watching them.

From Hurley's position, when he shook the bars in rage, he could see the mosque of death in the sun-scorched yard, the Mexican prisoners cleaning away debris, the dobe wall and over it the range of mountains he knew so well—The Miradores with snow capped peaks.

Beneath one peak, El Capitan, on its northern slope, he had prospected, become mill-owner, gone broke, come up again and then been tried and convicted for the murder of his partner, Wadleigh.

Dashing a clot of blood from one eye Hurley flung his weight against the snake-hole bars. He shook the walls (that were sunk five feet in the ground) so fiercely that dobe fell from around the hinges. A rattler wiggled away, up a flight of seven steps. The screw nearest the snake-hole brought his rifle's butt down on the sidewinder's neck.

In a cell nearby Billy the Kid No. 2 added encouragement to Hurley. The voice that cleft the air was like a breath from old Arizona.

"They ain't got no guts, Demon! Oh, gimme a shootin' iron, jus' one! I calculates about that would clean out th' whole corral."

"What are you in for, Kid?" asked Hurley.

"Motor-bus stick-up. I gotta chance—you ain't got th' chance that rattler had. I jus' seen th' doctor go in th' lethal chamber."

Twisting at the bars in agony Hurley tried to spread them.

"Say, Demon," came from the Kid, "we mavericks figured out last night, when we was calculatin' how to rush th' wall, that you hit this stir harder than it's ever been hit. Like a Texas Norther, so to speak. It ain't been done so neat since Jessie Grant wuz brung here, with Oregon boots on. He got away. But you—?"

"Me, what, Kid?"

"Acted wilder than a long-horn. We all calculates you didn't do th' job you wuz brung here for. Nothin' but an innocent tiger-cat could have done it better."

The Prison Demon had once heard a parson say at Silverdale that "Hell hath no fury like a man wronged." He held his swollen tongue for a time. There was a movement to the door of the lethal chamber.

Climbing on the lower cross-bars of the snake-hole Hurley glared at the doctor's form. He saw the prison medic stand, undecided, for a moment. Then he turned and peered toward the snake-hole.

"Here comes th' croaker," announced Billy the Kid No. 2. "He's th' only officer in this stir whose guts aren't green."

The doctor advanced toward the snake-hole and stood at the top of the steps leading down to Hurley. Admiration, like that of a beetle hunter examining a perfect specimen, lit up his eyes. "All set for the kick-off?" snarled Hurley.

The doctor smiled:

"It's an easy death, Hurley—easiest known. But I didn't come to tell you that. You, as a mining man, know more about cyanide than I do. I want to ask you one question, Hurley."

"You be damned!" spat the Demon.

The doctor went on in the same almost confidential tone.

"Hurley, what acid was used in the settling-tank your partner's body was supposed to be dissolved in? Quick. They found his teeth, his rings, his watch, his shoe nails—but not his bones. I'm a graduate chemist. I know of no acid or lye that acts that way. There is a doubt—"

Letting his fingers uncoil from the bars Hurley drew back into the shadow of the snake-hole, and lifted his hand to his head.

Was the little medic of San Jacinto trying to trap him?

"Won't answer, eh?" the doctor said. "Well, all right! Here's a little gift for you."

He tossed a sack of the makin's through the bars and walked away.

Hurley, distrustful of everybody in Jacinto, was a long time picking up the bag. As he rolled a cigarette he wondered why Dr. Pascal came to be so generous.

Late that afternoon Hurley spied a cloud of dust on the road leading toward the Miradores and Gun-Sight Pass. An auto was climbing the grade, its rear wheels churning.

"Goin' after your coffin?" said Billy the Kid No. 2. "Th' croaker's sendin' fer somethin'. I saw him chinnin' with th' chauffeur at th' gate." Receiving no answer from the Demon, he began singing:

"Oh, bury me out on th' lone prair—ee,
In a shallow grave's that's six by three—"

Death was a side issue with the Kid; his own or another's.

The attenuated air of San Jacinto suddenly grew static. A brass gong sounded. It was a signal for the inmates to file into their cells. Snaky lines wormed over the blistered surface of the yard. Screws came from the walls. The P.K. appeared. Behind him were the warden and doctor. The Demon saw them advancing to the lethal chamber, followed by four swarthy guards, built like wrestlers.

"Good bye, pal," sang out Billy the Kid.

The Demon crouched against the back of his cell, ready to spring.

His muscles were taut as bowstrings. The flats of his hands were pressed on the cold earth. His mouth foamed with blood and saliva. Once he beat his chest with his fist, roaring defiance.

Recoiling slightly the Mexican guards came on. One unlocked the door and sprang aside. He was not quick enough. A savage creature of two hundred pounds struck him, bowled him over and drove a heel into his neck. Then he engaged the three other screws. He flailed at them, ducked, uppercut, jerked his legs back and struck out fighting in three directions.

But the first screw had come out of his stupor. He got unsteadily to his feet, and struck the Demon over the right ear with a blackjack stunning him momentarily. The guards closed and bound his arms with rawhide.

"Sacré!" one swore. "This man—he ees El Diablo!"

Over the earth they dragged Hurley, toward the open door of the lethal chamber.

"In there with him, pronto!" snapped the thin-lipped warden.

The guards lashed the Demon to the chair, and went outside, leaving the warden, Pascal and the P.K.

Carefully, deliberately, the prison doctor made his preparation. He seemed to be taking more than the allowed time arranging the glazed bowl, the handful of cyanide crystals, the bottle of acid so that its cork could be pulled by one of four strings outside the lethal chamber.

Finally he advanced toward Hurley, adjusted a stethoscope to his chest, and made some notes in a small book.

"Hell! The warden exclaimed. "My dinner's getting cold. You never acted this slow in other executions, Pascal."

Bunching every one of his muscles Hurley attempted to wrench the double-stapled chair from the wall. His attempt was useless. He was hog-tied, diamond-hitched, lashed with cutting rawhide. He threw his weight forward. The chair held.

Suddenly he ceased his efforts.

There rose from the porcelain bowl a faint curl of vapor which spiraled up into the air, like some awful incense. Hurley resembled a hermit-like Buddha before a sacrifice fire. His eyes regarded the death smoke almost unseeingly.

"Ready," whispered the doctor. "I'll put this hood on him. You station your guards at the strings, warden."

The picture of the little medic coming toward him, coming past the white bowl with mincing steps, was the last Hurley expected to see in this world.

"It's the easiest way out," purred the doctor. "The easiest way—"

His voice broke off suddenly. The hood went down over the Demon's head, like a candle-snuffer. Something that tasted like rubber was thrust roughly into his mouth. Two rubber plugs entered his distended nostrils. He opened his eyes in wonder, seeing nothing.

Years before in the Great War, Hurley had worn a gas-mask. He was trained to put them on at Ypres.

Gripping the mouthpiece until his teeth sunk deep into the rubber, he heard the doctor hissing:

"This is our little secret, Hurley. There isn't much chance, but this neutralizing canister may save you. Pretend you've fainted. Don't let go your grip on that inhaler."

Going out of the lethal chamber, and stalling for time by consulting his watch, the doctor closed the door. Already there was a trace of gas in the air. The warden had stationed the four guards at the four strings. A pull at any one of them would jerk the cork from the bottle and set the crystals boiling and bubbling.

"All right!" called the doctor. "Everything is ready."

Four strings were pulled simultaneously. Pascal moved toward the little, sealed window and glanced anxiously from the spiraling fumes to Hurley. The Demon made no sign.

Pascal studied the road leading down from the Miradores, fingering his watch impatiently.

"That doubt in my mind about Hurley's guilt may cost me this job. If someone doesn't show up very soon," he was thinking.

And at that moment someone did show up.

Coming across the yard, moving as rapidly as a Mexican can, the doctor saw a trusty from the front office. He approached the warden and spoke in hurried whispers.

Pascal placed his watch in his pocket. He rather thought he knew what the trusty was saying. That's why he moved around the lethal chamber so as to be nearer the door when things started humming.

"A reprieve!" bawled the warden. "Phone call from the governor! There isn't a chance that the Demon is alive, is there, Pascal?"

The doctor shook his head. "Not a chance—but I'll see! Have Manuel go to the hospital and bring my pulmotor. Damn that governor!"

Pascal jerked open the door, stepped around the lethal chamber and smashed the glass window with a lump of dobe.

Green and yellow vapor curled from the openings. A slight breeze from the desert came over the prison wall and cleared away the cyanide fumes.

"Take ya time," suggested the warden. "Don't risk y'ur life, Pascal. I hope that Demon is deader than th' last sidewinder I killed. I don't want him on my hands."

To this remark the P.K. spat twice, once to the right and once to the left.

Pascal, holding a saturated handkerchief to his nostrils, glided into the chamber. He kicked aside the white bowl. Hurley sat hunched forward, all life out of him apparently. Quickly the doctor removed the hood and pocketed the rubber gag. He bent down and applied the stethoscope to the Demon's chest.

Suddenly he straightened. "You'll live, Hurley!" he cried, with feigned surprise. "It must be pretty darn hard to gas a smelter man!"

A shadow blocked the doorway. Pascal turned.

"Dead, eh?" asked the warden.

"No!" answered Pascal in a disappointed voice. "He's going to kick again. You'll undoubtedly have this Demon on your hands for the term of his natural life."

"Of all the rotten luck—"

The Demon was commuted to life, "doing it all" in the prison slang of San Jacinto.

With, good time, or "copper" off, life was usually twenty years. There was little likelihood that Ralph Hurley would earn any good time. He started as a Demon and intended to finish as one. A hell-roaring two hundred pound bob-cat as dangerous as death.

"You're a consistent devil," remarked the dry-as-dust doctor one day.

Shaking the snake-hole bars Hurley roared:

"I want to get out of here! I'll kill every man-taming gutless cur from the warden down, unless they let me free."

"You're lucky where you are. Those greaser screws would knife you, pronto. Cut that big-wind stuff. I'm getting along with my book concerning you, and others—including Billy the Kid No. 2."

"Is that why you slipped the gas-absorbing canister over on John Law?"

"Not exactly." Pascal was the one individual in San Jacinto who held any feeling toward his fellow man. "I slipped it over, Hurley, because of the doubt. They found a lot of evidence in that tank at Silverside Smelter—evidence that you had effaced your partner from this earth. He's gone. So is Cora—Cora big and Cora little. The wife and kid. You quarreled with her and with him."

"Damn the pair!"

"If he had been a trifle cleverer than I think he is, he would have thrown a tibia bone or two in the vat. The chemicals found there would not have dissolved them. The evidence shows they did. Therefore you've been framed."

"What's a tibia?"

"Largest bone in the leg."

The Demon's eyes grew slightly wistful. Somewhere in the southwest, perhaps in one of the dog-towns of the state, Cora was living with his partner and the kid. The failure to execute had thrown Wadleigh's plans out of gear. The partner figured on the lethal chamber doing its deadly work, then collecting everything of value pertaining to the smelter.

"The largest bone in the leg," repeated the doctor.

Back to Hurley's eyes came the demon glare. The doctor moved away visiting the other die-hards in the punishment cells.

Crouching in the back of the snake-hole, on the dirt, the Demon began planning an escape from San Jacinto. He could count on about a score of the most desperate criminals living. A few of these convicts were not under punishment. They sat together, peacefully making saddles for visitors, but in their hearts was the resolve to some day straddle these same saddles over the Miradores to freedom.

One of these men, Cisco Joe, possessed a trained lizard, which he exhibited to visitors. But these visitors never knew just why this lizard found so much favor with the prisoners, or that he was trained to do other things than they had seen—a thing such as the carrying of messages, for instance.

And so there came a night when Ralph Hurley heard a scaly something crawling over the snake-hole floor. Attached to its leg was a cigarette paper bearing this message, which the Demon read as soon as the morning light entered his cell:

> Why grow old, rotting in that black-hole? There is a new warden coming. The new guy is going to be tougher than the one we got now. His name is Flint. He's that fresh sheriff at Sandy Bend who shot Black Jack in the back with a sawed-off shot-gun. As ornery as that. Do you calculate you can help us fix Flint's hash before he gets settled on the job? Answer via Cordilla.

"Cordilla" was the name of the lizard. The Demon wrote one word, "YES," on the paper and attached it to Cordilla's right, hind leg. The intelligent animal ran scurrying over the baked yard, unnoticed by the greaser screws.

Rolling a cigarette with Cisco Joe's message, Hurley smoked it completely.

That day Hurley examined the bars of his cell by minutely scraping off every particle of rust that had gathered there since he had been thrown in the snake-hole. But he was forced to give them up as a bad job for him. They were over two inches in diameter, and made of tempered steel just below the point where they could be snapped. Inside them were revolving needles, set in glycerin. These needles possessed super-brittleness, so much so that a diamond-set-saw could not have cut through them. Such a saw would have revolved the needles without making an abrasion.

The Demon felt that some devil had invented the bars.

The door locks, too, were backed and riveted with steel bolts. The stone sills were uncuttable. The walls, roof and floor of the snake-hole were flint rock, covered by an accumulation of dobe mud.

One die-hard suggested by prison grape-vine that a silk thread coated with molasses and dipped in emery dust would sever anything. It had the advantage that a screw could not see it operating.

But the Demon knew that his particular bars were proof against emery.

He considered, over the months, some way of garroting the greaser who brought him food and twirled the pan under the door. But that was quite useless since the screw carried no gat or key, at the P.K.'s orders.

In the grind of time the Demon's mouthpiece arrived from Silverside. Billy Tilt was a raw-boned barrister who would never grow old.

"I've got some news, Ralph," he confided. He looked around for a place to sit down. There was none, save the steps leading to the snake-hole. Tilt chose the uppermost one of these. He crossed his long legs and assumed the air of a man who would like to stay and chin a while.

"The news ain't much, Ralph. Cora was seen in the east—down and out I guess. She was located in the back room of a speakeasy. I got a long letter about her." Tilt made a motion to reach in his pocket. He mopped his brow instead of producing the letter. "She went to hell—after she left you—and probably Wadleigh."

"Where she always belonged. The—"

"I wouldn't say that, Ralph. She's out of your life and his."

"The kid?"

"No trace."

The Demon took a turn about his cell. "Is that the news?"

"No, not exactly. The smelter proposition came up again. The bank has an offer for it. You're the sole survivor on that contract with Wadleigh, so the law says. Survivor gets all—but." Tilt acted like a novice sawing through a tough legal knot.

"Well—?" queried the Demon.

"But didn't the governor commute you to life, on a doubt Wadleigh might not be dead? That puts the question in the title. If you say you're guilty—I can a make a settlement and get you the money. If you—"

"No!" roared the Demon. "Not for all the high-grade ore on earth will I say that! I just won't, Billy."

"The money might spring you. A murderer can get out of here quicker than an innocent dupe."

Hurley gulped the suggestion.

"You don't want to get out for Big Cora's sake, Ralph. It's for—"

"Little Cora's?"

"Sure! That's a plenty, Ralph, and you're sure enough to find Wadleigh or Wadleigh's grave. You'll find that double-crosser if he's on this earth."

Billy Tilt recrossed his legs. The guards began casting dark scowls at him.

"We'll locate Wadleigh," he repeated, "if it takes ten years more. Silverside's had another sensation, Ralph. Crime again. I'm appealing the case. You know Old Pop's boy, Arlin? Pop of the Small Hopes Mine?"

"A freckle-faced kid?"

"He's grown up now! Went wild. Hooch, molls, cards. They trimmed him out of his eye-teeth at that crooked wheel in The Silver Dollar. Somebody told him it was crooked. He bought a gat and stuck them up, with a crazy mask on. Cleaned 'em out. Shot Winfield through the shoulder. They caught him, gave him five years. I'm appealing—he'll register in here soon. Kinda keep an eye on him, Ralph."

The Prison Demon wondered if Tilt meant the last instruction as a jest. How could he keep an eye on anybody? And young Arlin, especially.

"He had a right to stick up Winfield," said Hurley.

"A moral right—not a legal one. Keep him quiet in here. You have influence!"

Heavily the hand of a screw descended on Billy's shoulder. "Time up, *señor*. For you I lose my job."

The lawyer rose.

"Slug that greaser under the jaw for me," was the Demon's parting shot. "He's been sliding me moldy bread!"

That night the bread almost walked under the snake-hole's door. The beans were gritty from desert dust. The water was black.

"Slug me under th' chin, eh?" grinned the screw.

Arlin's arrival from Silverside was announced by grapevine as soon as the shackles were taken from his wrists. The Demon's first view of Pop's boy was when he was taken across the yard to the tailor shop. A finer specimen of young manhood never walked.

"Fresh fish," Cisco Joe called to the punishment men. "What they'll do to him is plenty."

The Demon saw the transformation when three days later Arlin was "skull-dragged," after a bare-back flogging with a sanded ash-stick, toward an isolation cell. Hurley grinned at the fighting spirit of Pop's son. Arlin landed blows on the enraged screws. He kicked and wrestled them until his door clanged shut.

Then he called through his bars to Hurley:

"Hello, old-timer. We're going to put Silverside on the map yet. They can't keep a couple of regular fellows down."

But before the problem of escaping San Jacinto was solved the new warden arrived. The prisoners, however saw nothing of him for several days. A trusty brought word that he looked like a bearded pirate with a record. But that didn't seem plausible since the warden's job at San Jacinto was no political favor. Nobody wanted it—the graft was small, the wage less.

Fiercely the Demon watched for a sign of Flint. But saw, instead, a colorful object that brought him standing upright on his toes. He blinked. Again he stared across the sun-scorched yard.

The object stood watching Cisco Joe making a saddle.

It was a girl, alone with the hellions inside of the stir.

She moved around Cisco, examining the other saddle-workers, who sat in yellow pants and shirts, their heads crowned by straw hats.

A girl—almost a woman!

The apparition sent the Demon's heart thumping. He felt the blood mount to his temples. Would she stroll his way?

Apparently she had orders to keep away from the snake-hole, for she vanished around the dobe corner of the mess-hall.

Letting himself relax the Demon began pacing the floor, his bare feet pounding down the dried mud. He heard one con sing out to another.

"That wuz th' warden's daughter—a swell moll!"

"That," thought the Demon, "may be my way of escaping this place."

Hurley began building air-castles. Time would allow him to sneak a "kite" to the girl. Sympathy might work wonders. He rapped on his bars, signaling the nearest die-hard.

"What's the girl's name?" he asked.

"Heard it wuz Arabella, or Bella, or Bell Flint. Sweet frail fer us hungry guys to be a-lookin' at."

Impulsively the Demon turned to a wall where he had scratched off the months and days of his incarceration. He counted the long strokes twice—the stretches.

"Nine," he said huskily as if making a new discovery. "Nine years since I've seen a woman—except them he-hen visitors."

The next day he again watched for the girl. Sooner or later she would approach the punishment cells.

When she did near them, she shied from the snake-hole like a timid bird and stood before the cell occupied by Pop's son, Arlin. Hurley sensed that they were talking together—girl and boy fashion.

He sent a kite to Arlin that night, by a trusty:

> That girl will fall for you. See if you can get a gat from her. It will take time. I can do it with a gat—by rushing the front-office.

Feeling sure Arlin could work wonders when a moll was concerned, the Demon got in communication with Cisco Joe, by whistling for the lizard.

The Demon explained that two mules used in construction work inside San Jacinto, could be used to drag off his door, since they were often used for heavy construction work and—what was even better—their driver was an ace-black die-hard from Texas.

Cisco Joe chewed up the message, raised his conical-shaped straw hat as a signal, and got up from his squatting position where he was hammering silver-buckles. He went to where the mules were leaning against a dobe wall, in the shade. The Demon saw with satisfaction that the negro nodded his head.

He showed his white teeth in Hurley's direction.

But at that moment the new warden appeared from around one corner of the lethal chamber, surrounded with guards. Leading the tour of inspection was the tobacco-chewing P.K.

"Th' 'Hessians' are comin'," signaled a lifer near the Demon's cell.

The party approached the snake-hole. Flint stared steadily at the Demon. Their eyes clashed. A curl came to the warden's lips. He laughed and said something to the P.K.

It was the tone of that laugh that drove a conviction home to the Demon. The conviction that he must escape before Flint could attempt to have him effaced by any one of the trusties, who were so handy with knives.

Back in the snake-hole Hurley crouched. He pressed his hands to his eyes, and tried to remember where he had seen Flint. Giving up the problem, he came to another—getting out of San Jacinto by rushing the front gate. It meant losing all the time he had served, if the attempt was unsuccessful. It wasn't an even chance for success.

He decided on the attempt. Arlin would get the gat. Cisco Joe and the die-hards would go the limit if they had a leader. The mules could be used to drag off the little gate leading to the front office as well as the door to the snake-hole.

Dangerous as it might be, the attempt would have to be made. Hurley became more than ever convinced of this that afternoon when he spotted Flint, tailed by the P.K., who carried a gat, coming directly to the snake-hole. The warden descended the steps, unlocked the door and backed up the steps again as though Hurley had rushed at him. But Hurley remained quite still, knowing that the slightest move on his part would be an excuse for the P.K. to kill him.

Disappointed the warden and P.K. strolled away.

"I'll fool that yellow pirate," the Demon mumbled. "Left that door open to catch me! But I'll stay in, instead of going out. That P.K. may be able to shoot as straight as he can spit."

Just then he saw the warden approach a guard called the Butcher, who had already killed several inmates with a knife.

Something resembling a yellow oblong of paper passed between Flint and the Butcher. A bribe for a quarrel and a slaying.

Hurley wondered again how he could escape this dangerous mesh and at once was given reason to believe that Cisco Joe was behind him.

Over the yard scurried Joe's lizard. It crept down the snake-hole steps and under the lower bar to the Demon, who took a note from its leg:

"Keep inside," warned Cisco Joe. "You wouldn't have the chance a cake of ice has in Mirador Desert if you fall for Flint's game. The stir is full of rumors he has ordered your guts slit."

"Ugh!" defied the Demon. "I'll take my time coming out. And I'll fix this door so they can't break in."

He tore strips from an extra pair of trousers and made them into a strong rope. Winding the strip around the bars, he waited. Behind him, set against the wall, was the iron leg of a cot, sent to him months before by a prisoner from another cell.

Deep, brooding suspicion covered San Jacinto that afternoon. The P.K. came in the evening and locked the door, after spitting at the rope. He left, saying nothing. Hurley glared at his figure, crossing the heated earth. The Demon's eyes swung toward the mule-sheds where the negro slept with his powerful charges.

He then called to Arlin: "They tried to trick me today. Were you wise?"

"Sure! Don't notice the damn fools. Let them play into your hand. Don't play into theirs."

"The whirl for six?" Hurley asked Pop's boy.

"Not yet. I expect it in a few days. *Ssh.* There's a screw sneaking around the edge of the isolation. I can see his shadow."

The next day, Bella, behind a tilted sunshade, appeared at the snake-hole. She had a basket of flowers and fruit for the isolation die-hards. The Demon kept his eyes on her. He had a feeling she was bringing the gat to Arlin. Her manner was more timid than usual.

This feeling was turned to conviction when Arlin called to him.

"Cheer up, big fellow," he said. "Here's a little gift for you. A banana."

Swiftly crossing the yard the screw intercepted the boy's attempt to slide the banana along the front of the cells. He snapped an oath at Arlin, and squashed the fruit with his foot.

But the Demon knew what it contained—a note saying that Bella had left a gat with cartridges.

Immediately the Demon sent a note to Cisco Joe, via lizard-post. He had changed his mind about using mules to drag open his door. The warden undoubtedly would order his door unlocked on the next day. Instead of coming out like a sheep to be slaughtered he would have Arlin's rod, and a pocket full of cartridges.

That night he paced the snake-hole's floor. He squatted down and gripped his jaws with his hands. He got up and stared at the southern moon. He worked the fingers of his right hand to make them supple. The plan he had formed was almost certain to be a success. Its virtues lay in the surprise.

Getting the gat and cartridges from Arlin's cell to the snake-hole was accomplished by a simple ruse—and the help of a trusty who removed the slop buckets, each morning, from the cells and emptied them out. The screw who went with him did not notice that an exchange was made. Arlin got Hurley's bucket. The boy's bucket, thick with quicklime at the bottom, was shoved into the Demon's cell.

Watching, while he bent over, Hurley ran his fingers through the lime. He drew up a .38. Again he reached. Fifty .38 cartridges brought a glitter to his eyes.

He was fanged! He waited for the tobacco-chewing P.K. to unlock the door.

Soon the man appeared carrying a great bunch of brass keys, which jingled like Christmas bells to Hurley.

No sooner had the P.K. unlocked the door than the Demon broke open the box of cartridges, loaded the gat, distributed the rest of the missiles in his pockets, and looked out, ready to rush the yard.

The screw near the P.K. sounded a warning too late. The bundle of hate that leaped up the snake-hole steps resembled a gigantic wild-cat. Over the blistered earth Hurley lunged, struck the guard a glancing, coma-producing blow with the .38, sliced again and went headlong at the P.K. All the man did was to spit once, in amazement. He went down under a series of blows that stunned him completely.

The excitement had been a signal for Cisco Joe and his die-hards who were waiting to be let out of their cells by Hurley.

Reversing his plunging direction, the Demon brandished the gat and dashed for the punishment cells. He flung the keys at Arlin after unlocking his door. "Beat it to the front office, kid, as soon as you open up! Let hell loose! Is the moll waiting with a car?"

"Horses," the boy exclaimed. "More romantic. We're going over the range—where no car can go."

• • •

Hurley led Cisco Joe's mob toward the front office. He passed the lethal chamber and fired at a Mexican screw. He reached the grating to the front office. Jabbing the gat through the bars he covered an old guard.

"Unlock this, Querida! Pronto! Get those keys from—"

"I no—know, where they are—"

"You lie, you yellow-livered coyote! Behind those books! Quick! Reach for them or I'll—"

The guard reached.

"Quick!" repeated the Demon. The bolt was thrown. Hurley shoved in the door. Behind him poured a mob of the post dangerous men in the west, most of them brandishing knives.

"At the warden!" commanded Hurley.

Flint was the only official who carried the key to the front gate. He lived with Bella in a suite adjoining the guard-room. The Demon lifted a carved chair and smashed through to a hall at the end of which were three rooms, painted and ornamented by life prisoners. Flint, in shirt sleeves, with his suspenders crisscrossing his huge body, was in the act of reaching for a rifle on the wall when the Demon flashed down his gat commanding:

"None of that, you! Get away from the wall! Elevate! Reach that ceiling! Where's the girl?"

Arlin went past the Demon and snatched at the rifle.

"She's in the other room," he explained. "I'll guard her. There's a door leading to the front-yard."

"Be with you in a minute," snapped the Demon. "Joe, you trail after us—you and the mob. I'm takin' this sidewinder for a hostage—a shield. This dirty double-crosser!"

From the walls of the penitentiary sharp shots resounded. The gun-guards were firing at the inner prisoners. There was sure to be a shower of lead directed outside when the Demon emerged from the little door.

"Go on!" Hurley commanded the warden. "Right, front! March! Through that passage! All set, Arlin?"

The boy from Silverside slid an arm from the girl's shoulder. "Ready," he answered. "We might as well take her along as hostage. The horses are straight from the wall toward that mesquite clump. Tethered close to that Joshua tree."

"Open the door! I'll keep Flint close to me. His screws dare not fire. They're bad shots. Come on Joe—and may the devil take the unlucky ones today."

Hurley prodded Flint in the side. Dust gagged the air. The screws churned the alkali with close ranging shots. Ahead, the Demon saw Arlin and Bella, running.

A sense for cover caused Cisco Joe and the die-hards to scatter when they were out of range-fire. They wormed through the mesquite like huge brown lizards. Ahead of them were the Miradores and safety.

Jabbing Flint fiercely in the back, the Demon came up to where Arlin and the girl were mounting the horses. Flint broke away from Hurley and approached Bella with curses.

Swiftly slicing the gat across Flint's cheek the Demon shrieked: "Away from that girl! She's not your daughter. Say that again, and you die!"

"She's not—his—daughter?" asked Arlin.

"No! I just found it out. She's—"

Flint started running toward the road that led from San Jacinto's front gate. The sudden appearance of a deputy sheriff and two under-deputies with handcuffed prisoners, had caught his falling hopes. The Demon shouted to Arlin.

"Ride hard! Good-bye! You only shot up a crooked gambling joint and you ought to have your freedom. Take care of her. She's my daughter!"

Hurley went after the warden with deadly intent. He leaped over the cactus, and gained on Flint. He took aim at his thick bulging neck. "Turn 'round!" he commanded. "Turn, I don't want to shoot you in the back. Tur—"

Flint tripped and partly turned. The Demon fired once—at the center of the forehead.

He stepped over the quivering form and offered the smoking gat to the deputy sheriff, from Silverside.

"Why, Hurley, why on earth did you do that? You had every chance of a parole next year—maybe sooner." The deputy sheriff took the rod. "Why, Ralph—?"

"Why?" The Demon laughed and turned.

"Why did I do it, Nate? That's easy. He is—was, my old partner. Jumped out with my wife. Framed me by throwing his false-teeth, collar-buttons and watch in the vat at the mine. Thought they'd finish me in the lethal chamber. When they didn't—he grew that beard and got to be warden. If I hadn't killed him he'd of killed me, Nate."

"Yes, yes, I know, Ralph—but now you haven't a chance to escape that lethal room. Not a rat's chance. They can prove this murder."

The Demon looked toward the sun-brown foothills of the Miradores. His lips curled in a triumphant smile.

"Oh, no, they can't, Nate! There's no proving to be done. I'll go free! How can I be condemned to be executed twice for killing the same man?"

The Warden's Dollar
John Harold Grove

*One dollar from a warden for six years' work—and five
grand from a gay-cat for a one-hour job! The first was hard
enough; the second much too easy. . . .*

BEHIND THE MAN WHERE HE STOOD ON THE DIVIDE WAS A PRISON; before him lay
a city, like a checkerboard, with straight streets, and narrow twisty ones for
those who would live beyond the law.

The law, which had taken six years of Redfern's life, left him bitter against
society. Society had paid the police who had captured him; society set the
judges on the benches; society furnished the penitentiary guards who had
made Redfern live six years of torment—six eternities in the jute mill until
he had wished every strand of okum was a rope around a screw's neck.

A silver dollar and a suit of shoddy was the warden's parting gift to him.
In disgust, Redfern pulled the dollar from his pocket and threw it against
a rock. It rebounded, struck another rock and rolled back to his feet. He

picked it up with a superstitious curse. The warden's slug had a dent near the head of Liberty; the unlucky piece was bent like counterfeit money from a defective mold.

"Damn them, I'll keep it!" Redfern decided.

He was a bulky man; his fingers, beneath the jute stains, showed nitro marks from blasting safes. His hatred against society dated from days when he was a punk kid guided by superior yeggs.

The okum had bound up the good seams in Redfern's soul.

He decided to put one over on the city that was infested with police. A river boat left the bay for Colmar, an interior mining town. The fare was one dollar. He possessed the warden's dollar. He would board the boat and disappear for a time until he had formed a plan against one of the city's strong-boxes. Distance would give him the correct perspective.

Redfern strode through the city's lower section and stood in line before the ticket window at the shore end of a dock. His bulk made him conspicuous among the farm-hands, berry-pickers and miners waiting to go aboard.

A touch on Redfern's shoddy elbow stiffened him with suspicion. He swung around and met the upward glance of an acquaintance—a weasel-faced gay-cat called Lavrey. Lavrey had never served time; he was too adroit.

"Thought I recognized you," said the gay-cat. "You better blow from here. Dugan and Dunhill always give the passengers on the Colmar Line th' once-over. It's a bum get-away for an ex-con."

The sight of Lavrey's ratty features was enough to make any self-respecting yegg turn straight. Redfern pushed forward and came up to the ticket-window, and thrust in the warden's silver dollar. "A ticket!" he growled.

The boat clerk eyed the dollar suspiciously, picked it up and dropped it on a marble slab put there to detect counterfeits. The coin had lost its ringing note. It might be good, it might be bad. The clerk took no chances. "Try another dollar," suggested the clerk. "You can't get a ticket on that one—unless it's to a Federal prison."

With a snarl Redfern snatched the coin. He hurried from the window. Fate was keeping him in the city; fate in the form of Lavrey, was again at his elbow.

"Shovin' th' queer, eh?" smirked Lavrey. "It's an easy graft if you don't know any better."

Redfern put the coin in his pocket. His glare at the gay-cat was calculated to silence most anybody. Lavrey drew his hand away from the yegg's elbow, the guile of a tempter creased his lips.

"Come on, pal, let's blow this dock. You just got out of stir; you need a drink an' a friend. I know a place, a scatter, where you can kip for awhile. It's run by a frien' o' mine. Th' place is called th' Eagle's Nest. It's over near Mission Street. An' Red, I—" Lavrey glanced around cautiously; he searched the dock for sight of Dugan and Dunhill. "An' Red," he whispered out of the corner of his mouth, thief-fashion, "I know a tough for you. It's right in your line—heavy work. Come on, forget hard work at Colmar an' let's sit on cushions."

Redfern allowed Lavrey to lead him toward Mission Street. They went through an alley and crossed the street on a long diagonal. Lavrey stopped, pretended to tie his shoe laces, and glanced backward. "No coppers trailin' us," he explained to the yeggman. "Duck for the door. This is th' Eagle's Nest."

There were vultures nestling in the dive. A few painted women sat with sailors; the bar was lined with offshoremen swilling beer, at two-bits a glass. Hookers of raw whiskey were upturned down parched throats. Fist-banged tables, a few flyspecked cromos, the model of a clipper ship atop the cash register, decorated the Nest. The air was stale—as in some prison cell.

Lavrey motioned for drinks. Over the furthermost table from the door he leaned until his lips were close to Redfern's face. "Th' job I got picked out for you," he whispered, "is at Paddy Doyle's boarding-house. Paddy has a room upstairs in th' boarding-house that he calls th' crow's nest. It's chock-a-block with swag. He's been collectin' gold chains, watches, fifty-dollar slugs, jewels an' foreign money until he must have ten thousand up there. There he sits an' sleeps most of the time with his parrot. His daughter, Margaret, sleeps downstairs. Paddy is the only one we got to look out for—an' Paddy is a bad actor."

Redfern, who had not had a drink in six parched years, gulped a whiskey and called for another. The fire of the poison flamed his cheeks; his eyes brightened. Lavrey grew more trustworthy to him. He became interested in Paddy Doyle.

"Gawan about that touch!" he throated. "You say it's good for ten thousand? Put me on it an' I'll fix Paddy Doyle."

Lavrey made a motion for a third drink; his rat eyes shifted from Redfern's burning stare.

"Sure," he smirked. "I thought you'd come around. Th' warden paid you one dollar for six years' work. I'll show you how to make five grand for an hour's work. I've been spottin' Paddy Doyle's boardin'-house ever since I can remember. Some day, says I, th' right man will come along an' help me take it."

A waiter brought the fourth round of drinks and hovered for his pay. Redfern drew out the warden's dollar. He fingered it. "That ain't no good here," Lavrey remarked. "Put it back in your pocket. I'll pay th—"

Redfern thrust the dollar toward the waiter. Lavrey's slippery fingers wheedled it from the yegg's palm. "It's bent," he said. "Maybe it's phony—I'll give you a good one for it. I'll keep this as a good-luck piece."

The silver token went into the gay-cat's pocket; Redfern crumpled a paper dollar in exchange.

"Drink up," insisted Lavrey, after feeing the waiter. "Then we'll go an' give Paddy Doyle's th' once-over."

The back way to Paddy Doyle's was through a barrel-littered alley, up a flight of steps and over a roof where securely-boarded windows marked the shipping-master's rooms. Above them was the crow's nest. Lavrey indicated a door, flush with the roof. "I got a key to that," he breathed. "Had it made by a sailor who was mad at Paddy Doyle."

"Paddy's goin' to ship some poor guys on a whaler," explained Lavrey. "He's collected one hundred bucks advance for each man. We'll cop that robber's kale—you an' I."

"When?" muttered Redfern savagely.

"Come on, let's blow. You've got the layout," Lavrey suggested. "Tonight will be a good night. As good as any. You got more beef than Paddy; you don't need a black-jack; you want to get your fingers around his neck and squeeze. He ain't a big man—he's about my size."

"Pretty soft," agreed Redfern. "I wuz goin' straight for awhile, but Lavrey, I'm glad I met you. You don't look like a copper's mark an' th' coppers will never think I'd turn th' job. They got me listed as a dragman, a peterman. I won't be suspected when Paddy Doyle is found tied up an' all his kale missing. Most of the bulls think I'm still back in stir."

Redfern lurched back to the Eagle's Nest and consumed more drinks. Lavrey spilled his drinks on the sawdust floor. The gay-cat began to fear the ire he was arousing in the brain of the yegg who banged the table with his fists and shouted threats against the prison guards—"screws" he called them.

Lavrey quieted him and stalled for time. Night came to the city. The offshoremen at the bar rocked back and forth as if on the deck of a ship at sea. The bartender slid them whiskey glasses like quoits in a game.

"It's gettin' time," said Lavrey after consulting the ship's clock, back of the bar. "I'll wait 'til twelve. Then I'll go on to Paddy Doyle's an' look th' job over. You stay here."

The ex-convict sensed a trap. "We go together!" he declared. "I'll wring that—hic—pipe-stem neck of yours—if you double-cross me."

The bartender appeared. "Another," ordered the gay-cat. He urged the drink on Redfern. More whiskeys were carried to the table. The yegg, who had drunk a quart of bootleg became pliable. Lavrey noticed the letdown in his actions.

"I'll go first," he again proposed as the ship's clock struck eight bells. "Ain't I a gay-cat? What's th' business of a gay-cat but to look over the lay of th' land?"

Getting up, Lavrey appeased Redfern by saying to the bartender: "Let my friend here, have all th' drinks he wants—on me. Put 'em on the slate, Fred. I'm goin' out to see a man off on that twelve-thirty ferry."

"See that you come back!" hiccuped Redfern. "For if you don't—"

Resentment against the gay-cat grew in the ex-con's brain as time ticked off from the ship's clock and Lavrey did not appear. Each five minutes Redfern ordered a drink; he had a muddled idea that all was not right. What trick was Lavrey up to? Why had he given him the bent dollar? It might be a clue left behind somewhere by that crook. The ticket-clerk at the dock would remember the silver piece if the newspapers dwelt on it.

Redfern lunged from the table at four bells. He overturned a chair and pushed aside the swinging doors of the Eagle's Nest. Out in the street the cold air cleared his brain slightly. Paddy Doyle's was north. He strode into the barrel-lined alley and looked around for sight of Lavrey. There was none.

"Th' rat got cold feet!" concluded Redfern. "He was afraid to come back an' tell me about it. I'll go up an' turn th' trick myself, just to get hunk wid them prison screws."

He climbed the steps, crawled over the roof and tested the door. It was locked. Lavrey had a key to it. Then the gay-cat was not inside.

Redfern knew he could break down the door. But that would make a noise. The windows were easy; but they would shatter and awake Paddy Doyle's boarders. Cunning came from the liquor. The ex-convict reached upward, clutched the tin-gutter and drew himself alongside the crow's nest, which had small, well-locked windows.

Rage against society gripped Redfern. He smashed one of Paddy Doyle's panes like a bear after honey. The glass frame hung from his neck; his fingers were cut in many places; he staggered upright, leaned forward with his hands moving in the gloom. He groped vainly, at first, for contact with the sleeper he was sure he had awakened.

"Where are you?" he muttered. "Jus' tell me where you are—jus' tell me—you!"

The convict's instincts were to coil his fingers on somebody's neck and constrict it until the vital spark was almost gone. He blinked and cursed the dark. He listened and suddenly heard a movement at his right. It was faint, but unmistakable. Paddy Doyle was there. Redfern hurled himself at a sound. His flying arms found a wiggling form.

Inch by inch his fingers moved upward; he was like a bull-dog getting a fresh grip each time. The soft flesh of neck and chin gave way before his grip.

But suddenly a pricking knife slashed along Redfern's ribs.

Just like Paddy Doyle to have a knife handy!

Berserk rage mastered Redfern. His grip would have twisted the life out of a stronger man than the boarding-house keeper. A limp form hung in his garrotter's hold. He let the body drop, breathed thickly a minute, and stopped until his fingers had searched two trouser pockets. The reward there was small—a few dollars!

"I'll find th' kale," muttered Redfern. "I gotta find it. Where is it? Where is a light?"

A girl's scream sent a chill through the ex-convict. It sounded at the foot of a ladder leading up to the crow's nest. The boarding-house of Paddy Doyle was aroused; it resembled a windjammer's fo'c's'le with a first-mate stirring things from above.

Redfern went quickly out the windows, over the roof, down the steps and toward the water front. Behind him sounded police whistles in alarm.

A dock folded him in its shadow. He sat on the stringer piece, his feet dangling near the inviting waters of the bay. Life was useless; the police hostile; he had committed a red murder; the best thing to do was to slip off the dock and drown. He inched forward; his fingers slipped over the slimy stringer piece. . . .

Just then two fishermen came sauntering in his direction. They were talking. "I dank dat was some murder, *ya!* Paddy Doyle found dead as a herring," he could hear one saying.

"So," breathed Redfern—"I *did* kill Paddy!"

He got up and lurched over the planks. The second fisherman remarked:

"And th' other fellow—who was he? Both choked to death. They must have done it to each other."

Redfern went blindly toward the Colmar Line boat. He was first in line before the ticket-office. Dugan and Dunhill would be on the double murder case—there was little danger of seeing them here.

He drew out a silver dollar which he had stolen from the man he had throttled. He was about to present it to the clerk at the window when something caught his eye! That coin looked familiar! Great Scott! It was the warden's dollar!

Lavrey, the gay-cat, had double-crossed him. Lavrey had gone to Paddy Doyle's and killed Paddy—expecting that the crime would be laid upon another. Redfern realized he had upset Lavrey's plan by coming on the job too early.

The man he had removed from this earth was the gay-cat. The warden's crooked, silver dollar was the clue to that.

The ex-convict laid the coin on a block of stone, and stamped on it with his heel. It straightened. He picked it up and approached the window.

"My last lucky dollar," he said to the ticket-clerk. "Gimme a ticket to Colmar."

Cell Number
Seventeen

Edward Letchmere

*"Who had done it? How had it been done?"—Seven times
these questions had been asked—and were never answered—
'til its eighth victim had spattered his brains on the wall of
Cell Number Seventeen!*

CELL 17 RESEMBLED TWENTY-THREE OTHER CELLS AT GRIMSDALE, as Chinamen resemble Chinks.

The sinister difference, however, was written in the front-office record book—or in the memory of the screws, the inmates and the hicks whose farms dotted the hills surrounding the big house.

When Tony Desparo, a beer racketeer, walked into self-punishment by planting a gat on his hip and insulting two detectives, he pleaded with the judge for a year at Grimsdale.

The Purple Gang had him distressed. He was booked for a ride. He chose the lesser of two evils.

He did not, however, choose Cell 17. It was chosen by chance when its occupant fell from the high gallery and broke his neck ten minutes before Tony Desparo registered in.

The exhaust of a murder car that followed his Rolls to the prison gate, was music to the millionaire baron's ears. John Law would see that he was protected for one year, less good-time off.

Tony's guts had forsaken him. He wanted that much time to get them back.

Unlike a monk who retreats to a cloister for meditation, the Beer Baron, after pulling political wires for a front-office job among the stir's silk-shirted elect, began mending his fences and directing his gang by grapevine telegraphy.

Greasy sweat covered his prison pallor one day when he saw a moll being brought in by a police matron. She brazenly stood lipping her pedigree to the chief clerk. Tony knew the Purple Gang had sent the broad to get him. Her sentence was a year and a day. She was called Goldie-Gertie, or Gertrude. Her other moniker was Anna Oakley, from the number of gats she could carry for the Purple Mob. This alias was copped from a famous female pistol-expert.

Desparo ripped the collar from his twenty-dollar shirt in his rage. He went to the warden about Goldie. "I'm goin' to be bumped off in m' cell," he puffed. "A gun-moll's goin' to do it. I saw her throw a dirty eye at me."

The warden shook his head. "Can't be done, Tony. Th' woman's section is isolated from the men's. The wall between is three feet thick."

A second fright shortly after seeing Goldie, drove another spike of fear in Tony's yellow heart. He saw a face at a barred window overlooking the inside yard that was line for line like that of Thug Murphy—the executioner of the Purple racketeers. Tony was carried to the hospital, then to Cell 17, after the record-clerk proved that Thug wasn't registered in the institution.

That night the count was wrong. Three times the gallery squeaked when a screw sneaked by the cells. "There's one over, somewhere," echoed through the block. Then, while Tony crouched in a corner of the stone-walled cell, he heard the bell clang that announced that the count had been corrected.

"One over," he bleated. "That one is going to get me!"

He wished from the center of his soul that he had had his two trusted body-guards posted in Cells 16 and 18. Mink and Abe Dolger might get to Thug and Goldie before those killers got him. Was the face he had seen Thug's? Tony cheered up slightly. It couldn't have been—he wasn't registered in.

Tony examined his cell, not like a felon who wanted to escape but like a con who prayed to be in. A slate slab, thick as a tombstone, comprised the floor. A similar slab made up the ceiling. They were impenetrable. The door had riveted plates at the bottom, narrow steel bars, a huge lock and a wire mesh so fine a lead pencil could not have been pushed through it.

The back and side walls were concrete blocks, larger than bricks, set together so precisely that they resembled the work of Roman stone-gravers in Caesar's time.

High up on the rear wall was a tiny ventilating aperture. Tony climbed on his cot, struck a match and studied this opening. Nothing lethal could spout out of it. Nothing large could go in.

He sprang down feeling certain that Cell 17 was the safest place in the world for him to be in.

Startled by a sharp tap of brass on iron, Tony's knees almost caved in. He slowly twisted his thick neck until he discerned the night screw peering in at him. "I thought I saw a light up here. Did you strike a match?"

"Yeah."

"Don't do it again, after nine. And did you make a noise?"

Tony shook his head.

The screw examined the lock. He peered at the many shadows above the gallery.

"I thought I heard one, up here—over there, somewhere. Guess it was the prison's ghost."

Tony did not sleep that night. He saw the warden again. "Cell 17, 8th Tier, West Block," the warden mused. "I haven't been here more than time to correct the discipline. I'll look into tradition when I get the opportunity. You're safe as hell!"

"Th' Purple Gang—" stuttered Tony.

"Show me one of then gunnin' fer you. I'll see that he's black and blue."

Desparo's henchmen had bribed the warden with a new car, which happened to be a stolen one. Therefore Tony stood aces.

One day soon after, the Beer Baron was given a tip by one of the silk-shirt inmates. "Go see a con named Mike Harrison. He's the stir's detective—an inside sleuth. Chess player, chemist, mathematician, psychologist, electrician. He graduated from three colleges before he reached this one. He won't rat on a con. He's th' talent I'd call in, Tony, if th' Purple bunch were after me."

Harrison was playing chess when Tony went to see him. Quickly the Beer Baron explained his hunch about Goldie and Thug.

"What's the number of your cell?" asked Harrison—and he frowned thoughtfully at the answer.

But he did not tell the frightened racketeer that he had a brochure written on Cell 17—an inside history of seven who had met with death, who occupied that cell.

The first was Mosely, the Rebel Raider during the Civil War. He was found shot, with a Union pistol lying on his breast.

The others all died violently.

Tony Desparo bleated a brace of questions:

"Could an extra gunman be inside th' walls?"

"Easy," replied Harrison. "The count was over last night—that interested me. Then it was corrected."

"You noticed it?"

The inside detective glanced toward the chess-men. "Yes, I noticed it. The odd man vanished."

Tony got out a silk handkerchief, and mopped his thick neck. "Could the moll get to me, from the women's prison?" he asked.

"Is she doing a bit in the women's department?"

"Yeah? She's behind the wall—from my cell."

"All right," said Harrison. "I'll get my magnifying glass and examine Cell 17, tomorrow. Meanwhile, Baron, go back to the front-office. This yard isn't safe for you."

Tony suggestively tapped his pocket. "It's worth a century note," he grunted. "You keep away th' Purple executioner an' that broad. If I'd known they'd follow me here, I wouldn't have come. My moll told me it was th' safest place in America."

Desparo carried a half dozen bananas when he entered his cell for the night count, that night. He shook his door to see if it was locked. At nine he extinguished his light, removed his outer clothing, and lay down with his heavy-lidded eyes watching the slate ceiling. Icy sweat covered his body. It seeped through his silk underwear. He fell asleep at midnight.

At two o'clock that morning a shot reverberated through the cell-block.

The hall-captain, the night screws and a deputy from the front office, got out their flashes and made an investigation of every cell.

The prison grapevine spread the news to the blanched-faced inmates.

Tony Desparo had been shot through the forehead—above the eyes. Whatever brains he had were spattered on his cell wall. Who had done it? How had it been done?

Mike Harrison sent a note to the warden at daybreak and, soon after he was led to him by a trusty.

The warden told him that the revolver that had slain the Beer Baron was missing. The door to Cell 17 had been inspected. No one had unlocked it, declared the warden, and he added with emphasis:

"I'll give you ninety-days' good-time off if you solve the puzzle. State Detective Davis has been workin' all morning. He struck one clue. Tony received a half-dozen big red bananas in a bundle yesterday. They weren't inspected, against my standing rule to inspect everything sent to a con. Outside of that, Harrison, the case is clueless."

"He was afraid of the Purple Gang," offered Harrison.

"Yes. But what is that? They couldn't croak one of my charges. Not with the splendid protection I'm giving them."

The inside detective obtained a one-day pass, to go anywhere within the four walls of Grimsdale.

He showed the hall-captain this pass and slowly climbed the iron steps leading to Cell 17. Before entering the cubicle he stood on the tier, sizing up the cell-house, the barred windows and the view outside, of guard-towers on a high wall.

The hall-captain came up to the cell an hour after Mike Harrison had entered it.

"Well, Harrison," he asked, "what have ye found?"

The inside detective came out of the cell, blinking through his cheaters. The outer light stunned him momentarily.

Harrison removed his glasses. He rubbed them with one corner of a prison shirt. Perching them again on his keen nose he interrogated the hall-captain.

"What was the exact position of Tony's body when you rushed up here?"

"On his back, doubled in a knot, about middle of cell. Hole in his head where the bullet went in. Blood all over his silk underwear. Powder burns around his eyes. Shot at close range—an' how!"

"An' how!" imitated Harrison. "I'll tell you *how*, shortly," he retorted. "I need all the facts to strike an answer. What was the calibre of the bullet?"

"Thirty-two. So th' coroner who dug it out, says."

"Hardly gangster-size. They use big gats." Harrison turned and examined the fine, wire mesh over the door of Cell 17. He got out his magnifying glasses, examining every opening in the screen. His glass moved over the key-hole, which was backed with a ¼ inch boiler plate. He tried to move the lock, but it was riveted securely to the lock-plate.

"Tony Desparo was shot," he detailed, "at close range by a .32 gat pointed at him from the sides or rear of the cell. He had no time to make an outcry. He was the kind who would, if he had a chance. Fear from the Purple Gang had turned his blood to water. The cell shows no evidence of another's presence. There are burnt cigars and cigarettes in the slop-bucket. He smoked both. The floor is scarred with heel-nails, probably Tony's. The ceiling is solid. The—"

"You ain't told me nothin' new, yet!"

"I didn't discover anything new, except—"

"Wot? —Spit it out!"

"Someone was outside this cell door, last night. Someone other than a screw."

"How th' hell d'you know that?"

"The hall-men scrub this tier every day. It's made up of cross planks, rather soft from long soaking with scrubbing water. There are imprints of heels, down there; see them?"

The hall-captain whistled. Sharp half-mooned dents circled the door-sill. "Tony had a visitor," declared Harrison. "It wasn't a ghost—it left deeper impressions than ghosts make. It wasn't a screw—they wear sneaks, don't they, in making their rounds?"

The hall-captain began to believe Mike Harrison wasn't overrated.

"It wasn't a con's heels that made those marks," continued the inside detective. "The state shoes have low paper heels. These cuts were made by real stuff—sharp, high grade leather cut fashionably."

"D'ye mean to say some outsider came up here an' chinned with Tony last night? With me an' two others down in th' guard-room watching the galleries?"

"Someone came up here—or," Harrison pointed upward, "or someone climbed down from the top of the block. Let's climb up and see. The dust must be an inch thick up there. Imprints in that will check my theory."

Mike Harrison shinned up an iron stanchion. The hall-captain followed him. He flung a leg over the edge and rolled through the gagging dust particles.

"See," pointed the inmate sleuth. "Tracks. Fresh tracks. Custom-made shoes. Leading—going. Why, there's a rope dangling from the sky-light."

"Cripes," the astonished screw coughed. "I thought I knew my onions. A rope in my cell-block?"

"More than that," added Harrison. "A silk rope. Notice its color?"

"Good God!" the screw shuddered.

"It's—it's—"

"Purple."

Harrison knew that the executioner of the Purple Gang used a purple silk cord to garrote his victims. Therefore a member of that mob had "broken-in" Grimsdale by climbing the side of the administration building at night, when the wall guards were called off. He had cut his way down through the cell-block's sky-light and sneaked to Cell 17—where he had left the heel imprints.

But how had this executioner shot Tony through a screen too fine for a bullet to go through? Also the Beer Baron was shot at close range—a few inches. The powder marks on a wall of the cell indicated he was shot with his back to the door.

The hall-captain went to the edge of the cell-block and called down to a screw, who came up, two steps at a jump. He shinned the iron stanchion.

"Fred," ordered the hall-captain, "climb that silk cord, and see if a bar is hacksawed up there. Go through to the roof. There may be another and longer cord, outside."

The inside-sleuth waited with the hall-captain. They saw the guard disappear, and reappear again in a few minutes. Calling down he cried: "There's been a get-away. Long thick cord tied to a cornice. It dangles all th' way down to th' warden's flower garden. Nobody noticed it—from outside."

"The bird has flown," croaked Harrison, sadly. "That gunman from the Purple Gang has been inside here for several days. Remember when the count was one inmate too many?"

"Sure! That's why. He must have doubled himself up with some inside pal. Next count he probably hid under a cot."

"More likely," deducted Harrison, "he was seen in a cell that's supposed to be empty. He wasn't wise to just when the count is made at night. He's gone—anyway."

Breaking in, instead of out, was a new problem for Harrison to consider. He suggested to the hall-captain, "Can you take me into the women's prison? I want to examine the cell directly back of Cell 17."

"Wot d'you expect to find there? Th' break-in guy?"

"No. He's out again—gone again. There's someone else I'm interested in."

Consulting a watch the hall-captain said: "Th' molls are all in th' shirt shop, now. Nobody'll be in their section, except a couple of matrons. I'll get the keys."

Mike Harrison trailed the captain through a staunch iron door set in three-foot stone-work. The door led to the floor of the women's prison. Rising to a sheer height of four galleries the cell block reached almost to the same roof through which the Purple Executioner had escaped.

"Go ahead," the captain ordered the inside detective. "That cell door is unlocked. The chief-matron says nobody occupies the cell back of 17."

"Then, if no moll occupied it—any of them could have gotten into it."

"If they had a key to their own door, yes—an' how!"

The precautions against escape on the women's side of the old cell block were not as thorough as on the men's. Harrison noticed that the cells lacked the fine-screen mesh that was on Cell 17. The lock plate was absent. A clever gun moll, like Goldie, could have left her cell during the hour the Beer Baron met his death, entered the cell back of Tony's and—

That was, Harrison admitted to himself, if she had a key. He knew of several ingenious inmates who sold keys for any door, at two dollars each.

Anna Oakley could have purchased one, reached out, opened her own door and sneaked into the cell under suspicion.

The inside detective polished his magnifying glass, snapped on the thirty-watt lamp in the cell and began an examination while the hall-captain watched him from the outside.

Nothing was missed by Harrison. Scratches on the walls loomed as big as turkey-tracks to him. The hall-captain impatiently pulled out his watch. "How long are you goin' to take, Harrison?"

Grimsdale's only sleuth laid his magnifying glass on the cot. "I've got something here," he announced. "This stone comes out. See, there's a hook, secured with lead, that some former inmate put in to hang up a tiny desk. Wait. Yes. It comes out. A tight fit. I—I—got it out. Neat work, showing recent disturbance. Ah—"

"What's the matter?"

Harrison was standing on his tiptoes, directly below the lamp. The first stone's aperture was about six inches by six by twelve. A second stone, leading to Cell 17, was jammed. Pressure from other cut-blocks held it rigid. A place at the bottom indicated where someone, probably Goldie, had scratched with a thin file or knife-blade. In time she might have removed this stone. That left but one more, and she would have been able to reach or peer into Cell 17.

"In some former time," Harrison told the hall-captain, "this opening went right through to Tony's cell. Two long-term prisoners, with this wall between, scraped and cut a channel to each other. A romance in stone! The barrier between a man and woman broken away. Long talks at night with the guards unaware. Hand clasps. Promises. Love, when neither could probably discern the other's features."

"Can that stuff, Harrison. Was Desparo shot from this cell?"

"No! He would have been—in time. He must have heard the moll scraping and scratching. That was enough to drive him wild."

"D'you think the wop did the Dutch act?"

Harrison backed out of the cell. His disappointed expression changed to new resolve. He wasn't that kind, captain. Tony Desparo, big-shot, Baron, leader of a notorious mob, a suicide? Never! The disgrace. The miserable funeral he would have. Not he. He loved a gat, always toted one, died by one, while the executioner of the Purple Mob was menacing him with a purple cord and Anna Oakley was digging in his direction.

"Who killed him—an' how?"

"Come on back to Cell 17," said Mike Harrison. "The answer must be there. This opening I discovered perhaps explains some of the bizarre things that have happened to inmates in Cell 17. It doesn't explain how Tony got the works."

While passing through the stone arch between the two prisons Harrison asked the hall-captain a question: "Those big, red bananas Desparo received, and carried to his cell, were not opened, were they, in the front office?"

"Likely not. Some inmates get their outside stuff uninspected. The important ones, like Tony. Did he eat th' bananas?"

"I found the skins of six in his trash bucket. There, also, which is important, was mashed banana pulp in the bucket, indicating he did not partake of all the fruit."

Mike Harrison entered Cell 17 and turned on the light. He set the bucket on Tony's cot. "These banana skins are a clue I overlooked. State Detective Davis also passed them over. See here, captain."

The hall-captain leaned through the doorway. "Those black lines in this peeling should have set me straight."

"Nobody in here's straight," the captain remarked.

"Straight to the truth! The lines were made by the action of some glue. Not waterproof, for it has dissolved leaving only the chemical reaction. Tony probably hummed 'Yes, we got no bananas,' when he opened these. It was his little joke, if he were in a mood to joke."

"What could he hide in a banana?"

"These big, red ones would hold considerable." Harrison peered through his cheaters, toward the ventilating duct. He tossed the skins back into the bucket. Rising, he took one step toward the rear of Cell 17. "I did find traces of powder burns, along this wall. Tony stood about here. It was dark with the exception of a glow from the moon, through the skylight. He had already put together the .32 that was hidden in sections in the bananas."

"But how—?"

"I'm getting to that. His hiding place for the rod was down that ventilating duct. It's not more than four inches by four, square. I can get my hand down it. Tony could—he had small wrists and slender fingers but a fat forearm. You couldn't. Few of the screws can—that's why they miss so much when they frisk these cells."

"What d'you mean, Harrison?"

Harrison thrust his hand and arm into the aperture. He twisted his body. The expression on his face changed to a smile.

"There's a little wooden cross-bar, way down here. Some con braced it there. The wood feels old, gritty from dust. And—"

The hall-captain leaned further forward.

"And," resumed the inside sleuth, "here is a broken piece of black thread. New thread. Thread probably brought by Tony from the front-office. Out of the warden's wife's work-basket, most likely. We can match it later."

Harrison held up the free end of the thread. He drew forth his magnifying glass. Turning he looked for scratches on the lower surface of the ventilating duct.

With Anna Oakley digging to the Baron, and the stealthy step of Thug Murphy creeping, with a purple strangler's noose, along the gallery, Tony agitatedly drew up the secreted .32. It is probably tied with black thread just back of the sight—the best way to lower it into the duct. He got it, muzzle first, past the wooden cross piece. He reached for it. It stuck. He let his hand slip. The trigger caught sufficiently to discharge the gat. Tony went over backwards. The rod recoiled down the duct, kept on falling and broke the thread with a snap."

"Gawan!"

"The proof," remarked Harrison, "is nestling in the loose stone and plaster below. How far is it to the bottom?"

"Nobody knows. Nobody can get under the cell block to find out. This block was built in 1834. We clean th' air holes outside, an' let it go at that."

"Their diameter is—?"

"A cat couldn't get in 'em. Maybe a rat could."

Harrison wasn't stumped. "While I'm getting the cross piece out, will you have the warden order about seventy feet of double-insulated No. 18 wire attached to a small magnet—one that will lift a pound or two? I'll plug it in this light socket an' go exploring for the gat."

The warden sent an inmate electrician with a shop order to make the device Harrison wanted. It was plugged into a two-way socket, leaving the light burning. Harrison lowered the flexible wires. He twisted and squirmed. Framed in the cell's doorway stood the warden and hall-keeper.

"I've got it—no I haven't. Here's something coming up. It dropped off. Probably a piece of plaster. I'll try again," mumbled Harrison. Sweat gathered in beads on his brow. His fingers tingled from their forced position.

Suddenly the inside detective grew rigid. "It's on. Something's taken hold of the magnet. A heavy—"

The warden coughed.

"Yes, it's coming up," continued Harrison. "I feel it—I hear it scraping the side of the ventilator."

Reaching far down his finger tips closed over a round, metallic object.

He ducked his head out of line with the small-bore of a .32, that appeared over the inner edge of the duct.

"Tony's own gat," he exclaimed, proffering an Italian-made revolver to the warden. "One shell is empty. Th' Baron died through carelessness brought about by fear. He lived by the rod and died by one. Say, warden, do I get my ninety-days copper off my sentence?"

"You bet you do, Harrison! But if there were as many sleuths as nifty as you outside, there'd be more cons in here fer me to watch."

Brothers in Stripes

A Novelette of Convict City

Henry Leverage

*A big bank official is a hard man to beat—but Tiger Nolan
knew there was a nigger in the woodpile—or rather in that
bank vault where he hadn't found the money he was after!*

ROCKPILE TONY LAID DOWN HIS HAMMER and squinted across the yard of Convict
City Prison. "Say, fellows," he said, "pipe the fresh fish being brought in."

A "fresh fish" in Convict City Penitentiary was a new inmate. Rockpile
Tony's pals appraised the handcuffed man who was being led to the warden's
office. He wore old clothes and had a spring in his stride that indicated
strength or youth.

A guard swung a rifle in the direction of the rockpile gang. Ten hammers
were lifted upward. The gang began tapping a tune and singing, below their
natural tones:

> "Bringing in the thieves, bringing in the thieves.
> We shall be rejoicing—when the warden leaves."

On the back of the third-grade striped-coats worn by the die-hards of
the rockpile gang was woven a red bull's eye, larger than any soup-plate in
the institution. Even an old screw, or guard, with sore eyes, could hit these
targets unerringly at a distance of half a mile.

Red Simone and Warden Grimshaw received the fresh-fish in their joint-
office. Simone was the Principal Keeper. He had every feature and action of

a soul-crusher. Dipping a pen in ink he glared at the new inmate.

"Your name?"

"Nolan."

"First name?"

"Tige."

"Tige, eh? A tiger. You'll be a little woolly lamb before you finish your bit! How old are you?" The Principal Keeper noticed that his new charge had twisted one handcuff chain almost loose, on the road to Convict City Prison. "How old?" he repeated.

"Thirty-six."

"Where were you born?"

"Boston."

"Boston, eh? Where they gave the tea-party. Got any living parents, father or mother?"

"What's that to you!"

Simone leveled the penholder like a revolver. He heard the warden grunt, and a cruel sneer exposed his teeth.

"Who were your parents?"

Nolan jerked at his handcuffs. He towered three inches over any man in the office. He leaned toward the Principal Keeper.

"You can't find out who my parents are, through me."

Simone entered Tige Nolan's record in the receiving book: "Nolan, Tige, or Tiger. Age thirty-six. White. Thirty years for bank robbery, Orleans County. Confine cooler for observation. Dangerous! Injured both deputies who brought him here."

The pen ceased scratching. Nolan tossed back a wild mop of hair and said through clenched teeth, "Damn you, I'm going to beat this prison!"

"You are, eh? Well, it's never been beaten since I'm P.K. Eh, warden?"

The warden of Convict City crooked a finger. Out from the shadows three guards sneaked and fell upon Tige Nolan. They blackjacked him, once to an ear, once across the eyes. He went down, crashing, squirmed and lay still, with his hands beating weakly on the carpeted floor.

"Take him to th' cooler!" ordered Simone. "Skin him to th' quick! Give him th' water-cure an' then th' hose. Add ten lashes. After that put that Oregon-boot on him an' let him cool off. Beat me, eh? Say, warden, every bird we've had from Orleans County has th' idea this is a soft stir."

The two officials watched the guards drag Nolan through a door. Simone jabbed at a buzzer button. To the shifty-eyed trusty that appeared he commanded:

"Go to th' tailor-shop an' tell Miguel, in charge there, to fix up a big-sized third-grade striped-suit, with a red bull's-eye. Tell him to send it over to the cooler. And jump!"

Cruelly laughing, the Principal Keeper leaned back in his swivel chair.

"We haven't a big stir here, warden, but it's complete. Yes, I figure it's got about everything. Why our condemned men have the choice of two ways of being executed. By hangin' or shootin'. Now, that's damn considerate of us, ain't it?"

Grimshaw enjoyed the joke. "This last con," he remarked, "struck me as being a first offender. Second offenders are tamed."

"I'll tame him! He'll eat out of my hand in a week."

In the cooler an iron door clanged shut. A stream from high-pressure mountain water struck Tige Nolan in the pit of his stomach. He revived and fell flat again. The manhandling he received from three guards would have slain a less rugged prisoner. It was an epic in torture.

Some time after he recovered consciousness, Tige was clothed in the shoddy suit, shaven bald, mugged and measured and stitched up by the prison doctor. The cooler cell into which they thrust him was the vilest at Convict City. A blacksmith appeared with an Oregon-boot, a detainer made from cast iron that was riveted to his left leg.

Principal Keeper Simone was an expert on diets. He could have reduced the fat man of a circus to a living skeleton. His orders, given to the two screws who guarded the coolers, were to pull Nolan's fighting spirit with bread and water. In the bread was a chemical that would turn red blood white.

Nolan did not receive the bread and water diet until the door had been locked on him three days. The light inside the cooler came from a ventilating aperture high up in one corner of the cell. Two iron slides, outside two peek holes, one at the front and one at the back of the cooler, allowed guards to inspect their captive without being seen.

They usually squirted a stream of tobacco juice through if Nolan was in striking distance. The red bull's-eye on his back was a fair mark.

Recovering from the brutal beating, Nolan took an interest in his surroundings. The Oregon-boot fitted less tightly as he lost weight. He had no cot to sit on. There was no way to climb up to the ventilating aperture. Insects, the size of silver pesos, climbed along the walls. Nolan watched them through hot, blood-shot eyes. His parched lips began to crack. His hate against the screws took a sudden turn when he began smashing the iron door with the heel of the iron boot.

The door was suddenly flung open. Back he was driven by pressure from a hose. The hose kept playing on his unconscious body. When the door closed with a clang and the screws laughed cruelly, Nolan lay in three inches of water.

"Want any more?" a screw sneered through the peek-hole.

• • •

Nolan, on gaining consciousness, lapped the water like a parched animal. He sat erect. His eyes discerned a small wrapped package that had evidently been shot out of the nozzle of the hose. It wasn't in the cooler before. Some clever trusty had sent the kite by an indirect method.

It read:

> PAL:
> Keep the scabs that come off your body until you get a handful. Show them to the warden's wife. She ain't as hard boiled as the rest of the half-breeds running this stir.
>
> WHISTLING KINCADE.

Nolan found out who Whistling Kincade was. He heard a screw brawl an order for Kincade to mop up the water between the cooler cells. A whistle trilled through the dingy isolation building as Kincade brought forward a bucket and broom.

The humorous inmate's tune changed to a song as he neared Nolan's cell.

> "Oh, I've been out east, I've been out west,
> Th' ladyloves, the ladyloves, they gave me no rest,
> Oh, bring them back to me!"

"Shut up!" commanded a screw.

"Oh, wait till I get you alone some night," continued the trusty, in a bated breath. There was no doubt Kincade had enough red blood in his veins to torment his tormentors. Nolan began to realize that even in a cooler there was life, and where there was life there was hope.

The three-day starvation period ended. It was followed by a bread-and-water diet extending thirty days, the limit allowed by law. At the end of this period Nolan could not rise from the stone floor of the cell. The weight of the Oregon-boot prevented that.

Simone, flanked by two screws, glared in one day. "Goin' to beat me, eh?" he spat at Nolan. "I've never been beat. And you're in a state where if you strike an officer with intent to kill you'll have your choice of dyin' by hangin' or shootin'. We're mighty considerate at Convict City, lettin' you take your pick."

Nolan didn't reply. The fight was out of him. The weakening process had done its work in body and mind. He rose on one elbow. Through Simone's legs he saw Kincade signaling at him, with a finger to his lips.

Keeping dumb, Nolan heard the door clang. The next day the blacksmith chiseled off the Oregon-boot. On the leg was a number of scabs. Nolan gathered these together, bound them in a strip of cloth and concealed them on a ledge at the top of the cooler. He might get a chance to show them to the warden's wife.

A period of solitude passed. Nolan caught fragments, now and then, of stir-talk between cons or between guards. Kincade sang apparently meaningless tunes which contained scraps of information. Piecing everything together Nolan's numbed brain became acquainted with Convict City. The warden was a drunken lush. His wife was a sister to the governor of the state. It was a state where many men had plural wives, by common-law consent.

Graft in the prison extended downward from the warden to the screws, who sold inmates pints of hooch, coke, or cigarettes. The stir's three hundred and fifty inmates were not allowed to form a league for self-government. They all were whipped shadows moving grotesquely under fear.

"Toughest can on th' map," Kincade sang into Nolan's cell. "Try to pull some wires or they'll let you rot. '*Starvation, starvation, lift up your eyes and see. Starvation, starvation for all humanity,*' " he said when a screw grew suspicious and came sneaking along the back of the cells.

"Pull some wires?" Nolan had no wires to pull. He had a moll, but she hadn't written or visited him. The bank job he had perpetrated was about the only 'wire' he could pull. There was something queer about it. His breaking into the vault of the First National Bank left him lootless when he was captured two days later. Someone had raped the strong-box before he blasted it open.

Its president or cashier was short the cash reserve. Nolan had blundered along in time to turn an inside job into an outside one, and cover up the real transgressor. He was convicted on an indictment charging him with making away with $22,840. The indictment was faulty; it should have been breaking and entering.

Nolan's release from the cooler came unexpectedly. The door opened. The warden and P.K. stood glaring at him.

"Too weak to stand up, eh?" laughed the P.K.

"Drag him out," suggested the warden. "Put him on the rockpile. I'm going to treat him like a gentleman. He knows where twenty-five thousand bucks are hid an' we'll sweat it out of him, eh?"

The trusty began singing when Nolan was dragged out into the sunlit yard:

> "Takin' out th' thieves, takin' out th' thieves—
> We are all rejoicing when a convict leaves."

Tony Genaro alias Rockpile Tony, and his gang, gave Nolan the silent-cure on his first day away from the cooler. Tony was in for life. His gang was made up of foreigners, or second generation culprits. They sledged little rocks out of big ones, with a sullen, suspicious motion. Above the rockpile, not a hundred feet away, a guard was perched in a wall-tower. A Winchester lay across his lap.

Over the outer world Nolan swept his eyes, like a man being permitted to look at paradise. He counted the wall-towers, seven in number. Three shops gave forth sounds of cons at work—a broom shop, a binding-twine factory and a machine-shop for repairing state work. The mess-hall and chapel stood near an ancient cell-block, whose many windows were barred. Beyond this cell-block was a stone oblong structure, with a skylight. The wall of this structure was defaced with a scaffold's arm. Marks on the dobe indicated where bullets had imbedded themselves at an execution.

Dragging his limbs and feeling pain in every finger, Nolan went with the gang, at sun down, into the mess hall. Utter silence ruled a crude meal of Mexican beans and black bread, washed down with chicory. Filing in the cell-block Nolan picked up a bucket, at a screw's order. The bucket was numbered 32, in white paint.

Cell 32 already contained an inmate. Nolan stood, with hands extended through the bars, when the hall-guard went by for the count. He turned slowly. The inmate was occupying the lower bunk.

"Take the upper," smirked a rat-eyed con. "What's the matter—no guts, eh?"

Nolan climbed upward, and fell across a damp mattress. Looking downward he closed his eyes in pain. The con below him was reading a smuggled-in paper, by aid of an oil lamp. He had on silk stockings and a fancy shirt, with a loud necktie.

"I work in the front-office," he explained to Nolan. "They convicted me wrong for assaulting a girl in Poga Springs. I'm only doing five. Hardly time enough to change my clothes."

Lugar, Nolan's cell-mate, was a second generation foreigner, from New York. He looked capable of squealing on his own mother.

"A stool pigeon, planted here by the warden," Nolan concluded. "I'll have to get rid of him."

Flashing a set of perfect teeth Lugar stood up near Nolan's head. The stool studied the many scab-marks in Nolan's scalp. "Blackjacked, plenty," he commented. "You can always tell when a con comes out of our cooler. Say, big fellow, there was a dame here to see you two or three times. A pretty little piece. She wrote some letters, too. Maybe they got them in the front office. I'll sneak them out of the drawer, if the mail-clerk is holding them. What's her name? Where does she live? I won't be long in this—"

Nolan reached out a heavy hand, and forced the stool-pigeon down on the lower cot. "Get me those letters," he said weakly. "I didn't mean to be so rough when I shoved you away. You'll get them, won't you?"

"Sure; maybe I'll have to copy them. Your Jane writes a swell hand—it'll be easy."

The thought that Babs hadn't forgotten him lifted Nolan's spirits. He dreamed of beating Simone and rejoining the moll. His awakening in the cold dawn was followed by an insistent clang from the hall-gong.

Somewhere along the gallery he heard Kincade singing:

> "In a prison cell I sit,
> Thinking, mother dear, of you.
> I wish I wuz in Ulster, I wish I was—"

"Can that!" roared a lifer. "You're where you belong!"

The cons of Convict City were treated to an example of how little the screws feared them when they filed in company formation out of the mess-hall. An inmate, Crazy Jake, drew a knife and started for a guard. He was stopped by two cons, thrown down and the knife taken away from him.

"Jeez!" exclaimed Nolan to Rockpile Tony. "Isn't there a man with any guts in this place?"

"Maybe plenty guts for eats," Tony grinned. "Wait until you're here as long as me, then you don't care."

The feeling of lassitude crept to Nolan's brain. The pitiless sun, the hammer-hammer on the rocks, the weight of the hand-sledge, and the ever-ready eye of the wall-guard, were like a Mongolian torture.

He was forced to follow Tony's advice. "Stall at breaking the rock. Take a smoke when the wall-guard isn't looking. Sleep plenty—maybe you will do your bit."

Tony's gang were adepts at stalling. The rock they broke was supposed to be measured each night. It had to pass through a mesh-screen. No one cared at Convict City about the production. There was finer and better rock scattered among the boulders on the outside of the prison.

"Cop a little from the big pile," Tony instructed Nolan. "Then you won't have so much to do."

Catching Nolan sneaking fine stones from the pile the wall-guard called for the assistant deputy, a brutal Mexican, who whipped out a black-jack. The blows that struck Nolan were punishing ones. Nolan went down across the rock pile, unconscious. Coming to he saw the assistant deputy rolling a cigarette and puffing it in his face.

Ordinarily a man who had blasted open a First National Bank's vault's door would have retaliated. Nolan lay quiet. He tried to rise in order to select a stone, when the Mexican strode away. His eyes caught the menace of the wall-guard's rifle pointed downward at him.

Cowed! Broken! Tiger Nolan a weakling. The stir had gotten him. He was no longer a man, he was a number.

Suddenly he heard a series of small explosions, outside the prison wall. Dust and powder fumes floated over the administration building.

"The Fourth of July," Tony grinned. "The warden's daughter and wife are celebrating with shooting, what you call those things?"

"Fire crackers," Nolan explained. "We shouldn't be forced to work on the Fourth."

"They do what they please." Tony watched Nolan's hand stray from a black-jack bump on his forehead to a slow salute. The Italian followed Nolan's eyes. An American flag fluttered from the Administration Building's flagpole.

"Why you salute that?" asked Rockpile Tony.

"Because I'm an American."

"Y—es?"

"To the bone, Tony! My parents were all-American."

"Yeah? Dat's so? Then you are the only American in Convict City."

The Italian's statement of fact started something stirring in Nolan's heart. It was as if a dormant vein had resumed flowing. The only one-hundred per cent American in the stir!

Behind a greasy newspaper that night Nolan's cell mate thrust out his rat-like face.

But the stool pigeon had forgotten to fetch copies of Nolan's undelivered letters.

"Those 'kites,' " Nolan suggested. "Won't you tell the mail-clerk to send them in to me. I'm out of isolation!"

"You got a striped suit and a bull's eye. You can't get mail when you'se in the third-grade. I'll copy them kites when I get a chance. And you can't have visitors, fellow! Our warden won't allow it."

It struck Nolan that Lugar liked the warden immensely. "Warden?" Nolan snapped. "He's a fine imitation of one. In my opinion he's a stool-pigeon fancier, lushed up most of the time."

Lugar felt the new strength in Nolan's voice. The cracksman had changed in a day. He might grow dangerous to himself, for Convict City was unbeatable.

Hiding behind the newspaper, within which he had brought a front-office lunch, Lugar saw the shadow of a calloused hand reach over the top and snatch the paper from him. "Orleans?" said Nolan. "That's where I was committed from. How did you get this paper?"

"Gimme it!"

"Not a chance, Lugar. That is, until after I read it. I wonder what my lawyer is doing about an appeal? Maybe there's an item about the bank I was accused of wrecking."

"Sure, you got the money!"

"I didn't! I got the name and not the game. What's this? Only a stick or two about President Francis, of The First National. He's bought a new car. Here's another item. Cashier Robertson went to the Orleans Hospital yesterday—that's a week ago. And—here's a third." Nolan buried his bruised features in the newspaper. "Another item. President Francis is going to marry Warden Grimshaw's only daughter, Lucile! She was shooting firecrackers today, outside the wall. Celebrating Independence Day."

"To hell with the Fourth of July and her! Yeah, to hell! We didn't get a bean more for supper tonight. That's why I copped the lunch."

Nolan jabbed his hand forward, and gripped Lugar's swarthy neck. It was like a pipe-stem in his grasp. "Take back that 'To hell with the Fourth of July,' you foreign dog! Take—it—back!"

Gulping a suave apology Lugar glanced side-eyed at Nolan. "I forgot you are an American," he choked. "I get my cell changed. The native sons don't like me. Never did."

The "rat's" declaration concerning changing cells started a train of thought in Nolan's brain. "You know," said he, "I used to be a boxer before I fell for the bank job. Yes, a pug with a wallop! An All-American punch. Like this."

Jabbing his left, Nolan's swollen fist caught Lugar under the chin. The stool-pigeon went over and fell upon the cell's bucket. He rose, feeling his jaw.

Again Nolan jabbed. He caught Lugar in the pit of the stomach. The white-slaver let out a yell that could be heard throughout the cell-block.

"Excuse me," smiled Nolan. "I didn't mean to hit you. Accident."

No guard came to the cell door. Fights among prisoners were too common at Convict City to bother about. Lugar sat dazed on the edge of the lower cot. "I want to get out of here," he whimpered. "You have gone stir-crazy."

Nolan was unusually active. "Now," he went on, "there was another wallop I used to know. The kidney blow. Stand up. I'll explain it."

Instead of standing up Lugar slid to his knees in an attitude of prayer. His pimpled features went chalk white when both of Nolan's fists swished the air.

"Lemme out! I'll report you to the warden. He's a friend of mine. Wait until I get to the front office. I'll—"

"I want you out," Nolan declared. "You double-crossed me with Bab's letters. Wait 'til I see my moll. You're so yellow-livered there isn't room on this gallery for you and me. Get that! I want a certain cell-mate. A white man. His name is Kincade. Irish to the bone."

"That singing fool?" Lugar stuttered.

"Sure! There's more manhood in his little finger than in your whole body. I'm going to have Kincade with me. You're going to turn the trick with the transfer clerk. Get this, Lugar. I'm shaping myself to my old time boxing form. Every night I'm going to practice—on you—until you jump off the gallery to get rid of me. Get me?"

"What d'you want—offen me? I'll get transferred in the morning."

"I want those letters, the originals. I want Kincade. I'm going to try and form a Convict League in this stir. They ought to have one."

"A league?" The white-slaver touched his fragile jaw. His shifty eyes grew larger in amazement. "Now I know you're crazy," he gulped. "The warden will put you back in the cooler if you start agitating the cons about a league. He's running this prison to suit himself. He's a fine man."

"He's a fine lush! A dressed up barrel-house bum who horned into state politics. He's ambitious to have his daughter marry President Francis of the First National Bank at Orleans. He thinks Francis has money. Say, Lugar, I've got something on Francis. You know it was his bank I'm accused of robbing. Tell the warden, when you cough up your troubles to him in the morning, just what I said. I've the goods on Francis."

"I'm afraid to tell him that."

"Then tell his wife. You have an opportunity to see her in private. I haven't. Cons with red bull's eyes on their back can't approach her without being shot."

Lugar realized that Nolan had changed. Back in the cracksman's brain, ideas were budding.

"I'll tell her," he promised. "She's a tough dame, but she always wanted the cons to have more freedom in here. She figures it would help her in society. What will she do to me if I say anything against Francis? I've seen him, visiting her daughter. They're kinda thick, yeah."

Silently a night screw, wearing sneaks, appeared at the cell. He made a mark with a white chalk on the door. He vanished. Lugar waited and thrust a small mirror through the bars. He studied the mark and smirked. "That's for you, not me. You're chilked-in fer talkin' loud. It's bread and water for three days. What are you going to do about it?"

"You get to the warden's wife. Tell her what I said to you, Lugar. That chalk mark will come off, all right."

The mark was removed at noon. The screw ordered Nolan to rejoin the rockpile gang. Tony gave Nolan one of his bland Italian smiles. "What you do?" he asked through one corner of his mouth, stir-fashion. "Maybe you gotta the pull now?"

Developments came fast for Nolan. The fear-of-God he had thrown in the stool pigeon's yellow heart had brought results. Babs came late in the afternoon, as a special visitor. She told Nolan, through two barricades of fine-mesh wire, about the letters she had sent him. Her bold and pretty features flashed fire when she discovered they had been undelivered. Suddenly she spotted the bull's-eye on her man's back.

"That was the reason," stammered Nolan, "I didn't get your kites. Third-grade prisoners have no privileges."

"Your lawyer in Orleans phoned me to come down here quick. Said I'd get in the visiting room. Who promoted you, Tige?"

"Did he say anything about the warden's wife?"

"So," fired up Babs. "That's it! You're stuck on her?"

Nolan leaned forward, out of hearing of a watching screw. "Never saw the dame, Babs. Honest! Don't know what she looks like. I got word to her that I had something on President Francis of the bank at Orleans. You know what I suspect of him? I almost know he's the shark that gutted the vault, just before I tried a hand at it. I didn't find anything but books. He's engaged to marry the warden's daughter. Her name is Lucile. Get me, kid? The old dame don't want to see that engagement busted up. She's a climber. I'm going to force her to help me start a league in here."

Babs showed her jealousy. "Have you connected with this Lucile?"

Nolan laughed. The American in him tempered the laugh with a little steel.

"I never saw Lucile. You're my moll. What are you doing in Orleans?"

"I'm hashing. Ain't that tough? It proves I'm no sugar-daddy's fool. Look at the coat I got. Bought it from tips. And—" Babs gave the guard the once over. "And," she breathed, "I bought a little gat. I can smuggle it in to you. These dumb-bell screws are easy."

"Wait 'til I send for it. Bake all the letters I write you in an oven. I may send you secret word written in lemon juice."

"I'm wise. What else can I do? I left some candy, cigs an' smoking tobacco with the receiving-clerk. And say—a fresh trusty tried to kid me. Dark haired, pimpled, no chin and thin lips. He—"

"Lugar! I'll get that skunk tonight!" gritted Nolan.

Babs rose when the screw growled that her time was up. A parting kiss, blown from her fingers, set Nolan's heart beating. He went out through the inner gate, after being thoroughly frisked, and saw that the rockpile gang were filing toward the mess-hall for dinner. Joining them he looked around for Lugar, but Lugar had vanished. Nolan set his jaw when he selected a bucket from the rack and marched with his company into the cell-block. It was his intention to break most of the stool-pigeon's bones when he entered the cell. A form was leaning over the lower bunk. Nolan swung the bucket.

"Hol' on!" cried a familiar voice. "Are you stir-crazy, pal? I'm Kincade! They transferred me to this cell. Why did they do that? Where's th' stoolie you were celling with?"

Nolan dropped the bucket. He thrust forward an impulsive hand.

"I don't know where that rat is. Got out just in time, Kincade. I'll make hash out of his body when I find him."

The Irish in Kincade brought a broad, thick-lipped smile to his mouth.

"Lugar's th' P.K.'s pet informer, Nolan. I haven't whitewashed and swabbed the coolers and isolation without finding that out. What th' boys they throw in there say about Lugar, is plenty."

Kincade began humming about a colleen while Nolan thought things over. He went to the door, looked up and down the gallery, with the aid of the mirror, and returned to the Irish trusty. He told him, under breath, of his forced play against the warden's wife. "I'm going to start a league," he added. "How's the best way to begin, Kincade?"

The trusty rolled a state-tobacco cigarette. "I'll give you th' dope on how to manage one, if you can start it. I've been in Sing Sing. That league there had a constitution, by-laws, secretary, a bunch of delegates, elections, token money, badges an' it worked swell fer a while. Th' trouble with prisoners' leagues is th' cons themselves. Sure it's inside! Wait 'til you get one goin' in Convict City. Then some stiff will get his mob together an' take it away from you. There's too many foreigners in here to rely on a majority vote. They'll pick a wop or Mexican leader, after you do all the work.

"But what you want," added Kincade, "is to get it started. It'll do some good—because there was never a hell hole worse than this stir."

In the morning while Nolan was sledging a boulder, with every one of his splendid muscles in play, a screw came across the yard and said:

"You're wanted in the front office. Warden's wife sent for you."

Nolan was frisked and let into a private room, off the guard-room. Mrs. Grimshaw sat stiffly in a chair that had been carved by a long-term convict. She held a bottle of smelling-salts to her aristocratic nose. "Sit down," she said to Nolan. "Guard, close that door. Stand outside. What I want to know," she said to Nolan, "is why you sent that trusty with that terrible message to me. I could have had you lashed for it."

Nolan cut in when he noticed a young girl, half concealed behind a screen. "I know you could, Mrs. Grimshaw. I'm a number here. I'm accused of stealing a large sum of money from a National Bank. Perhaps there wasn't anything in that vault. If that's the case somebody connected with the bank beat me to it. Suppose—" Nolan leaned toward the warden's wife. "Suppose the books that were taken away by the bank-robber are hidden somewhere now."

Mrs. Grimshaw jumped from her chair. She dropped the smelling-salts.

While Nolan was picking up the bottle he heard the swish of her silken skirts. A glare greeted him when he raised his eyes.

"Books? Account books? I didn't know any were missing?"

"I've heard that several important ones were," smiled Nolan. "I don't want to accuse any official of that bank directly. But, Mrs. Grimshaw, there was a nigger in the woodpile, or rather in that wrecked vault. A prominent citizen of Orleans—shall I mention his name?"

Swinging toward the screen the warden's wife ordered her daughter from the room. Lucile hesitated.

"Go, daughter!" commanded the warden's wife. "I want to ask this man several questions and one is about a convict named Kincade—the Singing Trusty, they call him. An Irish fool! You wrote notes to him once. I'm going to find out about him. This man here is now celling with that awful creature."

Feeling slightly dizzy Nolan waited until Lucile banged an inner door. Mrs. Grimshaw sniffed deeply of the smelling salts. Evidently she did not like the odor of a convict. "You," she snapped, "have no right insinuating that a splendid citizen of Orleans wrecked his own bank."

"I didn't exactly mention President Francis."

The woman flushed. "My daughter is engaged to him. You perhaps know that. You don't know that the cashier of the same bank is in the hospital with a nervous breakdown. He may be the guilty one, not President Francis."

Nolan played a desperate card. "I either know or can find out, with legal proof, which of those two men are guilty. That's something that concerns your daughter, Mrs. Grimshaw, doesn't it?"

The warden's wife stared at the convict.

Going on, Nolan declared: "I want to form a league inside Convict City. You have influence enough with the governor and your husband to sanction one. My bit is a long one. I can make things pleasanter for everybody. This stir is now a hell hole, dominated by one man, the Principal Keeper. He has no heart, soul or conscience. Just a man tamer, and proud of it. He will oppose me. I may be framed, locked up and denied communication with the outer world. They may fasten a murder on me. The P.K. is capable of that. All right." Nolan spoke in deadly earnest. "If that happens my signal to you is this. If I am shot, the cashier is guilty. If I am hanged—I have the choice of either, you know, in this state—President Francis is the one who gutted the First National Bank of Orleans."

"Perhaps you gutted it?" retorted the astonished woman.

"On my word I didn't get a penny out of it. The man who ripped that vault open may have carried away books that prove who did get the cash."

Breathing her smelling salts bottle again Mrs. Grimshaw bowed her head.

"I'll help you start a Prisoners' League," she promised. "I'll try to have the deputy warden removed. This Principal Keeper, however, is iron-willed and has my husband's complete confidence."

Nolan turned to go. "One thing more, Mrs. Grimshaw. There's an inmate named Kincade. He is a wonderful fellow. Not in for much, but guilty. They call him the Singing Trusty. He knows your daughter, well. Suppose President Francis was guilty. Would Kincade have a chance with her, if he was sprung, went out and made good?"

"My daughter would never marry a convict! How preposterous!"

Nolan whispered from the door. "Remember my signal if I can't get word to you any other way. I've served in the Argonne, Mrs. Grimshaw. I'd rather be shot than hanged, but a man on the point of dying tells the truth. Ask the prison chaplain about that. He knows a last minute's confession is stark truth."

"Why are you talking of dying?"

Opening the door Nolan replied, when he saw the waiting screw was out of hearing-distance.

"My bit is too long to serve. They may have me dead-bank-to-rights and it can't be appealed. I may lose my life defending the league. What can I expect from foreigners who hate an American?"

The fight ahead of Nolan was as severe as a skirmish in Flanders. He told Kincade that night exactly what he had said to the warden's wife. Kincade ceased humming. The Singing Trusty grew serious. "You have a face, Nolan, that destiny loves to toy with. Me old mother taught me how to read character. You're marked for a wild end. This bunch in here will fall for the league all right, then they'll start fighting among themselves. The Mexicans and foreigners can't stand prosperity."

"Tough Guss will be their leader?"

"Sure! An' behind him is another bird marked by destiny—th' P.K. He's a hawk of evil omen."

Nolan thought it queer Kincade had never mentioned the warden's daughter, Lucile. The Irish inmate was deep, in spite of his reputation for singing.

The battle for the Prisoners' League started at noon, in the mess-hall. Simone led the warden to a guard's platform.

The inmates laid down their tin knives and spoons. Grimshaw exposed a florid face. He thrust his fingers in the arm-holes of a fancy vest. His insulting voice carried far. "Men," he declared, "I'm going to give you a better break in Convict City. You don't deserve it, but I'll take a chance. How about a Prisoners' League with self-government, with limitations fixed by myself and the deputy warden? All those in favor of a league rise."

A faint cheer was mingled with foreign laughs. Most of the ignorant prisoners waited for some trick.

"Stand up, or sit down!" commanded the warden.

The population of Convict City was small enough to guess the count. The majority of the cons stood up. "That's that!" the warden said harshly, as if disappointed. "Now you have to have a leader and some delegates and a committee that'll confer with the Principal Keeper, my deputy warden. Maybe Sunday baseball can be arranged, and a little more time added to the exercise periods. But I'll break th' bunch of you if a riot or getaway is started. Pick your leader."

A dozen names were offered to the warden. A Mexican climbed on the mess-table, upsetting his beans. "We want Tough Guss!" he bulled above the voices.

"Kincade," was shouted from a score of convicts.

The Singing Trusty had a way about him that was compelling. He obtained a semi-silence. "Warden," he said eloquently, "my bit is too short to accept the nomination. I rise to propose a man! A he-man! A square-shooter doing a long term. He's educated. He's got everything the boys want in guts and resolution. For Captain of the Prisoners' League I propose Tiger Nolan. Stand up, Tige," grinned Kincade, bending toward his cell-mate. "Show them that you're big enough to be a real leader."

Nolan stood up with unflinching eyes. The P.K. scowled. He whispered quickly to the warden. The better inmates caught this gesture, and understood it. Simone didn't want Nolan to head the league. What the cruel deputy warden didn't want—they wanted.

"Tiger! Tiger Nolan!" racked the beams of the mess-hall and set the tin dishes rattling. "Give us Tiger."

"Tough Guss," echoed back.

Grimshaw suddenly stared at the open doorway leading to the prison yard. His wife stood there, protected by armed guards. She flashed a command at him. He nodded and mopped his forehead.

"Take a vote!" he ordered. "You cons sit down. All those for Tough Guss stand up now. Raise your right hands."

The Italian had no more than ninety votes.

"Sit down! All of you get down."

Impressively the warden waited. He again allowed the P.K. to drop a warning in his ear. He looked at his wife. Turning toward the inmates he shouted:

"All youse for Tiger Nolan, stand up!"

A majority jumped to their feet, or began rising doubtfully. Some were pulled back. "A fair count," sang out Kincade. "I'll bust a few of you saps who are using influence against a real man."

Counting slowly the warden came to a majority and stopped. He beckoned Nolan toward him. The disgruntled P.K. rested a hand on his hip.

"Congratulations, Nolan," lied the warden. "You got the run of the yard and shops from now on. Get together the better element and draw up papers for the league. Take votes for delegates. But remember this, Nolan, the first crooked move from you or any member of the new league—busts it up. Get that!"

Simone got it. He leered cunningly.

The odds were even, that the Principal Keeper would have the league dissolved within a month.

While Nolan brought together the inmates for an organization to lighten their lot, Babs appeared at the visiting room. Nolan was allowed to talk to her in private. She was still hashing, at a restaurant in Orleans, she told her man. The Orleans County papers had been full of accounts concerning the Prisoners' League. Babs produced a number of clippings from a beaded bag. "Swell stuff," she declared. "It ought to help to spring you, Tige."

Nolan shook his head. "I'm bucking the P.K. That's him standing over there, Babs. He's in with President Francis, I think. He's dirt mean, anyway. He'd rather have the stool-pigeon system than the honor system. I guess, Babs, there'll be plenty doing here in the line of rough work, before my bit is up."

"How long's that, Tige?" Babs cuddled up closer to Nolan.

"A century, almost."

The moll shivered.

"You—you can't do it, Tige."

"I know I can't. Unless you and my mouthpiece get busy!" Nolan dropped his head in his palms. He jerked up his chin suddenly. "Go out to Fingerboard Lane," he instructed the moll. "Go past Eaton's Garage, about two hundred yards. There's a curve in the road there. Underneath that curve is a dry culvert. I planted three books I took from the First National there. They're wrapped in oiled canvas. Take them to my mouthpiece. He's been a county clerk. He can tell at a glance if the cashier or Francis falsified the accounts and copped the money. I could have told, Babs, if I had time to look over those ledgers. I was in a hurry, believe me, babe, I was."

"I'll do that," Babs agreed. "How'll I send word to you?"

Nolan again dropped his head. He lifted it and eyed the leering P.K.

"Mail a box of candy if Francis is guilty, a box of cigars if the old cashier pulled that inside job."

"O.K." Babs got up to go. A petulant frown crossed her pretty face. "Oh, when are you going to get out?" she sobbed impatiently.

"I don't see when I am ever to get out, babe. Ripping open a First National Bank in this state is just about the same as throwing the stir key away."

The moll noticed, when she tripped past the P.K., that Tige's suit was no longer the hideous striped-and-bull's-eye-one.

"Thanks for dressing up my man," she flirted with the deputy warden.

Came back grimly: "He'll be wearing a wooden kimona, pretty soon."

Nolan ran into his first fight that very afternoon. Tough Guss had obtained some booze made from cactus by a Mexican con. The defeated candidate for league leader drew a knife. Nolan kicked it out of his hand. He followed up the kick with a punch in the stomach that would have felled a burro. Standing over the foreigner Nolan laid down the law.

"Any con caught with a knife, by a league delegate, will be given one chance. The second time he is caught he will be turned over to the P.K."

"*Si*, pig!" frothed Tough Tony. "Maybe I get my sheve from P.K."

"I wouldn't be surprised. He's probably passing them around."

Kincade came out of the isolation at the sound of the closing whistle. He went with Nolan to the mess-hall, then afterwards to their cell.

"You're doing a hell of a lot of good already," he said after the count. "A plenty! There's only five die-hards in th' coolers. Remember there used to be twenty. An', pal, I hear we're going to be allowed opera programmes over the radio. Think of it? Sure enough music, not the kind I warble. That old hen in the warden's house is all swelled up over this league thing."

"How about the pretty daughter?"

Kincade's Irish features flushed. He said nothing concerning her. Nolan knew Lucile and Kincade had been childhood friends in Orleans.

Before climbing in his cot Kincade imparted: "Saw your old cell-mate Lugar, chinning with the P.K. and Tough Guss, Nolan. Those three birds are going to put the evil-eye on our league, pal."

Nolan nodded. Kincade began singing softly, lightheartedly:

> "I dreamed I dwelt in marble halls,
> With vassals and serfs at me feet—"

He added with broad Irish wit. "Oh, hell, pinch me, pal! There's a 'seam-squirrel' bitin' th' middle of me back. A louse, an' I boiled the shirt only yesterday."

Apparently serenity laid a hand on Convict City. The league gained privileges from the warden. First-grade cons were allowed baseball Sundays and holidays. A movie-tone was installed in the chapel. Infraction of rules became scarce. The paddle and water-cure were seldom used. The Second Deputy, whose Mexican blood itched for torture, went looking for victims. He had invented a new punishment for victims, a quirt tipped with lead. He wanted to experiment with it.

"Wait, Manuel," the P.K. told him. "There will be a new governor soon. The sage-brush hen and the vino-soaked warden vamoose out their own gate.

Then you and me will put our boots on the league just like you smashed that scorpion, a minute ago. So!"

Down went the P.K.'s heavy leather heel, digging a depression in the sun-baked earth.

"Like that, Manuel," he leered.

The arch-enemies of the league separated when they saw Nolan approaching the rockpile gang, where he had formerly made "little ones out of big ones." Nolan paused before he reached the rockpile. He looked upward at the flag floating above the administration building. He slowly removed his prison cap, and saluted. Suddenly above the monotonous click of the sledges from the rockpile, Nolan heard Lucile's voice issuing from a grated window in the warden's quarters. "Mother," called the girl, "where is that book—*The Man Without a Country?*"

Nolan flushed. "*The Man Without a Country!*" A Philip Nolan, perhaps an ancestor, was the man—the outcast from America. Nolan remembered he also was without a country—an American without citizenship. He had lost that heritage when he was convicted.

Going onto the rockpile he studied the bull's-eyes and hideous uniforms of the hard-boiled gang. The guard above them had the lean face of a black executioner. He spat a stream of tobacco juice toward Nolan.

Rockpile Tony smiled the slow smile of Italy. "Screw up there," he grinned, "own all the water-rights. He spit plenty!"

"As long as he don't use that Winchester it's all right. I was thinking you boys are getting a tough break, Tony. I'll see the Second Deputy and have him change your uniforms and allow you first-grade privileges."

Manuel's face was stolid when Nolan made the request to him. The Second Deputy dusted off his uniform, which would have served for a Spanish general's. He moved his brutish body across the yard. A file of screws followed him, when he clapped a signal. They gathered up the rockpile gang and led them toward the tailor shop. Nolan waited. He almost choked with indignation when the mob appeared, each with a ball and chain riveted to his leg, each without cap, and heads shaven to the quick.

Kincade had noticed the balls-and-chains on the rockpile company. "They're trying to show you where to get off, Tige, eh? Look out for trouble. Manuel must have heard the new governor is an old school disciplinarian."

Lighting a cork-tipped cigarette the Singing Trusty began, counting marks on the wall of the cell. He counted for a second time, and lighted a second cigarette that had an aroma like a Persian garden.

"Sure," he remarked, "I'm all wrong in me calculations! With good time off I'm ready to start packing. That front office bunch will never tell you anything. I'll be buying a drink in O'Rourke's speakeasy at Orleans day after tomorrow. And I'll have an extra one for you, old pal."

Shading his eyes from the light at the back of the cell, Nolan looked at the Singing Trusty's regular features and curly black hair. He appraised and sniffed the cigarette the Irishman was smoking. A plush box lay on the sheet of the top cell. It was an expensive present for a con to receive.

"Mind telling me where you got those cigs?" Nolan asked. "Mind passing a few down? My throat's burnt brown from state tobacco."

"Sure, it is, I forgot." Kincade tossed Nolan the box. "Haven't heard anything from your moll?" he asked.

"Not a word, since last visit. I'll hear soon. This box," mused Nolan. "The cigs in it came from a dame. I'll bet she don't live far from here. Is she going to meet you at Orleans, Kincade—have a drink at O'Rourke's with you?"

"Cripes, not there! She and I know a better place. Say, oh, hell, I don't know any dame that lives near here!"

Nolan went out the cell next morning and braced the P.K. who stood with the Second Deputy. "It's state election day," he suggested. "Can the boys have the afternoon off? Two teams want to play baseball."

"They'll get baseball!" the P.K. snapped. "Get it, like the rockpile gang got theirs, eh, Mr. Manuel?"

Simone's little joke was followed by a brutal laugh, when Nolan made off across the yard. He ran square into Tough Guss, when he rounded the tailor shop. Guss' prison coat bulged. Nolan seized the gangleader. He ripped his buttons off and tore at his shirt. Out began dropping a score of needle-pointed knives. Boxes of cartridges followed the knives. Digging deeper, while the foreigner struggled helplessly in his grip, Nolan fished forth three Mexican-made gats, with killing calibers.

"I found these," stammered Tough Guss.

"To hell you did! You're distributing them for a riot. You want the league broken up, since you weren't elected." Nolan looked around. No one had seen his struggle with Guss. He began tightening his grip and, at the same time, shoving the guns, cartridges, knives under the covering of a long plank at the side of the tailor shop.

"You come along with me!" he ordered. "To the cooler. The delegates will decide what to do with you. One thing—our organization is saved."

Kincade was sewing buttons on an outgoing suit in the solitary when Nolan flung Guss through the door. The Singing Trusty tossed away a cigarette. "Bringing in th' thieves," he began laughingly. "Did you catch tough Guss stealing tobacco from the prisoners' cells. Were the goods on him?"

"I caught him with plenty!" Nolan glanced at the row of cooler cells. Most had their doors swinging wide. "I want to lock him up, Kincade, until I call a meeting of the delegates. He almost put the league out of commission."

"Try that double-cooler. Lock him in the front cell. There's one behind, a cooler that the assistant deputy designed. It's just like being buried alive. Manuel must come from a line of Inquisition experts."

After locking Tough Guss in, Nolan saw the foreigner's swarthy face framed at a tiny grated opening.

"He's all right," said Kincade. "But he won't stay long. His friend will sure spring him. Manuel and he drink out of the same mescal bottle."

Finishing a last look at Tough Guss, whose oaths were lurid enough to melt the bars, Nolan went out and called a meeting of the delegates. "Fellows," he told them, "our league was either going to be framed or accused of a riot. I want it to last forever. What'll we do with the rods and shivs?"

It was voted to bury them, and charge the prisoner with stealing tobacco, a serious offense.

Going from the league room a presentiment came to Nolan. His eyes swung toward the cooler. Guss should be instructed to plead guilty to copping state plugs. It was better than informing the P.K. of a more serious charge, which would mean Tough Guss stayed in Convict City for life.

Kincade was missing when Nolan stepped into the isolation building. A switch of a brutal whip sounded from the direction of a shower room. Tiptoeing over the stone floor Nolan looked in the room. The Second Deputy Warden had his brass-braided coat off. His flabby arm described circles, with the lead-tipped quirt. Each blow he struck was followed by a grunt of rage. Kincade, stripped naked, stood chained to a water pipe.

Taking a step nearer, Nolan caught the quirt handle when it swung back. He snatched it out of the Mexican's hand. Manuel wheeled his gross body. His breath was vile from mescal.

"Thanks old man," drawled Kincade. "This animal came in, found Guss locked up, accused me of doing it, and slugged me before he tried the whip. Said he'd give me a few marks to think about after I went out. He did!"

The Irish inmate's back was crisscrossed with bleeding stripes.

Nolan saw red. The sight of his pal's blood turned him berserk. He became a fighting Tiger. Manuel went down. Nolan constricted the Mexican's triple-chinned neck. He clenched too hard. He allowed his fingers to remain too long. When he rose slowly, the Assistant Deputy Warden was dead!

"Croaked," gasped Kincade. "You croaked him, pal. Get the keys from his coat pocket, over there, and uncuff me. We got to fix up an alibi. God, man, we gotta!"

There was no chance for an alibi. Tough Guss began screaming for the P.K. Another rat-featured inmate joined him. The yard-keeper happened to be passing. He came charging through the isolation door, with drawn gun.

More screws heard the commotion. They rushed across the yard.

It was the Principal Keeper who listened to Tough Guss' story and viewed Manuel's lifeless body.

"Execution fer you!" he spat at Nolan. "Get Guss out of the cooler cell," he snarled at a guard. "Unlock the inner door and throw this fellow in. Stand guard over him. It won't take a court long to sentence this man."

"I'm a witness he didn't do it!" came from the Singing Trusty.

Craftily the P.K. picked up the lead-fanged quirt.

"Died in performance of duty?" he asked, glaring at Kincade's back. "All right, then. Nolan tried to prevent a deserved lashing. For that his life ain't worth a tarantula's nest."

Apparently the deputy warden was right. The Convict City's local jury, composed of screws, friends and three swarthy hooch-runners, brought in a verdict of guilty after walking once around the jury room's table.

The last words Nolan heard from his trial judge were:

"You have the choice of being hanged by the neck or being shot, until you're dead, dead, dead."

"Isn't this a generous state!" Nolan shouted to the judge, before being led away from a courtroom where no spectators were allowed.

Babs had been kept away by force.

On the evening before he was to be executed Nolan raised himself from the damp, earthen floor and listened. Somebody had unlocked the outer cooler door. A second series of locks and chains fell from their staples. Framed outside stood the P.K. Behind him was a screw's leveled rifle.

"It is my duty," leered the deputy warden, "to find out how you want to die? You have no chance of reprieve. The new governor is with us. Old Grimshaw and that climbing wife of his'n is got the gate. Spit it out, Nolan. How'll I give it to you, with pleasure?"

"What happened to the league?"

"Suspended sixty days. Then I guess it'll go on. The governor favors some kind of inside government."

"Will I be allowed a visitor or a visitor's letters?"

"Not in here! You're only allowed to stretch a rope or stand against that south wall. How'll you take your medicine, Nolan?"

Nolan temporized. He did not know "how to take it." Neither Babs or Kincade, who was released after proving his splendid lying ability as a witness, had been able to communicate.

Coolly, icy-cold, Nolan whispered a question to the P.K.

"Did I receive any package at the front office, Simone? Any cigar, no cigarettes or candy? Did I?"

"Yep! It's there, if Lugar ain't made away with the box. Came before you were tried. Girl's handwriting."

"What—what was in the box, candy or cigarettes?"

Nolan felt that Kincade's fate depended on the answer.

The P.K. took an exasperating chew, from a state plug. He weighed his answer. Was there some trick in the condemned man's request? He could see no harm in telling Nolan.

"Well," he began, "I didn't open it. The box was given to the receiving clerk."

Nolan grasped the bars of the inner cooler. "Hurry," he said, "I haven't got long to live. I don't want to die wondering."

"There was a lot of torn sheets from a bank's record book—no good stuff in the box. Wrapped in them was—"

Before Nolan's eyes were closed by the law, at Convict City, a little party of four streamed into Orleans' best all-night restaurant. Mrs. Grimshaw led her charges to a back table, waited on by a pretty girl with tear-filled eyes.

The ex-warden of Convict City drew out a flask, in spite of his wife's protests. His daughter leaned across the table and spoke to a curly-headed man who had a number of bandages under his custom made shirt.

Kincade sent an Irish smile toward the waitress. "Any news, yet, as to how Nolan died at state prison?"

Babs started and recognized the group. She saw Kincade's hand stray toward the warden's daughter's wrist, when she announced:

"Y—es." Babs raised her apron to her swimming eyes.

"Nolan was hanged at daybreak. He chose that way. I wonder why? I knew him since he came back from France. Knew him too well!"

"Hello, Babs," said Kincade. "You're Babs, eh? Babs, this young lady and I are going to be married. We're going to Ireland on a wedding trip. She was going to marry President Francis of the defunct First National. She might have married him, if Nolan chose to be shot like a soldier."

Mrs. Grimshaw flounced out of her chair. "I can't eat anything," she protested. "I don't believe President Francis robbed his own bank. I can't believe it! Yet a dying man can't lie."

Babs' spunk came up. "Francis did rob the bank. He's going to be indicted tomorrow. I gave the prosecutor the goods on him, see. I sent Nolan a box of candy as a signal—who was guilty."

Clasping Babs' hand Kincade said with tears, "Good little Babs! Poor little Babs. You once loved a real man—an American!"

Babs stared at Lucile and Kincade. "You two are going to make up for what Tige an' I missed. Goo'-bye!"

Hanged by the Neck
Carl Henry

Something spooky about the whole business! The only wires leading to the house had just been cut off—there wasn't any other connection. And yet that voice kept hissing through the receiver, "You'll hang for it, by the neck, till you're dead—dead—dead!"

JIM BUTLER, THE TRUSTY, DROPPED OVER THE PRISON WALL, slid a shining pair of pliers from his pocket, and gleefully snipped the method of communication between Fargo Penitentiary and the outer world. Two strands of copper fell across a barbed-wire fence, and there was no chance that Warden Sedgewick would phone an alarm to anybody that night.

Jim's grin changed to determination. He advanced, peered through a curtain of sleet, scowled at the outlines of the warden's house, and began approaching it, stopping now and then with his prison shoes imbedded in mire. Once he blinked when he discerned fresh footprints on the warden's front porch.

Had someone beaten him to the job?

This was unlikely, since Fargo was off the railroad and far from the usual routes of predatory crooks.

Jim rounded a corner of a porch, felt along the side of the house and approached a window through which a light cast a glow on the falling raindrops. He rose to his full height and attempted to catch a view of the interior of the room. He rubbed the bristles of his chin. The blind was down within an inch of the bottom.

"I better not crash this one," he muttered. "Maybe th' warden is sittin' in that room. I'll mooch along to th' back of th' dump."

The rear of the warden's house ended in a screened porch leading off from the kitchen. Jim tightened his belt as he felt the drip of cold water from the eaves trickling down his spine, and took out a thin knife made from a file. He cut a tiny gash over the hasp to the screen door and tiptoed upon the porch. He listened intently but no sound came to him from the interior of the warden's home.

A scrutiny of the keyhole revealed light from behind a poorly fitting key.

"I used to pick these locks—before I wuz sent away," he chuckled. "I'll put my 'outsider' on this one."

Jim's outsider was a thin lead pencil with a slot cut in the tin sleeve where the eraser was missing. The trusty inserted the lead pencil into the keyhole, engaged the key, and slyly threw the latch. The door pushed open under his practiced pressure. He screwed up his nose and sniffed.

His eyes narrowed in calculation. Was it possible to cross the linoleum of the kitchen and peer into the room where the light was? He feared that the warden might have nothing to do but listen. An alarm could be sounded before he could present the business end of his knife to the warden's throat.

"I'll take a chance," Jim concluded. "Didn't I cut them prison telephone wires? Nobody can phone from this house either."

Shifting his weight to his toes, Jim started across the oilcloth. It crunched and creaked, but he made his way toward the inner door.

"I'm leavin' a trail," he thought, as he noticed the mud oozing from his "dogs." "This ain't goin' to be one of them perfect crimes you read about."

Suddenly a sound came to the trusty's ears, and froze him rigid as he was about to pull open the door.

He heard a tinkling that resembled far off sleigh bells. He strained his ears. Again he heard the tinkling—soft as a phantom sound, but seemingly everywhere.

"Hell," Jim muttered. "There ain't no snow near the prison. Maybe I'm like th' guy in th' play who wuz haunted by bells. Maybe I'm stir simple."

He took a chance and opened the door, at the same time extending the point of his hand-made knife.

All resolve melted from his right arm. It went cold. The knife described a circle toward the carpet. Jim almost let go of it.

His jaw opened agape.

There sat Warden Sedgewick in an easy chair—with his head split wide open.

A rural newspaper and a wood-chopper's axe lay at the warden's feet. A pool of blood was on the carpet.

Jim reclenched his knife. He closed his jaw to a muscular clamp. His eyes roamed the room, looking for a clue. Evidently the warden had been struck down from behind by someone who knew the lay of the house and Sedgewick's habits.

Behind the crumpled form in the chair loomed the opening to a front hall.

Butler recalled the muddy footprints on the porch.

"Some hick's beat me to it," he deducted. "Just couldn't kill that warden dead enough! Had to use—say, that axe must come from some chicken-house—there's lime on it."

A disturbing thought suddenly came to Jim as he approached the body. He would certainly be accused of the murder if he were found there.

Just as he was about to "blow," a thud came from upstairs, indicating that a sleeper had awakened. A door creaked. Water splashed.

Someone had gone to the bathroom—probably the warden's wife.

Moving toward the kitchen, foot by foot, Jim still kept his eyes on the carmine that stained Sedgewick's satin lounging robe.

Had the prowler who croaked the warden gone outside the house? The gun-guards would fine-tooth-comb the county and pick up everybody.

With his hand on the door knob the trusty gave a sudden jerk. He grew rigid. He blinked without moving his head. His eyes shifted toward the desk.

Again the sound of a bell had come to Butler's ears. Was the telephone ringing?

He turned when the room grew static with the menace of a loud clamor. Three times cold shivers ran up and down his spine.

"This is no place fer me," he concluded. "It's spooky. I *cut* the wires—they were the *only* ones leadin' to this house—there ain't a chance of *another* connection—and yet, there goes that damn *bell* again."

No one upstairs heard the insistent signaling.

Butler mopped his brow with the back of a shaking hand. Cold drops that were not from the outside rain dampened his wrist and fingers.

"Maybe I better listen in on th' phone," he proposed to himself. "A call that comes from nowhere is deep stuff."

He approached the telephone like a shaggy bear fearing a hornet's nest. Jim Butler was not usually timid, superstition was foreign to his nature, but the touch of the receiver, as he lifted it, shocked the nerves of his arm. Slowly he extended the ear-piece toward the side of his head.

The diaphragm clicked an awe-inspiring message:

> I know you murdered Warden Sedgewick. I saw you do it through the window.

Out from Jim's hand fell the receiver. He backed away. "Wot in hell!" he sputtered.

The voice that sounded in the instrument had a spectral note, like that from a cell. It resembled a "lifer" talking in a whisper.

Jim reached for the receiver and put it back on the hook again, with trembling fingers.

He turned and blinked at the warden's body.

"Nobody'll believe I done that," he mumbled. "There ain't a guard or a sheriff that'll say Jim Butler wuz a hatchet man. That's small town work!"

Growing bolder, Jim rested an elbow on the desk and slyly removed the receiver. The voice that whispered into his ear sent another dread message:

> You'll hang for it, by th' neck, until you are dead—dead—dead. I saw you when I peeked through the window.

Backing away the escaped trusty turned and lunged toward the kitchen. He staggered over the linoleum and burst out the rear way. He slipped and fell when he reached a gravel path and a muddy pool at one side of the warden's house. He averted his eyes from the penitentiary's gray wall and saw marks of a shoe-print. The trail led toward a flower bed, coming from the direction of the prison garage.

Jim mentally compared the footprint to one of his own. It was about the same size. Another prowler than the one who had tracked up the front porch, had been around. Both had worn gun-boat shoes.

It was time to be making a getaway through the rain. As Jim plugged in the direction of Fargo he could still hear a phantom ringing, and that insistent voice hissing:

> You'll hang for it, by th' neck, until you're dead, dead, dead.

Jim Butler shook his shoulders, dashed the drops from his prison cap, and fled through the rain.

It was after midnight and the way through Fargo's main drag seemed deserted. Jim hugged the sides of dripping buildings.

Back he recoiled, too late to escape detection. A night watchman was within inches of his own unshaven face.

"Good evenin'," Jim gulped, as he edged past the watchman. His hand slid into his pocket where the knife rested alongside the pliers.

"Say," cried the watchman. "You're a con, ain't you?"

"Can't stop, got a date!" Jim called over his shoulder.

"That wuz a bad rumble," he thought to himself as he ran along the sidewalk. "Th' old boy got a good gape at me map, and they're bound to use it against me later when they find the warden's body."

Jim could see garages, some with their doors open, at the back of most every residence in Fargo.

Whistling a reassuring tune, he sized up one garage, stepped on the grass and approached the rear end of a runabout, which could be backed into the street by a push from the radiator end. He released the emergency brake, and the car gained speed down a driveway that dipped over the sidewalk.

The trusty sprang inside, twisted the wheel, and headed the runabout to the bottom of a hill where he slipped the gears into high and engaged the clutch. The engine started after sputtering once or twice.

Without looking back he turned on a spotlight that illuminated a pike with hard concrete beneath the wheels. A sign indicated that he was driving north.

"This baby'll do seventy-five," he grinned. "Maybe a little more. It's a swell getaway from stir, an' from them bells."

He felt of his thick neck. There seemed not a chance in the world that he would hang by a rope 'til he was dead, dead, dead.

All that night, into dawn and daylight he drove up state, once buying twenty gallons of high-test gasoline from a sleepy garage attendant with money he had saved at Fargo penitentiary.

He struck a soft road that was narrow and slippery, and his speed abated slightly. Jim was a master with the wheel and knew how to avoid skidding.

As he flashed toward the outskirts of a town, there appeared before him an old model flivver which seemed to occupy the entire road. Butler gave the obstruction his horn and repeated the signal. The car did not turn out one inch.

"Ain't I got right of way?" he gritted. "I'll put that insect in th' ditch, where it belongs!"

Straight for the road-hog Jim went. He swung his wheels out in time to avoid a direct smash, but let the rear hub of his speedster catch the flivver under his left running-board, lift it, and swing it ditchward where it crashed into mire and water.

Jim slowed down and stopped at a house under construction. He found that the carpenters were at lunch somewhere, and used the opportunity to pick up a pair of overalls which concealed his prison uniform. He also found a slouch hat that fitted him.

Again he took the wheel and speeded down the road till he reached a railroad crossing where he brought up suddenly with his steaming radiator almost touching the black and white gate. A slow freight was coming.

The trusty backed the runabout with the intention of ramming the gate, and getting across before the train drew up.

"Stop! You're under arrest for speeding!" startled his ears.

He turned and saw that there was no way to avoid the unexpected speed officer.

He turned the runabout obediently, thinking he could slip the motorcycle cop a bill and prevent a pinch.

"How about it, kid?" he grinned. "Your moll must need stockings."

The cop grew indignant.

"Drive to the station!" he ordered.

The exhaust of the following motorcycle spelt menace to the trusty's ears. He slowed his car and leaned toward the officer.

"Say, kid, I'm well known in this burg. I'm a friend of th' judge. He'll break you fer pinchin' me. Take twenty and let blow."

"If you're well known you won't need bothering about bribing me. What's the judge's name?"

"I—I know him by sight. Met him up in South Fargo. Say, he'll fall on my neck an' weep, kid."

The cop looked along the pike. A muddy flivver with smashed bumper, mudguards and lamps, was just limping into town.

"You know our judge, eh?" asked the cop.

"Sure," chuckled Jim. "He's a particular frien' of mine."

"Well, that's him in the flivver. It's stopping in front of the station. The judge must have been ditched. He acts riled."

Jim's brows worked up and down.

Then the town's judge was the man he had shoved off the road, like an insect.

"Sufferin' soup!" he exclaimed. "I'm in fer it! They'll pinch me fer speedin', fer coppin' this car, fer escapin' an' fer croakin' the warden."

And Jim was right! Half of Fargo's gun guards took him back to the penitentiary.

"We got you dead bang to rights," the deputy warden said. "You were recognized in Fargo. You were leaving by a night watchman. You left your footprints all around warden's house—an' see this?"

Jim winced when the deputy displayed photographed finger-prints taken from the telephone receiver. "They're yours," snapped the deputy. "You split Warden Sedgewick's head open with an axe. You're goin' to hang for it on our scaffold—if you ain't lynched."

"Nothin' to it," Jim maintained. "Somebody else croaked th' warden. I ain't no killer."

Nearing Fargo, by a roundabout route to prevent a lynching, the deputy snarled:

"We come near arresting an innocent man who lived near the prison. A farmer who was going to have his place foreclosed. Wouldn't that have been a hell of a slip of justice?"

"What's that?" Jim exploded.

"Yes. This farmer owed the warden some money, and we thought that was his motive for murder—until we got *you!*"

Before Jim was thrown into a cell he caught a glimpse of a poster on the front office of the penitentiary, which offered $3000 reward for the capture of the warden's murderer, dead or alive.

Once in his cell, Jim heard menacing sounds outside that indicated a mob. For the first time in his life he hoped the pen was a strong one. He took hold of the bars, peered out inquisitively and saw a screw who carried a riot shot gun.

"You're indicted," the guard told him. "Fargo grand jury met when the deputy was bringin' you here. You go on trial in the morning. They're rushing you right to the scaffold, where you belong! Where you'll hang 'til you're dead!"

"Did you say dead more than once?" gasped Jim. "I thought—"

"I said it once, and I meant it!"

"Maybe I'm hearin' things. Maybe I'm simple. Me head ain't clear. Say, will you fetch me a cigar? One of them kind with a band on it. I gotta clear me head. I got to do some thinkin', I have."

Jim sat down on the edge of the cot, rested his jaws in his palms and stared at his stockinged feet while he smoked the cigar, before retiring for the night. The deputy had taken his stir shoes for foot-print comparisons in the mud about the warden's house.

The next morning, Jim awoke the entire cell-house with his loud demands to see the deputy warden. "Bring him here quick!" he shouted at a screw. "Th' quicker th' better. I ain't goin' to hang fer somethin' I didn't do. Tell him I know how to find out who croaked Warden Sedgewick."

The principal keeper came to Jim's cell, half undressed and surly. He was an officer with a brief way of saying things.

"What do you want?"

"Me?" Jim exclaimed through the bars. "Me, I want out! Did you ever see a con who didn't? You got me wrong an' I ken prove it. D'you want that pimpled-faced motorcycle cop to collect th' reward. You don't. *You* ought to have it—you an' me!"

The deputy warden lifted a suspender over one shoulder.

"Eh?"

"Sure! We split, fifty-fifty. Now listen. This is how to do it. You an' one of y'r deputies take me outside to th' warden's house. Right now. I'll trace out who croaked him. You ain't takin' any chances, 'cause you ken leg-iron an' cuff me."

There was no mercy on the deputy warden's face, but there was greed there, small-town greed.

"That cycle cop," Jim declared. "He gets th' reward if we don't get busy. I've been thinkin' all night, I have!"

Something in Jim's earnestness convinced the principal keeper that there was a chance to collect the reward. He had an excuse for taking Jim to Sedgewick's house for comparison of foot strides and for possible identification by the prison neighbors or fanners around.

"All right," he agreed, "but no tricks. No more midnight getaways."

The phantom telephone call was the clue Jim believed would help him save his neck.

"We'll trace them wires," he told the deputy when he was urged along the path that led from the front office to the warden's house. "I cut 'em in th' rain. You found pliers in me pocket, didn't you? There's where I used 'em. I don't mind admittin' that much."

The deputy strained at the handcuff chain and gaped, when he saw the two lines dangling loose as Jim had promised. One wire touched a barbed fence. The end of the other was deep in mud.

"When I wuz in th' warden's house," admitted Jim, "some ghost rang up an' said, 'I know you croaked Warden Sedgewick. You'll hang by th' neck 'til y'u're dead, dead, dead.' I don't know how many times he said 'dead' but it wuz enough. I got th' idea, somehow, that them two wires I cut formed a new connection. One is grounded; that's a good circuit in wet weather. Th' other is across that fence. Do these hicks around here use a fence fer short-distance talkin'? They do in Nebraska. They're too mean, some of them, to buy wire. Couldn't two hicks've been accusin' each other, an' I heard a phantom circuit in th' house? Couldn't they?"

The deputy knew nothing about electricity. Jim did.

"We got a swell lead," he went on. "All you got to do is follow that top barbed-wire, both ways from here. One way goes to th' guy who croaked th' warden, th' other to th' guy who seen it done through th' window."

The principal keeper studied the cut wires.

"Maybe," he admitted.

"Sure!" insisted Jim. "Ain't one of those farmhouses got a chicken shed? Th' one at th' end of th' fence. Th' axe that wuz used to kill th' warden came from here."

"That's Nate Simmons' place!" The deputy pulled out a handcuff key, with a reflective motion. He mused:

"He's got a telephone between his farm an' Sam Petitt's, down yonder."

"I'm an engineer, I am," said Jim. "I know when wires must be cross-circuited. Petitt must've called up Simmons' farm to accuse him and his voice naturally came over the warden's phone."

"Petitt ain't got nerve. He had no grudge against Warden Sedgewick, like Simmons has. Come to think of it, I've heard the warden say that Simmons was half crazy."

As the deputy went toward the warden's house, he called over his shoulder to a screw:

"Go to th' farm an' ring Simmons' 'phone when you get there. Don't waste any time. This is important! We're on the trail of a killer!"

Into the warden's sitting room Jim and the deputy strode. Jim eyed the warden's empty, blood-stained chair. He twisted his body and leaned toward the 'phone.

"If that gives a buzz we get three thousand berries, P.K."

Almost before he finished speaking a faint tingle came from the 'phone. A louder echo sounded. The deputy warden lifted the receiver.

"Hello?" he said sharply.

His features underwent a sudden change that Jim remarked gleefully.

"Simmons done it," roared the voice of the guard who had gone to the farm. "I got him! He caved when I busted in."

The diaphragm ceased clicking. Jim extended his handcuffed wrists.

"Take 'em off," he chuckled. "We get th' reward. That wuz a lucky break when one wire I cut landed across the wire fence leading between Simmons' and Petitt's farms."

"It's an alibi that'll save you from hanging. But you're wanted for escape. That's another year added to your list."

"Say, deputy, I don't mind that extra time. Ain't I goin' to get half th' reward?"

Big House Boomerang
Margie Harris

"—there to be confined until the end of your natural life!"
That was the order of the court—but that wasn't all, for from
the looks of things in Nut Avenue, the "rest" of Don's life
was a matter of hours!

DEPUTY SHERIFFS, FIVE OF THEM, FORMED A LIVING WALL about the stalwart form of Don Morgan as he entered the courtroom of Judge Ephraim Klamath, "the hanging judge," to hear sentence imposed for the murder of Chief of Detectives Alfred Bede.

There was a stir in the crowded courtroom, a craning of necks, feminine gasps of sympathy for the handsome racketeer who but two days before had heard the foreman of the trial jury say: "Guilty as charged, your honor, with

unanimous recommendation for mercy."

One of the deputies unlocked the handcuffs. Almost with the click of the tiny locks, Judge Klamath, his angry old eyes gleaming like those of a rheumatic eagle, leaned forward and rasped:

"The prisoner will come forward."

Don Morgan shrugged his coat-sleeves into place. His attorney, the slippery, resourceful Marsh Keough, fell into step at his side. They paused before the judge's bench.

"Morgan, it is the duty of this court to impose sentence on you for the crime of first degree murder," Judge Klamath began acidly. He cleared his throat, went on deliberately:

"In this case it is more than a duty—it is a pleasure. You have been a menace to the peace of this community for years. You have boasted that you were greater than the law. This court does not believe that Detective Chief Bede was the first—nor the fifth—nor the dozenth man who came to his death at your hands, or by your orders."

Don's handsome, aristocratic face was a cold mask; his powerful jaws were clamped tight. Rigidly he stood at attention, his gaze glued to the drapes over the dais. Judge Klamath's eyes sparkled wrathfully while he waited a long moment before he said:

"Has the prisoner anything to say before sentence is pronounced?"

Don's gaze shifted from the draperies; met that of the judge defensively. Their eyes locked. Each realized that he was probing the mind of an implacable enemy.

"Since the court chooses to show his hatred so openly," Don said in clear tones, "there is nothing for me to say—except that I was convicted on framed evidence. I did not kill Alfred Bede; I had nothing to do with his death."

Judge Klamath pursed his lips; sneered.

"It is in keeping with your character for you to add a lie to your other evil deeds," he snapped. "The jury has recommended mercy in your case. Why? I do not know. You understand of course that the court has the option to accept or ignore the recommendation. I have chosen my course.

"It is the judgment of this court that you be taken to the state penitentiary at San Quentin, there to be confined until—" He paused, ostensibly to consult a calendar.

A shiver went through the courtroom.

It was to be death, then! Next would be the date set for the execution, followed by the grim words: "to be hung by your neck until you are dead, dead, dead; and may God have mercy on your soul!"

The vicious, hate-filled old eyes of the judge raised from the desk, searched Don's face for evidence of fear. There was none; no telltale twitching, no cold perspiration. Don had set his features resolutely. Not by the flicker of an eyelash would he let this political and personal enemy have the satisfaction of seeing apprehension registered there.

They stared again at each other, the hot, searching glare of opponents set for the kill. It was Judge Klamath's eyes which fell first. He looked about the courtroom, gloating at the tenseness of the onlookers. Suddenly he cleared his throat and said:

"—until the end of your natural life!"

He rasped the words; rose from his chair.

A gasp of surprise went up from the crowded courtroom.

"Life!" Someone repeated the words in the doorway; "Life! Life!" "Life sentence!" The word billowed out along the packed corridors and to the waiting crowds outside.

Don let his tight lips relax into a taunting grin. The judge leaned forward, hands tense on the sides of the bench.

"Would—the—prisoner—share the joke—with—the—court?" he demanded slowly, choking with the rage within him.

Such sarcasm was common in Judge Klamath's courtroom. Few of the poor devils who passed before him escaped some scathing criticism, some acid satire.

Don nodded equably.

"Surely," he said. "There is a joke—on you." His head jerked up proudly, his muscular shoulders squared. "They don't make stirs strong enough to keep me from you," he gritted. "You know I'm innocent. You must know—you were Bede's partner in everything."

Judge Klamath dropped back into his seat, purple faced, stammering incoherently.

"You're a thief," Don continued, calmly, "a fake, a taker of crooked money. And I'm coming back—soon—just for the pleasure of wringing your filthy, poisonous old neck."

Judge Klamath pulled himself together with an effort.

"Take him away!" he shouted. It was a senile scream, the yelp of an aged jungle cat suddenly finding itself trapped.

Deputies tugged at Don's arms.

He shook them off; turned back to the bench.

He brought his powerful hands together in the gesture of a housewife wringing dirty water out of a towel; spatted them loudly; grinned again.

"Like that," he said—and extended his wrists to the deputies.

II
JOB TO BE PULLED IN NINETY DAYS

DEPUTY WARDEN MCVEY GRINNED WOLFISHLY as he perused the second of two personal letters the San Rafael stage had brought him a few moments before.

"Irish!" He shouted the word jubilantly. The door of the outer office opened and a diminutive Chinaman with a peculiarly monkey-like face sidled in.

"Get Cap'n Sam!" McVey ordered. "Scat!"

The door closed silently; opened again a few moments later to admit a bulky, red-faced man of forty-five, whose straight black hair and fiery black eyes proclaimed a trace of Indian ancestry.

Deputy McVey motioned toward a chair.

"Squat 'n' get a load of this!" he demanded. Sam Arndo laid aside the loaded cane, took a typewritten sheet from the deputy's extended fingers. After a few seconds his features broke into a broad grin. It was ugly, that smile; the expression of a Comanche as the torture fires began to flare.

"Read it out," McVey demanded. Arndo cleared his throat, began:

"Dear Mac: A word to the wise is plenty. Old frozen-face gave Don Morgan all of it today; threw the book at him. The punk said he'd crash out and come back to get him. I'm coming to see the gay-cat two months from now—and if he's over the hill it'll be jake with me. Five grand to you."

The signature was a scrawled "B."

The eyes of Deputy Warden and Captain of the Yard met understandingly.

"What's the split?" Arndo asked softly.

"Eighty-twenty—I'll have the explaining to do," McVey whispered.

"Seventy-five-twenty-five," Arndo said insistently, "for a quick turnover."

"Right—job complete in ninety days."

Arndo nodded reflectively. "We've got to work fast—right from the jump," he said after a moment's thought.

McVey pushed the second letter across the desk.

"Different," he said casually. "Chief Barney talks cash money; the judge gives orders."

Arndo took up the sheet, muttered softly as he scanned the lines. His voice rose occasionally.

"Morgan," he said, "dangerous—threatens escape—like a mad dog—should be killed—if he tries it—existence threatens safety—everyone—take no chances—be cautious."

He dropped the sheet on the desk top.

"Kinda givin' orders, eh, Deputy?"

McVey shrugged. "Why not?" he asked. "Him and Bede was neck deep until Bede crossed him up." He looked over his shoulder cautiously.

"You know, Deputy," Arndo said in a half whisper, "somehow I always thought the judge had Bede croaked, himself."

"Chop it." McVey snarled the words. "Who in hell keeps us on the job but him and his gang? How'n hell could we hang on if we didn't play with 'em? Keep your mind on your job and forget who croaked which."

The warning bell from the enclosure under the walls which ran from the Officers and Guards Mess to the inner yard, tinkled at McVey's elbow. He took down the intercommunicating 'phone.

"Yes, Janes," he said. "Who? Morgan? Receipt for him; send him to my office."

He turned back to Arndo.

"Wait in the supply room," he said brusquely. "The bird's checkin' in now. I'll send for you."

A moment later Don, preceded by a uniformed guard, stood on the threshold of McVey's office—truly the gateway of hell.

III

FRESH FISH

"MORGAN—SAN FRANCISCO—LIFE!" the guard mouthed roughly.

"Stand by," McVey ordered. He turned cruel, greenish-gray eyes on the dapper form before him.

"Morgan, eh?" he asked jeeringly. "The tough guy; cop-killer. So this is the bird they don't make stirs strong enough to hold, eh? We've been itchin' for you to get here, Mister Punk—we're all set to give you a rough time."

He came out of his chair, reached up and tweaked Don's nose roughly; tweaked it again and again. Don, hands at his sides, stared unblinkingly at the wall before him. No sound came from his lips.

McVey dropped back into his chair.

"Sullen, eh?" he grunted inquiringly. "We'll take *that* out of you, too." The deputy leaned back, rocked comfortably in his swivel chair. "You're innocent, huh?" he barked suddenly.

Don inclined his head gravely.

"Yes," he said respectfully.

"Say 'sir,' damn you."

"Yes—sir!" The pause between the words was a taunt.

"Fold your arms; never approach an officer otherwise!" McVey let his voice become soft, admonishing. Still in the same tone he went on.

"Innocent—yes! We know it over here." He waited, enjoyed the sudden flame in Don's eyes. "They fixed you up over there, dumbbell—and we're finishing the job here."

He snapped forward suddenly, spread his hands on the desk top while he glared into Don's face.

"You got in the way," he snarled. "So they put you away for all of it." He stopped, narrowed his eyes.

Don was scarcely breathing. His every sense was keenly alert for he realized that now he was face to face with the crisis.

McVey took a deep breath.

"And 'all of it,' in your case, means not more than ninety days." He muttered the words thickly.

Don tightened his lip muscles; gazed hard into the evil eyes before him.

"You mean I get the works?" He asked it without a tremor in his voice.

"Yeh! Klamath couldn't give it to you because the damn jury went soft. But—if I was in your shoes I wouldn't be makin' any plans for next year."

McVey grinned coldly, touched a call button. A moment later Arndo came shouldering into the room.

"Morgan," McVey said, twitching a thumb at the prisoner. "Take him,

Sam; make a damn snitch out of him."

Arndo's avid eyes snapped with anticipation.

"Pretty guy, eh?" he exulted. "Orders?"

McVey settled comfortably in his chair; licked his lips hungrily.

"Lots," he said. "Shave half his head—like we do the runaways we get back. Put him in red pants so the wall guards'll have something to shoot at. Put him to cell in Crazy Alley along with the rest of the stir bugs—and the first time you get a chance tear his head off with your cane. We can't use him here—long."

Arndo's hand pushed heavily against Don's chest; sent him reeling back against the wall. The other hand came up; crashed between the prisoner's eyes. He staggered again, came erect and refolded his arms. Blood was seeping slowly from a gash at the corner of his eyebrow.

"Come along, fish!" Arndo snarled the command, caught Don's arm and sent him whirling into the outer room. "Keep your arms folded," he went on. "Keep just three paces behind me—and if you wiggle so much as an ear I'll tear your noodle loose with my sap."

He whirled the loaded cane about his head, brought it down with a swish across the top of a packing case. The thin deal boards collapsed under the blow; flew into a thousand pieces.

"Heads don't sound so loud when I hit 'em," Arndo said meaningly. "Anyway, yours won't."

IV

NUT AVENUE

THE LONG PRELIMINARY JOURNEY through photograph room, Bertillon examination, barbershop, bath, then "dressing in" as a convict, all seemed a nightmare to Don.

Arndo followed orders. They clipped exactly one half of his head and gave him the hateful red trousers California's incorrigible criminals wear to make them conspicuous. A runner from the clothing room took Don to the supply department where he was given a mattress and pillow, straw filled, two heavy blankets and a night bucket.

Captain Arndo was waiting for them by the first of the open air cell-houses.

"Come along!" he growled. "Nut Avenue for you!"

Don fell into step behind him, gazed curiously at the fenced-in sector between Cellhouses One and Two which made of the ground floor cells a tiny village in the heart of the big prison.

Strange, lackluster eyes in pasty, expressionless faces peered out at him from between the ten foot pickets. Arndo's cane rapped peremptorily on the gate which was opened instantly by a deaf and seemingly senile guard.

"Mackerel, Jerry; put him in the cell between Goofy Brady and Merthen."

Arndo and the old guard exchanged knowing glances and chuckled.

"Merthen!" The name brought memories to Don. It was the insane killer from Calaveras County who had killed an entire family with an axe, and who had made the courtroom ring for days with his frenzied shouts.

Arndo shoved Don through the gate, clicked it shut.

"Come along," the old guard shrilled at him. "Step lively, fish!"

Don stepped out after him briskly, waited, mattress on his shoulder, while the guard unlocked the heavy iron door and motioned for him to enter. The cell, six by eight feet, lay in shadows.

"Mattress on the bed: spread your blankets; bucket at the foot," the guard growled. Don complied, straightened, folded his arms.

Old Jerry stepped to the door, looked out; came back.

"First fall?" he whispered.

"Yes," Don replied.

"Why the red pants and haircut?"

Don shrugged; kept silent. The guard stared at him curiously for a moment.

"Hell!" he gritted. "You ain't nuts. Who ordered you in here?"

"Deputy Warden."

Old Jerry scratched his head.

"Always say 'sir' when you speak to a guard or officer," he whispered. "You got 'em down on you, seems like. Do what you're told and maybe things'll work out."

Don blinked at him, sensing a trap.

Old Jerry peered out again before he went on.

"I been here thirty years," he said. "You ain't the first feller I've seen throwed into Crazy Alley when he wasn't nuts. Won't be the last neither, I reckon."

Don stared hard into the watery old eyes.

"What's the rules?" he asked briefly, added "sir" as an afterthought.

"Chaplain'll tell you. I'll make it easy on you as I can." The old guard edged closer. "Got any money?" he whispered.

"Some. Or at least I can get some."

Jerry spat into a corner of the cell reflectively.

"What's your name?" he demanded.

"Don Morgan."

"Hey, Morgan? Feller that killed the chief of detectives?"

"They convicted me of doing it; I didn't, though."

Old Jerry's lips twisted into a sour grin.

"That's what they all say," he commented. "But looky here. You got friends outside, hey? Folks that can do suthin' for you?"

Don nodded. "Plenty—except to get me free," he said.

"Give a hundred dollars to get word to 'em?"

The crafty old eyes were boring into his for the slightest evidence of possible trickery. Don met them evenly.

"Two hundred," he said. "And more laying back for other favors."

"I'll give you paper and pencil in a day or so. Write your letter and an order for two hundred 'n' I'll get it where it will do the most good."

"Double cross?" Don made the suggestion quite casually.

"Nope! I'm old; liable to be dropped any time. I'm fixin' Old Jerry up while I can. You're in a bad spot here; ain't got a chance unless your friends step in. I'll take the chance for two hundred. Meantime you keep quiet, don't get into no trouble with the nuts here in the Alley."

"Like to have twenty thousand?" Don thought to strike while the iron was hot.

Jerry shook his head briskly.

"Ain't runnin' no private parole bureau," he snapped. "Take what I'm offerin' and don't figger on flickerin' over the wall."

"But—" Don began quickly.

"Hell with that!" Old Jerry snapped. "I'm doing plenty the way it is. If I earn the two hundred you're in plenty of luck. Looks to me as if you was gettin' ready to be knocked off."

"Yes, you're right."

"Thought so. Watch out for Cap'n Sammy. He'll frame some nut to start a fight with you—'n' club your head off stoppin' it. Else maybe they'll dope your food 'n' slip you the black bottle in the hospital."

He started out, walked a few paces and returned.

"Got plenty money?" he demanded. "I'm liable to take some extra chances for extry money. Want a little snow, mebbe?"

Don shook his head, shrugged.

"Huh! Lots does—wa'nt no harm in askin'. I can take care of special wants sometimes, for cash money."

A second later, at the sound of leather scraping on the cement paving he moved nearer the door.

"Put them blankets on smooth," he screamed testily. "Didn't you have no raisin' to home? Keep your cell neat or you'll be eating bread 'n' water in solitary."

A monkey-like, wizened face came into view in the doorway.

"Morgan, No. 34,557" a voice said. "I'm the chaplain, 34,557; come to help you learn the rules."

Don removed his prison cap, pointed to the wooden stool.

"Will you be seated, sir?" he asked. Then he drew himself erect at the further end of the cell, folded his arms.

A pleased smile brought a thousand new wrinkles to the face of the man he was to know as "Holy Joe."

"You'll do," the chaplain said. "The first rule is courtesy to your superiors."

For thirty minutes he droned on and on—but his words did not register. Don's mind was on his letter to "Sundayschool" Manes.

V

CRAZY MERTHEN

DON'S GORGE ROSE IN INSTANT REVOLT at sundown when a trusty thrust a cup of lye-like tea, a shapeless hunk of bread and a tin plate of sour hash through the open cell door. Inmates of Crazy Alley were not allowed in the mess-line and their recreation yard was the cement floored enclosure between the two cell houses.

Don set the pan of hash on the floor and thrust it aside with his foot to avoid the odor. Tearing a crust from the bread, he soaked it in the strong tea and tried to eat it but succeeded only in swallowing one mouthful. A few moments later he heard the sound of heavy breathing; saw a hand and arm slide silently about the door jamb and lift the plate of hash. Seconds afterward the empty plate was set back soundlessly.

Despite his days in the county jail, Don shivered at the thought of hunger so fierce that even a demented prisoner could steal such a vile mess from a fellow unfortunate. Curiosity took him to the door.

A tall, loose-jointed man stood with his back to the cell building a few feet distant, wolfing his own and Don's portions of the hash. As Don emerged the other thrust an arm protectingly over the double ration.

"Finders are keepers," he growled. "Don't start nothin'."

"You're welcome to it," Don said heartily. "Want some more bread and tea?"

The other nodded his head vigorously; held out his empty cup. Don divided the tea equally.

"I'm Morgan," he said. "Get pretty hungry here, do you?"

"I'm Merthen—Crazy Merthen," the other said. "Hungry? You'll find out pretty soon."

"I'm doin' seven life sentences," he went on after a hasty glance over his shoulder. "Old Jerry says you got the book, too. You bughouse, too?"

Don met his eye squarely.

"As much as you are!" he said.

Merthen nodded. "Pay you to throw a fit once in awhile anyhow," he said. "That'll make it look good for them putting you in Bugs Alley."

The man's rational bearing, his unexplained friendliness aroused suspicion in Don's mind. Instantly there returned to him the tales of the stir snitches who sought for information to carry to the screws. Merthen's next words came as a surprise.

"Open up or not as you want to," he said in low tones, "but the word's all over the joint already that you're framed for a one-way trip over the hill quick's they can get to it."

"Yes?" Don contented himself with the one-syllable word.

"Uh-huh! Listen, guy; I'm tryin' to wise you. My folks pays Old Jerry ten bucks a week to slip me sugar, butter and chewin' tobacco. The old fox is gettin' more jack from outside than he draws from the state.

"The deputy 'n' screws is scared pink of him; he's been on the inside of too much dirt here. He's collectin' from everybody that's got a dime, but he gives value received for it."

"Square shooter, is he?" It suited Don's book to give no information to the other.

"Yeh, he'll drain you of your last nickel but he won't cross you." Merthen drew nearer, whispered: "He told me to watch out 'n' see no alley nut gets you in a jam, so I figgered you'd squared him already."

Don frowned; stared at Merthen.

"If that's so, then why did you hook the hash?" he demanded. "Why not ask for it?"

"A stoolie or a wrong guy would have squawked. I was tryin' to see was you reg'lar."

Merthen grinned, showing stained, tusk-like teeth.

"You come up to sample," he went on. "Fellers from across the bay's passed the word you was right, so I don't figger I'm takin' any chances." He paused, waited while he looked about for listeners.

"You won't cross me," he continued huskily. "If you did, I'd do myself a lot of good with deputy 'n' certain others by—by goin'—bugs—and—croakin' you!"

VI

A NEW FRAME

CAPTAIN ARNDO'S ORDERS TO OLD JERRY were that Don should be added to the cleanup squad in the alley. Several times daily he joined four other men and with coarse brooms and a hose policed-up the long concrete walkway.

While he was thus engaged on the fourth day of his stay, Irish, Deputy McVey's runner, came to the wicket gate.

"Thitty-fo, fi, fi, seven," he shouted.

"That's for you, fish," someone called from a nearby cell.

Don went to the gate, found Captain Arndo hovering in the offing.

"Lively, 34,557," he growled. "Deputy wants you."

Don, arms folded, passed out into the main recreation yard and thence into the beautiful landscape gardens on which the hospital, Cellhouse Four and the administration building fronted.

At the door of the convict bookkeeper's office the prisoner came to a halt. The elderly clerk crossed to some shelves, took down a book.

"Frame!" he whispered without moving his lips; followed with, "The Deputy wants you; go in." Don paused irresolutely. "Knock," the clerk said loudly.

"Come in, Morgan," a voice said from behind the closed door.

McVey sat at his desk, eyes narrowed and his face purple with anger. The door to the third office in the row stood open.

"Slick rat, aren't you?" he snapped. "Thought you'd run the stir from outside, huh?"

Don waited. "No—sir," he said presently, again letting an appreciable interval elapse between the words.

"You're a lousy, stinkin' con and a damn liar." McVey howled the words; went into a torrent of blasphemy and taunts. Don stood with arms folded until he had finished.

Sam Arndo shouldered in, thrust him aside and took a seat alongside the desk. Don, his senses keenly alert, felt a slight tug at his left coat pocket as the yard captain passed him.

McVey was talking again, hurling taunts and profane insults at him. Don, his arms still folded, moved his feet. A moment later he looked quickly down at the floor; back at the wall again. McVey and Arndo sensed the quick motion with which he seemed to rest his weight on one foot, kick something under the desk with the other.

"What the—?" Arndo began. Both officers bent as one, looked to see what Don was concealing. With the movement his left hand whipped to his coat pocket; felt and removed a small paper-wrapped packet. He crumpled it in his hand; flipped it out and to the top of a nearby cupboard.

Arndo came to his feet, thrust Don back against the wall. "Stand there," he snapped; helped McVey to move the desk. The floor was bare, innocent of any contraband article.

"Search him!" McVey ordered. Arndo plunged forward, frisked Don's pockets, felt under his armpits, ran his knowing hands up and down the prisoner's legs and arms. Mystified, he went over him again; turned with an oath to McVey.

"Nothing!" he snarled.

"Strip him!" McVey replied. Don, without waiting for further orders, slipped out of his striped coat, the red trousers, the red cotton shirt; dropped them on the floor beside him. Arndo picked them up, one by one, with the tip of his cane, subjected them to minute scrutiny.

"Shoes—socks—underwear!" was the next order. A moment later, Don stood in his birthday suit, arms folded correctly across his chest.

"Nothing!" Arndo said again after searching the remaining garments. He and McVey exchanged surprised glances; turned and searched the floor again. In a corner for a moment they conversed in whispers.

Arndo came back, leered in Don's face.

"You had a deck of gee in your pocket," he snarled. "Where is it?"

"I didn't have any—sir," Don said slowly. Suddenly rage shook him, almost mastered his caution as he realized how narrowly he had escaped serious trouble.

Arndo rapped him sharply across the hips with the loaded cane.

"Where?" he rasped.

"I didn't have any, sir."

Arndo, his eyes glinting evilly, stepped back, swung the cane high with both hands.

"Sam!" McVey barked the word, motioned the yard captain to a chair. "Not—yet!" he added. "Listen!" He turned to Don.

"How'd you get word to Sundayschool Manes?" he demanded.

"A friend, sir—in the county jail," Don lied jauntily.

"Why?"

"Safety—sir," again the maddening pause between the words. "I was framed over there; common sense told me I'd be framed here."

Arndo leaned forward, whispered something to McVey. The deputy choked down his anger; took a letter from his desk and reread it.

His thick fingers tapped the edge of his desk for a moment before he said, speaking to Arndo:

"All right! Cut the rest of his hair and move him to the first inside tier of No. 2 cellhouse. Put him in the jute mill in the morning on the breakers."

Arndo grimaced. "Stripes, too?" he asked.

"No, red pants and shirt and tell the wall guards to burn him down if he wiggles a finger. Tell Rats Halloran in the mill that 34,557's to be the official cleaner and he's to go to the hole if there's a shutdown on his account."

They looked knowingly at each other and laughed as at some grisly joke. Don felt new dangers closing in about him.

McVey, calm again, turned to say:

"Your friends are strong enough to get you out of Nut Alley, but that's all. We'll get you just the same—fuzz-tail. Now—where's the dope you had in your pocket when you came in here?"

Red fury blazed suddenly in Don's brain.

"I didn't have any dope in my pocket when I came in, sir," he said hoarsely. "The deck Captain Arndo planted on me is on top of that cupboard; I ditched it while you were looking under the desk."

Unhindered, arms still folded, he turned and reentered the outer office.

VII

THE JUTE MILL

THE SAN QUENTIN JUTE MILL! Dante's hell, Don reflected, would be a relief after the roaring machinery, the dust-laden air, the chattering, thudding breaker-machine to which he was assigned. All about him in the long building were scores of looms, each with its striped-garbed weaver with a daily task of one hundred yards of jute sack cloth to do between daylight and dark.

Near the entrance doors great calendaring machines, twenty feet high, reared their heads over the convict lines as they entered and departed. Back against the blank wall were the breakers, the spinners and the winding machines.

At the breakers, the raw jute was fed into the capacious maw, to be forced downward between countless serried rows of hooked teeth which tore it almost strand from strand and spat it out at the side in the form of downy gouts.

Dust from the dirty jute hung everywhere, filled the nostrils and throats of the workers with tiny hairy particles and the grime from far-off Asiatic hemp fields.

"Rats" Halloran, freedman mill supervisor, grinned maliciously as he turned Don over to the convict straw-boss on the breakers.

"A foine new cleanin' helper for yez," he said. "Wit' th' complimints av th' Deppity Warden. He's to clean, while th' bit machines is runnin'."

Again Don caught the look of understanding between the free and the convict bosses. A moment later came realization.

"I'm Miller," the straw-boss said. "Look!"

He loosened screw plates at both ends of the machine face, let down a metal window.

Don's eyes narrowed, squinted hard as he tried to make the blur resolve itself into units. Miller touched a lever. The big drive belt ran slower, slapping its slack together with decreasing spats.

Presently the streaks resolved themselves into the faces of huge drums revolving in opposite directions. Slower and slower the revolutions became until bluish blurs became hundreds of tiny steel needles, teeth of the machine which took strands of jute and macerated them into down which, in turn, became strands again in the spinners.

Don looked questioningly at the convict boss. Miller took up a three-pronged implement with a short wooden handle, set it at the face of the opening; jiggled it deftly. Instantly a powder of jute dust sprang out, followed by a shower of tiny bits of bark. He pointed meaningly, indicated the three-inch space on the drum he had cleaned.

He pressed the lever again and the great belt whirred noisily, sending the drums spinning again. Still wordless, Miller tore a foot-long strip of striped cloth from a discarded pair of uniform pants. Gripping one end firmly, he tossed the other into the maw of the machine.

His hand jerked twice; came clear. The end of the rag was frayed like a bit of pounded willow bark.

"That's what it does to hands," Miller said shortly. He whistled a single short, sharp note which sounded clearly over the roar of the machinery.

A nearby convict raised his head, nodded as though in response to a signal. Miller crooked his finger at him; pointed to his hands as the man came up. With a shrug the other brought up two maimed stumps, eaten down almost to the knuckles as though giant rats had been given their way with them. The palms and backs were purple and red masses of scarred tissue, mute evidence of the horrible hurts the man had endured.

"He was clean-up man, too," Miller said, putting his lips close to Don's ear. "And there's a dozen more like him in the mill. You'd better watch your step."

Don eyed him gravely, seeking some estimate of the man's attitude toward him. He saw only a lined, brutalized face, eyes expressionless as those of a snake.

Miller avoided his gaze; handed him the cleaning tool.

"Set the prongs at the edge; slide it in slow," he directed. "Don't let it drag through. That's a shutdown—and punishment. Try it now."

Don gritted his teeth; summoned all the iron resolution which had carried him to the top of the rackets in Frisco. Calmly he set the prongs as Miller had directed. He worked them in slowly until a tremor ran along his arm as the avid breaker-teeth beat at the edge of the implement. He turned his head to avoid the shower of dust and bark; stepped back and was resetting the scraper when Miller tapped his arm.

"You'll do," the other said. "Clean every fifteen minutes; oftener if the jute's dirty. If it is, the feeders'll signal you by raising both arms. Then don't stop cleaning even for a second."

Don finished the job for the first time, snapped shut the cleaning aperture and screwed the plates down. He was choking from the jute dust and particles of lint; his eyes ached cruelly. A convict at the next machine went through the motions of drinking, signed for Don to watch him.

Nodding his understanding, Don watched the man as he turned and raised his hand to a nearby guard, at the same time pointing to his mouth and then indicating Don. The guard squinted through the dust haze and jerked his thumb affirmatively toward the water tap fifty feet distant.

Others were ahead of them and for a moment the two stood waiting for their turn.

"Morgan out of Frisco, ain't you?" the man said. "The word's all over the joint that they're after you, guy. Don't be afraid of the cleaner job; you're just as big across the pants as it is. It gets most of 'em because they panic, or because somebody runs against 'em, accidentally-on-purpose."

Don flashed him a quick look of inquiry.

"Gospel," the other said. "They're layin' for the guy on my machine now—stoolie. He tipped off Dutch Miller for makin' a shiv out of a file. Keep your eye peeled and you'll see how it's done; they—" His voice dropped and he looked fearfully around him. "Then you'll know what to watch for," he concluded.

"Thanks," Don said crisply. "You're damn decent to—"

"Nix!" the other said. "We know everything here that goes on in the county jail in Frisco. You're highballed from there for a right guy. I'm takin' no chances."

"Can the chat!" a voice growled behind them. "Pop off in the yard if you have to; you know the rules."

At five o'clock Don formed one of the long cue of striped-clad men who staggered wearily from the mill, through the double gates, up past the laundry and into the recreation yard.

As he passed the calendaring machines, glinting light from a skylight was thrown back from the burnished surface of the five-foot main drive belt of the lower mill. It was mounted between two giant generators, running thence on a long slope to a great drive-shaft under the roof. Don wondered idly how many revolutions it would make before McVey and Arndo had their way with him.

VIII

DUTCHY GETS HIS SNITCH

DON'S NEW FRIEND ON THE BREAKER MACHINE adjoining his gave new evidence of his friendliness on the following day when he covertly handed him a lump of tar.

"Chew it," he said. "It'll keep your mouth wet and you'll swallow the dust and lint instead of breathing it in. Something about tar that licks jute right now."

An interminable morning, the noon mess and part of the afternoon passed. Don now was becoming expert at his task, but he kept careful watch of the other figures moving about him in the dust haze.

Presently he felt something strike his foot; looked down quickly. It was a rolled-up ball of cloth. He looked about him and caught the glance of the man at the next machine. Their eyes held for a moment and Don sensed an unspoken message as the other turned away.

Puzzled, Don kept a close watch about him for possible trickery. All seemed as it should be, yet instinct told him the signal was a warning for him alone. He opened the cleaning slot on his machine, put out his hand for the fork; settled back on his heels and braced himself as something rolled swiftly past him.

Then a scream of utter human agony rose over the whirring pound of the breakers; a form twitched horribly, grotesquely on the next breaker; came loose and fell to the ground. Dimly Don sensed that a stripe-clad figure caught at an empty warp-reel and dragged it between two of the looms as guards came running from three directions.

Don leaned forward, retched violently as the figure on the ground rolled over and waved a bleeding, torn stump of an arm wildly before its owner's unbelieving eyes.

A gong clanged. Convict stretcher-bearers came on the run and carried the maimed victim off to the prison hospital.

In the confusion Lyles, Don's newfound friend, sidled over to him.

"Be dumb," he said. "Dutchy got his snitch. It'll be hushed up for they'll figger somebody was tryin' to get you to make himself a pal in the outside office!"

IX

ANOTHER FRAME

DON, SICKENED BY THE GRUESOME SIGHT OF CONVICT VENGEANCE, elected to miss mess call that night, remaining in the recreation yard with the outside gang men who had eaten earlier. He strolled about aimlessly, eventually coming near the entrance to Crazy Alley.

A sharp hiss brought him to a halt, but his newfound stir wisdom warned him not to look about.

"Come over here and flop near the fence," a low voice said; added the word, "Merthen."

Don stretched, looked about him and saw others seated here and there about the yard with their backs against the wall. He found a place beside the pickets, waited while Merthen took up his place within the pickets.

"Listen close," Merthen said. "I'm going to throw a big fit in a minute so they won't think we're hatchin' anything. Old Jerry said to get word to you that Sundayschool Manes was over to see you and they turned him down. That means he'll come back with a court order and a lawyer. Watch yourself they don't get you."

Before Don could reply, Merthen leaped to a nearby cell, seized a bucket half full of water, and sloshed it through the pickets over his head and shoulders. A second later the killer was raging and shouting inside the barrier, hurling himself against the gate and making maniacal dashes at the ring of Alley inmates who had gathered about him, but at a safe distance.

Guards ran in, overpowered Merthen, slipped a broad strap about his waist and thrust his hands into leather mittens riveted to the belt. These closed at the tops with sewed-in handcuffs. Thus restrained, Merthen ceased his struggles and permitted a group of fellow prisoners to carry him to his cell.

Don heard a chuckle behind him and turned to find Arndo laughing at his bedraggled appearance. Don ceased his efforts to dry his face and hair with the prison bandanna and folded his arms briskly.

"We'll be pouring quicklime on you pretty soon," Arndo said evilly, "so get used to the feel of it." He came closer, leaned forward to fix Don with a snaky glare.

"You saw that rat get it in the mill today," he gritted. "Who rolled that reel over onto him, huh?"

"What's a reel—sir?" Don asked stolidly.

"Damn well you know," Arndo growled, "a warp-reel, fish; what hit him and knocked him arm-first into the breaker."

"I didn't see it, sir!"

"You're a lousy liar and I've a mind to tear your block off!"

Out of the corner of his eyes Don saw convict heads come up on all sides.

"The first I saw he was up to his shoulder in the machine, sir."

Don voiced the words crisply, plainly. Arndo's face was white with suppressed rage.

"Come on to the office; march!" he snarled; waved his cane as though to strike Don.

Don steeled himself for the coming interview with McVey, called on his reserves of determination for fortitude in the ordeal he felt was coming. Instead he encountered utter silence.

Arndo motioned toward a chair in the corner of the clerk's office. "Wait there," he commanded and passed into McVey's room.

For twenty minutes there was a suppressed hum of voices, then a burst of laughter.

Arndo came out, motioned for Don to follow him to the clothing room. There, in response to a muttered order, the clerk consulted his books and went to the shelves. Arndo, grinning in high good humor, turned to Don:

"Off with the reds," he commanded. "We're going to dress you all up like a dude—a stir dude."

Don had no choice but to obey. Puzzled he stood in his underwear and saw the convict clerk stencil his number on new striped shirts, coat and trousers.

"Into them," Arndo said jeeringly. "You're a pet now. Get it?"

An all-consuming rage swept Don. His mind flashed back to McVey's words on the first day: "Take him, Sam; make a snitch out of him!"

Now, to all appearances they had done it. A score of convicts had heard McVey question him in the yard; had seen him taken to the office in his red uniform, apparently bound for the straight-jacket and the solitary cell.

Now he was to be turned back in the yard, sans the red pants and shirt; seemingly accorded first-grade privileges and—for what?

The convicts over there in the yard would find the answer in their own suspicions. Henceforth he would be known as a stoolie, a rat. Despite his stoutness of heart, he shivered inwardly. For the thought came flashing into his mind:

"They'll figure I tipped Miller—and I'll get the next warp-reel."

X

RAT!

DON LOOKED APPREHENSIVELY OVER THE DOUBLE LINES of his fellow prisoners as he fell in for mess call the next morning. It seemed to him that men stared at him suspiciously on every hand. Then he saw the red-clad Miller quietly take his place in line and his heart leaped joyously. Thus far the lifer had evaded punishment for yesterday's retribution.

Don was reflecting that possibly judgment was being withheld when something struck his feet. He looked down; flared red with rage. A passing prisoner had squirted a stream of tobacco juice over his shoes—the stir gesture of hatred for the stoolie. Don's shoulders jerked. He started to fall out of line.

He looked up, saw Arndo with cane poised, ready—anxious to leap in and batter in his skull with the loaded cane.

"Easy, kid!" A hoarse voice hissed the word behind him. He half turned; looked over his shoulder. Lyles, the breaker-man, had exchanged places with another prisoner; now was staring nonchalantly off across the yard.

Don let his shoulders sag in token of understanding. Twenty minutes later he was in the mill, after a breakfast of chicory, oatmeal, bread and third-grade syrup.

As soon as the morning dust cloud had formed, Lyles moved over to him.

"What happened? Come clean!" he demanded brusquely.

"Jobbed," Don answered bitterly. "They didn't ask a single question. Arndo kept me sitting there half an hour; dressed me in stripes and said the rest of the cons would think I was his pet now."

Lyles ripped out an oath, slipped back to his machine without replying. As the noon mess-line formed, he whispered to Don:

"They've got you in a tough spot but I'll pass the word among the right guys that you're framed by Arndo." He stopped, stared hard into Don's eyes. "Know what that means?" he demanded. "If I'm wrong about you, I'm a rat, too."

Don grimaced wryly.

"Hell! Let it go!" he said. "They've made it look too good. Their thinking I'm a snitch don't make me one."

The same sense of utter helplessness oppressed him when he reentered the mill after noon mess. The broad, whirring drive belt on the main motors suddenly seemed to typify the forces working against him. The huge calendaring machines seemed the embodiment of fate, taking new, harsh cloth and steaming, molding and baking it into the same pattern for thousands of yards.

Reluctantly he drove himself to his task, dimly reflecting on the futility of it all. Once he miscalculated in handling the cleaner tool. The whirring teeth caught at its prongs, twitched the handle from his fingers; threw it halfway across the mill after it caromed off a rafter.

He passed between a double row of looms to retrieve the instrument, fell to his knees as he stooped to pick it up and something heavy and cruelly hard struck the top of his head. He scrambled erect. At his feet lay one of the weavers' shuttles. A loom tender behind him held out his hand, grinning.

"Sorry, pal," he called. "They fly out sometimes."

Don shook his head to clear it, looked about him. A row of grinning faces loomed through the jute cloud.

He sensed that it was no accident which had caused his hurt; cursed under his breath when the weaver before him caught his eye, laid two fingers on the newly woven cloth before him and depressed it suddenly.

The flying shuttle struck the closed strands of the warp, left the track and went screaming off across the mill, to fall at the foot of a guard.

The weaver looked back at Don with hatred in his eyes. Then he spat slowly, intentionally at Don's feet, slipping like an eel about the moving thumper-beam a split second later.

Something prodded Don's back. Pochecho, a guard, was jabbing at him with his cane.

"Back to the breaker," he shouted. "They're not dumb; they know you're a rat."

With the last word he shortened his grip on the cane he carried; made ready to bring it down in a deadly arc on Don's temple. For a moment they stood thus. Then Don's head slumped forward and he made his way back to the breaker. He sensed rather than saw the leering grins on the other prisoners' faces.

Miller, who had kept away from the breaker throughout the day, slouched up during the four o'clock shutdown, extended his hand to Don in a gesture of friendliness.

"Shake!" he said briefly. Don took the extended hand. A second later he found himself flying through the air as Miller brought the unresisting arm over his shoulder, whirled and bowed his back suddenly. Don struck on hands and knees, brought up against the side of a nearby loom. His head struck the cast iron base heavily. A deep gash opened just above the hairline.

Dazed, Don staggered to his feet as a guard rushed up.

"Who slugged you?" he demanded.

Don shook his head to clear it, dashed the blood from his eyes.

"Nobody," he said clearly. "I slipped—in that," he concluded pointing to a pool of machine oil which bore the mark of a prison shoe.

"Go to the office and get fixed up," the guard growled after staring unbelievingly at Don for a moment.

"May I just go and clean it at the trough, sir?" Don asked. Not for worlds would he go to the office of the Captain of the Mill unless forced to do so.

"Go ahead," the guard said after a prolonged stare. He turned to Miller who had reappeared quietly from behind the breakers.

"Hell of a con, that guy," the guard snorted. "If it was you or some of the old-timers you'd be on sick report for a week."

Lyles was waiting when Don returned, his prison handkerchief dampened and wadded over the wound under his cap.

"That'll help," the other said. "Stay in there and pitch."

Then the blow fell.

Minutes before the five o'clock whistle was due to blow and while Don was working at the face of the breaker, a convict ran from behind the machine and signaled to a guard.

It was Pochecho who responded. A moment later he came rushing about the other side of the machine, caught Don by the arm and dragged him, stumbling and protesting, to the office of the Mill Captain.

Carl Esterhale, a nephew of the warden, came to his feet with a loaded club in his hands as Pochecho catapulted Don into the office.

"What's the matter?" Esterhale demanded. "Fighting?"

Pochecho, panting from his exertion, stopped to moisten his lips.

"Worse," he grunted. "Murder! This man just killed Dutch Miller, the lifer. He snitched on him yesterday to Arndo, and Dutch took a poke at him earlier in the afternoon."

"Straighten out your 'he's' and 'him's,' " the mill captain demanded. "Who snitched on who?"

"This fish here snitched on Dutchy Miller for tripping Broyles into the breaker yesterday with a warp-roll," Pochecho recited. "Miller socked him with somethin' during the shutdown and just a few minutes ago somebody shoved a knife into Miller's neck—'n' this guy's the one that done it."

"Take him to the deputy," Esterhale commanded. "I'll telephone."

"March!" Pochecho ordered. As they passed through the lower gate and approached the sash-and-blind factory, Pochecho pointed with his loaded cane toward the east end.

"That's where they'll hang you, stupid!" he rasped. "You'll get your life sentence in damn quick, hey?"

Don, stumbling dazedly along behind him, went berserk at the taunt.

"Hanging's better than being ordered around by a lot of filthy, jobbing screws like you and Arndo," he gritted. A second later, as Pochecho slashed at him with his loaded cane, Don ducked in a low tackle and brought the guard to the ground.

A machine gun on the wall started its monotonous rat-tat-tat-tat but Don noted, subconsciously, that the bullets were passing high over their heads and striking in a corner of the yard. He had no doubt that if he did not die in the next few seconds, he would give up his life on the gallows. But now the wall guard did not dare to shoot directly at them for fear of wounding his brother guard.

Don tightened his clasp about Pochecho's knees, twisted him over; let hungry hands clamp fiercely on the guard's throat.

Then a great red-and-yellow light obscured the world; thunder crashed within his skull, and he went limp.

XI

THE SASH-AND-BLIND

SOMETIME, IT MIGHT HAVE BEEN CENTURIES AFTERWARD, Don came back to the realization that a giant machine was hammering inside his skull, that his mouth and tongue were dry as tinder, and that he was hanging by his wrists from bonds that cut him cruelly.

He managed somehow to get his feet under him; to drag himself upward until the horrible tension on his wrists was lessened. For long minutes he stood with his forehead pressed against cold metal until some of the buzzing went out of his brain. Presently he felt about with his fingers; found his wrists were held in handcuffs which in turn were riveted to the iron door of a dungeon.

No sounds came to him from outside except a monotonous rumbling from some place seemingly far in the distance. At last he realized what it must be—the big washers in the laundry. That meant he was in a dungeon in the lower tier of the sash-and-blind building. A shudder shook his frame. The sash-and-blind—San Quentin's chamber of horrors!

At one end was the execution chamber. Adjoining it, the death cells. At the other end, far removed from all other activities, the solitary confinement quarters where Morel, the bandit, Jake Sonnenschein and other incorrigibles had eked out a horrible existence for years.

His head spun madly as remembrance of the afternoon's events came to him. Dazedly he pictured what was to come. Hours, maybe days there in chains; then the trial, certain conviction; return to the prison, and then the long, long walk up the thirteen steps to the gallows-trap! He groaned aloud; hushed suddenly at the sound of jangling keys outside.

Instinct told him to simulate unconsciousness; that whatever protection he might gain must come from within his own brain power. Now he was in no fit mental or physical condition to cope with the vicious wits of his official enemies.

He gritted his teeth to fight back the pain, sagged in his shackles again; let his head fall limply toward his left shoulder. The lock clicked. Someone shoved heavily on the door, paused; thrust sharply. Don's body moved back with the swing of the door. His shoes scraped over the rough flooring. Piercing, throbbing pains ate into his brain as lights snapped on and their rays struck against his closed eyelids.

There were two men there. One fumbled at his head; the other felt the manacles at his wrists to see they were secure.

"Croaked, Doc?" one asked.

"Nope—and no fracture."

The questing fingers slid over his forehead; jerked at an eyelid. Don almost shouted with pain as the blinding light rays caused the eyeball to twitch vigorously.

"He'll be all right," the prison physician said. "That trusty sure bounced a pretty one off his head with a rock, didn't he?"

"Trusty!" Instantly the picture came to Don. The convict clerk at the lower gate had come to Pochecho's rescue; ending the fight with a blow from behind. But it was the doctor's next words which nearly caused Don to betray that he was conscious.

"Miller's all right, too," the other said. "The knife missed the jugular, but he says this con wasn't the one who did it."

XII

THE WARDEN

HANGING THERE IN CHAINS, HIS TORTURED MUSCLES SHRIEKING their protest in time with the crashing pains in his head, Don came to know in the next forty hours the true meaning of hatred.

Hitherto his resentment had centered about Judge Klamath and the political ring whose members had brought about his conviction. Now it expanded, grew to include society's whole punitive system; found new food in the persons of McVey, Arndo and the prisoners' code of conviction of a suspected stoolie without actual proofs.

At the end of the second day Pochecho and two trusties came to take him to the front office. Don's bruised wrists and discolored hands were incapable of movement when the handcuffs were unlocked. A moment later they were torturing masses of pain, as blood filled the veins and resumed circulation.

In the corridor outside the solitary cell, Pochecho swung a vicious blow to the back of Don's neck, the rabbit punch; sent hint to his knees, gasping with pain.

"Up—I'll tear your head off," the guard snarled. "That's pay for what you did to me. On your way now." He thrust brutally at the prisoner's spine with his cane; laughed jeeringly at the involuntary groan of pain which followed the blow.

A bath and clean stripes preceded the return to the yard. At the junction of the walkways leading toward the deputy's office Don started to turn.

"Straight ahead," Pochecho hissed. "It's the warden himself for you this time."

Don's heart leaped at the words. "Square Bill" Day was the head of the prison—and Square Bill was a boyhood friend of Sundayschool Manes!

Yard Captain Arndo was waiting in the warden's office. He fell in at Don's side, let Pochecho with his bruised face precede them into the room.

Warden Day was watching them appraisingly as they entered. His prominent, seemingly kindly brown eyes lingered overlong on Don's face; shifted to Arndo's and flickered for a moment with a strange light.

"What have you got to say, Morgan?" he said in a rumbling bass a moment later. "You are charged with assaulting a guard; the report says you tried to kill him."

Don's tense lips parted. He took a short step forward toward the desk. Arndo snatched at his arm; shouted, "None of that, Morgan; you can't scare the warden."

Again Don saw the flicker in the warden's eyes.

"No dramatics, Arndo," the warden commanded. "And don't try to influence my judgment." He turned his gaze back to Don. "Now!" he said.

"I did assault Guard Pochecho," Don replied. He was careful to modulate his voice respectfully. "May I tell you why, sir?"

Warden Day nodded. "I think I'd like to know what could happen in this prison to cause a convict to take such a chance," he said judicially. "I'll hear you out."

"It will take time, sir." Don replied. He watched the warden's face for signs of impatience. There were none. Suddenly it came to him that this man, political appointee though he was, would let him tell the true story of prison politics, or racketeer-influence brought within the institution.

For a brief moment he considered his course. He realized he might be stopped at any time; that he must get across to the warden the highlights of his tale before the others could interrupt.

"The order," he said incisively, "has come into this prison to Deputy Warden McVey that I am to be croaked. It comes from Judge Klamath, the crooked element of San Francisco, and from the police crooks who jobbed me into prison. McVey told me so in Arndo's presence, and Pochecho was framing me for the assault on Miller when I lost my head and attacked him."

Arndo chuckled. "Crazy, warden," he said casually. "I saw it the day he arrived; that's why I chucked him into Nut Alley."

Warden Day, back in his chair, studied the captain's face attentively.

"The persecution complex?" he asked. "Thinks he's innocent, eh?"

"Exactly!" Arndo's tone was unctuous. "Through with him?"

Day shook his head gravely.

"Not quite," he said. "If this man is crazy I'm wondering why his San Francisco friends are so sure he is on the spot here?"

Arndo's face went purple with fear and wrath. He did not attempt a reply. After a moment Warden Day continued:

"Morgan, you've committed a serious breach of the rules. An attack on a guard by a lifer means just one thing—solitary confinement for a long period of time, the warden to say when the punishment has been sufficient. That's what I shall do in your case."

He turned to Arndo, and now his eyes were cold with warning.

"The prison doctor will examine this man and will report to me on his condition. I will be notified of the slightest sign of illness as the days go by. Day and night guards will be changed twice weekly over the solitary cells. Every guard on the list will take his turn at this duty. That is all. Take him out."

Again, for a moment, he let his gaze linger on Don's face. Was there a message? Somehow, despite the punishment he faced, Don felt that he had gained a friend.

Thirty minutes later he heard the padlock snap to on the wooden shed which surrounded his cell, for the solitary was made truly so by the erection of a board barrier about the steel bars.

Within was darkness, complete except for the thin rays which reflected from the dim corridor light outside through chinks in the boarding.

A rat ran across Don's feet, waited, sniffing at the scent of the stranger.

Don drew back his foot to kick the rodent away; paused. A moment later he stooped and took the tiny, furred form in his hands.

A tame rat! Company in solitary! Probably the pet of Morel, Sonnenschein or some of the others who had spent years there.

Suddenly he grinned mirthlessly there in the dark.

A rat had come to him, the rat of a convict. Even in the dark cells there was a measure of friendship for him. The rodent wriggled from his hands, ran to his shoulder, nestled there squeaking its mute message.

Don lay back on his hard bunk, closed his eyes and slept.

XIII

SOLITARY

DON LOST TRACK OF TIME. He could identify Sundays by the clanging chapel bell. Wednesdays too, brought a change of guards. Otherwise the routine was the same. A sudden opening of the door, food thrust into his cell; the clang of the wooden barrier a second later.

For twenty minutes each afternoon he was turned out into the corridor for exercise. During these periods guards stood outside the hallway doors, weapons ready to batter him senseless if he attacked or sought to escape. At the order, he returned to his cell and pulled the steel door to after him. In all of the countless weeks no word was spoken to him, except the orders to leave the cell or to change his clothing.

Mentally he found he was becoming sodden, ruminative. To offset this, he began a fiercely tiring course of calisthenics in the darkness. One by one he exercised the various groups of muscles until sheer weariness sent him to his bunk for rest.

He became lean, rock-hard. His trousers loosened at the waist-band; his coat bulged over the new-born shoulder muscles. Gradually he put his burning hatred out of his mind; centered his thoughts on doing the impossible— escaping from the sash-and-blind solitary.

Once, prison legends said, Jake Sonnenschein had made his way out of a similar cell; had remained hidden for two days in the rafters before he was discovered. And then the Tiger Man of San Quentin killed a guard before he let them take him back to the cells.

Through it all, Don never lost hope. Daily he made the rounds of his cell, feeling here and there, testing joints, welds, seeking some flaw which could be opened into an avenue of escape.

Then came another Wednesday with its change of guards, a detail which long ago had ceased to interest him. Suddenly in the night hours he was roused by the sound of a key being inserted in the big brass lock of his door.

In an instant he was awake, crouching in a corner of his cell. Always he had known that Arndo and McVey would do their work on him at night. Rage flooded his mind. He had determined long ago that they would not find a willing victim.

He blinked his eyes; rubbed them fiercely as the blinding light struck against the distended pupils. A blue-clad form stood in the doorway; the man seemed to be motioning for silence.

It was Old Jerry from Crazy Alley, Jerry the con-grafter!

In two strides Don was at the door.

"Quiet!" Jerry whispered. "I've news for you." He paused to listen.

"I'm fired—first of the month," he went on after a moment. "Too old." He grimaced, stared craftily at Don. "You still got money?" he asked.

"Plenty, like before."

"Would you give five thousand to get out of here; go back to the mill?"

"I'll give twenty to go over the wall!" Don whispered. "Ten for a rod and two clips of slugs."

Old Jerry shook his head stubbornly. "Five'll put you back in the mill," he said.

"What—" Don began, hesitated.

"Legislature's investigatin' the straight-jacket 'n' solitary; your friends can do business for you now," Jerry answered. "Give me an order for five thousand and I'll tell 'em how to go about it."

He pressed paper and pencil into Don's hand, passed a flashlight through the bars; pushed the wooden door to but did not lock it.

Don wrote, eagerly. In a few moments he tapped quietly on the door and handed Old Jerry the order.

The aged guard took it with trembling fingers.

"Don't you fear," he whispered. "I won't cross you up—and listen, Morgan, you've got a friend in the front office."

"Warden?"

"Yeh, him. He's havin' Arndo 'n' McVey watched when they goes to Frisco. Things is brightenin' up for you—plenty."

XIV

FIRST-GRADE AGAIN

THE STIR-GRAPEVINE TELEGRAPH, that mysterious bureau of information which gets official news to the convict ranks almost as quickly as to the prison heads, buzzed a few days later with the rumor that Don Morgan, who had cleared himself of the stoolie suspicion by attacking a guard, was to be restored to first-grade.

Incoming prisoners from San Francisco brought the gossip of the legislative investigation; trusties from the offices told close friends of the other developments.

It was one week to the day after Don had "squared" Old Jerry for the five grand, when Warden Day's personal guard and a convict runner came to solitary for the prisoner. A bath, shave, haircut, new stripes and an issue of cigaret papers and prison tobacco preceded the interview.

Don's eyes ached intolerably from the glare of the California sunshine, but he held himself erect as he crossed the yard. Once he looked down at his trim waistline, felt anew the bulging muscles which covered his body from head to foot.

Warden Day was waiting alone in his office and instantly dismissed the guard and trusty when Don appeared in their company.

"Morgan," the warden said judicially, "you're going back to the mill, restored to first-grade. I want you to keep out of trouble from now on; will you?"

"I will, sir."

"You have powerful friends; it may be that they'll get you out of here one of these days, but they'll never do a thing with the governor or parole board if you keep on piling up bad marks."

"You think, sir—that—that's something for me to look forward to?" Don asked haltingly. Warden Day rose and walked to the window.

"I'm going to be honest with you," he said after a pause. "I'd like to say yes, but I don't know. Sundayschool Manes is trying to prove you were framed. You say that is the case, too. But reason tells me the only way you'll get clear is for someone to smash the whole rotten political system, and send the crooks here to take the places of less guilty men they've sent here by jobbery and worse."

"I could prove it, sir, prove it in a week if I could go free."

Warden Day shook his head.

"They'd never let you get off the peninsula," he said glumly. Suddenly he flared about, his ordinarily placid face convulsed with anger.

"They're even bossing my prison," he thundered. "They gave orders to give you the works here." He nodded angrily. "Yes, I've proved that part of your story. I've stopped that, but I can't control their plots with the other prisoners."

He crossed the intervening space, put his hand on Don's shoulder.

"You're going back to the mill," he said, "this time on a loom. I've given orders you're to be treated fairly. The rest is up to you. Keep away from the yeggs and hard guys; keep to yourself—and don't talk to anyone. Maybe, who knows, you'll get a break yet."

Don turned, started for the outer office.

"Wait!" the warden said. "Sundayschool Manes'll be over today to see you. You're first-grade now and can have visitors. I'll let you have an hour with him."

XV

KI—TAI

YARD CAPTAIN ARNDO WAS WAITING at the yard deadline when Don was turned back into the recreation enclosure.

"Hung with horseshoes, eh?" he snarled.

Don stopped, folded his arms, looked the other full in the eyes.

"Yes," he said. "Percheron horseshoes—sir!"

Arndo twitched his wrist, swung the loaded cane brutally across Don's shins. "Answer by 'yes' or 'no,'" he said in a loud tone. "Get fresh with me, zebra, and I'll send you to the hole."

Irish, the deputy's runner, appeared at this juncture, calling Don's number.

"Cell fo' you—numbeh fo-fo-two, Cellhouse Two," he said. "You go ketchum blanket." He fell into step beside Don, squinted over his shoulder at Arndo.

"Him plenty goo' flen' fo' nobody," he whispered. "Plenty ki-tai, him."

"Right!" Don said. "But it sounds better in English."

Merthen was waiting at the Crazy Alley palings when Don returned to the yard again from his new cell.

"Come on over and talk," he said in a low voice. "I've been rational for a week now. They won't suspect nothin'. How'd you make it, boy?"

"Fair," Don said. "But it looks like a long grind for me. No chance of getting out."

Merthen pressed close to the palings, let his voice die out to a whisper.

"They're putting on the stuff for me outside," he said. "I'm to have a mental examination, and I'll make the mill. Once down there you 'n' me can crash out. Game?"

Don eyed him reflectively for a moment.

"Make it snappy," he whispered. "I've got places to go and things to do."

It was while he was still in this frame of mind after lockup that a guard came to take him again to the warden's office. There he was met by the lugubrious face, the hearty handclasp of Sundayschool Manes—his mentor in the early days of the rackets, and still a political power in the Bay Cities.

"Don!" Manes exclaimed, drawing the other to two chairs in a corner. "Day's given us an hour together. We've got plans to make, for times are changing over across the bay."

A guard sat in an opposite corner of the room. Yet another paced, sentry-fashion, in front of the lighted office. Occasionally a late detail of convicts, house servants in the homes of the officers and guards on the reservation, came swinging up to the gate and passed through into the prison proper.

Presently two red spots glowed in Don's pale cheeks. He began talking excitedly. Manes put out a hand to touch his.

"Easy, Don," he warned. "They've got spies everywhere. I was followed on the boat. Right now they know I'm here to see you. I've got a fast car and two rod-men waiting for me outside the reservation gates, but I may have to fight my way through if I get home safely."

Warden Day entered at the moment, nodded pleasantly.

"Hour's up," he said to Manes. "Morgan'll have to go in now. I'll do the best I can for him; the rest is up to himself."

Don tossed on his hard bunk, wide awake, for the remainder of the night. Every time he closed his eyes he heard the roar of machinery, saw the great, five-foot drive belt at the mill whirring from floor to roof, the sunlight from the roof windows glazing its black surface.

XVI

BREAK!

THERE WAS NO DOUBT OF THE WARMNESS OF DON'S WELCOME back into the mill. Convicts, men he never had exchanged words with before, winked, waved a hand surreptitiously or nodded to him when he went to his loom with a stripe-clad instructor to learn the art of weaving. Before night he was operating the loom alone. Next morning he undertook his first hundred-yard "task" unassisted.

During the recreation hours he became the center of grinning groups of fellow prisoners. He was coldly courteous to all, except when Miller, now also recovered and back in first-grade stripes, came up and extended his hand.

"Glad you're out," the latter said. "Lyles and I want to talk to you in a day or so when the others get through ganging up on you."

"Don't hurry," Don grinned. "I'm doing life, you know."

At the end of the week he had become an expert weaver but he made it a point to be among the last each day to finish his task. Warp breakdowns, bad cobs of woof, broken leather bands on the kicker-arms, all seemed to conspire to delay him. His cloth, though, was first grade, and he made but one trip to the inspector's table for warning.

Before the second week was done the guards had come to recognize him as certain to be one of the last half dozen men to leave the mill at night. The fall evenings were at hand now and dusk was falling when the mill line entered the recreation yard to await mess call.

Few saw the effort Don put forth to take the last few steps between the calendaring machines and the huge drive belt. Each trip in a different section of the line had taught him new facts he wanted to know—must know. These had to do with the main drive belt, slowing into inaction as the motors came to a stop.

Then came Thursday. The day was raw and cold. A high wind sent squalls of rain beating against the stripe-clad lines wending their way from mess hall to mill. The ventilators already were closed; the skylights battened down.

Don's loom ran with the obstinate perfection of an ancient Ford auto. Once he depressed the cloth with his fingers, let a shuttle tear its way out through the warp. The noon hour saw his task less than half finished. At three o'clock he seemed to be weaving furiously in order to catch up.

Three minutes before whistle time the inspector's ruler showed the necessary seven and one half inches on the cloth roll and he signaled for Don to shut down the loom.

The head of the mill line already was through the lower gates when Don fell into line with Jones, one of the loom guards, at his heels. Just short of the line Don stumbled against another prisoner, caught himself and took the place on the left the other had occupied a second before.

"Watch yourself—hep! hep!" the guard shouted and the last four men of the lines quick-stepped to merge with the others ahead.

Don's heart was pulsing rapidly. Despite his iron will he felt his hands trembling as he trod quickly along through the new mill, down six concrete stairs to the old building and thence to the turn into the doorway.

Ears alert for the sound of the dying motors, Don paced ahead. Click-clack-click-clack! The big belt was slapping its way merrily onward as yet. Ten feet more and the sound had lessened to a click-click-click. It was slowing. Five feet farther and Don's eyes fastened on the smooth surface.

Slower and slower the huge web traveled. Now he could see the metal lacing; could trace its course up to the big pulleys under the roof, each revolution decreasing its speed.

And then he acted!

His enemy-guard, Pochecho, stood in the doorway, waiting for the final units of the line to pass through the portal. Jones, the young screw from the looms, was behind them. All of the other guards were at their appointed places beside the line. The other free men in the mill, captain and assistants, were at the doorway in the new mill structure.

Like a flash Don whirled in his tracks, caught Jones a stiff arm blow in the throat with his left hand, and leaped over the prostrate body.

Three steps brought him to the big motors. Then his body went up in a curving, upward leap, arms and legs extended to their limit. Like a giant crab he struck the surface of the slowly turning belt; found hand holds at the edge; braced his feet and knees against slipping.

Uproar broke forth behind him. He had time for the merest glance over his shoulder. Pochecho was shouting, gesticulating in the doorway. As Don looked, the guard turned and raced to the foot of the belting. His arm went back and the heavy, loaded cane slashed through the air inches from his head.

It all was done in the space of seconds while the slowly moving belt with its human freight traveled obliquely from the floor to the skylight forty-five feet ahead and above. Now Don thanked the foresight which had enabled him to build up almost superhuman strength.

Though the belt was forty-five degrees off the vertical, it still required every atom of his strength to cling to it. Something heavy whizzed past his head, crashed out through the skylight; send a shower of glass down onto the belting.

Suddenly the skylight seemed to rush downward at him. Now was the final gamble.

With his right hand he snatched for a hold on the turn of the pulley, pulled his knees upward; loosened the grip of his left hand before the fingers were crushed, and ducked his head forward.

Dully he heard a splintering crash. Something struck him heavily across the neck and shoulders. Broken wood and glass rasped at his arms as he pitched through the skylight and out onto the flat roof.

Six feet away was the wall, rising five feet above the roof level. At the corner was a guardhouse and an armed screw.

Don came to his feet like a flash, tore across the intervening space and threw himself to the top of the wall as the door of the guard tower opened and a 45.90 carbine spat twice at his head.

Seemingly unhurt, he sprang like an unleashed spring straight at the guard in the doorway, knocking aside the muzzle of the gun and raining heavy blows on the startled screw's head.

Guards in other towers and the cheering, shouting prisoners in the lower yard, stared aghast a moment later as Don, unscathed, slipped from the tower doorway, dropped feet first to hang by his fingers from the top of the sixteen-foot wall—then disappeared.

XVII
CROSS FIRE

FOR A MOMENT DON LAY HUDDLED IN THE PROTECTION OF THE WALL and fought off the shock of the long drop. Meanwhile he cast his eyes about to find the landmarks he had memorized long days before.

The mill guardhouse lay at the extreme westerly corner of the long wall. At the other end of the mill it jutted east sharply, with a guardhouse situated also at that spot. On higher ground over the prison yard proper was a third guardhouse, which like the further one on the mill contained rapid-fire guns.

Five hundred yards to the northwest—five hundred yards of ground which offered the fugitive no cover—lay the jute storage building and the pier at which the prison packet, Caroline, put in daily with supplies.

Don came to his knees, fingers touching the earth like a sprinter on the mark; lunged forward into the mist as a new squall blew in over the prison headland. A storm was gathering in the west and occasional flashes of sheet lightning gave promise of a downpour at any moment.

Ten, twenty, thirty—forty yards without a shot. Don slowed for a quick look over his shoulder as the prison bell started its clamor notifying all that a convict was loose on the peninsula. The searchlight on the administration building winked on for a split-second; went out again. At the same instant a stream of fire leaped from the upper guard-post and a chattering row of explosions came out against the wind.

Don heard the hum of slugs high above him; saw tiny eddies of sand as the bullets dug into the earth fifty yards ahead and turned back the damp surface. Still he kept on doggedly, waiting for the gunner's range to shift. A new series of explosions behind him, but now from the right, came to his ears and lead began singing along from that direction.

Ahead of him now the sand eddied redoubled, and with the realization came understanding.

He was pocketed by machine-gun fire!

The two guards were firing from an equal base. Their bullets were meeting at the point of a triangle into which his running feet were carrying him inexorably. At the apex he would be riddled. To turn aside would be merely to encounter one of the single sprays of slugs.

Still his feet thudded onward. The machine gun fire was striking the

He leapt like an unleashed spring straight at the startled guard.

ground forty feet distant. Calmly, coolly, he calculated the lines of fire; the relative heights of the slugs above the ground.

Suddenly he stumbled; fell. For a full two seconds he lay still; waited for the shift of weapons he felt must come. The fire from the southern tower paused, swept back toward him. That from the north continued appreciably longer. In a flash he started rolling over and over to the right, chancing all on the possibility that he might cross the line of fire in the semi-darkness before the distant gunner could see his movement.

Arm close at his side, shoulders and hips thrusting mightily, he rolled on and on. Now lead was singing but a few inches above his body; then it was passing at the left. He rolled over thrice more; then for a moment lay still.

Raising his head a few inches he looked to the north. The little spurts of sand now were rising eight feet away, but the gun at the north was directly in line with his body. A half inch of elevation would send the slugs tearing and snarling into his body.

With a quick twist of his body he swung parallel to his former course, rolled desperately along for another ten feet. He was out of the double line of fire; past the deadly triangulation of slugs they were laying down for him.

At the same instant a new squall struck, and with it came a flurry of raindrops which changed in a second to what seemed almost a cloudburst. Don looked behind him. For the moment the prison walls were almost blotted from sight.

Something like a shout of triumph came from his lips as he sprang erect and ran at top speed toward the prison pier. Yard after yard he progressed until the huge woodpiles waiting for the axes of the choppers, lay between him and the menacing tower guns.

In another moment he was sheltered by the great jute piles on the pier and running to the string-piece of the wharf.

There, without a second's hesitation, he went over in a jackknife dive, came up spluttering; then swam overhand to a corner of the warehouse piling. He felt about in the darkness, growled in disappointment and made his way onward.

Presently his hand touched moving wood—the gunwale of a boat. Carefully he drew himself aboard, threw out a bow-load of tule leaves which had concealed the small craft from sight, and felt for the cord-starter of the outboard motor.

The mechanism coughed once; whirred sulkily the second time. Then it caught and began roaring its power-song. Don cast off the bow painter, took the tiller and using his hands as buffers, worked the boat out into open water.

When the first group of guards reached the waterfront, an outboard motor was chattering derisively at them—somewhere out there in the channel which led toward San Quentin Point and the open bay beyond.

XVIII
CONFESSION

TWO HANDS, HARD AND RELENTLESS AS VISES, clamped down on the scrawny neck of Judge Ephraim Klamath, brought him to the ground, choked him into sudden insensibility. Two brawny arms lifted him, bore him swiftly to a clump of shrubbery but yards from the doorway of his own residence; held him there until the jurist's chauffeur had put the limousine away and had gone to his own quarters over the garage.

A muted, single note sounded on Don's lips. An answering chirp came from the direction of the street. Don rose, stepped lightly to the darkest corner of the hedge.

"Pass him over to me," a voice said out of the darkness.

Three minutes later a big town car, moving without lights, turned into an intersecting street. Judge Klamath, gagged with a rolled handkerchief, sat huddled between Don and Sundayschool Manes.

"Old, experienced kidnapper—you," Sundayschool wheezed. "Gettin' him almost pays for the drenchin' you got out there in the bay before I picked you up, huh?"

Don switched on the dome light, stared stonily at the prisoner's contorted face.

"I'd go through it a thousand times more for the privilege of having him at my mercy," he gritted. "I'm going to make him wish he'd hung me when he had the chance—damn his filthy, rat heart!"

Sundayschool looked at Don over the judge's bowed head; winked.

"Where you goin' to hide the body?" he demanded.

"Right back in his own yard." Don snarled the words viciously; continued: "I want to take my time with him—almost strangle him a dozen times before I finish him off."

The words brought an inarticulate moan of terror from the prisoner.

"Don't blame you a damn bit," Manes replied. "Gonna do the rest the same way?"

Don's reply was lost in the screech of brakes as the driver brought the car to a halt before a studio bungalow near the top of Russian Hill. There Manes had kept Don in hiding while the hue and cry of the search subsided. Only today the newspapers had advanced the theory that Don had drowned in the squalls. In proof of the theory they cited the finding of an overturned boat with outboard motor and the further fact that the police stool pigeons had found no trace of Don in his old haunts.

Once within the house they carried Judge Klamath to an upstairs room, tying him securely to one of twin beds. Don took the handkerchief from the prisoner's mouth, let a few drops of raw liquor trickle down his throat.

"Muh? Morgan!" the old rascal gasped. "What—what—"

"Shut up!" Don barked. "I told you that day in the courtroom that I'd be back some day—just to wring your damn old turkey neck, didn't I?"

The judge gurgled weakly.

"You—you were—guilty!" He managed to stammer the words.

"You lie!" Don's hands hovered over the wrinkled throat. "You know now—you knew then—that Big Kennedy and the cops had framed me. You were in on the play because you'd been in on the graft for years. You knew that I had the dope on you and you were ready to hang me for something I didn't do."

The prisoner rolled his head from side to side weakly.

"Nuh—no—untrue!" he gasped.

Don set his hands about the quivering throat, fumbled for a killing hold; stayed there—waiting.

"Don't lie to me, you rotten ghoul," he muttered thickly. "It's all true, isn't it?"

He let his fingers compress for a second; flexed them. Judge Klamath shuddered but remained mute.

"Three, before I choke the life out of you," Don growled. "One—two!—"

"Yes—true—true—"

It was a mere whisper, skeletons of words.

"What will it be, confess, or choke?" Don snarled the words viciously, dropped his hands to the shaking shoulders and shook the judge as a cat worries a mouse.

"I'll deal with you, your life for a confession—written."

The judge gulped, went into a fit of coughing. His crafty eyes ranged the room, came to rest on Don's face. Nowhere could he see chance of escape, hope of pity.

"I—I want to live," he husked. "Do I go free?"

"I'll see that you don't go to prison," Don promised, then called over his shoulder, "Paper and something to write with."

Manes came from the adjoining room, with a cheap tablet and an indelible pencil. "Good as ink," he said, "in any court."

Don untied Judge Klamath's bonds, lifted him from the bed; gave him a slug of raw whiskey.

"Write!" he snapped. "And remember—your neck cracks if you slip away from the facts. I know them, and you know it."

For ten minutes the judge wrote steadily in a spidery, shaking hand. Don watched the formation of each letter, glowed happily as the tale of rascality in high places was unfolded.

At the end Don twitched the tablet about, signaled to Manes.

"Sign as a witness," he commanded, "then put it in a safe place."

Judge Klamath half arose. "I can go now?" he asked, quavering.

"Not yet," Don snapped. "You've a few chores to do yet." He stopped to grim triumphantly at the prisoner. "You're going to back up your confession, damn you."

"But you said—"

"I said," Don interrupted sternly, "that you wouldn't go to prison. There's a worse fate for you. You're going to be the state's star witness—its chief stool pigeon."

He turned to Sundayschool, grinning.

"How the boys'll love him!" he jubilated. "He's going to tear Northern California to pieces."

XIX

SERVING THE STATE

A SAN FRANCISCO AMBULANCE, purring at high speed along the state roads through the night hours; met at the Sacramento outskirts by an ambulance from one of the capitol hospitals. A quick transfer of a blanketed form from one stretcher to another, under the supervision of an athletically proportioned, white uniformed interne while a hard-faced, portly individual who answered to the name of "Sunday," stood by carrying a physician's bag.

Then a hurried run to the beautiful grounds surrounding the State House, a sudden stop at the side door of the executive mansion. The doctor and interne carried the stretcher into the governor's own library while the driver of the ambulance slid noiselessly out and back to his station at the hospital.

Governor Graeme, despite the lateness of the hour, was fully garbed. His kindly, sensitive features were set in an expression of granite hardiness, but there was a quizzical light in the gray eyes he turned on the group before him.

"I hope we're not making a mistake, gentlemen," he said gravely.

For answer Don opened the doctor's grip and brought forth the tablet on which Judge Klamath had written his confession.

"His statement, sir," he said tersely, "and the writer." He pointed to the stretcher.

Judge Klamath opened his eyes, nodded weakly to Governor Graeme.

"It's all there," he said and closed his eyes wearily.

The executive went to a table-desk, read and reread the confession. For long moments he sat in silent thought, then took up the telephone. A moment later the listeners heard him say:

"That you, Lindsay? Graeme speaking. I want you to bring your chief deputy and come to the mansion at once. It's a state matter of the most urgent sort—otherwise I wouldn't be routing you out at this time in the morning."

He turned back to Don and Manes.

"You've served your state well, gentlemen," he said solemnly. "Now it's up to me to carry this thing through, and I promise you it will be done to your fullest satisfaction. Rooms have been prepared for you; when you're needed I'll let you know."

Don advanced at a gesture from the executive, took his hand.

"When the case is completed," the governor said, "and before your testimony will have real value in court, it will be necessary for you to go back to prison voluntarily and surrender yourself."

He smiled significantly.

"It would be setting a bad precedent to pardon an escaped prisoner—and a pardon is your just due. In the meantime I don't think you'll be punished—the warden chances to be Mrs. Graeme's brother."

XX
"I HOPE THEY HANG YOU!"

HOW WELL GOVERNOR GRAEME AND ATTORNEY GENERAL LINDSAY labored through the remaining hours of the night was evidenced during the morning hours while the papers still were shouting the news of the disappearance of Judge Ephraim Klamath.

Two state detectives dropped in informally on the Chief of Police of San Francisco, whispered in his ear that Governor Graeme was considering a new post for him; that the governor wanted a conference immediately.

Simultaneously Warden Day notified Yard Captain Sam Arndo and Deputy McVey that he wanted them to take two parts of an important and highly secret message to the governor. They were, he explained, to travel by different trains, and to keep their mission secret.

"Big" Kennedy, San Francisco's underworld boss, presented a different problem. A onetime stevedore, he yet boasted of his physical prowess.

"I want no bodyguard but me own good fists," he was wont to brag. "I kin lick any five men in Frisco today—an' I'll take 'em on wit' bare knuckles, billies or gats."

To make the boast good he went on periodical rampages. Once he cleaned out a tough bunch of sailors in a waterfront dive. More recently he had downed three thugs who had attacked him with blackjacks. He left the three on the battleground; two unconscious, the third with a broken neck.

Absolute secrecy was the vital need of the officers detailed to take him before the governor. Finesse was the only answer. So Kennedy was awakened by a mysterious telephone call that the federals had discovered one of his liquor caches and were preparing for a raid.

When he came charging out of his apartment house ten minutes later, five men materialized seemingly out of thin air, covered him with gats held significantly in side pockets and directed him to a curtained limousine waiting around the corner.

Before his arrival at the capitol, Chief of Police Barney Maginn already had broken down under questioning; had admitted the facts detailed in Judge Klamath's confession, and had added to them. Then Maginn, broken and facing a prison cell inevitably, went to join the disgraced judge under close guard in the executive mansion.

McVey and Arndo arrived within an hour of each other, McVey waiting importantly for his audience with Governor Graeme until the yard captain appeared. Then a sleek, low-voiced secretary came through a door and motioned for them to follow him.

Arndo, smiling in oily fashion, thrust through ahead of his superior. A moment later he leaped back, trod heavily on McVey's toes.

"Hell!" he snarled. "Morgan!"

"Come in, gentlemen," Governor Graeme called. At the same moment three state detectives shouldered in after them, passed inquiring hands over their clothing. Arndo's pockets gave up a slender knife; his shoulder holster a heavy automatic.

Both prisoners were staring at the smiling, well poised man sitting beside the governor's desk. It was Don's moment of triumph. He let his smile rather than words, express his satisfaction.

Arndo was the first to recover.

"We came after that man—an escaped lifer," he said, pointing at Don.

"Sorry," Don replied softly. "I'm after *you*—and I got here first."

Governor Graeme touched a button, called for Attorney General Lindsay.

"McVey—Arndo!" he said crisply. "Read the confessions and Morgan's statement."

Lindsay selected three of a pile of papers from the governor's desk.

"Statement of Donald Morgan," he began, "concerning unlawful official and private control of law and order in San Francisco." His voice droned on and on for many minutes. When he was done, he looked at the pair.

"Lying statement of a convicted murderer," Arndo snarled, but his face had lost its ruddy color; his Indian eyes twinkled with fear and hate. McVey sat twisting his hat-brim. He did not look up.

"Confession of Judge Ephraim Klamath," Lindsay continued. Arndo's head came up angrily; he looked about over his shoulder. McVey sagged still further in his chair, fumbled at his vest pockets.

"Confession of George, alias 'Big' Kennedy," the attorney general said, and cast a shrewd glance at the two. He waited for a moment to give the bluff time to have its effect; thrust the document aside.

"We'll let that go until later," he said. "Instead, I'll read the confession of Chief of Police Barney Maginn, of San Francisco."

Arndo, the stoic now in the face of disaster, interrupted.

"Why read that junk to us?" he demanded.

Governor Graeme thundered the answer, rising and pointing an accusing finger at the two before him.

"Because we've got you two for murder—men you've killed in prison—killed them brutally because your brother crooks in San Francisco wanted them out of the way," he said. "Go on, Lindsay."

Then McVey cracked.

"Stop it! Shut up!" he screamed fearfully. "They've got us, Sam, Klamath, Kennedy, Maginn! They've turned on us, they'll get us hung—hung!"

He fell to the floor, slavering with fear; rolled on his face at Arndo's feet. Arndo kicked him brutally in the side.

"I hope they do hang—you!" he snarled. His right hand flashed to his lips. He swallowed hard; grinned evilly.

A moment later he was out of his chair, charging with outstretched hands at Don.

"I'm going—cyanide," he snarled, "but I'll take you with me, you damned punk!"

Don met him with an overhand right delivered with all the force of his powerful body; a right guided by hatred—the recollection of the man's bestial cruelties.

Arndo raised on his toes, pitched to his face at Don's feet. A second later his body went rigid as the poison clutched at his heart, crushed it and sent the black soul questing out into eternity.

Governor Graeme raised his hand for silence.

"Lindsay," he said sternly, "arrest every man named in the confessions. Take over the Frisco city government as long as is necessary. When Kennedy arrives, get his confession and then send him back in handcuffs. Smash the ring, and smash it forever."

He turned to Don. "San Francisco and all of California should thank you as I do. Now go, remember you have a date with the warden. Your pardon will follow you."

"Thank you," Don said softly. "What I've given you was 'inside' dope—and I didn't like the scenery!"

The Electric Warden

Peter Singer

*Pretty queer goings on—a hobo picked up by the warden
for his butler, his teeth filled, his mole removed—and acid
spilled on his leg to make a long scar . . . just like the warden!
That's what he was now—a ringer for the warden!*

"YOU AND I ARE GOING TO TAKE A LITTLE RIDE TOGETHER." Dan Tully, ex-gangster
and ex-con, stiffened like a ramrod when he looked up from a bench in
Balboa Park.

"A little ride together," repeated a stranger in a raccoon coat. "Come on,
there's money in it for you!"

"Wot? Money? Kale?"

"Exactly, come on with me. I'm the warden of Bridewell Prison."

Feeling his spine turn to a jelly-like substance Dan Tully relaxed. "Pinched
again," he sighed. "Th' warden! Hell!"

"You're not pinched. I want a man with your honest appearance for a job at Bridewell Prison. I'll pay you a fair wage. Follow me to the entrance of this park where we'll get in my car."

"Is this me lucky break?" Dan Tully asked himself when he trailed the raccoon coat like a hungry cat after a mouse. "Maybe this warden is afraid tuh trust his trusties. Most of them squeal on squealers."

Dan recalled that Bridewell Prison was located out of town, in a lonely spot seldom visited by anyone except those who remained to stay. He had never done a bit there.

Reaching the park entrance Dan spotted the warden's limousine, with the warden giving instructions to a gray-uniformed chauffeur, who was undoubtedly a convict. The monogram on the car was G. It had a low license number, 71.

The warden remarked when Dan had stumbled inside and sat on a pillow-like seat:

"My name is Gangler. You've heard of me? Of my soft-hearted way of treating deserving inmates?"

"Soft-hearted, eh?" thought Dan. "Dat's a hell of a thing for a warden to brag about."

The limousine glided away from Balboa Park, with the purring exhaust of sixteen cylinders.

The warden's eyes were hard ones, framed by gold-rimmed glasses. His face was broad and heavy. His neck bulged the expensive collar of a ten dollar shirt. Dan Tully noticed his large patent-leather shoes and spats.

"I could wear some of his clothes," he mused. "I wonder where he's takin' me to?"

The warden read Tully's thoughts. "I was attracted to you," he explained, "by your neat appearance. It is often my habit to visit Balboa Park and study the flotsam. You have seen better days. I can aid you at prison by giving you a position. We'll say as butler. I want a loyal man to protect me against the inmates."

Dan felt like pinching himself to see if it was all a dream. His gorilla-like eyebrows worked up and down. Suddenly his ears were startled by a voice, other than the warden's, in the interior of the limousine. He turned around.

"A radio," explained Warden Gangler. "A short-wave one I had installed in this car. I believe in keeping in touch with Bridewell when I'm away."

Dan Tully knew that the police did not allow short-wave radios in privately owned cars.

"This fellow must be a nut," he concluded. "Or maybe one of them reformers."

Twisting on the cushions Dan flattened his nose against a side glass of the limousine. The car had left the city's suburbs. It was purring in the direction of the hills, where expensive, solitary mansions sat perched above the plains.

Some of these mansions had been used by bootleggers for observation stations and liquor caches.

The four-wheel brakes went on when the car snaked up a driveway. It stopped at a high gray wall. Dan, at the warden's command, lumbered out. Before him was an iron gate.

"Take him through the guardroom," the warden said to the trusty driver. "Feed him in the mess-hall. Then, show him the way upstairs, over my quarters. He can have that last butler's clothes."

The inmate touched his cap. He looked at the warden interrogatively.

"Yes!" Gangler snapped. "The butler is leaving. This is our new one, if he proves worthy."

Tully saw that an understanding had passed between the driver and the warden. The trusty had not known that the butler was leaving.

"I'm in soft," thought Tully. "From Balboa Park to a swell job as a warden's butler. I ken do butlerin'."

Dan's transformation to a smug-looking servant took place rapidly. He sat on the edge of the old butler's bed and considered his surroundings, after the inmate chauffeur had departed, tiptoeing downstairs.

The warden's quarters had once been an old mansion. It was surrounded by part of the prison wall. A radio antenna, consisting of many wires, held by loops at each end, ran across the roof and to a cell block.

Puffing at a cigar, Tully ran one hand under the coverlet to feel if sheets and blankets were there. He had not slept between these luxuries in years. His hand came away with a peculiar warmth in his fingers.

"Still warm," he gasped. "Somebody wuz kippin' here, not more than ten minutes ago. They must have given that other butler th' raspberry."

He squinted at the books on the shelves. Most were about advanced radios. Some had electrical titles. A very few concerned prison reform.

Getting off the bed Dan Tully admired himself in a glass. He smoothed down his iron-gray hair and sneaked to a window. Raising this he peered down, three stories, to the warden's flower bed.

To him here was a getaway, by water-spout, ledges and a leap to the prison yard. He scowled upward at the radio wires. The antenna was too large for an amateur set. It had sending connections. Tully cocked one ear and listened.

He heard a whine, somewhere in the warden's house, that indicated a generator being operated. Undoubtedly it was sending out short-wave lengths.

Deciding to prowl the house early in the morning, before the inmates were let out of their cells, Dan softly pulled down the window.

He went to bed and slept until four.

His dreams were all about crooked, smiling prison wardens and eight-tube radios.

Shaving off his chin stubble with the old butler's English razor, he dressed, all but his shoes. He gave the top floor the once over before descending to more dangerous levels. The light he used was a fat cigar, reflecting in the palm of his hand. He inspected keyholes, and opened doors. There were five convict servants on the top floor of the warden's house. The inmate chauffeur was missing. He might have a room above the prison garage.

There was one room next to Dan's, fitted with three locks. Two of these locks were unbreakable, except with a jimmy. Dan stepped back from the door. He listened and heard the sinister whine of a radio generator. It was somewhere in that locked room.

"Th' warden uses juice all of th' time. I wonder why?" Tully studied the door. He had an idea something worth inspecting was secured by the unpickable locks.

It came to him that the builder of the door had been careless. There was a slit underneath. Getting down on his haunches Dan tried to screw one eye low enough to see the room's interior.

He got up, dusted his trousers at the knees, listened and went into his room where he removed a mirror from its frame. Dawn and a soft light had arrived.

The mirror fitted under the door, then Tully pulled out a hall runner. He squatted again. There was little he could make out from the angle reflected on the mirror. Wires crossed Dan's vision. He saw the oblong of a window. On one side of this window was a shelf and a workbench. The shelf was bent with technical books. The bench supported a long beam, made of copper, that ended in a mahogany-box, the size of a modern radio cabinet.

Around this box was scattered pieces of paper.

Dan Tully returned to his room and placed the mirror in its frame. He appraised the former butler's patent-leather shoes. He might wear them, but they would pinch his calluses.

"I'll try the sneaks!" he decided. "Them slippers won't make much of a rumble when I give th' lower floors th' once over."

Passing the doors on the second floor, without opening any of them, Dan descended the staircase and began nosing into a library. Another room was off the library. A faint glow there indicated an all-night lamp burning. The windows were all crisscrossed with staunch bars.

Opening a morocco-covered book, Dan was startled to see many signatures on its pages. His thumbs went through the volume. He believed he was peering at *Who's Who*, in financial circles. Banker's names were there. Express companies' officials had autographed that book. Under each signature was a notation, explaining who the signer was, with a brief history.

Twisting his features, Dan noticed the gold-stamped title on the book: "Contributors to Prison Reform."

"Dis is a stall," he gulped. "Dis book is queer! Whoever heard of a banker givin' kale to a warden? This is a autograph album that a swell forger could use to advantage. An' there's plenty in this prison!"

"I'll cop it!" he said loudly.

A cough swung him around. He dropped the autograph album. A prim-looking girl stood in the doorway.

"I overheard you!" she exclaimed. What did you mean by that remark?"

"Nothin', nothin' a'tall, miss."

"You did! Put that book back, exactly where you found it. Are you the new inmate butler?"

"I ain't no con!" Dan retorted. "I wuz hired from outside the prison."

The sharp look the moll gave Tully upset his nerves. She seemed to have something on him, as if the warden had told her a secret.

"My name's Miss Prim," she smiled. "I'm the warden's private secretary. I have charge of his accounts, other than those of the prison."

The sound of dishes from a private kitchen told Dan that it was time he should eat. He heard the warden's voice in the dining room. Going in, Dan palmed a tray. The warden was joined by Miss Prim at the table.

Screwing his eyes Dan was pleased to see a black bottle in front of Gangler's plate. Out of it, the warden poured a glassful of aged stock. He grasped the glass with shaking hands and gulped the drink.

It was such a "shot" that Dan did not believe he could have gotten away with it himself. "Nice old party!" he thought. "I'll watch where he hides that 'belly-vengeance.'"

Miss Prim ate her grapefruit. Her fingers, Dan noticed, belonged to an artist or a forger.

"Maybe she's an ex-con," he thought.

After breakfast the warden called Dan into the library. "There are two things I ought to do for you," the warden suggested. "One is the shocking condition of your teeth. Here, take this letter and go to my dentist. He'll fix you up. He has my orders. He lives two miles away from Bridewell at Duffee City."

"I ain't got any kale to pay for dental work." Dan was proud of his remaining molars.

"I'll pay for it. Go!"

The convict chauffeur motored Tully to the dentist. Dan looked backward when they rolled from the Big House. "Swell wireless mast," he suggested. "Th' warden must be nuts on radio."

"That's busted! The warden hasn't had it fixed yet."

Recalling the whine of a motor generator, Dan glared at the convict. "They ain't spillin' much information around here," he mused to himself. "Wot's th' big idea ov me gettin' me teeth fixed? They've been me best friends fer years."

He made four trips to the dentist before the job was pronounced complete. The dentist kept consulting a dental chart each time he made a new drilling or capped a tooth. He was as non-committal as a clam.

The warden examined the completed work. He rubbed his hands and wrote out a check for the dental bill.

The moll mailed the check. She remarked hesitatingly: "The warden wants that mole on your chin removed by a dermatologist. He says it disfigures you. You must have it taken off at once."

"Wot ho!" Dan Tully sputtered. "Removed? Say, babe, if any beauty doctor takes that off, he takes part of me chin wid it. I got that since I was born."

"You'll look much handsomer, Mr. Tully."

Dan rubbed the mole, reflecting. "Suits me, then. I wuz always going to have it looked into, but didn't have th' price," he grinned, flattered by the secretary's thoughtful interest.

It occurred to him after the dermatologist had finished the job that the oily warden was getting too solicitous concerning his personal appearance.

"Tryin' to make a dude out of me! Wot's his game? He's deep as any con he's got in stir. Deeper, maybe!"

An accident, while the warden was carrying a bottle downstairs, startled Dan into the realization that he was being prepared for some event. The convict-chauffeur mentioned that his auto batteries required electrolyte. Gangler brought a small carboy out of the double-locked room.

Tully felt a burning sensation along his left leg when he helped the warden carry the acid to the prison garage. The burning increased to hell fire. Cloth, underwear, shoes and skin turned yellow.

"Ouch!" cried Dan.

"Oh, that's too bad," smirked Gangler. "How careless of me!"

Hopping about on one leg Dan exploded: "You did it a purpose. I resign from being butler in this stir! Gimme me pay an' I'll quit."

"Go see my doctor first," the warden ordered. "When you come back I'll give you fifty dollars out of the safe in the front office."

After pouring oil on the wounds, Dan went with the chauffeur to the doctor's, who remarked as he applied bandages:

"The warden has a burn in this same spot, on the same leg. Queer!"

"Ye—s, too damn queer!"

It came to Dan that early evening while he sat on the edge of his bed and dragged at a prison-made cigar, that it was time he was blowing from Bridewell Penitentiary. He had noticed enough swag in sterling silver, worth fifty cents an ounce, to go first class to Tia Juana, Mexico.

"I'm bein' framed! I better beat it before somethin' happens," he puffed. "Somethin' is goin' to be investigated 'round here—but I ain't goin' to be th' fall guy. Not me! That slick warden has one or two 'cons' visitin' his private quarters. Wonder if they are professional scratchers, like th' moll?"

Dan liked the job. The inside of the pen interested him. He had often talked to desperate prisoners. They declared the warden was a crook, working a secret racket, by aid of inmates. He was liable to be pinched at any moment by government operatives, for having that low-wave wireless.

Getting up from the bed, Tully started a prowl that would have been a credit to Bill Sykes. The warden's silver was bundled in a rug. Dan thrust two bottles of rye in Gangler's best overcoat. He selected a ten dollar hat.

Then, going through the front gate he blinked at the darkness. Turning, he studied the high gray walls, with its guard towers. Suddenly he grinned at a larceny thought. There was a nice runabout in the prison garage, that he could roll out without awakening the convict-chauffeur. It would convey the silver to a fence, fifty miles away from Bridewell Penitentiary.

Dan laid down his plunder. He slyly opened the garage door. He sniffed and smelled gasoline and oil combined.

A sound caused him to stiffen until he was rigid. Another and similar sound came from a clump of geraniums. Both sounds were remarkably like cocking of Winchesters. Dan knew the difference between a gat and a rifle when being set for action.

Bridewell was surrounded!

Slipping sideways, doubling up, getting down on all fours Dan crawled toward the warden's gate. Inside it he turned a key with shaking fingers.

"They ain't after me!" he mused. "If they were they'd of said, 'Get 'em up!' They don't act like gun-guards."

Continuing, Tully deducted:

"Them wuz fly-mugs, or Secret Service dicks. It's Gangler they want, or that moll, or them inside forgers."

He decided to go to his room and stand pat in case of a raid. His right foot was on a lower step when he heard a call from a window. The warden stood looking outwardly.

"Come here!" he commanded. "Come over here, Tully. Tell me what you see over that wall."

"Look! That way. Not toward the quarry. Through those trees. Do you see a peculiar light on that hill?"

Tully strained his eyes. He pressed his nose against the glass. A greenish flare shone from the highest hill. It was an actinic ray, focused toward Bridewell.

"This window," said the warden, "is covered with non-mist like is used on auto windshields. I had that done in case of rain. The ray is a warning."

"A warnin' fer wot, warden? I don't get you!"

The warden's knees began shaking slightly. He gripped Dan Tully's arm.

"Come upstairs to the radio room. I'll show you everything. Yes," he whispered hoarsely, in a tone that chilled Dan's blood. "Yes, everything! You'll know the reason I selected you from that bench in Balboa Park. The 'Hessians' are coming!"

Tully knew what Gangler meant. "Hessians" were Secret Service agents.

Following the excited warden, Dan almost stepped on his heels as they mounted to the radio room. Gangler got out a bunch of keys. His hand shook when he opened the door. He switched on the lights. Each window of the room was double-shaded inside the steel bars.

Dan squinted around the room, while the warden moved a heavy chair. This chair came under Dan's squint. It was a duplicate to the chair in Bridewell's death house. The warden adjusted four brass tubes that were screwed to the floor. "A new invention!" he remarked cunningly.

"Have a drink. I know you like my private stock. Have known it for some time. Here's how! And, Tully, damn the Hessians!"

Tully felt menace everywhere. The drink he gulped was to steady his nerves. He felt fire running down his throat. Gangler watched him through glittering eyes. These eyes began to dance before Tully. He reeled and reached swayingly for support.

"If you don't mind," he gulped, "I'll sit down. Wot did y'u put in that drink, chloral hydrate? If you did, warden, I'll kill you!"

"You guessed right! You've taken twenty grains of chloral. Sit down in my chair, or lay on the floor, if you'll have it that way. I have prepared you for an experiment in my new hot seat."

The warden turned around when Dan fell, face downward. He threw a glance at the door. Miss Prim stood framed there. Her features were aflame.

"We are surrounded!" she cried accusingly. "I knew it would come! Your influence isn't strong enough to save you now."

"You knew, did you? I'm ready for them. Turn your back, while I change clothes with this 'butler.' "

Again Gangler ordered: "Keep your back to me. If you weaken I'll spill what I know about your penmanship. Get that?"

Unable to protest, Dan felt Gangler stripping the clothes from his body. He was lifted, and his body propped in the chair. Straps were drawn tightly around his waist and across his mouth. The warden stepped away. He selected two wires from a bench.

"These," he chuckled, "are the terminals carrying high tension current. The current will burn your head. It'll be unrecognizable when the Secret Service operators arrive. They will conclude I committed suicide."

"The pantagraph!" exclaimed the moll. "The checks? I've two ready now for transmission in the machine. The Secret Service men will find them here."

Gangler reached for a switch.

"They already know about them! Somebody tipped me off. I've felt it coming for weeks. Now, this man in the chair will be blamed for everything. The current will singe his head so that only the teeth and skull can be identified."

The warden took his hand from the switch. He advanced toward the moll. She backed away from him. "Wait," she pleaded. "You are about to commit murder. The entire prison is surrounded by detectives. Where is your getaway?"

"I'm supposed to be the suicide. Don't you see I've changed clothes with Tully? I must destroy his features."

Dan came out from the effects of the chloral. He opened his eyes. He felt the moll's hand run something under his hair, when the warden strode to the wall switches.

Sizzling sparks crackled. The air was filled with ozone. Struggling and expanding his chest Dan tried to break a strap. It gave a little. He renewed the struggle.

His eyes roamed the room. Gangler and the moll had fled. "I'm done fer," Dan gasped. He ceased his efforts. Pounding thumped at the door. The door burst open letting in a squad of men. The warden followed. The chief of detectives brought up standing before the electric chair.

"Gangler's electrocuted himself!" he exclaimed. "See the electrodes. He went stark, starry mad."

Disguising his voice, the warden said: "My master's acted queerly lately. He spoke of killing himself."

Tully glared at the warden. The moll stood in the shattered doorway. Going to the wall switch the chief of the squad yanked it out and swerved toward the chair. His attention was attracted to the cabinet on the bench. Picking up two pieces of paper he hastily examined them, and passed them to an assistant.

Suddenly he swung on Tully. "That forger captured out west—the one who passed those certified orders, had a suitcase receiver with a pantagraph in it, smaller than this one here. Warden Gangler's confederates got their signatures, forged to perfection, from this room, via wireless. It's the same idea as the apparatus used in banks and department stores for sending handwritten messages. A signature could be sent from here to Denver, via air, and written on a check. Many such electrical forgeries were passed in various states."

Dan Tully drew a breath, twisted and broke the straps around his chest. He jerked loose from the electric chair. Running his fingers over his singed head he roared:

"Grab that two-faced warden! He's Gangler! I'm no warden. He tried to throw you dicks off from pinching him by substituting me. He gave me the job as butler 'cause we were almost ringers. He knew he was going to fall hard some day. Didn't he have me teeth filled with gold, jus' like his own? He did. Didn't he spill acid on me leg? Sure! Fall on him before he draws that gat! He's half crazy!"

The gun Gangler drew from beneath the butler's coat was wrenched from his hand by an operative. Dan began to chuckle when the warden was handcuffed.

"You ken fingerprint th' two of us," he suggested, "if you want to see who's guilty of air-forgery. Me mug ain't never been took. I ain't so burned so you ken see who's who, even if we look a bit alike."

The chief of operatives asked Tully, "Why did the warden want to use a gat? To murder the moll, eh?"

Tully explained: "Sure, chief, that's it. He wanted to croak th' moll 'cause she slipped a short-circuit through my hair. It's a steel strip like is used in old-style wireless earpieces." And Dan added: "I beat the chair by it, thanks to her!"

Bull's Eye

Henry Leverage

Hate is sometimes a good thing—if you hate a guy you don't give a damn whether the lead poisons him or not!

THE RIOT AT BLACK RIDGE PRISON had all the elements of a battle in France. Seventeen hundred convicts held the prison and the walls. They were armed with machine guns, rifles and revolvers taken from the arsenal. Smoke from burning shops floated above their impregnable position.

Surrounding Black Ridge was a ring of steel. Soldiers, gun guards and a detachment of the state militia occupied dugouts and trenches, under a withering fire from the rioters.

They sat down to starve the inmates out, at governor's orders. He was a reform executive who didn't want "his boys" slaughtered.

Most of the convicts were not "boys." They were "die-hards," demons and lifers.

The desperate prisoners who had started the riot had on third-grade suits. Black Ridge Prison clothed its charges according to grades. First-grade inmates wore gray. Second-grade wore hideous stripes.

The demons had, in addition to stripes, a red bull's-eye sewed on their backs. This was a target in case of a getaway.

Nearest to the prison, a sergeant of militia and a state trooper, dubbed Bigboy, lay protected in a dobe hut with three more troopers. They held this post against the rage of the convicts.

Corky, the sergeant, had a biting tongue. He hated Bigboy for the airs that trooper put on. Perhaps it was because Bigboy wore a gold medal for marksmanship. Bigboy often crawled out of the hut toward the prison.

"He's out there somewhere," a trooper said to Corky. "Why don't you tell him you hate him when he comes?"

Corky twisted his mouth into a loose purse.

"He's got the side of a general, he has. You wait! I'll drive a big fist in his face, I will! He's trying to see how many cons he can slaughter."

"He claims he shot five, Corky."

"He does, does he? Well—it's a lie! I hate him and he hates me. If hatin' wuz love, I'd be Romeo and he'd be Juliet."

Corky got a hand from the troopers. He bowed in mock comedy, strode toward the entrance, then backed and stood to one side. Bigboy, with a Winchester under an arm, stepped in and walked over to the farther corner of the hut where an empty gasoline can stood.

The sergeant sniffed with disgust as he saw Bigboy making preparations for a bath at the side of his bunk. The huge can was lifted, a place cleared. Bigboy set the can down, and turned.

Again Corky sniffed, glanced at the troopers, then plunged out the door opening between the hut and trench for a breath of air. He did not stop at one breath. He took several deep gulps. He shot a shrewd eye toward Black Ridge Prison.

"A bawth," he snickered. "A bawth, a bawth! He'll have a room and bawth, he will. He thinks he's in Plattsburg."

Corky spat to the white ground. He had worked himself up into a proper mood for anything. The riot, the waiting cons were forgotten. Bigboy had enraged him almost beyond the limit of his endurance. The idea of a man taking a bath in a tin can was enough to make a top-sergeant eat bullets.

"I knew it the minute my captain sent him to me. I knew what kind of a ranker I had to live with and sleep with and see taking a bawth."

Corky had the saving grace of self-intoxication. He had relieved himself of pent-in venom by his tirade. He felt better as he started toward the hut. Bigboy had probably finished his toilet and was cleaning his rifle. He always did this before going to sleep. It had become second nature with the man.

The door of the hut was sheet iron. Corky breathed on his hands before he stooped and peered through the keyhole.

Bigboy, in the uniform of Adam, was still bathing. He was bending over the can like a statue of Hercules at the Fountain. Corky blinked, dropped his jaw, and took a second peep. He breathed into his hands, winked his left eye, then closed it entirely. His open right optic swung to the top of the hut. He raised his heavy brows, lowered them, then raised them again in the manner of a hairy gorilla getting an idea.

"Damn it, if that ain't the limit!" he exclaimed. "Strike me cold and blue if I'll stand for that!"

"Maybe he'll kill me someday," Corky said to himself. "It's them quiet kind that are dangerous."

He stepped into the hut, removed his outer clothes and rolled into the blankets. He heard a sentry change with another, then he drowsed into a slumber that was complete and satisfying.

Daybreak found the squad alert and intent upon their duties. Corky officiated in a host's capacity as he served out the breakfast from pans on a sheet-iron stove. He hesitated as he reached Bigboy. The trooper had left his plate and coffee cup on the edge of his bunk. Corky filled these two utensils with more than ordinary care and generosity. Bigboy had turned and picked up his rifle. A volley from Black Ridge Prison indicated the cons were more active.

Tactfully the members of the squad moved in between Corky and Bigboy. They all liked the little sergeant. He was the very life of the dugout. Without him the days fighting convicts would have been too dreary to face. They had a week of outpost duty.

Corky finished his coffee, cleaned his plate with a piece of whole wheat bread, then stepped to the door. The dawn revealed a deserted expanse. The safety and security of the night was gone. A ditch showed like an ugly lip midway between the hut and the prison. It was a long rifle shot from the hut.

Bigboy rose from his bunk and had breakfast. He slung the Winchester under his arm and moved toward Corky, who was still glued in the doorway. A trooper dropped a cup, stepped forward and placed himself between the two men.

Bigboy hesitated, fixed a deep browed glance upon Corky, in which was bottled all his contempt, then, with a firm tread, he strode out of the door of the hut, and crawled along a hollow toward the outlet.

Corky wheeled, bowed with a grimace, then snickered through his long nose:

"I had me eye on him. I could see him in the reflection of the shaving mirror. He'd better look out! He's a-shooting daggers with his eyes. He hates me. Well, I hates him. I hates him 'cause he don't say nothing. He's madder'n an hotter'n—I can see that with one eye open!"

Noon arrived, and with it came an interruption from the general monotony.

Corky was boiling a meal when there came a tap at the door of the hut followed by a stout command.

A trooper crossed the floor, lifted the bolt, and peered outside. His salute that followed this action caused Corky to stop cooking and come to stiff attention with his right hand on his forehead.

Two figures in long black coats strode in, glanced round, then called Corky imperatively to one side of the hut. They gave orders which necessitated frequent trips by Corky to the ditch.

One man was the warden of Black Ridge Prison.

They left after a final whisper of caution, to which Corky nodded vigorously. The door had been closed all of five minutes before Corky stepped in, squinted with one brow raised to the roots of his hair, then turned and let his companions into the secret.

"It's a blasting hole they're going to have. Old Rummy—the warden—says, 'we want a wire from this hut out toward the prison.' So it's up to us. We got to put on dark shirts. One of us has got to crawl out there."

"Who's going to do it?" asked a trooper.

"I'll go," said Corky. "The warden didn't suggest me, but," he hesitated, then added, "for a buck I'd send Bigboy, but what's the use? He'd only look at me in that 'damn your soul' way and go. What would I get by it? Nothing! I'm going myself. The wire will be here pretty soon. I know we're up against a hard job. Them cons got machine guns, and they're mad."

Corky studied the situation.

"Yes," he continued, "I know them. The leader, Sing Sing Dan, is a terror."

To Corky a "terror" was a con with a bull's eye on his back. "It ain't no trick at all to crawl out there. They can't see me, you know. I'll be slicker than a bed bug. I'll be in a black coat. The wire will be insulated with black silk."

Corky stopped chattering long enough to cross the hut's floor, stoop, and raise a diagram.

"It's all marked just as the warden said. I'm going to blow up the south wall."

It was two o'clock when Corky crawled out, and started across the surface toward the prison. He lugged fifty pounds of dynamite with him.

The little sergeant was aided by a general pepper-and-salt appearance in the heavens overhead. He took advantage of every mound and depression in the ground. He wormed forward inch by inch. He reached a point midway between the hut and the prison.

There he lay flat, thrust a keen pair of eyes upward and wondered if he could crawl up to the wall and plant the dynamite he carried.

He got up, rolled down to the bottom of a pool of water, then stood erect and eyed the penitentiary. He was congratulating himself upon the success of his venture when a busy whine sounded overhead, followed by another bullet fired at him.

Realizing that the convicts had seen him, he dug with frantic haste till he had burrowed a foot or more under the mud and water. There he waited for quiet to come when he could shove the dynamite forward.

The firing ceased after the convict marksmen had straddled the wall, and dropped behind it.

Corky crawled from his shelter, shook himself like a terrier, then worked up the slope until the corner of his eye was over the edge. He chuckled in satisfaction. The wall with its barbed wire top and cunningly arranged guard houses was revealed like a curtain above him.

Corky moved to the bottom of the depression, a matter of twenty feet, found a spot under the wall, and planted the explosive. He adjusted a fuse.

The squad in the hut had followed his operations with burning concern. They had seen him drop down into the depression. A trooper worked a telescope through the front of the hut and braced it in position to watch for any developments from the convicts.

Minutes passed with the squad taking turns at the telescope and counting the time when Corky would set off the explosive. The convicts fired now and then to where the warden stationed.

The trooper at the telescope had just turned away when a shout from the back of the hut caused him to glue his eye on the stretch below the prison. He dropped a curse as he saw the reason for the warning shout. Out from a side gate, through barbed wire and across the earth, a snaking demon crawled on Corky. This demon was the rioter's leader, garbed in a third-grade suit.

Darting through the semi-darkness, the convict closed with Corky under the wall. They swayed, with the convict holding aloft a huge knife. Corky bent backward under the prisoner's weight. He sank to his knees with one hand clutching the wrist that held the blade over his heart.

A groan and a long-running roar of rage rose from the troopers. A score of men started across to Corky's assistance.

The troopers in the hut realized the situation. The rescue party even if it could have advanced, would never reach Corky in time to save him. The convict was toying with the little sergeant, like a giant bear with a terrier. The blade of the knife was at Corky's heart in a straining position.

A trooper jerked the telescope from its position, wheeled and glanced about the hut for a rifle. Bigboy and one of the squad were by the stove. The trooper shouted, sprang half across the hut and snatched up Bigboy's Winchester.

"Is it loaded?" he asked as he dashed to the opening.

Bigboy raised his brows.

"Yes, it's loaded."

The trooper dropped to one knee, thrust the barrel through the opening and drew a sight by the aid of a telescopic attachment. He saw in the tiny circle Corky and the convict. His finger touched the trigger. Its cold chill numbed his arm. His eyes strained, blurred, then filled with tears. He rose, leaving the rifle.

"I can't shoot," he sobbed. "I'll hit Corky. They're close together. Damn it, man, I've lost my nerve! Yet I can see the bull's eye on the convict's back." Again the trooper tried. He let the rifle waver. His voice shook. "I'll kill Corky if I touch the trigger," he exclaimed. "The poor little devil's going to be knifed to death."

Bigboy had turned, when the trooper seized him by the arm.

"Good God, man—you do it! You try! Don't let a con kill Corky like that!" he begged, entreatingly.

Bigboy turned, brushed the hand from his sleeve, raised the rifle and took aim. His fingers held the barrel like twin steel claws. They compressed and whitened, as a flash struck from his eye, and at the same moment the Winchester jerked backward with a sharp report.

Bigboy smiled, set the rifle against the side of the hut, and stepped over to the stove.

He was watching the water in the can when Corky was brought in the doorway of the hut. The little sergeant slid from willing arms and stood swaying back and forth, his eyes fastened upon the troopers.

"Who clipped that con?" he asked.

A trooper turned and nodded his head toward Bigboy.

"You ought to thank him," he said. "He did it! I tried and couldn't. It was too close for me. I was afraid of hitting you, buddy."

"It was a fine shot!" exclaimed the sergeant. "It went through the bull's eye. I'm going to beg Bigboy's pardon. He couldn't have hated me when he could shoot that close—when he could draw a bead on the prison demon!"

"Your psychology's wrong, Corky," said Bigboy. "Hating you was just the reason I could do that! I had no feeling concerning you. Therefore you didn't disturb my aim."

The Black Warden

Thomas Bell

Human life was cheap to Brute Madden—that is, until his own worthless life was at stake—then he whistled a slightly different tune.

THE TROUBLE WITH BRUTE MADDEN WAS THAT HE WAS A KILLER.

A killer in Chicago and a killer in New York, Madden was forced by the police to make a getaway in order to escape the hot-seat at Sing Sing or a noose in some nearby state.

Abysmal in thought as a stone-aged ape, Madden decided to fade out of his old haunts and make for South America where one country on the east coast was reputed to be free from extradition. Mixed with the Spaniards, half-breeds, negroes and refugees from other hothouse republics, were reported to be gangsters, public enemies and crooks living the life of Riley.

Once in Madden's life he had qualified, under Finger Conners of Buffalo, as a lake sailor and a bucko mate with a wicked punch, right or left. That was before his surly disposition changed to a killing instinct.

He shipped as an A.B. aboard the southern schooner *Golden Shell*, and dreamed through the fumes of a shore-bottle, the first watch out, of escaping the yawning gates of every prison from Joliet to Dannemora. He woke, turned in his bunk, squinted out into the gloom of the schooner's fo'cas'le, then spat savagely at a wind scoop in a port hole.

Already the south wind was blowing around Hatteras. It was a half-gale that did not exactly worry Brute Madden.

Nothing mattered as long as he was getting away from his old life. No moll bothered him. He was too untamed to hold the love of any of them.

Over Madden's head sounded the stamping of the starboard watch who were shortening sail upon the *Golden Shell*. Above the howling wind and the beat of the sea rose the shouts of the mates, the singsong of the sailors, and the creak of blocks.

Madden glared at the tiny fo'cas'le light that swung above a molasses barrel which was the principal ornament of the place. This light irritated him. He blinked at it as some tawny beast in the presence of fire. His jaw blocked aggressively, and he snarled.

It would soon be time for the post-watch to take the deck. Madden listened for the bells. Seven struck overhead. He cursed as he flung his huge legs over the edge of the bunk. He would be called at eight with the rest.

His getaway called for hard labor on the schooner.

The fo'cas'le of the *Golden Shell* contained bunks for eighteen men— nine to a watch. Two of these bunks were under the fo'cas'le ladder that led to a small hatchway that was covered with a slide. Eight bunks were upon the starboard, and eight upon the port side of the ship.

The litter of the *Golden Shell's* fo'cas'le was the hallmark of sea scum. Boots, sou'westers, dungaree jackets, pans, cups, caps, loose bedding and empty flasks comprised the collection. The stench and odor of the place was that of some waterfront shock-house made more shocking by the grunts and snores of eight seamen who were bound to have their last inch of the watch. They resembled convicts in a cooler.

Madden dressed swiftly. He had an object in view. The third bunk at his right upon the lower tier, contained that which would wet his lips and at the same time keep out much of the cold and the rain overhead.

The gangster had seen a member of the other watch place a flask well within a "donkey's breakfast," which was slang for bedding. This fortunate one would never fight. In fact, Madden was willing to meet the entire watch on deck at any time. They reminded him of ten or twelve he had cleaned up in a dive. Poor weaklings who had gone down to sea to escape the coppers.

Madden felt his way along the bunks, reached and found the flask which he up-ended in one thirsty swig of joy. His shoulders lifted then, as he heard the companion-slide open. A face was framed there. Madden snarled. He dashed the flask to the deck, and squared his jaw. The figure crept down the ladder, and turned at the bottom in weak protest. It was his flask the Brute had stolen.

Madden bent his arms as if exercising. The play of great cords and muscles showed under the silk and satin of his skin. His lips curled, revealing an uneven row of teeth—curd-creamy and animal-like. His short, blond pompadour bristled.

The man who faced Madden had that upon his face which the world stamps on its misfits. Weakness was in chin and soft brown eyes. The nose was long, thin and tender at the nostrils where red veins showed in tiny crisscrosses. The cheeks were hollow, consumptive. The stoop of narrow shoulders might have been of student days or of weight added to years. Slender hands tapped nervously against the rough hem of the dungaree trousers. They were the hands and fingers of a poor thief, perhaps a pickpocket.

"Ugh!" The voice of Madden was challenging. He grinned down at the pseudo seaman. The thrust of his jaw was an invitation for blows. The clenching of his fists sounded throughout the fo'cas'le, as knuckle bones cracked aggressively. He was going to muscle his shipmate.

"Ugh!" he repeated, reaching and thrusting the crook's chin up until their eyes met. "What are y'u goin' tu do about it?"

"It was my flask—I brought it out with me."

Madden dropped his hand three inches. His fist closed. His elbow crooked. He measured the distance.

The fugitive from justice attempted to escape. It was too late. The blow that came up would have lifted the deck. The cry of pain that resounded was followed by the fall of the man across the litter at the foot of the ladder. Madden leaned in careless strength. He peered down at the white upturned face where it quivered. His great fist came open reflectively. An ugly grin widened his features. He stood erect and slowly turned his head, resembling a prison demon.

"Guess none of youse want to protect this guy, ugh?" he throated.

The sailors drew back their heads. Madden stumbled across the lurching deck. From the pan on top of the barrel he took a double slice of bread. Stooping, he drew the peg from wood and allowed a thin stream of molasses to drip upon the meal. His great teeth crunched into it.

Eight bells struck. The companion-slide was thrown open.

"All hands on deck, quick now!" came the stentorian voice of the first mate. "Lively there, men! Stir your stumps!"

A blur of muffled, blanket-covered oaths and protests greeted the call. Feet came out from the bunks and reached down to the deck of the fo'cas'le. Men yawned, glanced at the tiny light over the barrel, then stretched their arms in the awakening. Boots flew on, coats were buttoned, caps jammed over unshaven features.

"All out!" shouted the waiting mate.

Madden believed that force was greater than destiny. He turned and peered down the companion. Others of the watch paused about the figure of the crook at the foot of the ladder.

The mate asked: "What's th' matter? Clear out an' give th' deck-watch a chance to go below."

"There's a—sick man here, sir," a sailor answered. "Looks as if he had fallen down."

Madden grinned and closed his fist as the mate snapped:

"Fallen—hell! He's been struck! Throw him into a bunk, an' come up—all of you! What d'ye think this is—a yacht?"

The mate glanced at Madden.

"Take th' wheel," he said sharply. "You're a thug, eh? That fellow was knocked out—cold!"

"There's more will be," replied Madden, "before I reach port."

"Look out, Madden! Some day justice will get you!"

"Western ocean weather," grinned Madden taking the wheel. "Full an' bye, eh? She's a rum hooker and a rum crew. I'll smash 'em proper if they monkey with me." He pushed the wheelman aside.

He spat to the deck. The good that had been in him in the younger days was dead. He would bully the crew, and particularly the weakling whom he had knocked out. That would be his pleasure, mingled with whatever whiskey there was in the fo'cas'le.

Weeks passed, when suddenly the flying schooner struck a reef and staggered with the impact. Mountains of brine cascaded upon the deck. An avalanche of water drove the *Golden Shell* down and under. The three masts ground through the deck and churned like toothpicks in a hopper.

The fore part of the ship opened. The capstan upon the fo'cas'le deck crashed through the keel and kept on going down. Two lookouts crept up the deck and reached the wheel in time to ask the Brute what had happened.

Madden cursed his luck, glanced back once, with eager-twisted face, then plunged overboard, where he struck away from the wreck with both giant arms reaching over and over in tremendous strokes.

The suck of hollow space that followed told him that he had escaped in time. The *Golden Shell* had gone down. Some wreckage followed.

Daybreak found Madden clinging to a booby-hatch. His attempt to make a getaway seemed destined to fail. He was still two hundred miles from his destination—the Republic that did not grant requisitions. The hatch he was on was big enough for one man, provided the wind went down. The wind, however, strengthened over the morning hours.

Madden doubted if he could last out the day that was dawning over the harrowed western ocean. He knew that the coast was a hundred miles below the horizon. Toward this the booby-hatch was drifting. There were coast guards and police on the coast.

A voice came to him. He lifted himself upon the hatch, strained his eyes, then grunted as he saw the figure of the crook he had struck in the fo'cas'le, swimming dog-fashion in his direction. The weakest and the strongest member of the crew of the *Golden Shell* alone had survived.

From hollow to hollow of the waves the crook came—tired and almost spent. He reached up a thin white hand, scratched the edge of the booby-hatch, then rested an elbow upon its planks. He breathed heavily, his watery eyes fastened upon Madden's face as in a mute question.

Madden gave no notice. It was as if a worm had crawled into his ken. He had scant thought for the crook. He rose and peered about the wind-churned sea. He saw no other swimming or wreckage. The booby-hatch was the only floating thing in the wild waste of waters.

The crook took Madden's silence as permission to crawl up from the sea and spread himself across the hatch. His soaked legs and feet dangled over the side. He was careful not to disturb Madden. He was half in and half out of the water—tired unto death and thankful for the brief respite of life.

The current was cold, tinged with an icy nip that spoke of floes or bergs to the north and west. The outlook, if rescue did not come before the following dawn, was hopeless for the two men on the drifting hatch.

Madden weaved a piece of line about an eye-bolt in the center of the hatch. This he had fastened under his arms. It served to hold him without effort on his part.

He studied the hatch in the manner of a man who had nothing else to do. The eye-bolt in the center, the six planks, one of which had *Golden Shell* burnt deep within it, the rim of harder wood, resembled a trap door to eternity.

Madden's head went down. He glared, loudly cursed the crook, then thrust out his fist.

"Quit cryin'," he spat, "or I'll drop you cold with me fist!"

The crook moved to the slippery edge of the hatch. His teeth chattered. His weak eyes wandered in a hopeless appeal to Providence. He seemed like a punished dog, miserable with fear and terror of the gangster.

His fingers slipped from his hold—he went down and under the sea. He came up with weak strokes. He rested his elbows on the edge of the hatch. He knew that it was sufficient to support the weight of two men. He eyed Madden.

Madden allowed an idea to form within his brain. There was a spot upon the crook's chin where he had connected with it once before. He grinned as he eyed it, fascinated with a thought.

The wind freshened to a gale. The sea reached and dashed against the hatch. The crook hung on desperately. He whined once or twice. Madden heard it. It fired the blood within his veins. It was as if a worm or slug had crossed his vision or gotten in his path. He snapped his jaw shut, thrust out his chin, crooked his thick, right arm, and crawled across the booby-hatch. The crook saw him coming and whimpered.

The Brute waited. The crook's fingers seemed to be slipping from the hatch. His eyes appealed for a moment of life. Madden chuckled, hooked his fist upward, and crunched the frail jaw.

"Ugh!" said Madden with the force of his own effort. He did not watch the crook disappear beneath the sea.

Dawn came with Madden sleeping upon the hatch. With the dawn came a slight lowering of the wind and the sea. Madden woke with the sun beating down upon his salty face. He grunted as he lifted himself upon one elbow and surveyed the horizon. He rose, and shaded his eyes as he peered sharply to leeward where a speck was bearing down upon the booby-hatch that had been sighted by sharp eyes aboard a pearling schooner.

The boat's crew who took Madden to the shelter of the pearler, asked few questions. They did not guess he was a public enemy fleeing to a tropical port.

Madden climbed to the fo'cas'le deck, glanced back at the floating speck that marked the booby-hatch, then turned and faced the mate of the pearler.

"I want some dry duds!" he snarled savagely.

"You'll want a lot if you talk that way on this ship," said a half-breed mate.

"You heard me ask!" snapped Madden, clapping his hands on his case-knife.

The mate's answer was a quick, double snap of two flying fists. One caught Madden on the ear, the other drove into the Brute's stomach like a pile-driver.

Madden stepped backward, attempted to draw the knife, caught his feet in a coil of line and crashed to the deck. The mate was over him with the swiftness of a panther. His heavy heel ground against Madden's face as a hand reached the knife from its sheath.

"Now get up!" ordered the mate, as he backed away from the Brute. "Get up!"

Madden rose and felt of his ear.

"Give me my knife—that's all I want, matey. It's me knife I want. It's got me name on it."

"I'll keep it," said the mate of the pearler. "Knives are not allowed on this schooner. Men like you shouldn't carry them."

The Brute slouched to the fo'cas'le companion. He lowered himself down to the deck-planks, and surveyed the members of the pearler's crew, who were off watch.

Then he swaggered to a bunk and took possession by dumping its contents out upon the deck. Into this he crawled, glanced out once, then stretched himself to his full length.

He awoke and groaned as he moved his stiff limbs. He turned over and glanced out craftily. The crew of the pearler were making ready for the landing, which would take place in the morning. The fo'cas'le was almost deserted.

Madden knew that the country from which there was no extradition was several hundred miles farther south. It was destined that he was to go ashore on unsafe sands, not far from the reef where the *Golden Shell* struck.

He climbed to the deck, stretched himself, then glared around. The crew were lined along the rail. A thin wet fog shielded Madden's figure as he worked aft toward the galley. He ducked under a main-boom and crawled to a deck-light.

This was open. His eyes lighted with satisfaction as he made out the form of the mate directly below. The soft intake of breath, the flutter of lips at the exhaust, told the Brute that his quarry was sleeping. There were other forms in the gloom of the galley. The one nearest the opening was the mate's, however.

Lifting his head from under the boom, Madden turned slowly. None of the crew had noticed him. He lay flat, reached and ran his fingers over the mate's side in search of the knife. Feeling nothing, he strained and groped under the straw pillow. A cold chill at his finger's tip was his reward. It was the knife, placed there in hiding.

Again Madden raised his head and searched the deck. All eyes were intent upon the shrouded sea. He thrust half his body through the opening, hooked a leg about the sharp corner of the deck-light's coaming, and reached. This time his fingers moved between pillow and mattress with the caution of a professional thief. The point slipped once, he renewed the pincher grip, and drew his arm back slowly. The knife came with his hand.

He was grinning in satisfaction, when there sounded an interruption. It was from the fo'cas'le deck of the pearler. A shout had been followed by the stentorian cry:

"Reefs ahead! Starboard! Hard-a-starboard! Throw her hard-a-starboard!"

The mate woke and lifted his arm. It struck Madden's in the act of bringing out the knife. The half-breed's fingers seized the Brute's elbow. He struggled to free himself. He strained with knee against the deck. The point of the knife was over the mate's throat. Then, as a mallet strikes a ball, the main-boom of the pearler swung and as the course was changed, it drove Madden's arm and shoulder downward in a lunge.

The quick spread of blood across the white pillow—the quiver of the mate's body—the wide-staring eyes, told the Brute that the knife had gone through the jugular. He cursed the swinging boom and the red blade that gleamed upon the deck of the galley where it had fallen after the thrust.

Madden dropped to the deck. The shout of surprise and amazement within the galley told that the mate's body had been discovered. The red-stained knife, the opened jugular, the staring eyes and the open deck light all flashed before him. He swaggered forward, turned at the fo'cas'le companion, then climbed below and crawled into the bunk. He felt as if a thousand coppers were about.

There followed a silence as the pearler rolled. Afterwards came a hushed order. Then heavy feet stamped the deck. Madden waited like a convict in a cell.

The companionway was blocked as the skipper came down. An ugly automatic was in his hand. He curled swarthy lips.

"Madden," he said, "I want you! I am going to lock you up—put you in chains. Do you come quietly, or do you want some of this?" The skipper thrust out the automatic suggestively.

"So help me, Gawd. I didn't knife him, skipper!"

"Come!" The voice was iron.

"I went after me knife."

"You can tell that to the port judge. You're under arrest. You're going to be put in *carcel* ashore."

Madden knew "*carcel*" meant jail.

"Also," added the skipper, "I want to warn you that anything you say from now on may be used against you in the trial. You stabbed my mate!"

"What d'ye mean?" growled Madden, darting his eyes about like a rat cornered and trapped. "What d'ye mean by what you said? I'm innocent."

"Just what I said! You murdered the mate because he took your knife from you. He was following orders. You'll hang for it. That is the law of Tropicador."

Only destiny could explain the swinging of the main-boom of the pearler.

"You got me dead wrong. I didn't croak your mate. It was an accident."

"Throw down the cuffs, Bill," said the swarthy skipper, glancing up through the companion. "Throw them down—he's nice an' quiet—he is."

Danger weighed heavily upon the Brute's brain. The pitching pearler, the sound of the lapping waves, the shouts of the sailors and the creak of the blocks worried him. What had he done that he should be railroaded to the gallows?

The pearler made port on the coast of Tropicador. The police flag flying, brought a throng to the beach. The shore boat that put out was rowed by six negroes. In the stern of this sat three men in bright uniforms.

They minced words as they advanced on the Brute. One of the officers grasped Madden's arm with the assurance of authority. It was then that the Brute realized that he was to be taken to a black-and-tan court.

The fight that followed stirred the Porte. Madden charged his captors, with lowered head and a roar that a bullock might have made. His great, gnarled fists flayed about him in the manner of a bear in a swarm of tormentors.

The officers were dashed against the rail. One, Madden seized with a giant's strength, and hurled overside the ship. He turned and charged the crew who were approaching with belaying-pins and knives. Into their mass he lunged, bowled them over, then charged again.

Blows rained down upon his thick, bullet-like head. He brushed them off, rose to his feet, and bellowed with rage. There seemed no stopping him. The skipper held away until he saw the chance.

Madden, covered with blood and wounds, was getting the best of matters when the captain dashed into the squirming pile, poised the butt of his revolver, then brought it down just over the top of the Brute's swollen ear. The blow was well delivered. Madden grunted, milled in a circle like a scorpion, then fell, got erect, crawled to the rail and dove into shark-infested waters. He swam toward shore.

A group of soldiers were waiting near a breakwater. Out from tropical palms sprang more soldiers. The officers in charge shouted an order. Rifles went up. They swayed. They covered Madden's head as he reached the sands and staggered up the beach.

A flash came from a Mauser rifle. Bullets chipped stone from a sea-wall. Madden turned and twisted. He dodged between bags of coffee and bales of hides. He leaped over stones until he was driven into an ambuscade near where a courthouse loomed with sinister significance. Boats that had been lowered from the pearling schooner blocked the way to the sea.

Madden made for the leader of the soldiers. He resolved to sell his life in one bull's rush. A native in a poncho proved his undoing. He snatched a rifle from a soldier. He turned it, ran forward, and upended the butt beneath the Brute's outthrust jaw as Madden heard someone cry: "Look out, Captain Santander."

The blow was known in the Coffee Countries as a crusher.

Madden spun, fell face forward, and quivered on the sand. His right leg moved. He was very still.

The Brute had a vague memory of being dragged like a pig toward the breakwater. He felt arms under him. He was shoved forward. A dark period followed until he woke to partial consciousness.

The Captain of the Guard, flanked by two soldiers, stood talking with the sentry before a barred gate to a prison. Madden took an immediate dislike to the tropical officer.

The sentry shouted. A man appeared at a grating set in a stone wall. He had the air of authority. It was the warden. He came over the stones to Santander and exclaimed:

"*Señor*? You sent for me. What have we here? An American murderer? We can attend to him. Put him in a dungeon! He will have a fair trial and then we will build a gallows and hang him, American fashion."

This order, Madden overheard. He tried to get at the warden. A soldier raised a gun. He brought it crashing down on the Brute's shoulder.

Santander ripped Madden's shirt off.

"What muscles!" he exclaimed.

The warden curled a black mustache.

"Open the gate," he said to the sentry. "I'll call the witness from the pearling schooner and we'll try this white dog in the morning."

Madden was stripped in a stone-flagged court. His money was taken away by the warden. A dirty shirt, a long sash and trousers were tossed to him. He was led to a dungeon at the land end of the breakwater.

He turned his head. Bayonets followed him. He saw the naked blade of a saber. He eyed the high gray walls and heard the sound of the sea on the sands of Tropicador. It seemed a dirge to all his hopes. What had he done to be hanged in a foreign port? He expected his trial would be a kangaroo affair.

He heard the prisoners marching out on the breakwater. A guard unlocked the dungeon door. Madden stared in the sunlight. He was led to the courthouse. Santander, the warden and a score of sailors from the pearl ship were waiting.

The proceedings were perfunctory. Santander showed the knife. He explained how it had been used. The captain of the pearler gave his testimony.

Madden, the Brute, strained between his keepers. They dropped guns on his bare toes.

A judge, Santander and the warden, stood with their heads together. The warden glanced up. His mustache bristled.

"Hang him at daybreak," the judge said to the sergeant of the squad.

Madden leaped toward Santander. A bayonet pricked his legs. A gun was jabbed into his stomach. He went down.

Santander turned at the grated door that led from the courtroom.

"So perish all murderers!" he exclaimed.

"*Gracias a Dios!*" echoed the judge.

The Brute, on his way to the dungeon, heard the braying of bloodhounds. They were kept in a kennel attached to the prison. They vied with the guards to protect the shore end of the breakwater.

The guard pointed out a surer means to hold prisoners, when they reached the stones before the dungeons.

"Look there, swine," he grinned at the Brute.

Madden followed the bayonet point. It marked a spot on the water where swam a man-eating shark. The fin of this shark was notched.

"Our Black Warden!" remarked the guard. "Try and beat him, gringo."

Madden felt weak suddenly. He thought of the schooner that had struck a reef far from the hostile shore. Then he recalled the accidental killing of the pearling mate, nearer yet to shore.

"Wot in hell?" he sputtered. "Wot have I done fer Providence to treat me dis way?"

He noticed that the long breakwater was thrust out over the waves of Tropicador like a bent index finger. In its shelter, where it was calm, floated the navy of the Republic, the converted yacht *Admiral Cervantes*.

The guns of this ship commanded the breakwater and the prison. They were loaded with shrapnel. The gunners slept by the breech-blocks. There seemed no way of escaping.

Back of the Porte—from horizon to horizon—stretched the green walls of the jungle. Over the jungle, here and there, could be seen the spires of churches and the yellow walls of the city.

The bells of the cathedral towers rang for mass. Silently the worshippers hurried, bent head and devout, entering the cathedral door, one by one, as they would have entered the gates of Heaven.

Some knelt to the Virgin's shrine. Some bowed beneath a picture Murillo had painted, but most of the worshippers prayed long and earnestly for those who were appointed to die.

Had not Brute Madden slain a favorite pearlman? He was going to be hanged in the northern fashion. The *calles* that evening were filled with citizens. The band played on the *Prado*. Santander, who would be the hangman, showed his yellow teeth in a grim smile.

Out on the breakwater, after sundown, a scarlet-capped sentry walked before the dungeon doors.

The prisoners of the Republic were quartered like land crabs, in holes hewn in the rock. The way toward the shore was guarded by many soldiers. The sea was shark-infested. The chief of these sharks was the Black Warden. He made his meals from sun-bleached men who were foolish enough to attempt escape by diving into the sea.

Madden discovered the strength of the prison into which he had been thrown. The breakwater was built out of cubic-meter blocks of concrete. The stone where the dungeons had been quarried was part of the land rock.

His cell was a perfect cube—two meters long, and high and wide. He measured it by stretching out his long arms. An iron door was fitted into the stone at the front of the dungeon. A small hand-hole was well up in this door. It was used by the guard to pass in food or inspect the cell. A slide covered it on the outside. It moved now and then when the guard looked in, then dropped the slide.

Madden felt the walls. They were damp and solid. He examined his clothing. Captain Santander had furnished a shirt, a scarf and a pair of frayed trousers. His feet were bare. A stream of blood coagulated where the bayonet thrust went through to the bone in his leg.

His shoulder ached and his stomach was weak. He lay on the stones and wondered if there was any chance of escape from the gallows trap.

An escape must come, if it came at all, from his own exertions. The door would not be opened until daylight. That hour would bring the file of guards, the hangman, and an open grave somewhere on the beach.

"Wot a tough break!" thought the Brute.

He thought of rushing the guards and taking a chance of swimming from the breakwater. But there was the Black Warden with his blacker dorsal fin.

Rising from the damp floor of the dungeon at midnight, the Brute examined the door. It was set with huge hinges that pivoted on the wall. There was no getting at them. The lock was also on the outside. He had not noticed what kind it was. There was a band of thick iron, a hasp and a chain to break before he could get away. He waited, listened, timed the guard and attempted to reach his hand through the small hole in the top of the door.

He could not feel the lock because it was far down. He drew back his arm and let the slide fall. It made a slight noise that brought the alert sentry across the stones. This man hammered on the door with his rifle, then went away.

Madden heard the call of the other sentries.

"All's well!" they said in Spanish.

He grimly waited and walked back and forth. The spirit within him was not broken. He repeated over and over: "Wot a tough break! I didn't croak the guy I'm to be hanged for!"

An hour passed until it was one o'clock. The silver bells in the cathedral chimed and the sentries repeated their call from the watch-towers.

Crouching beneath the small hole in the door, Madden worked out part, but not all, of a plan for escape. Much depended upon the sentry. He was weak-chinned. He reminded the Brute of the crook aboard the *Golden Shell*.

Madden went over his adventures since he had fled from the States. He wondered how he had escaped the police's dragnet, only to fall for a job he never was guilty of.

The sentry passed the door on his walk to the edge of the breakwater. Madden listened and heard the roar of the surf on the river bar. The bell on the *Admiral Cervantes* struck the time, while the trade wind moaned.

Raising his right hand, Madden stretched his fingers wide. He crouched on the balls of his bare feet. His breath came swiftly, when he detected the sly approach of the screw.

The slide on the outside of the hand-hole was moved an inch. It moved another inch. A face blocked the light of the tropical stars. Eyes burned through the gloom. A swarthy neck showed over a red uniform.

Madden struck swifter than any jungle creature. He closed a gagging grip over the sentry's throat. He had done this same thing to many gangsters.

The rifle clanged to the stone. Madden extended his arm through the hand-hole. He worked his elbow out and, tightening his grip, braced his right knee against the door. There was no working loose from his fingers. Life was at stake. The Brute took care, however, not to slay the sentry. The man might be useful in an escape.

Hearing a choking throat-rattle, Madden relaxed his grip a little. He let the sentry down until the sharp iron of the door cut his arm. With his free, left hand Madden unwound the scarf from his waist. He looped this, thrust out the ends, and succeeded in noosing the sentry's neck whose tongue hung out like a black piece of leather. His eyes popped from their blood-shot sockets until his weak jaw clattered.

Testing the noose, Madden let go his grip on the sentry's throat. The screw's weight was now on the scarf.

Slowly the screw came back to life. He muttered a curse and tried to draw away from the noose. Madden jerked the scarf, braced his knee against the door, and pulled with both hands. The sentry relaxed in every muscle.

Waiting, Madden heard slow breathing outside the door. He wrapped the free ends of the scarf around his wrist, and said distinctly:

"You'll croak as sure as the sun rises tomorrow, if you don't do what I tell you. Yeah, y'u croak!"

The sentry shook his head when Madden stared through the opening.

"Where is the key to the lock?" asked the Brute.

The screw reached upward and tried to unslip the noose. Madden jerked it tighter.

"Where is the key? You yellow dog!"

"Santander—has the key, *señor*."

"Is the lock on the door? Spit it out!"

"No, *señor*."

"Is it on the bar, eh?"

"*Si, señor*."

"That's swell!" exclaimed Madden. He felt that his luck was getting better.

The sentry reached and grasped the sash. The Brute jerked it until the screw's hands dropped.

"What kind of lock is it?" throated Madden.

"A bull-lock, *señor*."

"What is the shape of the key?"

"Round."

"How large is the key-hole?"

"Big, *señor*."

Madden's brain worked rapidly. He had less than an hour before the sentry would be missed by the guards on the walls of the prison. The lock could not be smashed with a gun. The bayonet was not strong enough to twist the staple and hasp from the iron bar that crossed the door.

Drawing on the sash, Madden asked the sentry:

"When will the warden come?"

"At daybreak, *señor*."

"Who will be with him, you dog!"

"About twenty soldiers, and Santander the hangman."

Madden bared his teeth. He pressed his face against the iron of the door.

"Listen tu me!"

The sentry felt death in the gangster's tones.

"Turn the lock upward, yu!"

The screw reached, groped in the darkness, and upended the bull-lock so that its key-hole was on top. He held it in that position.

"Take your hands away!" snapped the Brute.

The screw's hands raised to the silken sash. Madden drew back his right arm, and hunched his muscles. The sentry's head was dragged against the opening. His cap fell off and rolled over the stones.

"Give me one ov your cartridges," growled Madden.

The sentry fingered a webbed belt and drew out a Mauser cartridge which he offered to the Brute.

The bullet was cupro-nickel steel. Madden bit around the cartridge, and compressed the brass shell. He succeeded in dragging away the bullet between his teeth.

"Now pour this powder into the lock, yu!"

The sentry's hand shook when he took the cartridge, filled with loose powder.

"Pour it all in! Hear me?"

Madden could not see the lock. He waited until the sentry dropped the empty shell, then he demanded another cartridge. He bit this open with his teeth.

"Fill the lock!" he ordered.

The sentry filled the lock and showed that the cartridge shell was still half full of powder grains.

Jerking at the sash, Madden eyed the sentry's top pocket. A bag of tobacco showed there. He gauged the length of the scarf. It was almost time for the guards to make a round of the breakwater.

"Quick!" grinned the Brute. "Your life is hanging by dis scarf. I'm going to choke you if you don't do just what I say. Have you matches?"

"*Si, señor.*" The screw's teeth chattered. He reached to his pocket and drew out a block of sulphur matches. He showed them to Madden, with a shaking hand.

"Swell! Light a scrap of paper. Touch th' powder off by it. I'll let you move to the end of the scarf. You won't be croaked, if you're lucky."

The guard's knees knocked together.

He tried to protest until the Brute jerked his sash. It throttled the screw until he gasped.

"I'll do it, *señor.*"

Madden loosened the sash. He was ready for any treachery. The screw tore a strip of paper from his tobacco bag, and laid this on the top of the lock. One corner touched the powder around the key-hole.

"Light it!" bulled Madden. "I'm gettin' tired ov stayin' in dis can."

A jerk at the sash indicated the sentry's attempt to escape. Madden drew him to the door—like a heavy fish on a line.

"Light that paper—y'u yellow-livered cur!"

A match was held in shaking fingers. It scratched upon the iron of the door. The sentry's teeth chattered like castanets. He held one hand over his eyes when he reached and touched the match's flame to the paper.

The flame crept toward the lock until a blinding flare was followed by a muffled concussion. The lock broke into a hundred pieces. The door shook and the sentry flung himself down. Madden pressed with all his weight and the door flew open. The iron bar clanged against the stone with a note of menace.

Untwisting his wrist from the sash, Madden leaped from the dungeon. He gulped the acrid air and sprang over the sentry. Shouts sounded from the land end. A rifle was fired. A bullet clipped the stones.

Intent on freedom, Madden raised his hands, took one quick step, poised a moment on the edge, then glanced at the dark waters. He saw distinctly the dorsal fin of the Black Warden. The shark had heard the explosion and turned toward the breakwater. White foam showed where it swam.

A second bullet rang from the land end.

Turning away from the edge of the breakwater, Madden lunged to the sentry, lifted him, hurled him into the cell and clanged the door shut. He picked up the rifle, twisted the bayonet and pulled it from the barrel. The bayonet was a dangerous weapon in his hands. He leaped into the sea, on the opposite side.

A third shot was fired at him as he swam with overhand strokes and dove

under water. He held his breath as long as he could. Coming to the surface
and glancing back, he saw lanterns moving from the direction of the barracks
where the screws were quartered.

The white line of cubic-meter blocks of concrete extended fully a mile
from the beach. It blocked the way for the Black Warden to reach him.
Madden started swimming vigorously away from the breakwater.

The tropic stars were bright. No moon was to be seen. Waves slapped
the Brute's face. He thrust the bayonet through the front of his shirt, ducked,
swam, and came to the surface when the current was setting toward a reef.
Black rocks lifted their fangs above the waves.

Often before Madden had swum a mile in surf. He reserved his strength.
The fortunate set of the current was with him and the screws had no mark
to shoot at.

A cannon's roar from aboard the *Admiral Cervantes* announced that word
of the escape was communicated to the warden and ports officers. Madden
had no fear from this gunboat. It would take it some time to get up steam.
The lax condition aboard South American ships was to be counted on. He
swam on, and his arms did not seem to tire.

Midway between the dungeons and the reef of rocks, the Brute trod
water. He glanced toward the sea end of the breakwater. He saw distinctly
the rushing wake of the Black Warden.

The shark had rounded the barrier. Its dorsal fin cut the waves as if it was
being denied its prey. Its speed was faster than Madden could swim.

He pulled the bayonet from his shirt when the shark disappeared. A swirl,
a leaping body, a flash of white belly marked the Black Warden as it started
circling Madden.

Again it closed upon him. He slapped the water and dove suddenly, grasped
the bayonet, and thrust upward, but missed the man-eater by an inch.

Alternately swimming and treading water, Madden waited for the next
attack. He threw himself to one side, went down, then turned his face upward.
He struck with an underhand sweep to his arm. Something menacing passed
between him and the surface of the sea. The sharp point of the bayonet went
through flesh and was almost jerked from his hand.

Blood stained the water. Madden realized that the shark would have to
turn over in order to seize him in its mouth. He took advantage of this fact
and jabbed into the dull-white belly.

No ripple showed on the surface when he lifted his head above the sea.
Madden paddled toward the rocks, then turned, doubled his knees, allowing
himself to sink, and opened his eyes wide.

The chance that came was not to be overlooked. The Black Warden—
twenty feet of gleaming hate—tried to seize its prey. Madden could not see
where to strike. He jabbed the bayonet upward and repeated the stroke. The

blows were not as deadly as his first ones. The bayonet's point turned and it was pulled from his grasp. He lay, floating, wondering if he had a chance for life.

The shark milled in a crimson sea and lashed the water. It turned over with the bayonet showing beneath a fin. Madden's last blow had reached the sea-cougar's heart.

Slowly swimming toward the rocks, the gangster turned once, threw himself on his back, and shook his head. The drops of water described a circle around him.

There were lights on the breakwater prison when he reached the first of the jagged rocks. A bell rang in the city and a flare of fire from the *Admiral Cervantes'* funnel indicated that she had steam up.

A jungle showed—alluring with its security. The stars began paling. It was almost daylight. Madden dragged himself upon a rock and rested a minute, then stopped and waded toward the beach. He cut his toes on sharp shells and pieces of coral when he reached a marshy place.

Through this swamp he staggered until a shelf of sand was beneath his feet. A fringe of cocoa-palms lined the coast and hid the breakwater from view.

He turned toward the security of the jungle.

Silver bells in the cathedral were calling the worshippers to early morning mass. Hammering indicated that carpenters were building his scaffold.

"Jees!" he swore. "I beat them!"

His joy was short lived. Out of the foliage rushed a squad of prison screws. They fired at the Brute, re-fired, and brought him down with a dozen wounds. They pounded him to unconsciousness, then dragged him toward the scaffold.

His shriek of defiance rang throughout the town when he came to life. His voice dropped note by note. His throat gagged as he declared to Santander that he had not slain the pearling mate—that the mate had come to death through the swing of the main-boom of the trawler.

He could not remove the thought from his mind that they were going to string him up because of an accident. The many blows of his life, the many punishments he had been able to endure were fair, for they were what was coming to him. The thought of dying like a dog at the end of a rope for something unnatural was what rankled. Madden wondered in his dull way why. Providence was working against him.

The place chosen for the Brute's taking off was upon the sea-beach. Willing natives had built a scaffold out of drift-wood. The finishing touches of this scaffold, consisting of the trap and the nine-stranded noose, had been adjusted by Santander.

Madden, two screws, a priest with a little book, and Santander climbed the scaffold. Santander adjusted the hemp with care. He stepped back then, and asked if there was anything to be said, as he rested his foot upon the trigger of the drift-wood trap.

Madden cleared his throat. His eyes lowered inch by inch in the weight of thought. He searched for speech. He counted the planks of the trap. There was a ring-bolt in its center. There was a burned place with a northern schooner's name there. His great jaw gaped. He shrieked in terror as he realized that—

He was standing upon the booby-hatch of the *Golden Shell!* On the hatch where he had wantonly murdered the little crook. It had drifted ashore near the prison on the breakwater.

Wait Outside

Don Murray

The men called them "rats," the warden "informers"—and they couldn't last long if anyone knew them. But until someone did a little informing as to who stabbed Jake Biddle, the whole third floor would pay for being square.

THE LONG PRISON DAY WAS DRAWING TO A CLOSE. In the chair factory, the men on the hand-sanding line were finished with their daily task, and had gathered around "Orphan" Blue's work bench, begging for a song.

Orphan grinned at the ring of faces.

"You guys don't wanta hear the song I've got for you today."

"Aw, yes we do, kid!" chorused the group. "Come on, let's hear it."

"All right, here goes. One of you keep an eye out for the supe or a brass hat. The name of this one is: 'You Can't Win!' "

Orphan had a pleasant voice and the men were always glad to hear him use it, even when on occasions the things he sang brought unpleasant memories to his listeners.

> "We know it's hard, but we know it's fair,
> To be caged in here like a grizzly bear.
> But we didn't tell you to pack a forty-four,
> Or break the window in that jewelry store.

We didn't tell you to crack that box,
We didn't tell you to lift those rocks;
But you did all that and then some more,
So here you are, behind the iron door!

The road of sin is a long, hard road;
And those who travel it carry a heavy load.
The road is long, the road is wide,
But the Law is waiting somewhere beside.
They are always waiting to bring you in,
And say to you, "You Cannot Win!"

So you come to the end of the road, and then,
Why, here you are, in the Meadville Pen!"

As the song ended there was a sudden commotion among the men, and a moment later a burly figure burst through the ring and confronted Orphan. It was Jake Biddle, the worst convict in Meadville.

"Hard" Jake Biddle was well deserving of his title. For most of his twenty-six years he had lived in places where he *had* to be hard to survive. The waterfront, the alley, and the reform school had been his home. His education was gained in the school of kicks and curses. But for all of that, he grew to prodigious size, tipping the scales at two hundred and twenty pounds, and standing six-feet-three-inches tall in his socks.

His feet taxed the limit of shoe sizes, and his hands were huge and knobby, but his head, set on a thick bull neck above massive shoulders, was curiously dwarfed, tapering to a point at the crown, giving him somewhat the appearance of a huge jug.

Few men cared to defy Jake Biddle, and to those who did, his methods of retribution were typical of him—brutal and direct, as more than one man in that group could testify.

Now, bursting through the circle, he planted himself directly in front of Orphan and thrust his chin to within six inches of the other's nose. He was forced to stoop considerably to do this, as Orphan could never have been called a giant, for he stood less than five-feet-six-inches even in his shoes. Jake glared at Orphan for a full minute, then rasped out:

"Yuh think yuh kin do as yuh dam' please aroun' here, don't yuh? Well, listen, yuh measly little deputy's rat. I told yuh tuh stop singin' them damned preachy songs or I'd bust yuh! Now, by cripes, I'm gonna do it!"

Orphan rocked back on his heels and grinned mockingly at the bully.

"Yeah?" he drawled. "Listen, Windy, it would take a real man to bust me! Don't forget, we're in a place now where we don't always fight with our fists. If you think I'm gonna stand my fists against your damned hard head you better think again! But—if you want to start something"—he jerked his thumb over his shoulder—"now's the time. The screw's asleep!"

"Yuh better wake him up, then," sneered Jake, "and tell him tuh watch out fer his little rat."

"Don't call me a rat, yah big baloney!" stormed Orphan.

"Who says not? Thet's what yuh are, an' that's what I'm callin' yuh! RAT!!"

Smack! Orphan's fist, backed by a hundred and thirty pounds of concentrated fury, smashed full in the snarling mouth, battering the thick lips to a bloody pulp.

With an insane bellow of rage, Jake lashed out, both fists flailing, but they met only empty air, for Orphan, blessed with that lightning-like agility which most small people possess, was easily able to evade Jake's bull-like rushes. He retreated warily until his groping hands encountered his work bench. He ran one hand swiftly across its top, seeking a weapon. After what seemed an eternity, his fingers touched a heavy rasp, used for removing glue from chair legs. Instantly he closed his hand on it and swung it before him.

"Now, Hard Jake!" he said in a low but nevertheless deadly tone. "Start somethin'!"

Jake, blind with fury, kept up his ponderous advance, his huge arms spread wide, fingers extended like monster talons. Once in that fierce grip, all would be over with Orphan. The smaller man knew it, but he was reluctant to use his weapon. That, he knew, would in all probability mean a murder rap to face. Still, thought Orphan grimly, "it's Biddle or me."

He grasped the file more firmly and drew back his arm. But the blow was never delivered. As Orphan raised his arm something whizzed past his head and buried itself full in Jake's chest!

The giant screamed hoarsely and clawed wildly at the thing which had struck him. With a superhuman effort he wrenched it free and a stream of blood spouted from the gaping wound, drenching the horror-stricken Orphan.

"Yuh did it!" he choked through frothed lips. "No, not you, kid—it was—" But before he could finish, his head sagged forward. He took a tottering step or two and crashed down against a pile of chairs, a ten-inch file grasped in a bloody hand.

Orphan, heedless of the protests of his fellow convicts, dropped to his knees beside the fallen giant and was attempting to turn him on his back when the floor guard, awakened by the crash, came running up.

Jake was attempting to speak again, but now his words were only broken whispers, so low that only Orphan could hear them.

"He got—me this time—" said Jake faintly. "He said he would—when I—beat him up—last time—" The words died away as a fresh gush of blood came to his lips.

"What's going on here?" blustered the guard, seizing Orphan by the shoulder. "Did yuh do this?"

"No!" raged Orphan. "And if I knew who did I wouldn't tell you!"

"We'll see about that!" he shouted, yanking Orphan to his feet. "Come along!"

He strode to his desk and jerked the telephone receiver from its hook. "Send a special and a couple of hospital men!" he directed, when he was connected with the hallmaster. "We've had a knifin' over here."

In a few minutes a special officer from the main building arrived and took Orphan in charge, while two hospital orderlies removed the stricken Jake. When they were gone, the guard lined the rest of the convicts up for count. It was a sober and frightened group of prisoners who lined up that night. Hard Jake Biddle was dying, struck down by someone in that group, and until that man was found and punished, the third floor would suffer.

Deputy Warden Joel Sanderson raised his eyes from the report sheet and gravely inspected the blood-spattered Orphan. The deputy was used to scenes such as this. Fourteen years as a prison official had accustomed but not reconciled him to them.

Deputy Sanderson was an enigma to the convicts. His granite-like face, with its thin, pale lips, never changed expression, whether he was passing judgment on a man for some minor infraction of the prison rules or for inciting a riot. His eyes, too, behind the rimless glasses he always wore perched on his beak of a nose, never changed; cold eyes, as bleak and gray as the dismal walls surrounding the prison, they stared alike at everyone, a blank, gray mask, hiding his moods from the anxious-eyed men haled to his office. No man ever knew, after the deputy had weighed his case, whether he would hear the curt but welcome "Go to your cell" or the fateful "Wait outside."

"James Blue," began the Deputy. "This report states that you were involved in a brawl which ended in the stabbing of Jake Biddle. What have you to say?"

"Jake and I were fighting," admitted Orphan. "But I didn't stab him!"

"I said, 'which ended in the stabbing of Jake Biddle,' " replied the deputy sharply. "Do you know who *did* do it?"

"No, I don't! And—"

"That will do!" cut in Sanderson. "You were going to say that if you did know, you wouldn't tell. Now, let me tell you something. The guard on the third floor didn't know for sure that you had been fighting. You were covered with blood—all Biddle's—but that meant nothing, as you were kneeling over him at the time. No one would think you would go up against Biddle, but we were subsequently supplied with the information that you did!"

"A rat, eh?"

" 'Rat' is a hard word, young man. Let us say an informer, because I want you to do a little of it. I want you to inform me who stabbed Jake Biddle! Wait!" he said as Orphan was about to burst out. "I'm giving you your choice. You are due for a parole next month. Whether you get it depends upon whether the man who stabbed Jake Biddle is found and punished. We will find him eventually, but it will help you mightily if you tell me what Biddle whispered to you—" He was interrupted by an urgent knock on the door. "Come in!" he said sharply, and an orderly from the prison hospital burst into the office.

"Beg pardon, sir, for interrupting you," he said breathlessly, "but Hard Biddle just died. The doctor said you'd want to know it right away."

"Did he talk?" asked the Deputy.

"No, sir, not a word," replied the trusty.

"Very well, you may go," and he turned to Orphan and finished his interrupted sentence.

"I was about to say 'before they took him to the hospital,' but now, what did he say before—he—died."

"I—I didn't hear what he said," replied Orphan slowly.

"Are you sure?" questioned the deputy. When Orphan nodded his head, he said calmly, "Perhaps a night in the hole will refresh your memory. Wait outside!"

At nine o'clock the next morning, after spending a sleepless night in the dungeon, Orphan, hungry and thirsty, was again led before the deputy.

"I have some news for you," said that official shortly. "The informer whom I had counted upon to supply me with the name of the man who murdered Jake Biddle was killed this morning on the third floor as he stood in line for the count!"

"He had it coming!" exclaimed Orphan bitterly. "Whoever he was, he was a rat and he deserved it!"

"I beg to correct you," said the deputy coldly. "He was an *informer!* Get that through your head! No prison can be run without them! Once more, and only this once, I offer you the chance to tell me the name of the convict who is responsible for these killings. You are due for a parole next month, and as a married man you should do everything in your power to earn that parole.

"After what happened this morning, I cannot have you sent back to the hole in connection with this affair, but unless you tell me what Jake Biddle said yesterday afternoon and help to clear up this mess, I must consider it my duty to refuse to recommend you at the commission next month! You are married, but your wife may consider that twelve years is too long to wait for you. You will do best to tell me."

Orphan was white to the lips, but he clenched his fists and shouted: "Not by a damn sight! You'd 'a' done better to have left my wife's name out'a your rotten talk! She's stuck by me this long and she'll stick until hell freezes over, but there's one thing she wouldn't do, and I sure as hell wouldn't want her to, and that is to stick by a rotten damned *rat!!*"

The months went by, and Orphan still sanded chairs, but he no longer sang for his fellows when the day's work was done. Instead, he sat on his bench, or stared out of the window at the green fields, the trees, the yellow ribbon of the highway; brooding.

Frost came; the trees changed from green to yellow, from yellow to brown, and finally to gaunt black skeletons stretching their arms to the bleak skies of winter. Snow blanketed the fields and the highway, but still he sanded, and stared, and brooded.

Small progress had been made toward apprehending the third floor killer, but the third floor, and especially Orphan Blue, suffered. A few men were paroled from that floor, and no one could say whether or not the killer was among them, but they were still ruled by the deputy's iron law: "Tell or take the consequences."

Slowly the weary days dragged by until the first of February and the night of the fourth annual all-prison talent show.

A light snow was falling that night as the seventeen hundred convicts marched from their cells to the auditorium. As he crossed the yard in the slow moving line of gray-clad men, Orphan looked up at the black sky, and for the first time in many months he smiled.

It was not pleasant, that smile, and if Deputy Sanderson could have seen it he doubtless would have ordered Orphan back to his cell. For trouble was brewing in Meadville. Everyone knew it, but no one, not even the deputy, knew who was behind the trouble. But he was almost certain that it was the third floor, and as he sat in the balcony of the auditorium watching the men file in, he was trying to decide who might be plotting.

"There are four men who work on that floor who might be responsible," he mused. "Blue is the one I most suspect, but there is Sam Benevelo and Jud Higgins, each with fifteen years hanging over him. Too, they are known to be trouble makers. Benevelo led the '26 riot, and last year Higgins led a break from the dining hall. Then there is Joe Ager, the one the convicts call 'But' Ager. He is cautious, but—"

His thoughts were interrupted by the arrival of the warden and his party. The party consisted of the warden's wife and daughter, the deputy's wife, the state parole commissioner and his wife, the governor's secretary, and perhaps twenty-five more ladies and gentlemen, friends of the warden.

The deputy bowed to the guests; then he turned to the warden.

"May I have a word with you, Mr. Wells?"

"Certainly, Mr. Sanderson," acknowledged the warden, motioning his guests to seats. "What's on your mind? Nothing serious, I hope?"

"Well, not exactly," replied Sanderson. "But it may be before this show is over." He lowered his voice and pointed to the slowly filling area of seats below them. "Look at the men—sullen, restless, growling at each other. I am afraid—"

"Nonsense!" broke in the warden sharply. "They're just impatient for the show to commence."

"You may be right," answered the deputy in a level tone. "I hope you are. But remember, I am in daily contact with these men and I *know* them. Those men are brewing mischief—four of them in particular, and those four I am having carefully watched."

"Perhaps it is a good plan," agreed the warden. "Well, there goes the curtain; I must go and give my speech." And he hurried downstairs and toward the stage.

He mounted the platform to greet a stony silence. In other years there had always been at least a ripple of applause when he stepped on the stage, but tonight he faced a sea of set, grim faces, and for an instant he felt a twinge of apprehension. But he was a brave man, perhaps *too* brave; and certainly too confident of his power to rule these men, as he was to learn, all too soon.

"Boys," he began, "once more we are assembled here to witness the efforts of the best talent in the show world. The fact that they are confined in this place does not lessen their fame. We have some of the best known names in the theatre here, men who, like you, have made mistakes. It is our endeavor tonight to make you forget for a time where you are, to cheer you and to give you courage to continue, until the day when the gates shall open for you, and you will once more take your places in the outside world. If any of you carry a burden of sorrow or anger tonight, I ask you to cast it aside, and give us your wholehearted help to make this, our fourth annual entertainment, a huge success. I thank you."

As he stepped from the stage a faint, half-hearted ripple of applause arose, but the first-act curtain lifted before eyes of men that were, in the main, still sullen and morose.

The show was made up of a number of short features similar to a vaudeville program. The first act went off well enough, and received a fairly generous hand, and the deputy relaxed a trifle; but when the curtain rose on the second act, featuring Gustave Martel, the deputy, the warden, and all the guards sensed the change in the men.

Martel was not a popular man in the prison. Perhaps it was because he had little to do with his fellow prisoners. Therefore, they all considered him "stuck up," and some even went so far as to refer to him as an "informer."

But, be that as it may, Gustave Martel was a wonder violinist, and because the warden wished to impress his guests, he, with more egotism than discretion, included him in the program.

Martel started playing a weird, mournful selection, excellently rendered, but decidedly not the type of music suited to the convicts in their present condition. As the first note floated out in the vast auditorium it was echoed by a murmur from the prisoners.

At first it was only a faint whisper, as that of a breath of wind, forerunner of a mighty storm, sweeping across a forest; but like the wind, it grew until it was a mighty volume of sound, drowning the feeble notes of the violin, ever increasing, until the deputy, in desperation, rose to his feet.

But he had waited too long. As he left his chair, two figures in that vast group below him leaped from their seats. They were Sam Benevelo and Jud Higgins, the two worst convicts in Meadville, and, at the instant they left their seats, every light in the prison went out!

No one was ever able to satisfactorily explain the lights failure, but that it was part of a prearranged plan was proved when, in the stunned silence, the voice of Sam Benevelo roared out:

"Well, what're yuh rats sittin' here for? Let's go!"

For an instant following his words the convicts, still too stunned to move, sat there. Then with a shout which carried clear to the outside walls, the seventeen hundred freedom-mad prisoners surged to their feet, throwing chairs aside or seizing them to beat down the guards who opposed them.

Everywhere was confusion, it being impossible in the intense and complete darkness to tell friend from foe. In the ensuing melee many of the convicts were crushed and trampled by their fellow convicts mistaking them for guards. Everyone was shouting at once, the guards imploring the men to be quiet and resume their seats, the convicts answering them with curses and demands to be let out. It seemed impossible, but above that bedlam of sound rose a voice, vibrant, compelling, momentarily halting the crazed men.

"Listen, you halfwits!" came the voice. "This is Orphan Blue. All of you guys know I got as rotten a deal as any of you, but let me tell you—you're a bunch of damned boneheads to think you can get away with this! You can't win, and you know it. Most of you have been in riots before. How many of you got away? Not a damned one! What did you get when it was all over? Six months in solitary for the guys who led the break; loss of all privileges for the rest of you. Rotten grub, soup—beans—more soup! Hard work—damned hard—and a hell of a lot of it! And you do it on moldy bread, and beans, and soup! If there's anybody with a brain in this gang—SIT DOWN!!"

The deputy listened and marveled. Orphan Blue, one of the four men he had suspected of being at the bottom of all the trouble, was actually trying to avert the riot! For a moment, when the shuffle of feet and scrape of chairs told him that some of the men were heeding Orphan's words, he had a wild hope that Orphan might succeed, but Benevelo's words dashed that hope and sent him rushing into the thick of the struggle.

"Tuh hell wit' yuh!" shouted Benevelo. "Anybody what ain't got guts enough tuh git in this, stand aside or git hurt. Let's GO!!" And again the clawing, fighting mass surged forward.

They were still confronted with the problem of the door. It was locked from the outside, and the only one who could open it was the guard stationed outside. But the rioting men soon solved this difficulty. At Benevelo's shouted command, a hundred or more of them, led by Jud Higgins, groped their way to the balcony, where the warden's party huddled in a frightened group.

The warden heard them coming and drew a pistol from his pocket. "The first one of you who comes a step nearer gets this!" he shouted. For an instant there was a dead silence on both sides, then one of the men in the warden's party broke under the strain of waiting in the darkness and lighted a match.

"Put that out!" exclaimed the warden. But his words came too late. The flare of the match revealed him, pistol in hand, to the convicts. A chair, hurled by one of the rioters, floored him, the pistol flying from his hand. There was a rush, a quick scuffle, and when it was over everyone in the warden's party found his hands pinioned by convicts. Then Jud Higgins scratched a match and held it so its feeble rays fell on the warden's face. He spoke rapidly.

"Yuh're goin' downstairs wit' us an' tell that screw at the door tuh open it—see? If yuh don't, we croak these guys"—he waved his arm at the male guests—"one at a time—an' the women—"

The warden returned the leering gaze until the match flame died down.

"You win," he said grimly; "this time—but—you can't win in the end. What have you in the way of weapons? My pistol. Perhaps one or two more. A few knives. You think you can go against our rifles and machine guns with that?"

"That's enough out'a yuh! We—"

His words were cut short by a fusillade of shots from outside the building. Special officers, armed with Thompson guns and repeating shotguns—riot guns—and carrying electric lanterns, had arrived from the central guard tower. The first burst was fired as a warning; then John Delmar, the Head Keeper, stepped to the door and shouted: "We're opening the door now! Come out; and come peaceably, or we'll mow you down!"

But the armed guards had not reckoned the devilish cunning of the men behind the riot, for when the doors opened only a few score convicts marched out, and before each one was a human shield, the warden, the deputy, the parole commissioner, the other guests—both ladies and men—and the guards!

Benevelo was in the lead, the warden before him. He stopped just outside the door and snarled at the guards:

"Listen tuh us! Youse birds march right back intuh the main hall, an' stay there! But before yuh go, yuh kin lay them toys down—we'll need 'em. Git goin'!"

Seething with rage, but helpless under the menace to the womenfolk of the group, the warden nodded to the guards to comply with the convict's order.

"They've got us for now," he said. "Do as they say."

The machine and riot guns were surrendered, to be seized upon by convicts who poured from the auditorium. The mad rush across the yard to the wall, and freedom, began.

As the wildly shouting mob neared the wall, a flame stabbed the darkness from the wall top. There was a roar from a convict-manned machine gun; a scream, and a dark shape hurtled to the ground, to be soon trampled into an unrecognizable bloody mass by the convicts milling at the base of the wall, shouting for ladders, ropes, anything to use in scaling the wall.

Two ladders were found and thrust upward, and in an instant they were both crowded with men frenziedly seeking the wall top. One ladder broke under the tremendous load, pitching men in a sprawling heap on the frozen ground.

Instantly Benevelo, on the other ladder, lashed out with his foot at the face of the man below him.

"Git down, damn yuh!" he raged. "There ain't no room fer yuh on here!"

"There ain't, huh? Then yuh don't go over, either!" and the man grabbed Benevelo by the legs and twisted him from the ladder. The leader's fall was broken—at a frightful cost—by the men on the ground. There was a sickening crunch as he fell among them; and when he staggered to his feet, four men lay on the ground, screaming in agony, while two more lay still, their necks broken.

At last one man gained the top of the wall. He carried a rope to affix to a wall light standard to assist him in reaching the ground safely. But as he reached out to fasten the rope, the lights, with the same startling suddenness as when they had gone out, flamed into dazzling brilliance. Taken utterly aback, the convict stood blinking foolishly for a moment, and only a moment, for the guards, armed again, had mounted the wall and a withering hail of bullets blasted him down.

The convicts answered with a fierce barrage from their machine guns and the deep boom of the riot guns added their battle note. On top of this, and the fierce shouts of the convicts, the prison siren added its terrifying note to the general uproar.

The guard's terrible fire soon drove the convicts from the wall, and as the merciless hail of death continued, their courage broke and they began a confused retreat. The chair factory was the only place that offered refuge, and toward this they fled, only stopping long enough to seize some heavy timbers from the drying shed to use as battering rams.

Once inside the building, the convicts milled around their leader, uncertain as to their next move.

"Now we're in here, what do we do?" growled someone. "Why in hell didn't we go through one o' the gates?"

If the leader heard, he gave no notice of it. It was evident that whoever asked the question was a new man, unfamiliar with the operation of the gates.

Once, years before, when the gates were fitted with individual locks, each operated by a turnkey, the prisoners had staged a break, overpowered the turnkeys and gained the outer gate. There, if their courage had not failed before the threat of the riot guns and rifles in the hands of the wall guards, they would undoubtedly have succeeded in opening the last gate and making a wholesale escape.

Soon after that, the new type of electrically operated automatic gates were installed. Every gate in Meadville except one was of this type. In the event of electric power interruption, the gates remained locked, and in an emergency, that one gate, manned by a guard in a bullet-proof cement cage was the only exit from the prison—unless one scaled the walls.

Orphan Blue was among the rioters. When Benevelo roared out in the auditorium: "Come on or git out!" he had followed the mob in a desperate hope that he might still stop the riot. Now, his brain in a whirl, he found himself trapped with the five hundred or more convicts who still defied the guards.

A raking volley from the guards who had pursued them across the yard finally drove the convicts from the first floor to the second, and at last to the third—the top—floor, where they prepared to make their last desperate stand.

A number of them were wounded, and downstairs, on both floors, men lay, still and lifeless, mute testimony to the folly of their attempt to win. The guards, too, had suffered, for all of the dark forms sprawled on the frozen ground of the prison yard were not convicts.

Outside, the wind was mounting in a rising gale and snow was falling, sweeping across the yard and eddying around the factory building, cutting the faces of the guards crouched in the lee of the drying shed, waiting for a sign of surrender on the part of the convicts. Now and then they fired at the dark third floor windows, drawing intermittent flashes from the besieged men.

At last Benevelo broke under the strain.

"Listen, youse guys," he said in a rasping whisper. "We ain't gittin' no place here. Some o' them screws might be comin' up the stairs now! Whadda yuh say we make a rush fer it?"

"Yeah?" asked Jud Higgins. "An' git hell shot out'a us? Why, hell an' damnation, Sam, we wouldn't git out of the door 'fore they'd mow us down!"

An uneasy silence followed his words. From somewhere a match flared and a cigarette glowed. At that, Benevelo flew into a sudden rage.

"Put out thet damn match!" he shouted. "Yuh wanta burn us outa here?"

"But" Ager, the man who had lighted the cigarette, ground it beneath his heel and said querulously: "But what the hell, Sam, I bin smokin' downstairs. I *gotta* smoke!"

"Like hell yuh gotta— *What's that?*"

An acrid odor assailed the convict's nostrils, and a moment later a thin wraith of smoke rose before the windows!

FIRE!!

The shout was echoed by a half thousand fear crazed men. For the space of perhaps ten seconds fear held them paralyzed.

Orphan was the first one to recover. With a cry he leaped for the stair door and flung it open. A fierce wave of heat accompanied by a terror-inspiring snapping and crackling made him fling it shut instantly.

The men crowding behind him turned and raced for the two elevators situated in the center of the building, but by the time they reached them, flames were already pouring from the shafts.

They were trapped!

An ear-splitting crescendo of shouts, curses and screams arose as the frightened horde battled their way through the choking smoke to the windows. The iron bars precluded any possibility of escape there, but at least there was air, cool, fresh air, and the weaker men were trampled under foot as the windows were jammed with choking men.

The prison siren, silenced when the rioters were driven into the chair factory, again started its wailing, but this time in a different tone, and in a series of short, screaming notes—the fire-signal.

Five miles away, in the town of Meadville, the firemen dashed out in the storm in answer. The non-rioting prisoners manned the prison fire department and rushed to the battle, but from the first they realized it was a hopeless fight. The building was old, and with wood stocked on every floor in addition to the paint on the third floor, on the finish line, the flames, fanned by the fierce gale, roared their way upward, every second bringing them closer to the trapped men.

Benevelo, when it seemed certain that no help could reach them, lost his head completely and dashed away from the window toward the fiery stairway. The stairs themselves were of steel, and perhaps he had some wild idea that he could fight his way through the flames. But for the second time that night Orphan's voice halted him.

"Get something to use for a ram!" Orphan was shouting. "Saw down one of these posts—anything. Break down that door to the roof! I'll get you birds out'a here if you'll listen to me!"

Men rushed through the blinding smoke frantically seeking something which would serve to batter down the door, and after losing precious seconds in their mad search, they broke into the tool locker and secured two saws.

One on each side of the square timber, they attacked it feverishly and at last succeeded in severing it at the base; after which it was but the work of an instant for a score of them to wrench it from the ceiling. A single blow of the ram, manned by the terror-driven convicts, tore the door from its hinges, and they poured through to the temporary safety of the roof.

"What're we gonna do now thet we're here on this damned roof?" gasped Benevelo.

"Follow me," said Orphan confidently, "and you'll be on the ground in no time."

"Whole?" asked Ager, doubtfully.

"Whole," repeated Orphan. "But we've gotta hurry!" And he led the way through the clouds of smoke and around the blazing penthouse to the end of the building.

Below him was a two-story addition, housing the first and second floor sawmills. From the roof of this building ran a huge, galvanized metal pipe, supported from the ground by stout beams. It was a sawdust conveyor, drawing dust from the hoods over the saws to furnaces in the powerhouse.

"Get the idea?" asked Orphan, pointing to the snow covered roof below them. "It's an easy drop down there, and you can scramble down those beams easy. Let's go!" And he leaped out. He landed in the deep snow on the almost flat roof, and waved to the waiting men.

An instant later the air was filled with flying bodies, and too late, Orphan opened his lips to shout a warning for not too many men to jump at once. But someone struck him, throwing him to the edge of the roof. He clawed wildly for a hold on the slippery surface but to no avail, and an instant later he felt himself sailing through space. He landed on his feet with a force which sent a jarring shock through both legs, followed by stabbing white-hot needles of pain. Then things went black before him.

He opened his eyes to a white ceiling from which hung a shaded light. Slowly, painfully, he turned his head. White walls and white cots met his gaze. Slowly it dawned on him that he was in the prison hospital. As his mind cleared he tried to remember what had happened to him. He became aware of a dull throbbing in both legs and an ache in the back of his head. His exploring fingers encountered a swathe of bandage on his head, and when he tried to move his feet he cried out sharply.

"Come out of it, have you?" It was Dr. Bradshaw, the prison surgeon.

"You took quite a tumble a while ago," he said, his voice gentler than Orphan had ever heard it. "I'm afraid Benevelo here, though, got it worse than you did."

Orphan's eyes followed the doctor's hand. On the next cot a figure writhed in agony, muttering unintelligible sounds. Slowly the words formed themselves into phrases, and the doctor moved closer to catch them.

"He wants to talk to you, James," said the doctor presently.

"Yuh—beat it—Doc—" gasped Benevelo. "Jus' fer a—minute—I—gotta tell the kid here—somethin'—"

The doctor looked at Orphan thoughtfully. "You are supposed to have heard Jake Biddle's last words," he said slowly, "and you wouldn't tell what—"

"Listen, Doc—" broke in the dying Benevelo, "beat it, or—I don't talk—see?"

The doctor shook his head doubtfully, but moved out of hearing, giving attention to the injured and fire scarred men on the other cots.

"Kid?"

"Yes, Sam."

"I'm goin' out—in a minute. They'll be no more—'Wait Outsides' fer Sam Benevelo— But—I threw thet file—an'—knifed thet rat. Tell the deputy—so's the third floor won't ketch—no more hell—fer it. So long—kid."

As the lines of pain in Sam Benevelo's face eased out in a faint smile of content, the mournful notes of "Taps" echoed faintly from the prison rotunda. The riot was ended.

Next morning, Deputy Warden Sanderson stood before Orphan's cot, a telegram in his hand. His eyes were still a blank mask through his rimless glasses, but a faint smile lurked in the corners of his mouth.

"Well, Jimmy, I believe I've said my last 'Wait Outside' to you! And I sincerely hope I have. The governor is rushing you a full pardon for your work last night, in attempting to avert the riot, and for leading almost five hundred of your fellow prisoners to safety."

"I'm glad, Mr. Sanderson," said Orphan simply. "But before I leave I've got to tell you something. Sam Benevelo asked me to tell you that there is no one now who worked on the third floor who is responsible for the murder of those two men."

"I see—" said the deputy. "And I thank you. I will not retract my statement that a prison must depend upon informers, 'rats,' as you so aptly name them. But I will say this much—that day in my office when you defied me, you won my respect by taking the part of a man! And now"—the smile was threatening to break forth—"I am asking you, as Joel Sanderson to James Blue—why, when you had been so sullen all winter, and had every prison official keeping an eye on you, did you try to stop that riot last night?"

A mocking smile curved Orphan's lips for an instant, then he became serious.

"Mr. Sanderson, as convict No. 76483, I would never tell you. But as Jim Blue, it was because I was all set to go over the wall last night—alone—and that riot knocked my plans all to hell!"

December 1930

To Our Readers

EVERY "STIR" IS A VOLUME IN STONE.

Without Law this country would be a howling wilderness peopled by savages.

The laws are the backbone of our great civilization.

There would be no advancement if some sort of punishment was not meted out to those who violate the code of fair dealing.

We have fines, work-houses, prisons and electric-chairs to keep men good. A penitentiary is a place of exile wherein the transgressor is removed from the tribe until the tribe believes he will behave himself.

There is considerable human interest connected with the man inside. Half of literature contains something about a crime. The body is penned in prison, the mind may soar to heights such as were dreamed of in Jack London's *Star Rover*.

PRISON STORIES tells how it feels to be a four-time loser, a die-hard, a demon, a lifer or a desperado. It relates about the so-called innocent man of whom one warden found so many, that he concluded he was the only crook in the Institution.

You will find no cheap maudlin sympathy in PRISON STORIES. The day of the Reformer is gone. The penal world of today relies on education to lift an inmate out of his position. The fierce white light of applied justice now fuses the crucible of crime.

This magazine is a lamp on a dark subject that concerns everybody.

We are our brother's keeper and we should know more about the man inside.

Faithfully yours,

HAROLD HERSEY,
Publisher.

[This monthly column started in the second issue of PRISON STORIES (December 1930). Following are selected letters.]

(In the argot of the Underworld a "kite" is a note or letter sneaked in or out of "stir" or prison, by a guard or trusty.)

•• December 1930 ••

Sister Liked It

Dear Editor:

Just finished digesting PRISON STORIES and turned it over to my kid sister to see if she liked it. I think you got a bright idea in that mag and I hope you continue giving us as good or better stuff in the next issues. I never did a bit myself but I got a brother in the can and visit him every other Tuesday.

From what I can see of the inside of those places you have hit the nail on the head with PRISON STORIES. A lot of big Movies lately like *The Big House*, *Numbered Men*, *The Last Mile* and *Condemned*, were about prisons. Who gave you the idea of starting a magazine along the same lines? I particularly like the Burkholder story about Molly O'Hare. The shorts were good too.

P.S. My kid sister wants more about girls in the magazine.

JAMES MCCLEAR,
Larimer Street, Denver, Colorado.

From a Detective

Dear Editor in Chief:

I happened to pick up your magazine yesterday and finished reading it this morning. I am a detective connected with the Kansas City Police Department. We Dicks are too critical about underworld stuff, I guess, but there were a lot of good moral lessons for the poor suckers who try to beat the law, in PRISON STORIES. Most of the grafters and crooks I've helped send up would have made a lot more money at honest jobs. You got the prison atmosphere all right in your magazine. I suppose you got your idea of starting a PRISON MAGAZINE by seeing so many Detective Magazines on the newsstands. I ain't going to crack too wise, but when there's so many Dicks written about there ought to be one magazine concerning what happens to the boobs they catch.

Yours faithfully,

M.J.B.,

Ward Parkway, Kansas City.

A Boosting Knock

The Editor:

Say, the best thing to do with your new PRISON STORIES is to call them all in and throw them over the walls to the boys inside.

They read anything they can get. I don't!

LAVERE SHAFER,

New Oxford, Pennsylvania.

A Hard-Boiled Egg

Dear Chief:

I ain't signing this letter for the good reason I'm a four-time loser and am laying low from the Coppers just now. I read your new magazine and like it as well as I do GANGSTER STORIES, maybe better. Your writers made a bunch of blunders about prison slang, but maybe I'm wrong because I ain't been in all the big houses yet.

Say Ed, why don't you run a novel like *Monte Cristo*? That was some prison escape. And there's another one, "Foul Play," that's about a guy on parole. He went down to Australia like they send them to Devil's Island, these days.

As I said, I ain't signing this letter because there is a warden out west who missed me once, maybe more than once, with a Winchester.

A FOUR-TIME LOSER.

Always the Under-Dog

Dear Mr. Hersey:

One of the cons in this penitentiary handed me PRISON STORIES and asked me how I liked it. Frankly I'd say yes and no. I've been a guard here going on eighteen years. It always struck me in reading about prisoners that there were too many innocent ones and too many brutal guards. Why don't you begin right in your magazine by publishing a story now and then with the guards as heroes, or the wardens. They have a hard life, like firemen and policemen. Ask the life insurance companies what risks we run.

Am going off duty now. Going to a wife who never knows whether I'll be brought to her on a stretcher. So Mr. Hersey, consider that there are two sides to the prison question.

"JACK —,"
Canyon City, Colorado.

Dear Hersey:

Go to it, old boy! I've seen your work before. This new "PRISON MAGAZINE" looks great. It ought to hit about a million men on the outside who have done time and are keeping it under cover. I think there is a little bit of larceny in all of us. I copped PRISON STORIES from a corner newsstand. Didn't have the price when I spied it. Maybe I'll slip it back when the newsdealer isn't looking. When is the second issue out?

FRANK OMSTEAD,
White Plains, New York.

•• January 1931 ••

Dear Editor:

I liked your opening issue of PRISON STORIES so much I know you are going to shorten my bit by me perusing the magazine as it comes out. Wish it appeared more often. Can't you make it a weekly? Time, and I've got plenty of it, would pass quicker. I intend to join the Navy some day, if they will let me. Do you think they will?

HUNTER STREET,
Ossining, New York.

A Brief Kite

Editor Prison Stories:

I am writing this on a postal-card because I only got a one-cent stamp. Your new magazine is great. I am wondering how this fellow Hersey gets out all the mags he does. Does he read all the stories sent in by cons? I hope he don't have to. There are some bad penmen inside of prisons.

JACK COLLINS,
Utica, New York.

From Old Arizona

Dear Editor:

I never stole anything in my life. I have never been nearer a penitentiary than ten miles. Can you explain why I like to read about prisoners and prisons? I ate up your first issue and just got the second. PRISON STORIES, to my mind, satisfies an appetite I've always had. Gee, print something about

Billy the Kid and Tracy. I think Billy was a better shot than Jesse James. It takes Old Arizona to turn out the bad men.

ED SCHAFER,
Rural Box 276.

From Hollywood

Dear Mr. Hersey:

I am a movie extra and get a call now and then from Central Casting to do a bit in prison stories. Why do they pick me out as a convict? Is crime stamped on a man's face? I am as honest as can be. Think Leverage's and Burkholder's stories would go good in the talkies. Both those writers understand dialogue. "The House of a Thousand Doors" [December] is certainly inside stuff. Out here we are lucky to have one door to our bungalows.

NIGEL FRENCH,
Care of Universal.

A Heart Story

Dear Mr. Hersey:

I just came out of a woman's prison and saw a copy of PRISON STORIES on the newsstands. I bought it, although I'm living now in a Home for Old Women. Could you, through PRISON STORIES, help me find my son who was last seen in a court room at Boston? He may be wealthy now. He goes by the name of Claude Armstrong, because I disgraced his right name. Do you think he will see this letter? If you hear from him please communicate with MARY DELANEY, Home for Old Women, formerly called God's Pocket, New York.

A Hot Grouch

Editor Prison Stories:

You have got a crust pretending PRISON STORIES is the real dope on prisons. Them what served time don't write about it. None of your writers did a prison bit. I can tell.

JAMES OLIVER,
Atlanta, Ga.

From a Sailor

Hello Captain Hersey, or are you only an editor?

I'm a gunner's mate aboard the Lexington. Saw PRISON STORIES and bought it two days after they let me out of the "brig."

Don't blame them. I beaned a fresh guy with a marlinspike. That's my only experience in prison, that brig aboard the Lexington. Can't you give us a naval-prison-story where the hero is always getting framed and put in the brig? That ought to go big with us guys.

Maybe a story about The Prison Ship would hit us. I saw one of your mags in the cockpit of one of our bombing planes, the other day. The pilot or some passenger went up to find a quiet spot to read it. We got a lieutenant who does a lot of sleeping in the air. He says it's too noisy about ship.

GORDEN JONES (not Davy Jones),
U.S.S. Lexington.

Queenie Says a Word

Editor in Chief, Prison Stories:

I have a little Maltese terrier who carries the newspapers and magazines home from the drug store, where I buy them. I bought PRISON STORIES and Queenie, my dog, refused to carry it. Why? I whipped her, but it didn't do any good. I don't believe in signs, because I thought the magazine was pretty good. What struck Queenie?

GRACE HOLLINGER,
Houston, Texas.

A Gold Digger

Dear Editor:

I'm a gold-digger, right on Broadway, and I live at one of the best hotels. I've got a sugar daddy and a boy friend. Sometimes I'm back in my hotel rent. The other day I carried in a copy of PRISON STORIES. You ought to see the dirty look the house detective gave me. The fresh thing. I guess there was a lot in the magazine that sleuth don't know about. Don't use the name of my hotel if you publish this letter.

TESSIE,
Just Broadway.

From Montreal

My Dear Mr. Hersey:

Been reading your magazine, PRISON STORIES. No fault with it, old chap, at all, except we in Canada like to read a Canadian story once in a while. We get fed up on American stories. The history of the Canadian Mounted Police ought to furnish your writers with an idea about a Northern Prison. Some of the most dangerous scamps in the world are in durance vile, up here. And, Mr. Hersey, we have no second timers or recidivists. Once is enough. They are always printing stories in American Magazines about "Get Your Man." There is a movie in Montreal this week about a long chase by a Mounted Policeman after a criminal. He got his man! The kind of prison he was put in afterward, would make a good story.

• • •

Chicago

Editor Hersey:

Just went through PRISON STORIES, from cover to cover. I like it and most of the prison yarns. This town isn't as bad as New York, but the gangsters here are more given to the limelight. I saw one hanged in Cook County Jail, years ago, who had to be strapped in a chair in order to be carried from his cell. I never got over that experience, neither did he.

ARCHIE GRUBB,
Union League Restaurant, Chicago, Ill.

He Likes Our Mag

Dear Editor:

Just finished PRISON STORIES. Big idea you've got, Mr. Hersey. I would suggest you have some reformer buy a copy for every prisoner in this country. It would do them a world of good. Why don't you send samples to the wardens and ask if your magazine will be allowed in prisons? I see nothing derogatory in PRISON STORIES. Each yarn teaches a lesson, and a bitter one. Can't sleep until I see the second issue. Hope it is on the newsstands soon.

JAMES CONNOVER,
Regent Post, Scarsdale, New York.

Rough On Rats

Mr. Editor Hersey:

I read PRISON STORIES and one thing I like about it is the reason it is "rough on rats." I had an experience once where a "rat" squealed on me, and got me in a bad jam. I wonder how many so-called square-guys outside would become stool-pigeons and warden's pets inside? A plenty. Most wardens use them, but hate their guts. So do the police. I did one bit, Up-River. Kerchway was warden then. He was a gentleman. Gave me a whole box of cigars when I left. Toddle along with your second issue. I'll eat it up, like a squirrel eats nuts.

TED COX,
Harwood Grange, Upper Mountain Avenue,
Montclair, N.J.

•• February 1931 ••

Rough On Pugs

Dear Editor:

I just devoured your second issue of PRISON STORIES. It hit me right above the belt. I'm a prize-fighter and have knocked out a few tough babies here in Los Angeles, but you got one or two in your mag that are tougher than I ever ran up against. That guy in "The Prison Demon," for instance or The Tiger, in Burkholder's story. The wardens ought to turn those kind of guys loose and let them earn an honest dollar in the prize ring. We have bouts out here, now and then, when we sic an American against a Chink, a Negro and a Mexican, all at the same time. That's just like some of your stories. Give us more of them, red-blooded with a punch in each page.

THE FRESNO KID,
Walker's Training Camp, La.

This One Is Nervy

Mr. Editor:

How do you feel about letting me do some writing for your magazine, PRISON STORIES? I have been in three workhouses, a county jail and was once two months on a chain-gang near New Orleans. I know what prisoners do and say but don't know exactly how to express myself. If I don't get a job writing I'm liable to get pinched when I get out, because I'm broke. My present address is:

J.R. DENNING,
Parish Prison, Louisiana.

The Queue Hold

Editor Prison Stories:

You haven't given us the real low-down on prisons yet. How about China? I was a prisoner there during the Boxer trouble and the only reason my life was spared was because I, being an American, didn't have a queue. The executioner absolutely refused to cut off any prisoner's head who didn't have one. He used the queue as a hand-hold.

H.J.C.,
San Diego, Calif.

The Principal Keeper

Dear Editor:

Your second issue of PRISON STORIES is a hot baby, and I like it because all the convicts don't say they are innocent. I hate a story about prisons where everybody is innocent. I don't believe two percent of the inmates of prisons are really innocent, and most of them had guilty knowledge. Give me some more of that kind of stuff. Do the initials P.K. come from his habit of always "peeking"?

SAM LARNER,
Indianapolis, Indiana.

Speaking About Speakeasies

Editor Prison Stories:

After reading your last copy of PRISON STORIES I went out and got a drink at a speakeasy—you know, one of those kind of basement places they look through a knothole and let you in. I started out and the bartender shouted at me, "Say, do you want to go to prison?" I asked him why. He said for not paying for the drink, which I forgot to do. I paid for it, but don't you think he was more of a lawbreaker than I was? How would that case go in court?

PHIL SHERIDAN,
Cottage Grove Avenue, Chicago.

Ace in the Hole

Editor:

I liked "City of Numbered Men" in your last issue of PRISON STORIES. The warden going down and becoming a convict to find out what was actually going on in his prison is a bright idea. But wouldn't his cellmate or the inmates recognize him? I think that's the weak part of an otherwise good story.

NATE BUSHELTON,
Rural Free Delivery, York, Pa.

A Snow Storm

Dear Editor:

The address at the bottom of this "kite" is from near a penitentiary where they think they can make men better by making them worse. They got the wrong idea in the can I am in. The Deputy Warden was a political plumber. The warden hasn't an ounce of brain above his neck. The screws come to work every morning after milking the cows. That's what we're against. We have a night school taught by a grafting banker who couldn't pass a third grade examination.

The other night when I had my cell light lit a pal of mine sent me PRISON STORIES, by a trusty. I knew what was inside of it, besides the stories. Three pinches of coke. I started sniffing the "happy-dust" and reading on. I came to a yarn about A Prison Demon. The pages danced before my eyes, the convicts became real, the lethal chamber's door opened and a big Mexican screw, in uniform, beckoned to me. Ugh! Say, I woke up and came out of it. Funny, wasn't it, I smelled cyanide, or something like it. How do you account for all of that? Maybe some con had smashed a peach-pit with his heel and released prussic acid vapors. Did anyone ever write about a doped book that made a slave of its reader? Such a thing could happen.

FRED CONDICT,
Ogden, Utah.

Kites and Molls

Publisher Hersey:

All of your writers in PRISON STORIES use the word "Moll" frequently. I would think some Mollie, a good English name for a girl, would storm your office and bust your head. And "kites" for smuggled notes is foolish. You are going to have bad luck if you don't quit trying to remake our language. See if you don't.

JANE OSBURN,
Rural Free Delivery, Route 12,
York, Pa.

Teasing the Kid

Dear Editor Prison Stories:

I am a regular reader of your *Blue and Red Band Magazines*, including the new one, PRISON STORIES. My profession is plastering, although I am out of work, just now.

There is a sad case back of us. A widow and one son were left without a penny when the widow's husband was hanged at our State Prison. I think he was hanged wrong. He was arrested after a robbery in a department store where the night-watchman was clubbed to death. Some of the dry-goods was found in his shack. A slick friend of his did the job, I think. He got away, although the police are looking for him. What I was going to protest against, if you can spare the space, is, why don't our state give the widow a pension if her husband was innocent? They do that in Europe. Her son, we call him "Freckles," came to my house the other day bawling his eyes out. He was afraid to go home, as he played hooky from grammar school. I asked him why he played hooky and he told me that all the boys and girls at school held up little pieces of string tied in a noose every time he came near them. I think there ought to be a law against that, don't you, Mr. Hersey? Maybe Freckles is a chip off the old block, but he doesn't deserve being reminded about his father. It will end up in making him a crook; see if it doesn't.

FRANK BLAINE,
Jersey City, N.J.

From a Hotel Man

Editor Prison Stories:

I notice quite a number of your PRISON STORIES left behind by guests. We collect all magazines and give them to the help. One guest that skipped without paying his bill had the following magazines in a pasteboard suit-case: Two issues of PRISON STORIES, one THE BARTENDER'S GUIDE, three DETECTIVE STORIES and a BIBLE. Can you tell me if the defrauder was an ex-con, a bootlegger or had just used the magazines and book to make his "luggage" look heavy? Our house detective would like to know.

JAMES MCPEARSON,
Hotel Walden, Chicago.

A Marine's Protest

Dear Mr. Hersey, Publisher Prison Stories:

After reading your second issue of PRISON STORIES I selected "The Prison Demon," by Carl Henry, as the best story in that issue. The gas-mask idea used in connection with a Lethal Chamber is certainly original. I do not think, however, that any chemical cannister slipped up under a death-hood would save a man from cyanide poisoning. The story was stretched there. We Marines all enjoyed your new magazines.

FRED LOVEJOY,
Kearney Street, San Francisco.

From a Coast Guard

Dear Hersey:

I am a coast guard stationed near Sea Bright, New Jersey. We patrol the beach, looking for rum-runners. One of your magazines, PRISON STORIES, was picked up on the sand. In it was a notation—"12 Cases Rye. 16 Cases Scotch. 2 Cases French Champagne." Whoever wrote those notations must have brought that load ashore. Or else his rum-boat was lost in a storm we have had recently. We are keeping the magazine as a curiosity or a possible clue, as there was a man's name written on the cover of it. It was the issue with a girl and two death-house guards on the cover.

EDGAR LEVITT,
Sea Bright Post Office, New Jersey.

From a Cowpuncher

Dear Mr. Hersey:

I have been reading your *Blue Band Magazines* for some time. The other day I bought PRISON STORIES. It has a *Red Band.* It ought to have a band of blood around its cover. Of all the murders and shooting I ever read about— that magazine has it. Say, are there any closed seasons for killings? I mean it. The other night I got up, after losing my month's wages at Black-Jack, and woke all the outfit declaring I was cheated by an ex-con we got with us. We searched his bunk and found "strippers" and loaded dice and a lot of crooked stuff in his mattress. He confessed and gave me back my money. Then we "took him for a ride," all right. He is riding yet toward Mexico. If he reaches Tia Juana I've written a friend to "ride him" some more. All ex-cons ain't saints, as we found out.

JACK O'ROURKE,
Sentinel, Arizona.

A Jim Dandy

Brother Hersey:

Collecting PRISON STORIES fast as they come out at the drug-store. They are as snappy as a dose of prescription whisky. Why I wrote this short note is that I have a brother in a prison in the east somewhere. He will recognize my name and let me know where he is locked up. Can you publish this screed?

TOD LOCKWOOD, JUNIOR,
Steamboat Springs, Colorado.

Mother Got the Mag

Dear Mr. Hersey:

I started something in our house when I brought home your magazine, PRISON STORIES. Dad is a professor at State College. My brother Ned is reading law with Seamour and Hicks. My sister is interested in prison reform. They all made a grab for the magazine. Some of the pages were torn. We went to dinner and afterwards Dad and Ned and my sister started looking around the parlor where we read at night. We all, including myself, looked at each other foolishly. We couldn't find the magazine.

I went up stairs to bed. There was a light in mother's room, later than usual. I opened her door. There she sat, propped upon two pillows, with her glasses on her nose, reading PRISON STORIES. Can you beat it?

BETTY O'LEARY,
Dodge City, Kan.

A Big Kick

Dear Publisher Hersey:

That's a dirty dig you handed us in the last issue of PRISON STORIES. I mean that story "The Prison Demon." Do you mean that a doctor in a western prison, where they use lethal gas, would go so far as furnish a condemned man with a gas-mask instead of a hood? Wouldn't that be noticed by the prison authorities? I'd say it would, unless they were very careless. That story may go all right elsewhere, but it won't go in Nevada.

TIM WINFIELD,
Goldfield, Nevada.

From a Professional Writer

Editor Hersey:

I saw a man reading one of the issues of PRISON STORIES on the train coming down from Camden, Maine, the other day. He had torn the cover off.

I'm a professional writer and I bet my next check that man was an ex-con. He had hold of something so "hot," he wanted it kept quiet.

Keep up the good work.

FRANK DON Q.,
Camden, Maine.

From Newport News

Say Editor Hersey:

What's the joke they put over on me yesterday when I came ashore from my ship? I got stewed and went with two first-class seamen to a newsdealer, after we left the speakeasy. I asked the guy in the news-store if he had a copy of *The Newport News*. He didn't crack a smile. He handed me PRISON STORY MAGAZINE and said I better be reading that. Did he mean I was going to be pinched for taking a couple of drinks—the first I'd had in five months?

CHUCK LUCK JOE,
U.S.S. Lexington.

A Window Washer

Editor Prison Stories:

I am a window-washer and was working on the windows of the tallest building in Frisco the other day. Inside the window I was washing, while my belt was attached to a hook, I saw a man leaning back and reading one of your PRISON MAGAZINES.

Suddenly he got up and threw the magazine in the waste-paper basket. Then he saw me. He went to the waste-paper basket and got the magazine again. I heard him say: "Well maybe they *could* climb a wall like that. Look at that human-fly on my window sill. How did he get there?"

I grinned in at him and he handed me two bits. "How did you get up here?" he asked. I showed him a ledge running around that entire floor that was over a foot wide.

We window-cleaners see so many queer things. I hope someday to graduate to flagpole climbing. That's a big paying profession. Is there any call for flag-pole artists in New York or Chicago?

AMOS BRADFIELD,
Union No. 6, San Francisco.

A Wise Kid

Big Chief:

I am only nine years old but I buy PRISON STORIES every issue it has come out. Will you publish this letter of mine so I can see my name in print? It is RALPH DUDLEY SEYMORE, JR., Dallas, Texas.

Assessment Work

Brother Hersey:

I want to tell you about a crooked piece of business I did once and wonder if any of the readers of PRISON STORIES can tell me how I can square it so I'll keep out of prison. This is under cover and in the quiet and I have changed the names so nobody'll be hurt.

I was released from a western stir after doing five years with "copper" off to the extent of over nine months. While hanging around a boom-town the coroner gave me a job of burying a Mexican who had been bumped off in a saloon. There was a regular fee of $25 for digging the grave. I drags the corpse out on the prairie, and it being hot as Hades, I didn't dig a grave but dumps the Greaser into an assessment hole and covered his body up.

Along comes the owner of the assessment hole which he has lost because, apparently, there had been no assessment work done. He hell-roars about camp and the Mexican is dug up, proving that he did the assessment work required. They get after me, and I beats it for parts unknown.

Now I want to go back to Goldtown, cause I staked a claim there that looks rich. How can I? The coroner is wild at me. The sheriff claims I cheated the town out of $25, and the owner of the assessment hole has attached my mine for damages. Can any reader suggest how I can get to Goldtown, and finish my assessment work?

FRED DE GROTTE,
Care of Planters Hotel, Globe, Arizona.

Editor's Note: You got yourself in too deep for us to help you out, old pard. Better sell the rights to your claim and forget about it.

•• March 1931 ••

A Double-Ex-Con

Editor Prison Magazine:

I'm a double-ex-con and don't write many letters, but here goes one. I was tickled to death when I saw your PRISON STORIES on the newsstands. I didn't like the first issue as well as the second; and the third, the one with the cell door for a cover, is a swell piece of work. That serial by Byrd, "Public Enemies," promises to be a crackajack.

A bunch of Chicago Big-Shots ripping dear old London wide open and working their rackets there is sure-fire stuff. I read a story once about a guy who stole a storage warehouse, so if the "Public Enemies" from Chi do cop the Crown Jewels, they're in the same class. What I hate to waste my time over is crooks pulling petty larceny stuff.

DUDLEY TUPPER,
Spokane, Wash.

A Real Boost

Say, Hersey:

You're getting to be the guy who don't know when to quit. Here I runs across PRISON STORIES the other day, and I thought they had used up all the titles. PRISON STORIES is a great title.

I get so mixed up on Detective Magazines that I think there ought to be a law stopping them using the word "Detective." I bought one, at the same time I bought PRISON STORIES, and it wasn't the one I wanted at all. I know what I'm getting when I see your mags. And you've published plenty.

THEODORE HOOPS,
Glens Falls, New York.

Christmas Turkey

Dear Editor:

We were short a couple of pounds on the turkey I bought the old lady and kids for Christmas. I happened to stop at a newsstand first and bought PRISON STORIES and two other of your magazines. So I went shy six-bits on the bird to liven things up with the kids, for they are all great readers.

FRANK PEARSON,
Trinidad, Colorado.

Taken From Truth

Editor Prison Paper:

Saw PRISON STORIES on the newsstand and glanced through it while I was waiting to take a bus to work. I ran across a real fact in that serial called "Public Enemies." The author has a character there called "Joe Beef."

I knew a Joe Beef in Montreal, who was said to be strong enough to push a freight car. They used to say in Montreal: "Joe Beef, you know Joe Beef? He's strongest man in Canada. He regular switch engine."

CHARLIE YOUNG,
White River Junction, Vt.

A Bright Idea

Dear Editor-in-Chief:

Writing this "kite" to tell you I struck a bright idea the other day which you can have for ten dollars, cash. I'm on the level with this and you got to come across if you use the idea. It is new. And I am with a gang that will pay a "call" if you don't come across with the ten bucks, providing you use my idea.

It is this: Keep it under cover. Sell your PRISON STORIES to gangs that need fall-money and kale to spring pals. Have them go around peddling your mag for all they can get. You give them the low-down price on your mag, they get top dollar. You ought to sell thousands of copies that way. Now come clean if you don't think that's an idea.

TONY BURKE,
General Delivery, Hoboken, N.J.

Why Is It?

Dear Hersey:

I done two sentences in stirs and I have often wondered why there are so many cons inside for selling stolen goods and none for receiving? They used to say in Moundsville, Pa., that if there were no crooks there would be no fences, and we'd come back at the screws by saying if there were no fences there would be no crooks. Why, I know a mob that ships truck-loads of copped stuff to Chi where the fences are thicker than speakeasies, and that's going some.

HUGHIE GANNON,
Indianapolis, Ind.

A Slick Trick

Publisher in Chief:

I want to put some of your readers wise to a slick trick that was worked on me when I was greener than I am now. I was trimmed by two ex-cons who claimed they won a big bet at Saratoga, but had to have five thousand more to show the bookmaker they had the cash when they made the oral bet. I chips in five grand and we all goes up on the Hudson River Boat.

When we went ashore I puts up a squawk and notifies the police. The simp I was. I swore I was trimmed in Albany. It was in Troy, a few miles up the river from Albany, where I was nicked. They had me so stewed I didn't know one town from the other.

JIMMY TETLEY,
New Brighton, Staten Island, N.Y.

From a Rocking Chair

Dear Editor:

I'm a great reader of your magazines and often sit for hours chasing gangsters and racketeers and escaped prisoners through the pages. I used to knit considerable. I had a cat that killed my pet canary, and afterwards got tangled in a ball of yarn and was strangled to death. I believe as you do that justice is retributive.

ALICE CARSTAIRS,
Boston, Mass.

A Hot Kick

Dear Editor:

I liked that story by Carl Henry in the December issue of PRISON STORIES. The one about the lethal chamber and the prison demon. "The House of a Thousand Doors," by Henry Leverage, was kinda punk. The demon in that yarn threw too much dynamite to suit me.

TERRY O'BRIEN,
Hays City, Kansas.

Gentlemen:

May I tender my congratulations upon the fine magazine which you are putting before the American public? One can see that the stories you print are not mere wanderings of the imagination of some jaded writer, but real-life narratives of things which go on around us every day.

That is refreshing in this day of "thrillers" and stories that really belong in the category headed "Trash." I read your magazine with keen interest, and await each issue impatiently. Sincerely,

DR. J. COOPER.

The Truth

Dear Editor:

When you mentioned The Stove Contract in one of your yarns about Sing Sing I began to believe one of your authors, at least, knew what he was writing about. Keep it under cover but I spent two years making stoves Up The River, and that was a hellhole. It's so long ago I had forgotten it.

The shirt-shop, run by contract labor, was just as bad, I could scoop a handful of moisture every morning from the lower tier cell walls. Yet I never had rheumatism. I guess we old-timers were too tough to kill. Across from the stir was an old mansion, where they kept the women appointed to die.

Couldn't a story be written about that old house where a condemned woman went batty and thought she was living in a palace? I'm doing prison work now and am connected with a Parole Board, making investigation of paroled prisoners. Most of them are making good.

GEORGE SHIRLEY,
New York City.

•• May-June 1931 ••

Border Stories

Dear Mr. Hersey:

I would like to see more stories in your PRISON MAGAZINE about the far-countries, like China, India and South America. In other words, I am curious to know how the other half of the world settles penal problems.

JAMES DUFFY,
Sacramento, Calif.

A Complaint

Mr. Editor:

I am an old woman, living in a house about the size of a shoe. I have three children. I want to know why I, who lost all my savings in a bank, have to see the president of that bank ride by my door almost every day in his limousine.

Last I heard of him was that he was sent to prison for five years. That was less than a year ago, soon after my youngest boy was born. Are the prisons just stalls to blind the depositors? And what a haughty look that banker has.

JANE MACARDLE,
Andersonville, Ark.

A Booster

Dear Publisher Hersey:

Keep a-coming with your excellent PRISON STORIES, and the remarkable covers. They stand out on the newsstands like clubs in public riots. I like Levy, Leverage, Byrd and Burkholder's stories.

MONTROSE DOOLY,
Albuquerque, New Mexico.

Competition

Dear Editor:

I suppose you think your magazine PRISON STORIES is the latest thing out. Guess again, old Ed. I got a copy, the only one written, by a bunch of cons in a New York prison. Hot stuff and how!

What they think about the grub isn't fit to mention above a whisper. And stool-pigeons getting paroles. Say they rip it into the prison board. I suppose you'd like to see my copy of the mag? It's for sale, all inside dope, for fifty bucks.

The subscription manager and the treasurer went to the death house, but any kale I can collect will go for a big funeral for them. They both want a wreath with a harp. Could any of your readers donate for the flowers? The execution comes off next month.

JACK KNEFE,
Paddy's Cafe, Utica, N.Y.

Here's a Woman Hater and How!

Dear Sir:

I have just been reading your February issue of PRISON STORIES.

I read the story of the convict which, I presume, was written behind the stone walls. I finished up the issue reading short notes of what others had written. One guy spoke of how unfair it was to imprison women. If he read the story of Jane Allen in "The Big House Blues" [February] he would soon change his mind.

Why have women any more right than men to murder and get away with it? Just because she has money, she shouldn't get off with it more than anyone else. If this one in New York ever got out in the wide open world, he would know something.

I have been in twenty-one states in the United States, and have learned a lot from experience and no doubt I still have lots more to learn. I want to write this party a note and if you will print it, I will appreciate it very much.

I am calling your hand. If you are not yellow, you will print it. If you don't I will say you are yellow to the core. I want this one party to see it in print. I am cutting his out so you'll know the one I mean.

I will close hoping that you are not a coward but a man.

Very truly yours,

W.H. WINTER, JR.,

Scott City, Kansas.

The Light Within

Publisher of Prison Stories:

There is a needy case in the county jail of a young newspaper man who went wrong and is serving eleven months and twenty-nine days. He is broke and his old lady went broke trying to save him. That boy can write good special articles about China and ghostly English castles.

Is there any way to get him a typewriter and a market for his special articles? I saw the warden and he is willing to let a typewriter in the prison. I will furnish the paper and postage if anybody sends me a typewriter for this inmate.

ELSE FURGENSON,

Snake Hill, New Jersey.

Short or Long

Mr. Publisher:

In looking over a large number of magazines on the newsstand, and reading most of them, I think your magazine PRISON STORIES stands out very well, as to newness of material and freedom from hackneyed stuff. I no longer care for Mexican Border, rum-running, dope-smuggling, hero-wins stuff.

ALFRED McGANN,
New Orleans, La.

Swell Sentiments

The Editor:

Glad to get third issue of PRISON STORIES. It's like seeing an old pal, with stripes and ball and chain, come in for a chat. I've done a couple of bits in stirs. The sentences didn't worry me much.

First bit, I learned to manipulate cards until I was a shark. Second bit, I took to religion and got a job which pays me twenty-five dollars, enough to live on. On the dead, Ed, I never knew a con who was made happy with stolen money. Not one. It went too fast. There is something wrong with crooked kale. Keep up the good work.

ARNOLD JOHNSON,
Salt Lake City, Utah.

More Molls

The Editor Prison Stories:

I am only a young girl, sixteen last birthday. I ran across PRISON STORIES at the village drug-store and purchased a copy. In its "Do You Know Columns," I read that more women were going to prison than ever before.

I wish you would publish more stories about what happens to them in prison. Poor souls. We have a jail, near where I live. There is one woman in it, a colored one, who scrubs the floors every day. She don't want to get out. She killed her husband because he was unfaithful to her. Doesn't she deserve to be freed? Please run prison stories about women.

TINY McALLISTER,
Hays Center, Kansas.

Reformers

Mr. Editor Hersey:

I don't often write about magazines I have read but I am making an exception of PRISON STORIES. I never had any use concerning the "sob-stuff" about hard boiled ex-convicts. I haven't any now, but I think the era of the new Reformer has arrived. Not the wealthy man seeking publicity, at the expense of the inmate, but the new Prison Boards and enlightened wardens and Governors. They are doing a world of good.

The recent riots in prisons stirred things up. Who wouldn't riot when they didn't have the chance of being released, even for exceptional behavior.

PRISON STORIES is and can be made a great factor for good, inside of penal institutions. It is a mirror to hold up to the public to show what is going on inside prisons. More power to you, Hersey. You have hit on an unhappy theme and are making it a happy one.

GUSTAVE BLUMFIELD,

Hoboken, New Jersey.

A Good Suggestion

Publisher Prison Stories:

As a suggestion I would ask that in some future issue of PRISON STORIES you publish a novel or novelette about a Federal Prison, like Atlanta or Fort Leavenworth.

I understand they are getting most of the Big-Shot gangsters in those prisons on account of evasion of the income tax.

MICHAEL PELL,

Phoenix, Arizona.

Short and Sweet

Dear Editor:

I would like to know if the prisoners of this country would vote wet or dry if they had a chance to vote? My guess is they would vote wet and wet and wetter. It must be dry as dust where they are.

JACK MacGILL,

Produce Exchange, New York.

False Ideas?

Editor in Chief:

Oh, dear Editor, how often that name has been used by people who ought to know better. I think your magazine PRISON STORIES is just about the best, the finest, the sweetest bunch of wood-pulp I ever took the trouble to look through. All pulp and ink and false ideas concerning prisoners. All the cons I ever met were meek as Moses; you've made lions out of them and demons and terrors. If you want to know the low-down on prisoners, go ask the police chiefs, or look at the records.

A Cop Who is Dying to Croak a Thief.

TOM HEALY,

Chicago, Ill.

A Bum Reporter

Dear Editor:

I'll tell you the toughest break I ever had. I am a reporter and was sent to a Big House where there was no chance to mail copy out. I got the news of a coming break. It grew larger and eight inmates were going over the wall.

In addition the shops were to be set on fire. I knew the names of the men concerned in the riot and escape. I couldn't get the news out because I would have been either a stool pigeon or a violator of the prison rules. I kept my mouth shut. I still am a bum reporter.

And nobody gives me credit.

ALANSO TWAIT,
Joliet, Ill.

Index

OFF-TRAIL PUBLICATIONS
Specializing in the era of American pulp fiction

THE WEIRD DETECTIVE ADVENTURES OF WADE HAMMOND
By Paul Chadwick
Volume 1: 10 stories, 180 pages, $18
Volume 2: 10 stories, 172 pages, $18
Volume 3: 10 stories, 202 pages, $18
Volume 4: 9 stories, 232 pages, $18

> *The Wade Hammond stories complete in four volumes. In these chilling adventures, all from the classic 1930's pulps,* Detective-Dragnet *and* Ten Detective Aces, *freelance investigator Wade Hammond battles a series of weird enemies. Some of the best of the '30s pulp fiction.*

DOCTOR COFFIN: The Living Dead Man
By Perley Poore Sheehan • Introduction by John Wooley
8 novelettes, 178 pages, $16

> *Weird stories from* Thrilling Detective, *1932-33. A former character actor who faked his own death, Doctor Coffin runs a string of mortuaries by night and fights crime at night. One of the strangest detective series.*

SUPER-DETECTIVE FLIP BOOK: Two Complete Novels
From the pulp *Super-Detective*:
"Legion of Robots" (November 1940) by Victor Rousseau • Introduction by John McMahan •• "Murder's Migrants" (March 1943) by Robert Leslie Bellem and W.T. Ballard • Introduction by John Wooley
2 short novels, 174 pages, $18

> Super-Detective *started as a Doc Savage-like adventure pulp, then changed format to hardboiled detective. The* Flip Book *features a novel from each of the two phases with intros exploring the historical background. Exciting!*

PULPWOOD DAYS: Volume 1: Editors You Want To Know
Edited by John Locke • 180 pages, $16

Numerous articles from the writers' magazines by and about pulp editors, with ample biographical profiles. Editors include: Frank E. Blackwell (Detective Story, Western Story), Ray Palmer (Amazing Stories, Fantastic Adventures), Edwin Baird (Weird Tales, Detective Tales), and many more.

GANG PULP
Edited by John Locke • 19 stories, 294 pages, $24

Hardboiled stories of the criminal underworld from the first year (1929-30) of the gang pulps: Gangster Stories, Racketeer Stories, *etc. These violent tales came under immediate censorship pressure; the history is explored in an in-depth essay. "A remarkable work of popular-culture scholarship"*—MYSTERY SCENE, *Fall 2008.*

THE GANGLAND SAGAS OF BIG NOSE SERRANO
Volume 1: Dames, Dice and the Devil
Volume 2: Horses, Hoboes and Heroes
Volume 3: Hell's Gangster
By Anatole Feldman • Introductions by Will Murray
Each: 4 novels • **Volumes 1-2**: 266 pages, $20 • **Volume 3**: 224 pages, $18

The complete Big Nose Serrano novels from Gangster Stories, Greater Gangster Stories, *and* The Gang Magazine, *1930-35. Feldman was the best of the gang pulp authors, and Big Nose was his most inspired creation, the berserking king of Chicago gangsters.*

AMAZON STORIES
Volume 1: Pedro & Lourenço
Volume 2: Pedro & Lourenço
By Arthur O. Friel • Introductions by John Locke
Vol 1: 10 stories, 222 pages, $18 • **Vol 2**: 10 stories, 286 pages, $20

Collects Friel's first twenty stories from Adventure *(1919-21), following the strange experiences of two Amazon Basin rubber workers as they explore the jungle. The best of pulp adventure fiction.*

GROTTOS OF CHINATOWN: The Dorus Noel Stories
By Arthur J. Burks • Introduction by John Locke
11 stories, 194 pages, $16

The complete adventures of Dorus Noel from All Detective Magazine *(1933-34). Burks' Manhattan Chinatown is a place of dark mystery, riddled with secret passageways, menaced by hatchetmen. Introduction discusses the history of* All Detective *and the career of the Speed-King of the Pulps, Arthur J. Burks.*

THE GOLDEN ANACONDA: And Other Strange Tales of Adventure
By Elmer Brown Mason • Introduction by John Locke
10 stories, 260 pages, $20

Ten fantastic stories set in the exotic corners of the world, all of them known to their globe-trotting entomologist author. Includes all five Wandering Smith *stories from* The Popular Magazine; *and five tales from* All-Story Weekly, *topped by the horror-laden two-part saga of Borneo, "Black Butterflies" and "Red Tree-Frogs." All published, 1915-16.*

Shipping: $3.00 media mail; $6.00 priority
Check or MO to:
Off-Trail Publications
2036 Elkhorn Road, Castroville, CA 95012
Paypal: offtrail@redshift.com

www.ingramcontent.com/pod-product-compliance
Lightning Source LLC
Chambersburg PA
CBHW030356020726
47493CB00003B/841